THE CIRCLE

Welcome to the Circle, Krysta!! Happy Reading!

Steve Galgon

STEPHEN J. GALGON

The Circle
Published in the United States by MJE Publishing, 2019

ISBN 978-0-578-53876-1
This book is available on Amazon.

Editing, Book Design, and Self-Publishing Services by
Heidi Connolly, Harvard Girl Word Services
harvardgirledits.com

PUBLISHING

THE CIRCLE

— STEPHEN J. GALGON —

For Maria, Mallory, Jocelyn, and Emilia

PROLOGUE

New York City, Four Years Ago

Well-dressed couples don't wait long for a table at The Four G's where reservations, or a well-greased palm, are the only way in. The man in his late fifties in an Ermenegildo Zegna suit of the finest Australian wool arrived at his rooftop table with his companion at precisely the same moment as their waiter in a naturally unrehearsed choreography. The waiter bowed slightly, politely pulled out the woman's chair, and then the man's. Normally, the rooftop's view of New York's East River elicited an exclamation or two, but Orson Hughes and his daughter were not ones for displays that only stated the obvious.

The young woman was striking, as much for the obvious pleasure she took in her father's company as her natural beauty and poise. The velvety dark blue of her evening gown brought out the color of her eyes, which sparkled like the ocean reflecting the moon. Her vibrant strawberry-blond hair, falling to the small of her back, bounced as she moved. Hughes was focused on the vision across the table, breaking his gaze only to peruse the wine selection. After a moment he beckoned the waiter, who had been hovering discreetly in the background.

Eduardo, tux impeccably white with black lapels standing out in crisp relief, glided effortlessly to the table, congratulating himself. To have Orson Hughes in his section had taken a bit of haggling with Pietro, the waiter who'd normally be serving this table. The debt wasn't small, both drugs and money involved, but what was the point if you weren't willing to take a risk to meet the opportunities that came your way? Eduardo had a fondness for risk. Risk, that is, tempered by meticulous planning.

"Good evening, sir, madame. Welcome to The Four G's. My name is Eduardo. It will be my pleasure to serve you this evening."

Hughes inclined his head benignly in the waiter's direction. He had little interest in the people who served him. A billionaire who had made New York City his home for more than three decades, he was one of the city's most notable citizens, and haughty as they come.

Orson Hughes had panache, true, but Eduardo saw the rift behind the man's eyes. As if his body was there but his thoughts hadn't come along for the ride. But hey, as long as they liked what Chef cooked up, the bill got paid, and Eduardo got what was coming to him, the man could crease his Botoxed brow all he wanted.

Hughes cleared his throat pointedly. Eduardo came to. Oops. No matter how long you had to wait, Server's Rule Number One said you never, ever let the guest feel you weren't riveted to every word he spoke, every move he made. He plunged in.

"Might I recommend a '61 Latour? The bouquet is unmatched anywhere in the city and, coupled with Chef's salsify-truffle soup and the roasted partridge decadently topped with *foie gras*...." Eduardo waited discreetly for a moment that hung in the air until its thickness became a tad uncomfortable. "Unless, of course, you have already made a selection...."

The woman acknowledged Eduardo's pitch with a subtle nod to her father.

"The bottle of Chateau Lafite," Hughes said. "Still in the cellar, I presume." He made an infinitesimal adjustment to his diamond cufflinks, easily two karats each. He and the waiter both knew the price of the wine was not listed. And true connoisseurs knew that Chateau Lafite was the vineyard that produced the wine of choice of Thomas Jefferson.

"Yes, sir," Eduardo said, again with the little bow he'd perfected to show temerity and respect. His suggestion of the Latour had been a good one. Albeit not good enough.

"Then right away, please."

Eduardo was inwardly self-congratulatory. Courses in wine-tasting and history kept him in the forefront at The Four G's and ensured steady employment for as long as he wanted it. The Bordeaux Chateau Lafite was a famous winery in France occupied since at least the fourteenth century, the majority of its vineyards planted around 1680 and its wine first sampled by Thomas Jefferson on one of his many diplomatic trips to France. So impressed was Jefferson by the wine's quality that it remained one of his favorites for a lifetime.

The waiter also knew that one particular bottle of Chateau Lafite, the one found in Monticello and had a *Th.* J etched into the glass, had sold at auction for somewhere over one hundred sixty thousand back in 1985. The bottle in The Four G's' cellar did not have the mark of Thomas Jefferson, but at six thousand bucks was still a major night's coup for a waiter from Secaucus, New Jersey. The pricey wine would add many thousands to the check's bottom line. The other night Eduardo's pal Pietro had served a rock star who ordered a bottle that went for two grand, but for Eduardo this was a first. He hurried off to tell the owner of The Four G's.

Vincenzo Guadagno, real name Vincent Glick—no one wanted the owner of an exclusive Italian restaurant to have a name like Vincent Glick—had owned The Four G's for years. He would handle the transaction himself.

Eduardo, real name Edward Kaminsky—all the waiters who work at The Four G's were also given "real" Italian names and taught how to speak with slight Italian accents—swallowed his disappointment, standing to the side as instructed. As long as the change of plan wouldn't affect his tip...well, *c'est la vie*.

Guadagno approached the Hughes' table with the bottle brought up from the wine cellar on a bed of velvet.

"Vincenzo," Hughes said, "you know my daughter, Elizabeth."

Elizabeth extended her hand and Vincenzo placed a delicate kiss upon it. "Of course," he said, "the pleasure is all mine. "He held out the bottle of wine and displayed the label. "An excellent and ambitious choice, sir. If you will permit me."

Hughes nodded. Guadagno began the pomp and circumstance of opening the bottle, a normally commonplace affair for the seasoned restaurateur. But opening the six-thousand-dollar bottle of wine in his hands—with no one to blame but himself if he were to drop it—required finesse. Taking a deep breath he retracted the cork without mishap and soon the aroma escaped and filled his nostrils. After years of wondering, he now knew why the price was so high. It was too bad he wouldn't get to taste it for himself.

Orson Hughes sniffed the cork and again motioned for Vincenzo to proceed. The owner poured a sip into a large crystal glass, set it down before Orson Hughes, and waited. Mr. Hughes slowly lifted the glass of wine and swirled it in front of his eyes to release the full-bodied scent. He closed his eyes to breathe in the bouquet.

Guadagno was the epitome of patience. One did not rush moments like these. Hughes tilted the glass and a small amount of wine passed his lips. Vincenzo held his breath. Even with a price tag so high, if the selection did not meet the standards of the guest, especially this one, the wine would not be poured, and another bottle would have to be selected.

"Magnificent," said Hughes.

At Hughes' signal, Guadagno obediently poured Elizabeth Hughes a glass and returned to finish the pour for her father. He placed the bottle in a stand next to the table and excused himself with the utmost discretion.

The sniper peered through his high-powered binoculars. The irony of the situation tickled his fancy. One hell of a last meal for his mark, the wine alone, he assumed, costing more than some would pay for a car. At least the poor bastard would get to go out in style.

In the darkness, the sniper was invisible. Dressed like a Navy Seal in his preferred disguise of all black, he was totally hidden in the shadows of the rooftop almost a full block away. The pigeons taking off and landing took no notice of the immovable object in the dark, nor he of them.

The sniper took aim with his Dragunov SVDN3. Through the cross hairs he saw the man and woman toasting with crystal goblets. The woman is stunning, invoking the Venus de Milo in a tasteful blue velvet dress with a nice hint of cleavage.

The man and his lady friend touched glasses as if in some kind of celebration. The sniper withdrew a picture from his front pocket and studied it one last time. Confident with the accuracy of his sighting, he took aim again.

This time he pulled the trigger.

The 7.62 caliber bullet made its way silently, steadily, across the river and through the immaterial glass barrier of The Four G's rooftop. The killer picked up his binoculars without hurry, luxuriating. Confirming the results of the hit was the best part.

Perfect. The bullet struck the man's head. Blood formed a Rorschach across his daughter's exposed neckline. A silent scream, and then another. Orson Hughes' body went limp and fell from his chair, knocking over the wine bottle from its stand by the table. Never one to waste money, the killer tsked over the waste of the fine vintage. Blood and grapes mingled as they spilled onto the carpet. The patrons of the restaurant had erupted into panic and were tripping over each other in their chaotic path to the exits.

The sniper, pleased with his handiwork, packed up his rifle, shed his dark camouflage, and packed it securely into his duffel bag before descending the metal ladder back into the building. Once outside on street level, he was nothing more than a man on his way home from the gym. He looked over his shoulder and took one last look at the site of the pandemonium he created. A satisfied chuckle echoed in the quiet street after he'd gone.

PART I

I

The forest is still verdant from the summer growth. The sun shines brightly. Because the thick canopy allows little light to penetrate, however, it remains relatively dark for the time of day. This is as close to deer country as you can get and still be only a few hours north of the city. For Doug Goodwin, this haven of nature just south of Albany is a taste of home, and just what the doctor ordered after several long weeks in the mad swell of people and things that is Manhattan.

Doug is a young man in his mid-twenties. His athletic posture and long stride, together with his well-defined musculature, reveal confidence and comfort with an environment that would send most New Yorkers running for Fifth Avenue. He's been described as handsome by many, his face all planes and angles, his eyes an arresting shade of hazel. His friends back home always said he could double as Val Kilmer. A nice compliment. Personally? He's never seen much of a resemblance.

As Doug breathes in the fresh scent of pine his thoughts turn to Grover, Colorado and the ones he left behind in his one-stop light community. Did they miss him? Were they still shaking their heads and thinking what old Mr. Dowd at the hardware store had said out loud—that Doug would be back before another hunting season began? He never thought he'd feel at home in a clanging, thrilling, willfully exotic metropolis like New York, which might as well be another planet compared to his hometown, but he's surprised himself with his adaptability. Still, up here, away from the crowds, it's familiar territory. A few hours' drive to go hunting was nothing new either. Driving sets the stage and puts him in the frame of mind to prepare for the ritual of the hunt. It's almost like being home again.

Hunting has always been more than a sport to Doug. He feels a kinship with the animals of the forest and has the utmost respect for them. After all, they were here long before humanity, and would probably be here long after humankind had found its way to messing it all up for good. Doug's upbringing had taught him that man was meant to be one with nature, and his regular trips upstate ensured that living in New York City would not dissuade him from that belief.

The hunt was a lot more than a thrill or a game of conquest, too. That's why he never used a gun. The first men had no form of weaponry other than what they were able to build with their own two hands and Doug didn't want to be any different, to have what he considered an unfair advantage. The gift of technology was great, but not one shared by the designated prey of the forest, and it was Doug's sincere opinion that if hunting was not about the skill, then you weren't really hunting at all. Like his father always told him, "Shooting isn't hunting."

Doug left his silver Jeep Wrangler a few hundred yards away, and set up a makeshift base camp in a small clearing where he began performing maintenance on his hunting equipment...attaching feathers to arrows, restringing his longbow, and sharpening his knife. His deep-forest camouflage was all but complete as he applied a dark green face cream, kneeled before his arranged weapons and bowed his head. His silent prayer is always the same. *Lord, who hast bidden us be merciful as Thou art merciful, I pray to thee. Steady my hand and bring peace to my heart. Bring good fortune upon me and to all the creatures of the earth. Just as You have given unto Adam, the earth, and all its creatures, so I go forth to honor You and Your Kingdom. Amen.*

When he was done he crossed himself and kissed the golden cross that he wore on a chain around his neck, rose, and began to gather the implements of the hunt.

A sound that didn't belong broke his concentration. A couple more seconds and Doug recognized Led Zeppelin's *Ramble On* coming from the clearing he'd just left where his Jeep was parked. He looked back to see who the idiot was who thought it was okay to disturb the sanctity of the forest with hard rock.

A shiny Lexus convertible with vanity plates that read "E MAT ESQ" was noisily making its way through the rough. In a few seconds it stopped behind Doug's Wrangler. The music ceased abruptly as the engine cut off. There's a moment of stark silence until the birds settled enough to start twittering again.

In a moment Doug heard the familiar voice of his best friend.

Eric Matthews, and Eric's law career, was the reason Doug was in the Catskills rather than back home somewhere within shouting distance of his small family. Despite Doug's persistent invitations, however, Eric had never once joined him on a hunting trip. As a matter of fact, as long as he's known Eric, Doug can't ever recall a time when Eric has even set foot in the wilderness.

Eric was carefully navigating his way down the beaten path that led from the cars to Doug's current position wearing what looked like his work attire. A Mont Blanc pen was hanging on for dear life in his shirt pocket and a Bluetooth was glued to his ear. The guy had less business in the woods than a polar bear in the Sahara. Whatever he wanted this time, it wouldn't be to partake in the male bonding ritual of the hunt.

"Dougie! I found you."

"So, you've finally decided to join me. I hope you brought a change of clothes, Matthews. The deer'll be hunting *you* looking like that."

Three men were taking up the rear.

The four were soon a few feet away. The unexpected visit brought on a nagging disbelief. Why would his BFF drag his sorry-assed metrosexual self—and three men in full hunting gear, including way too hi-tech and over-the-top face camou-flage and goggles, no less—with him? Why would he bring three total strangers into Doug's sacred hunt?

"Nah, you know me," said Eric wincing. "I'll leave all the blood and guts to you. But aren't you always telling me I should try to appreciate the beauty of nature?"

"And aren't you always telling me how much you hate the great outdoors, and that the only beauty in nature is when *Sports Illustrated* shoots the swimsuit issue on safari?"

"Bro. Me, hate the outdoors?" Eric directed this comment to the three men, who hadn't spoken. He grabbed Doug's arm to pull him aside.

Doug leaned away. "Okay, enough bullshit, *bro*. What the heck are you doing here? And who, in the name of Artemis, are these diffuses with you?"

"Who's Artemis? Never mind, it doesn't matter. They're new clients."

"What're you up to, Matthews? You off your Ritalin or something?"

Eric raised his eyebrows. Doug waited. Eric would get around to telling him what was up in his own good time. Pushing him only meant waiting longer and getting less.

Eric had always been high strung, even as a kid. How he managed to pass the bar was still a mystery, but Doug suspected the honor system got a run for its money that day. He consciously gave Eric the benefit of the doubt, but he'd never seen Eric cross-examining a witness or staying calm in a heated debate. Nope. Didn't compute. On the other hand, Eric was making good money and was apparently headed for partner if he played his cards right. So maybe it was Doug who had the problem. Maybe Eric had a lot more up top than Doug had ever given him credit for.

Finally Doug's thin veneer of patience gave way. He shrugged at the men. "I'll introduce myself, then?"

"Yeah, about that," said Eric.

Just as he thought. With Matthews, there was always a catch. With Matthews, it was just a matter of how big.

"Look. These guys are potential clients, very big time," Eric said urgently. "I mean, this could mean serious money for the firm. The senior partners put me in charge of making sure they have a good time while they're here on the East Coast. They're hunting fanatics, too. You know me, dude. I can't stand this kind of thing. But I had no choice."

The pleading was pure calculation. Eric knew how much Doug hated it when he begged.

"I need you to show them a good time, Doug. Please, man. Show them your skills. You know, win them over for me."

"Let me get this straight," said Doug. "You want me to show three guys I don't know a good time, but you don't want me to introduce myself. And that might be because—why, exactly?"

Eric shuffled his feet. "It's just that...well, you can try, dude. But they won't talk to you. They're big on anonymity, won't even show *me* their faces. I drove them here like this. Three hours, man, and not a word from any of them. I don't know. Maybe it's a test or something. Come on, I mean, you like quiet. How bad can a few hours with a bunch of really quiet dudes be?"

You've got to be kidding me. Masked mute men? Whatever Matthews had going on, Doug would bet it wasn't on the up and up. He'd have a reason for it, he always has a reason, but this time it might just be the one that crossed the line.

Once, back in Grover, fourteen-year-old Eric had tried to get Pepsi to sponsor Grover's baseball team and sent out a convincing letter to Pepsi's central office that caught a senior executive's eye. The exec himself actually flew to Grover to meet with Eric, not realizing he'd been communicating with a teen-aged pipsqueak. Eric was always really good on paper. In person, not so much. When Eric panicked at the last minute, Doug, to save face for the team, had to pretend to be Eric, while Eric pretended to be a "Coke representative." As if. But Eric was adamant. "You know," he'd said, "to inspire competition and all that." Not all that good a plan when you live in a town with two hundred fifty-three people. Needless to say, the sponsorship died on the vine for numerous reasons, but mostly on account of the fact that Eric looked just like what he was: a pimply teenager trying to put one over on the man. The experience had one significant result, though. It got Eric started in the area that would make him sure money: bullshit. Eric Matthews could bullshit his way into or out of anything.

Apparently, this was going to be another one of those times. It was strange, though, even for Eric, and Doug didn't want any part of it, whatever *it* was.

"All I need you to do is show them around, man." Eric was back to pleading. "No names...so? What's the big deal? It's not like you're going to be pen pals or anything. And you're not a Facebook kinda guy." He lowered his voice. "I think they're using code names anyway."

Doug swore. "What are they, Mafia or something? I'm telling you, Matthews, I swear to God, if you...."

"Mafia? Nah, they're legit, I swear. That's why I love you, man, always looking out for me. "

Yeah, like he could believe the guy who told his mother his jacket was stolen rather than admit he'd lost it. Doug was trying very hard to remember why he was still friends with him.

"I don't know, Eric. You don't see something bizarre about this? Asking me to go hunting with three guys who won't show their faces? All because you say they're okay? I don't think so. What if there's an accident? What if *I'm* the accident? Then what?"

Eric arranged his face.

Uh-oh. There's that look. The guilt card was about to be played, and dammit, it always worked.

"I'd trust my best friend," Eric said. "And if he said some guys are legit, they're legit."

Doug was quiet. Eric held his breath. "Come on, what do you say? For me, man, come on."

"Fine. No wonder you're a damn lawyer."

Eric relaxed visibly. "Thanks, Doug. Really. I owe you one." He pulled Doug to him in a brief one-armed clench and checked his watch at the same time. In another second he was sprinting back to his pristine Lexus faster than a fish spinning off a hook.

Unbelievable. Doug had just agreed to do something stupid for people he didn't know and his best friend had flown the coop. And what was that bizarre aborted hug about?

"You're the best, dude, I'll call you later," called Eric over his shoulder. His phone was already ringing. "Ye-llo. Eric Matthews here...yeah...I understand...right...yeah, hang on a sec." Hand cupped over his earpiece, he turned to the men standing in a tight group. "Mr. Johnson, Mr. Williams, Mr. Smith, you're all set to go. You're in good hands with Doug Goodwin here. I'm sure I'll be hearing from you next week. I wish you all a...um...successful hunt. Or whatever."

Eric gave Doug a little salute and redirected his attention to his phone. "Yeah, Bobby, you still there...? No, no, I'm out in the fuckin' woods. Yeah, no, it's like *Lord of the Flies* out here...." The conversation became unintelligible for a second and then there was a loud "fuck!" as a tree branch smacked Eric in the face. A minute later the car door slammed and the Lexus engine cranked. Eric was gone with a squeal of the tires.

Doug couldn't believe it. Eric had really left him here with these—Doug didn't even know what to call them.

He shifted his attention to his newly acquired unwanted companions. It was a bummer, but now he was committed. The three of them were all about the same height and build. Brothers? Maybe, but with their faces covered, who knew? Even with face camouflage, their expressions were stone-cold and not a word had left their mouths. By some kind of tacit mutual agreement they began to gather their things and approached Doug. They stood before him side by side like some crazy trio of terminators or something. His skin crawled with discomfort.

"Okay, well, I guess we're stuck with each other," he said. "And it's time to go. You know my name. If you need anything, just say so."

The three nodded a stilted acknowledgment.

Why the heck had he let Matthews put him in this position?

"Do any of you guys have weapons? I don't think you're going to be able to catch anything with your bare hands."

More silence. The dude on the left raised his arm in the slightest gesture to indicate that Doug should proceed into the forest. Doug didn't know whether to be offended or pissed off. Eric implied they were "out here" from somewhere else. Maybe they didn't speak English. Still, that didn't answer why he would bring them all the way out there to *watch* Doug hunt. And if they planned to hunt themselves, why would they come without weapons?

Doug was damned if he'd go up into the woods with guys who might pull something funny. "Before we go, I need to know what you brought with you. You know," he said at their blank stares, "*weapons*? Hunting knives? *Anything?*"

"Johnson, Williams, and Smith" looked at each other. Finally, again by some kind of mutual yet imperceptible communication, they obliged Doug by emptying their respective pockets. Besides a couple of dollar bills in one of them, they were empty. All the trappings, none of the essentials.

That's not even normal.

At least they understood English. Maybe they had concealed weapons. "Listen, there's some pretty thick forest up ahead. It would have been smart to at least bring knives." The men rolled up their sleeves and pant legs; no concealed weapons of any kind.

Doug's face heated up. This was so wrong. Was he going to end up on the ground with a blade stuck in his back? When—if—he made it home, Matthews was going to pay big for this.

"Time to go," he said, unenthusiastically moving toward the trail. "Stay close to me. Watch where you step. You seem pretty good at the silence thing, but you're unprepared. And I don't want you to scare off the animals."

Doug and the three camouflaged men had ventured into deep forest. Doug was leading them through some jagged Adirondack terrain. As the wind blew in the tree tops, birds hopped from branch to branch, scavenging for their next meal. Smaller creatures crossed their path, but were quickly scared off by the giants in their woods. This time of year the mosquitoes were still out in full regalia, and Johnson, Williams, and Smith swatted at them without effect, though they didn't voice any complaints. Doug kept his tittering to himself.

To this point they still had not spoken a word to him or one another. As they made their way toward the Mohawk river, the powerful 149-mile-long tributary of the Hudson River, one of the men, the biggest one, the one Doug had already named Terminator One, slipped on a wet patch of moss. He reached for the support of a tree branch, a hand to catch him, anything, but hit the ground hard on his tailbone and let out a grunt of pain.

"Hey, you okay, pal?" Doug doubled back to see if the guy was hurt. Accidents in the woods were never a good thing. The man picked himself up with a groan and dusted himself off. His companions didn't offer assistance or ask if he was okay. Their eyes continued to hold the same blank stare, the kind you'd give a dog when he went to the bathroom in the house. The man on the ground simply gestured impatiently for Doug to keep going.

The men continued on, heavy breathing and footfalls the only sounds. The sun tracked its way across the afternoon sky. A buck drinking from a narrow trickling stream in a small clearing far from civilization jerked up his head, startled by the interlopers. Doug turned, peeved. His "guests" again, not a clue in the world about what it meant to respect the hunt.

Until that point, Doug had been focused on his own stealthy tracking of the animal. But now the buck at the water's edge didn't hesitate. It fled.

Doug was already on the move. He chased after the buck and kept pace. As the animal increased its speed, Doug matched it. From their vantage point the men looked on, fascinated. It was like watching Tarzan up close and personal. Doug ran straight for a big tree with a low branch. He leapt to grab the branch, the motion carrying him in an arc off the ground. With the agility of an Olympic gymnast, he landed gracefully on the arms of the tree, unsheathed his long bow, drew an arrow, aimed, and released.

The arrow hit the buck square in the head with deadly accuracy. The animal tumbled in a death spiral and the momentum carried its already near lifeless body forward until it came to a sliding stop. Doug swung from the tree and landed like a cat on his feet. He walked toward the animal carefully. He kneeled, waiting for the final puffs of breath to cease before removing the arrow from its head, then crossed himself. He kissed the gold cross hanging around his neck and moved his lips in silent prayer.

The men looked at each other. They'd just seen a man track an animal and near outrun it. Not to mention the acrobatic maneuvers he employed to kill the powerful creature.

Doug Goodwin would do quite nicely.

2

It is early in the morning on the first Monday of July. The sun has barely gotten the chance to kiss the skyscrapers on the horizon, so it is still cool enough to be outside without roasting. The city was already bustling. Taxis drive as if the rules of the road don't apply to them. Apparently, they don't. People are waiting impatiently at bus stops and pedestrians with coffee cups and cell phones are moving with determination to get where they are going.

Doug is sitting at one of only five tables in the *Bread Basket Cafe*, an upscale coffee shop on the Upper East Side of Manhattan, the kind of place the upper echelon frequented. That is, of course, if the upper echelon stood in line to buy its own coffee and muffins. It had occurred to Doug on more than one occasion that most of the people waiting for their lattés and espressos and mocha frappés were assistants and interns fulfilling the daily fixes of others, the ones who gave the orders. Every day the worker bees obediently stand in line hoping that the cup of coffee or mocha java grandé supreme they bring back to the office will change their lives, get them noticed, maybe even put them one step closer to a promotion or their dream job.

Doug might be the exception. He is no executive and he is no intern. What he is, though, is out of place, and he knows it. He is not dressed like they are for one, and he is sitting alone. At a table. The tables in this establishment are more or less for show. The people who come here are always in a hurry, on their way to or from someplace fast, and never have the time to sit and enjoy their pick-me-up of choice and rest at the same time. The fact that Doug does have the time, or makes the time, gives him the aura of either entitlement or wayward screw-up. He's never sure which.

There was a reason Doug had parked himself at this table in this fancy café drinking his not-too-great, over-the-top crazy expensive coffee, the way he had been doing for many weeks, and she was in line now. In all this time he has never spoken to her, never learned her name. He knew only a couple of things for sure. One, that she was more beautiful than any other woman he'd ever seen, and two, that she dressed for success. She was around 5'7". Had long flowing hair and dark green eyes. The total package was magazine material, a slender, tight body complete with a chest of perfect proportion. She was way out of his league, but it didn't stop him from coming back for refills every possible chance he got.

Today she was wearing her Gucci dress suit, which Doug loved because it accented her best feature—at least he assumed they were her best feature, although he was dying to learn otherwise—legs that went on forever. Around this woman Doug hardly knew his own name, and has been one hundred percent incapable of asking for hers. The closest he'd come was a couple

of weeks ago when she'd dropped her *Wall Street Journal* in front
of him and he'd mustered up a croaked you're welcome to her
thank you. He winced at the recall. Doug's persistence was one
of his good qualities. Sadly, his shyness with women was one of
his not-so-good ones. Despite all his confidence in other areas
of his life, he still felt like a high-school kid when it came to the
fairer sex. Sure, he'd had his share of adventures in high school
and college, but that was a whole different ballgame. Now that
he was out and on his own, he was in uncharted waters. At least
he was smart enough to know that the lines that used to work
at frat parties were useless. Especially now...in this city, on this
street, in this coffee shop, with his pay grade. With this woman.

And there she was, as always, waiting with infinite aplomb,
for her extra tall latte. When it was delivered, she moved to
the condiment counter and added her standard two creamers
and two blue packets of sweetener. She never hurried, always
seemed to have everything under control. Held herself in a way
that broadcasted she could handle anything life could dish out.
To Doug's way of thinking, if you can't wait a few minutes for a
cup of coffee, you're wound too tight and can probably afford to
miss a cup here or there.

Doug watched some more, trying to decide which approach
out of the hundreds he'd been practicing to take. It was a perfect
opportunity for the casual contact maneuver. He had another
few seconds to make his move. All he had to do was pick up his
own cup, join her, and start up a conversation.

Swallowing the lump in his throat, he planned his advance.
Hi, I've noticed you here before. No. *Hi, I'm Doug. Latté, huh?* No.
Hi, can I buy you a coffee sometime? Despite vowing not to disappoint himself again, the possibility of rejection was making him
sweat. Before he'd gotten halfway to the counter he'd already
swung around and made a hasty retreat, a beeline to the door.

Lame, lame, lame.

He didn't stop until he was almost across the street. When he looked back his mystery woman was adjusting the leather satchel on her shoulder and sipping on her hot drink. Doug paused for so long that the light changed. "Hey, get outta the way," shouted a cabbie about two inches from Doug's behind and gave him the finger. Doug jumped onto the sidewalk to bemoan his pathetic lack of chutzpah.

Misters Johnson, Williams, and Smith stood in the center of a dimly lit room, their faces concealed behind the same camouflage they'd worn on their excursion with Doug. They were waiting to be beckoned, as usual.

In a far corner of the room a solitary man in his late sixties sat in the shadows smoking a fresh Partagas cigar. The smoke from his and all the other cigars was thick in the enclosed space and threatened to supplant what little oxygen was left. No one seemed to notice. The man was wearing a black turtleneck, the sleeves casually pushed up to the bottom of his forearms, and a pair of perfectly creased khaki pants.

"Gentlemen, what do you have to report?"

Johnson bowed his head respectfully. "Mr. Black, we've completed recruitment of a Mr. Douglas Goodwin."

"Is he worthy?" Mr. Black asked, disposing of some of the ash on the end of the cigar.

"Worthy would be an understatement, sir," said Williams.

"We feel confident with the selection," added Smith.

Mr. Black's eyebrows lifted. He took a small sip from the highball glass that sat on the table next to him. Seven and Seven, as always. "Very well. Extend to Mr. Matthews an invitation to the lounge. Be sure he brings the new member."

"Yes, sir," the men replied as one.

When they were gone Mr. Black leaned back in his soft leather chair, took the last slow drag of his cigar, and wished he were young again.

3

The architecture of the American Museum of Natural History is only part of what makes it one of the most famous tourist attractions in New York City. There's the bronze statue of the original roughrider President Theodore Roosevelt on horseback, signaling to the people of New York to "stand tall" right outside the Central Park West entrance, for one, and the sheer massive size of the museum for another. Hundreds of rooms that hold slice after slice of history, including relics of medieval weapons and skeletons of prehistoric dinosaurs.

Behind the scenes, of course, is the heart and soul of the museum, the research laboratories and offices, of which Doug's is one.

Doug's shared office is the epitome of unintimidating, even with the several letters of accreditation on the wall, including a diploma that acknowledges the successful completion and acquisition of a Bachelors of Paleontology and Archaeology from Colorado University. It was small and sparsely decorated with a desk more like a door on legs and, as his mother would say "hardly enough room to change your mind." Still, he figures he's lucky to have it.

He'd made feeble attempts to decorate the space, but in waffling all he'd managed are a couple of mementos. One, a picture of his old house back in Grover. The tiny specks in the lower right corner were his parents. Two, next to the photo currently adorning the makeshift desk, the *pièce de resistance*, a collector's plate signed by all seventy-five students from the Pawnee School and wishing him best of luck in college. Eric's is the only name written upside down inside a crude drawing of a Pepsi logo. Doug remembered, quite clearly, signing Eric's plate first, also in the center. After Eric signed Doug's, all the others intentionally signed their names in the other direction, making Eric's name the only one to appear upside down...as if Eric needed any help looking like a dork.

He and Matthews were the first to leave Grover and go to college in almost a generation. Grover was full of people who simply recycled back into the population, tended to their home and farm, and then died at the end of a life of hard work. It was a very big deal that not just one but two Pawnee graduates were moving on to greener pastures. Lastly, next to Doug's signed plate was a coffee mug with the interlocking CU and a buffalo, the Colorado University logo. Aside from these few keepsakes, which he kept to one side, Doug's desk was habitually cluttered with museum paraphernalia.

In the center was a pile of circulars about one of the museum's upcoming exhibits, another exhibit of which he will undoubtedly be forced to sit on the sidelines. As a tour guide at the museum, he was well aware that his expertise was way under-utilized. Not to mention that saying the same things over and over to groups of relatively disinterested parties was not the most rewarding job in the world. If he were to work an exhibit, on the other hand, he'd have the opportunity to show off his full potential to the top brass. Unfortunately, tour guides didn't tend to climb up the ladder fast. Outside work he talked about "his office," but everyone at the museum knew that two or more tour guides shared a space, and that offices were more like glorified janitors' closets. At least he had a place to keep his coat, even if it was on the back of the chair that was built for a Smurf.

Doug shared Room B21 with his partner Michelle, another lowly tour guide on the museum's totem pole. Michelle was in her early twenties, a few years younger than Doug, and was not only attractive but brilliant. Sadly, like so many attractive women, she was often taken less seriously than their male counterparts in this line of work, her two masters degrees, one in history and one in theology, notwithstanding. She'd double-majored at Villanova and finished her undergraduate work in only three years. She was as smart as she was driven, applying her astute sense of logic and design to folding circulars and stamping them with free postage.

Why did Michelle tolerate being stuck in such a go-nowhere job? Every day, doing what was asked of her and then some. Why didn't she look outside the museum? If she expanded her mind and thought about working somewhere else in the field, she'd go straight to the top. Of course, the same thing could be said for Doug. Which was why her answer—that you can't appreciate the top if you don't start out on the bottom—is always an effective plug on the subject.

Doug walked to his desk, set down his coffee, and fell into his chair with a sigh. Michelle, at her desk, a clone of his, didn't look up, but continued to lick and stick. "Well, nice to see you, too."

How could the woman possibly have so much enthusiasm for licking and sticking? "Sorry, g'morning."

"What's wrong? Oh, you saw her again, didn't you? What'd you do this time?"

"What do you think? Froze. As usual. I have nothing to say to her. I have no opening line. You're so lucky you're married. You don't have to do this anymore."

Michelle and her husband had been together since high school. No two people belonged together more than they did, the perfect complements.

"If only I could meet her on neutral turf. I'm tired of spending big bucks for a coffee just to catch a glimpse of her. But I'm desperate."

"You're nuts, Doug. Fageddaboudit," Michelle said in her best Italian mob imitation. "Just talk to her. I mean, what have you got to lose? Other than your self-esteem, of course."

Doug stuck out his tongue at her.

"What's the worst that can happen? If she rejects you at least you'll save a few dollars by getting your coffee at a normal place like the rest of the world."

Valid point. "You're right. I know you're right. But it's easier said than done."

Doug took another sip of his medium-sized regular coffee, all he could afford at the Bread Basket. "Tastes like buckwheat," he said disgustedly, "the worst coffee I've ever had in my life."

Michelle laughed as he got up from his desk and walked a few steps outside the office. He dumped the remainder of the coffee into the water fountain and returned to discard the cup into the recycling bin. Their office was often overlooked in the empty-the-bins department, as evidenced by the four or five other empties there already.

When Michelle left for her lunch hour Doug sat alone at his desk, staring at the wall, specifically the diploma that proudly displayed his name and asked him every day *what if*. The words of one of his favorite professors back at CU came to mind. Professor Balachi was more than just a professor; he was a mentor and a good friend. Doug felt more at home in the prof's office than in his own dorm and they'd often shared a beer together at the campus pub after classes were over for the day. Balachi never showed impatience at Doug's long-winded and resolute deter-mination to make a ground-breaking discovery, never seemed put out by the fact that Doug did most of the talking. Toward the end of his college career, Doug began and then widened his job search in Colorado. Unfortunately the results had been pretty darn disappointing.

Balachi had sensed his discouragement. "Listen, Doug, whether you stick with this or not, make sure what you do makes you happy." At the time he couldn't imagine abandoning his chosen field; he knew what made him happy. But on a day like today the professor's words have a different ring to them altogether.

Sighing, Doug returned to the tedious task at hand. Jenkins was likely to check up on them at any time and it wouldn't do for him to look under-utilized. Fold, stamp; fold, stamp; fold, stamp. He'd much rather be reminiscing about his college days.

Ralph Jenkins, his boss, knew how to make an entrance. Most people would extend the courtesy of a knock before entering a closed office, but that wasn't Jenkins' style. His was more of the I'm-going-to-catch-you-at-something style. Which was probably why, at a short stocky 5'4" with a paunch to rival John Goodman's, Jenkins still managed to command the atten-tion of those in his presence. Would things be different if he met Jenkins outside the workplace? Would Doug willingly step back—or would he push back faster than a dissed Marine? He doesn't know. Jenkins might look like a pushover, but that assessment would be wronger than wrong.

Sure enough, Jenkins stepped into the room. "The next group is waiting for you," he said without preamble.

No *Good morning.* No *Hi, how are you, Goodwin, nice to see you this morning.*

"My turn already? What about these circulars?" Maybe by the time the tour was over and the day was done the circulars would be finished—by someone else.

"Tour first, then finish the circulars," said Jenkins. He turned on his heel and was gone.

In a second he stuck his head back in. "*Now,* Mr. Goodwin. And see to it that those circulars don't wait until tomorrow. Schools are big business for us; we've got to get the new exhibit advertised."

"They'll be on your desk by the morning."

"See that they are." This time Jenkins executed his famous Gestapo-like heel-turn before starting out the door.

"Wait! Mr. Jenkins! Did you get a chance to talk to Dr. Von Haven about moving me to Paleontology?"

Jenkins stalled. Not promising.

"Look, Mr. Goodwin," Jenkins said. "You are a hard worker, and I respect that—"

Here it comes. The old you're-great-but-it's-not-going-to-happen speech.

"—but I can't very well walk up to a distinguished scientist like Dr. Von Haven and recommend someone with your...lack of experience. Why don't you give it a year or so, keep working hard like you are now, and I promise you, we'll sit down and evaluate your future then...yes?"

Sure we will. After we've cleaned up this pile of BS you're dumping that stinks from five feet away.

Doug nodded and extended his hand, full well knowing Jenkins' reputation as germophobe.

Jenkins hesitated for a long moment, but then gave in. His grip was firm, too firm. Like Doug's hand was a baseball bat. Overcompensating for his lack of height?

Don't overdo it, Doug. Choose your battles. Now is not the time. To Doug a handshake was a bond. On the other hand, if Jenkins thought that he was willing to wait "a year or two" before moving upward, he was sorely mistaken. On the third hand, Doug needed this damn job.

Jenkins walked quickly for a man with his girth and was already off down the hall before Doug had locked the door behind him.

But then, Doug wasn't in any particular hurry to meet one more tour group of thirteen-year-olds.

4

Eric Matthews sat back in his leather chair with his feet up on the wide expanse of desk in his plush office, talking into his Bluetooth. "You honestly think I'm going to settle for anything less than the fifty-yard line? You must not think much of me Ricky.... No, I don't really give a damn how much she wants them, all she did was bring you into this world. I'm the one that kept you out of jail. A deal is a deal, Rickster, and we're still in mini-camp here so you still have a few weeks to pull out a miracle."

"Mr. Matthews, there's a call for you," his secretary interrupted hesitantly.

"Hang on there, Ricky," Eric muted the phone. "Tell them I'm in a meeting, Mary Ann."

"Sir, he says it's urgent, he says he's calling on behalf of a Mr. Black."

Eric went pale. "Tell him I'll be right with him." He spoke into the headset. "Listen, Ricky, I gotta take this. Just make it happen."

For a brief time Eric had actually allowed himself to believe this call would never come. Slowly, he removed his headset and picked up the receiver of his desk phone. "Mr. Black? Oh, I thought…no, of course not, sorry. Yes, of course he's too busy to call me…. Tonight? Well, no, actually I have other plans…. Oh. Yes. Fine. Yes, I understand. I'll change them…. Yes, the same place, I understand," he said again, but the call had already ended.

Eric slumped his head into his hands on his giant desk. Then, as he'd been doing every day for the past month, he opened the top drawer to withdraw a plate, signatures scrawled all over it. It was too painful to look at. He shoved it back into the drawer, the force shattering it into pieces. Where the words "Your Friend" and "Doug Goodwin" met there was now a clean split between the two.

Doug stood before the crowd of thirty-five, all with cameras at the ready to snap a shot of Billy with the T-Rex or Sally next to the mummy from Egypt. Most groups sported a decided lack of intellectual curiosity and this one didn't look any different. He took a deep breath. The speech was the same one he had given hundreds of times. "Hello, everyone. My name is Doug Goodwin. I will be your tour guide this afternoon." The respectful ones let their idle conversation dwindle as Doug began his usual intro-duction. "I see a few of you are holding cameras. We ask that you refrain from flash photography when we enter certain wings of the museum. Flashes can damage some of the older artwork and obviously we do not want this to occur. I will alert you when we enter such wings. Failure to comply may result in expulsion from the museum. If you will follow me…."

Being a tour guide in a museum did have its privileges. Doug got a chance to spend most of his time among history's most astounding artifacts, which he loved. It had always surprised and bothered him, therefore, that no matter how rare the piece, unless it had something to do with dinosaurs, most people didn't really care. So, here he was, guiding a bunch of mostly uneducated (or uninterested) people through one of the most educational buildings in the world. He is well equipped with all the information he needs to answer most any question; seldom is he tested.

You never knew when you'd get a live one, though. A few months back, for example. A girl, maybe fourteen or fifteen, on her class trip from Hoboken, New Jersey. She'd walked alone for most of the tour, isolating herself from the rest of her classmates, only speaking to Doug when she had a question or comment. Doug's assessment was that she was too smart for her own good; pretty, but not interested in the boys her own age. He felt for her.

Her first question came as they walked through the Hall of Human Origins. To their left and right various displays were designed to stimulate conversation. *Understanding Our Past* encouraged a debate on the extinction of early primates. *The History of Human Evolution* explored early man from Neanderthals to Homo-Sapiens. One particular display always made Doug nervous. The "Didn't God create man?" question came up more often than any other and was never an easy one to sidestep. Involving himself in a religious debate with people on his tours was always a lose-lose proposition. Next to that, though, was the *One Human Species* display, a favorite. Explaining, especially to children, that we were all from the same species of man, regardless of skin color, was a high point.

That day when they reached the *What Makes Us Human?* display, the girl with long black braids turned to Doug. "Mr. Goodwin, it says here that the human brain reached its current size 150,000 years ago, but it took tens of thousands of years before it started to work. Why did it take so long for humans to begin to use their brains?"

"That's a great question," he told her. Although when he'd heard "Mr. Goodwin," he'd actually turned around expecting to see his father. "Scientists are still debating that today. You have to look at ten thousand years in perspective. It's really not such a big number when you compare it to 150,000 years. Or, let's look at it another way. You've had a brain your whole life right?"

The girl nodded.

"Well, then why weren't you talking when you were a baby?"

A look of understanding came over the girl's face. "Right," said Doug, "It takes time."

"I see. Thank you, Mr. Goodwin."

"You're welcome, and thank you for the question," Doug said, and meant it. If only every tour group had that girl's thirst for knowledge, he'd be a lot happier at his job.

No such luck with the group today, busily looking for the next *Jurassic Park* artifact. Still, this part of the tour was a real treat. Doug led them to an exhibit of early man where he stopped before a reproduction of a woolly mammoth. Most of the group members were carrying on their own conversations, but he went on with his speech anyway. "This is the woolly mammoth, *mammuthus primigenius*. It walked the earth thousands of years ago. Its extinction has been the subject of controversy for decades. However, new evidence suggests this animal was hunted to annihilation by prehistoric man. Such a magnificent beast and such a sad demise...."

Doug paused for a second, closed his eyes, and bowed his head just slightly, absently feeling for his cross through his shirt. "An interesting fact about the woolly mammoth, too, one that most people don't know, is that they were actually walking the earth at the time King Tutankhamun was ruling over Egypt." This sparked a few oohs from the small crowd that had perked up at King Tut's name. "And he ruled only 2000 or so years ago. Sounds like a long time, but is it really?"

As they returned to their starting point in the museum's lobby, Doug saw Eric waving to him from the circular information desk. Doug acknowledged him with a slight nod. The crowd had grown impatient at just the right time.

"And that concludes our tour for today, ladies and gentleman," he said with the over-the-top smile the museum's staff had probably trademarked. "Feel free to visit our gift shop off to your right. It should be open for another thirty minutes. I would like to thank you for sharing your day with us and, on behalf of the museum, I wish you all a pleasant day." The crowd dispersed.

And another one bites the dust.

Eric the fashionista, flashy as ever in another trim suit and a pair of dark Ray-Bans, was flirting with the receptionist. It was late but the sun was still out, peering in through the stained glass windows of the museum. The varying shades of green, yellow, and purple resembled some kind of toxic sunset that was still too beautiful to ignore. Doug patted Eric on the back. "Hey, Matthews, what are you doing here?"

Mr. Jenkins walked by at that moment, gracing Doug with a thumbs-up sign followed by a tap on his wristwatch.

"I hate this damn job sometimes," Doug said through his teeth. "But hey, what's up with you? You haven't returned my calls all week. I was kind of worried...thought maybe you got whacked or something."

"Sorry about that. I've been really busy at work."

"You get that account?"

"What account?"

"What account? You know what account. Those clients you brought out to 'hunt' with me the other day. The ones you left me with. The ones who were spookier than Michael Myers on Halloween. Those clients."

"Oh, them. Yeah, we got it. Big money, too. The firm is now officially their company's legal representation. Um, thanks."

"Yeah, I deserve a lot more than thanks this time, Matthews. 'Cause I got to tell you, those guys were not normal. Didn't say a single word the whole time. And those masks. I mean, who wears masks in that kind of heat? And who doesn't bring any kind of a weapon—not even a frickin' key chain. And I didn't appreciate having something like that sprung on me by my best friend."

Eric didn't answer. Something was up. Eric without a comeback? Eric always had a comeback. Unless something big was going down. He wouldn't get anything out of Eric here, though. He'd worm more out of him later, once they'd left the museum and had settled in with a pint or two.

Eric fidgeted with his earpiece. Dougie always could see right through him. And this time little Eric Matthews had fucked up so good that not even Doug Goody-Two-Shoes Goodwin would be able to set it right. "So, uh, wanna go for a beer or what?"

"You read my mind. Oh, wait. Shoot. I can't. I have to finish these circulars and have them on Jenkins' desk by tomorrow morning."

"Come on, man, screw the circulars. Jenkins works you like a dog because you let him. Show a little backbone. I don't have to come in here dressed like a museum executive from MoMA do I? 'Cause I'll do it. You know I will."

Eric would, too. March in here like the director of the board of the Museum of Modern Art. Doug admitted defeat. "You know what? You're right. I'll come in early tomorrow and get it done. Just let me go punch out."

"Now that's the Dougie I know and love. Hurry up man, we're checking out this new hot spot I know."

Doug scurried off into the bowels of the museum and Eric was left alone with his thoughts, his picture-perfect grin quickly retreating into a look that, if you didn't know him, you might think was fear.

These days the museum was not a place Eric liked to be. He'd been there too many times to meet Doug, so many that it had almost become a home away from home. He removed his sunglasses, but the light from the reflection of the stained glass was too blinding and he shoved them on again.

The performance of my life, he thought, and it wasn't close to the final scene.

5

Mass transit fascinated Doug. The way one subway could hold more than twice the population of his hometown. Its aroma, so unappetizing to most, enchanted him. The smell of roasted peanuts that never faded away, even in the summer, along with all sorts of other earthy smells. It reminded him of cold winter nights out by the fire back home in Grover, when it was below zero but no one noticed or cared. Too far from the fire, you froze your butt off; too close and you sweated like a pig. That one perfect spot—heaven on earth.

Normally Doug would rather walk wherever Eric decides to drag him. This time, however, Eric was insistent. As soon as they stepped out the museum doors Eric checked his watch. "Way too far to walk it," he said. Fast-moving, fast-talking, fast-thinking Eric. Almost everywhere was too far to walk. Always in a hurry to get where he was going, and walking could never get him there fast enough. Rush hour in New York City was a sea of occupied yellow cabs as far as the eye could see. "We'll need to take the subway," Eric said. "Come on, there's one in three minutes."

With anyone else Doug would be skeptical. But Eric had memorized the subway schedule to and from his favorite destinations within a month or so of moving to New York. It was OCD even for him. Without the funds to support taxis in the beginning, though, it had been a necessity. And he was so protective of his new Lexus that he only took it out of the garage to impress his parade of "female companions."

That is, until his unlikely trip to Doug's hunting zone.

As they descended the stairs of the nearest subway entrance at 72nd Street they heard the sounds of a struggle. Two kids, young teenagers by the looks of them, in pants so loose Doug was seeing far more of their asses than he wanted, were harassing a homeless woman on the station platform. Since subway workers weren't allowed to leave their bullet-proof Plexiglas cubicles, aside from making a phone call there was nothing they could do.

"Hey!" Doug yelled. "What the hell do you think you're doing?"

When they saw Doug's size the kids took off. They hightailed it to the other end of the station, hopped over the turnstiles and hustled up the stairs. If the police ever caught up with them, they'd likely get no more than a slap on the wrist. There was too much crime of much more serious consequence in the city.

Doug approached the woman slowly, taking in the bleary look in her eyes and her mumbled diatribe. When he reached out she jerked back as if expecting another attack. "It's okay, ma'am, I'm not going to hurt you. Let me help get you up."

It was hard to tell how old she was, what with the effects of the street so deeply etched in her face, but early sixties was his guess. Layer upon layer of ragged clothing made her body seem twice its size. The woman looked up suspiciously, but after a minute offered Doug her arm and let him guide her up off the filthy ground. Doug assumed it was her shopping cart he saw leaning against the wall in the corner loaded with dirty garbage bags full of who-knew-what. It was hot down in the tunnels right now, too. She'd die of heat exhaustion if she wasn't careful.

Doug helped her to a bench. "Are you okay, ma'am?"

Eric watched from a safe distance. Revolting homeless people. Shouldn't be allowed near the public. "Hey, Dougie, I wouldn't be putting my hands on someone like that, man. She's crazy, just look at her. And what if she bites you? She's probably got AIDS."

Idiot. Telling Eric that you couldn't get AIDS from a bite was useless. His tolerance for logic was notoriously low when it didn't meet his needs. "Shut up, Matthews. Call someone on your cell. She needs a doctor."

"Damn right she needs a doctor. And a shower, and probably a bottle of vodka just to even out. It's not our job. Let's go."

"Terry, is that you, son?" The woman peered out from swollen eyes in Eric's direction.

"No, lady, I'm not your son." Eric rolled his eyes.

Doug's face was a mask of piety. "Why are you looking at me like that?"

"I'll tell you why. We're due at this club and this good Samaritan act of yours is getting old fast. I mean it, Doug. Let's get out of here."

"Terry went to the store," said the woman. "But he never came home. The circles got him."

"Doug, it's time to go!"

"Back off, Matthews." The woman had a few screws loose, sure, but how could Doug leave her there where she was so vulnerable? He turned back to the woman. "Ma'am, stay here for a while. Someone will be here to help you, I promise." The woman went on mumbling. She didn't seem to hear him.

He rose, feeling a strong yank on his arm. The woman's grip was unrelenting. Her rheumy eyes met his. "The circles got Terry. You hear me, boy? You'd best be careful or they'll get you, too."

A chill traveled straight up Doug's back. The woman was crazy, it meant nothing, but tell that to the hairs on his neck.

"We'll be fine, lady," Eric said loudly, leading Doug away toward the tracks. "We'll be real careful, won't we Doug? ...Of the triangles, the squares, and all the other shapes."

He turned on Doug. "Listen man, we're not in Grover anymore. You can't get involved with everyone you see. That woman's probably crawling with disease. This is New York, man. You have to learn to look the other way."

"I can't do that, Eric."

"Then you're going to end up in some bad situations. Even if we got that woman to a hospital, in twenty-four hours she'd be right back on that bench and there's nothing you can do about it. People have bad luck or make stupid choices and you can't change it. And I definitely don't need you dragging me into your pathetic little do-gooder routine."

So that's the way it was, then. Eric Matthews was glib, sure. Selfish, definitely. Not to mention a well-earned reputation for self-aggrandizement. But this was new, an over-the-top contemptuousness that Doug had never seen in his best friend before. He doesn't like it.

"*You* look, man. Whatever's *really* bothering you, either tell me what it is so I can help you or keep it to yourself and suffer in silence. You and I both know that's the way I was brought up, and I'm damn sure it's the way you were brought up, too."

The flash of guilt in Eric's eyes wouldn't have registered on a lightening meter. "Look, man, just be smart. This isn't Grover, okay? Everyone in this place is out to screw you, not help you. They'll step over you, or on you for that matter, if you give them half a chance."

Doug sighed. It was true, at least to an extent. Back home, if someone had problems, the whole town knew about it. Grover was so small it was impossible to keep anything a secret. But someone was always there to lend a hand. New York, on the other hand, had over six million people who were all fighting to get ahead. And Doug had become one of them. If he didn't change to keep up he'd be the one getting trampled. Eric was right about being smarter, too. As much as Doug epitomized the "country boy in the big city" thing, it was getting old. Then again, if he didn't watch Matthews' back the way he always had, who would?

The train came and they sat across the aisle from each other swaying with the movement of the coach.

"Suffer in silence?" Eric finally called over.

"I guess," Doug said. "Your dad must have said that every day of our lives."

"And now you carry the torch, huh, Goodwin. Makes you sound like an old man."

Which is exactly how Doug felt.

6

The remaining beams of sunlight were still fading into the evening sky, taking with them the beautiful but ironically smog-induced oranges, yellows, and blues, when Eric and Doug arrived at their destination. Lost in the moment, it took Doug a minute to realize that Eric had descended three stone stairs and stopped in front of a big wooden door. Doug would have walked right past it. The sign above the door was simple, light wooden letters against a darker wooden backdrop with no illumination of any kind. Like the type of work he did as a kid in shop class. It read "Tasker's" with the final "s" dangling at an angle off the end. On purpose or poorly constructed, who could say. Either way, its only character was in the fact that it was falling apart. The entrance itself was akin to a sixteenth-century dungeon, the wooden door without windows, layered brick walls. What was it doing here on the Upper East Side of Manhattan?

Eric went up to the door and pushed. The door didn't give. Doug waited for a head to appear from a slot in the door to demand a password or to tell them to go away like in the *Wizard of Oz*. Finally, Doug elbowed Eric aside and pulled the handle. "Suave, dude. Very suave."

Eric gave him the finger. "How was I supposed to know it pulled out?"

The interior of Tasker's was small and smoky. Scattered about were comfortable-looking chairs and tables, many of which were empty. Doug's eyes adjusted to the dim interior slowly. The place had a surprisingly intriguing layout, like an upscale ski lodge. Along the wall closest to the door was the bar itself. There was only one tap dispensing beer and a soda gun attached to the bar; rows of liquor were stacked against the mirror behind it. Even from here Doug could see that the bottles on display ranged from expensive to off the charts. A one-drink kind of place, then. So much for a couple of pints.

The stools were well-maintained, no scratches, no tears in the cushions the way they were in most of the other places Doug usually drank, and all had three solid legs to ensure a steady perch. On closer inspection what looked like wood paneling turned out to be actual wood. Classy. A fully stocked humidor sat along the wall closest to the door. Romeo y Julieta, Porto-fino, Montecino, Fonseca, La Gloria Cubana, and a few brands he couldn't even pronounce. He only knew their names because Eric had a recent obsession with the disgusting things. There was no visible lock on the humidor.

One of the male patrons went over and debated over the selection. He chose a big fat cigar and then took a seat near a small stage and lit up. No money exchanged hands. Curious and curiouser, thought Doug. He was wasting money by just standing around.

A blond man, mid-forties, took the stage accompanied by a small band. His crooning performance wasn't great, but he did a fair-to-middling rendition of *My Way* by Frank Sinatra. There were a handful of patrons at tables, enjoying cigars, engaged in conversation, listening to the performance.

"Where are we, Matthews? How did you find this place?"

"Great isn't it? Lots of atmosphere, right?"

The bartender waited patiently for them to get comfortable on a pair of adjacent stools. Guy was around 5'6," looked fit. His face was deeply lined, but his hair was dark and full, albeit with a silvery wave of maturity and distinction. His long-sleeved button-down shirt, bow tie, and apron, the kind that slides over the neck and ties in the back, were leftovers from the 1920s. Could probably run a marathon and top it off with fifteen rounds in the ring. Doug made a mental note not to get in the guy's way.

"What'll it be, boys?"

"What kind of beer do you have?" asked Doug.

"I only carry one type of beer on tap and that's Weihenstephan. The oldest brewery in the world, you know, started in the year 1040. Imported from Germany. Costs a pretty penny, but then, it's for my customers."

"We'll have two," said Eric.

"Coming right up, gentlemen."

So this was how the other half lived. "Come here often, Eric?"

"Me? Sure. Love that Vine-er-soppin they got here...."

"Because this doesn't exactly seem like your kind of place. Or at least it didn't used to."

"Two beers," the barkeep declared.

Doug went for his wallet. "How much?"

Eric had his phone out. He was already punching the buttons. "I gotta go make this call."

Unbelieveable. "How much?" asked Doug again, shaking his head.

"First drink is on the house for all new customers."

"New?" Doug looked back at Eric. Had he been to the bar before or not? But why would he lie about it? What would be the point?

"Well, I'm not going to turn down a free drink. Doug Goodwin," he said.

"Nice t' meetcha. Known Mr. Matthews long?"

"Who, Eric?" *So, the guy knows Eric.*

"Since we were kids."

Then why is he treating us like new customers? And why is Eric running around like a lunatic?

"So…he comes in with his partners from the firm then?"

"The firm?" the bartender said, looking puzzled. "Oh yes, that's right, the firm."

What the heck? Doug didn't know what to make of the bartender's response. He put out his hand.

The bartender's hand was small but strong, a good grip for a man his size. A don't-underestimate-me kind of grip.

Doug's boss did that macho thing, and Eric always managed a kind of weird non-handshake, where he sort of dodged it, clasping Doug's thumb in an arm-wrestling pose. It had never really bothered him before, but lately Doug was getting a little pissed off. Eric was all about getting noticed, and this quasi "bro, I'm so cool" handshake made them both look ridiculous. The bartender, on the other hand, had a confident grip, cool and dry. A bartender who wanted to know his patrons. Hmm. Doug had never known a bartender who wanted to be acquainted with anything but his—or her—tips.

"So, where you from, Mr. Goodwin?"

"Colorado. Little town called Grover. Just outside Boulder."

"Ah, mountain country, magnificent. Peaceful?"

"Very."

It had taken Doug weeks before he could finally sleep though the night in his place in the city. The noise never quit. Garbage trucks at 5:00 AM, elevators moving night and day.

"Not much to do except ski during the winter and hunt during the summer."

"Sounds like you miss it. What brings you to the big city?"

Doug jerked his finger over his shoulder to indicate his pal, Matthews, who had conveniently disappeared. "My friend, there, and his law career."

"Oh?"

"Ever since the O. J. trial he wanted to be a lawyer. I swear he was glued to CNN for the entire thing, mimicking Johnnie Cochran's walk and talk—the whole nine yards. Before the verdict even came out his mind was made up. He was primed for the big time. Let's just say that Grover isn't a hot bed of legal activity. When he passed the bar exam it was New York City all the way. Gotta be where the action is, that's what he said."

"And you came along for the ride?"

Doug nodded. He'd helped Eric move and then stayed. Sometimes he wondered why. What life would be like if he'd stayed in Grover or gone somewhere else.

"I do miss the simpler life back in good ol' Grover, though."

"Well, look at that, a real fish out of water," the bartender said with a wink.

"I guess. But Matthews tends to, um, live life to the fullest."

"Oh, yeah? How?"

Doug drew back, aware he was on the edge of TMI. "No offense, but I think I've already said too much."

"No offense taken, Mr. Goodwin. But if you're trying to protect his gambling problem, it's okay, I already know."

Gambling problem? Eric had a gambling problem? A deep burn began to grow in the pit of Doug's stomach. What the heck was Matthews into now? He reached for his wallet. A paltry hundred and thirty dollars stared back at him. All of it marked for utility bills. "How much is he into you for?"

"No, no. It's not like that." The bartender held up his palm. "He and I made...other arrangements. He's okay in my book. But how'd he end up with such a good friend like you anyway?"

Trying not to show how relieved he was that he could keep his electricity going, Doug put his wallet back in his pocket. "Just got lucky, I guess." As soon as he got a hold of his "good friend," they would be having words.

He drained the last of his beer, appreciating its yeasty quality and the hint of cloves, but tasting bitter disappointment over his discovery. "I wonder what's keeping him."

A framed photo of a man who looked identical to the bartender, only with a tiny mustache and goatee, caught Doug's eye.

"My dear departed father," the bartender said, bowing his head and crossing himself. "There to watch over me. He used to run this bar, and his father before him. Someday, my son will be sitting here with a picture of me looking over him. Tradition, you know."

"Cool," said Doug. "Like he's always there for you." He raised his empty glass. "To your dad."

"Thank you, Mr. Goodwin," the bartender said, "but I never toast an empty glass." He pulled out a shot glass, dispensed himself and Doug a small amount of beer, then clinked glasses with Doug's. "*Na zdraví, Papa!*"

Doug smiled, but he'd had enough. Where the heck was Eric? Doug's fingers tapped impatiently on the bar as his gaze went from the door to the back of the bar and back again. No Matthews. A man in the far corner of the bar was nodding at him, though. Doug looked closer. He didn't know the guy.

The bartender nodded back.

Doug flushed. The guy was nodding to the bartender, not him.

The man got up and the bartender reached down under the bar. A second later one of the wood panels slid open in the wall. A woman, a real knockout in a lavender mini-dress, emerged. Behind her Doug caught a glimpse of a smoky room, men engaged in billiards and playing cards. So many beautiful women it looked like a fashion runway.

The woman in purple winked at Doug as she passed by. His eyes tracked her as she made her way toward another man sitting by himself in the corner. From this distance, the man looked old enough to be her father, but with all the smoke who knew? His tuxedo was expertly cut and, even from this vantage point, the cufflinks at his wrists were giving off a sparkle worth at least a couple karats each.

Doug's attention was rooted to the mystery woman's every move. She was like a page out of *Maxim*, voluptuous and seductive in a short skin-tight dress that barely covered her you-know-what. One of her shoulder straps had fallen loosely down her arm. As she fixed it, she bent at the waist to whisper something in the man's ear. She tossed her long glossy brown hair seductively. She looked directly at Doug in the process boldly, unapologetically. It was unlikely she was unaware of how high her dress had hiked up in the back. Doug gulped. *Be still mine heart.*

The man rose from his seat and followed the woman back through the bar. As she passed Doug for the second time, her sidelong glance was packed with nuance. Doug felt a further flush on his neck and the blood rush to the part of his body that had been neglected for much too long. The door slid open and then closed again soundlessly. She was gone. Doug was left sitting there, mouth open, like a schoolboy with his first crush.

"Mr. Matthews probably had to take a conference call or something."

The bartender was talking to him. "What? Oh, yeah, right. Hey, so, um, what's up back there?"

"Back there? Oh, that's the VIP parlor. For our more distinguished guests."

Distinguished? That meant dough. And not the kind Doug had in his wallet to pay his utility bills. Oh, well. There was always the woman at the coffee shop. The one who never gave him a second look.

"Listen," said the bartender. "I don't usually do this, but you seem like a good kid. I'll vouch for you. Go check it out."

"Yeah?"

"Sure, why not?"

"Well, I shouldn't, but..." That's what credit cards are for, right?

"And don't worry. I'll let Mr. Matthews know where you are too when he returns."

The bartender waved, nodding to the man behind Doug, the singer, who was singing *Tell Me It's Not Over* by Johnny Gaines. The singer nodded back at him. The bartender deployed the button, and the door to Doug Goodwin's future opened without a sound.

7

A fraternity for adults who can afford the upkeep. That's what the room looks like. Doug scanned the women, but the one in the purple dress wasn't there. He swallowed the blow to his ego.

The décor was simple, a few scattered game tables accompanied by leather chairs and small coffee tables. Maybe fifteen men, each with one or two women at his side, each more exotic than the next. The woman with the sexy, um, hair might not be there, but the selection blew him away. Four of the men were playing pool. Five or six were engaged in a roundtable discussion over a game of what appeared to be Baccarat. A couple were playing a game of darts, while the remaining few, including the man with the diamond cufflinks, were sitting in cushioned leather chairs talking. Their suits were not off the rack. They held glasses of brandy and cigars. The smoke in the room was thick, and Doug's eyes watered. He felt a cough form in his throat. With all eyes upon him, he stifled it. After a brief moment of scrutiny, the quiet rumble of voices picked up again and the room returned to its former level of activity. Doug was still standing at the door, which had magically disappeared into the wall behind him. He leaned on it. He'd fade into the woodwork until a plan of action came to him.

The man wearing the cufflinks had a certain air about him—self-satisfied—the owner of the place? A 007 type, good-looking, debonair, sophisticated. The type of man who got exactly what he wanted when he wanted it. To his left a chubby guy, also in his prime with a full beard that hid his features, was unsuccessfully attempting to disguise the tire around his stomach with a loose jacket. Where 007 was confidently suave, this guy lacked all the finishing touches. Doug moved on. The third guy caught his eye, and not in a good way. A distinct look of menace lit his face. A reddened indented patch of flesh just below his right eye looked raw, as if the skin had been ripped away and had never healed right, maybe from a war injury or a fire. Somehow the deformity made it hard for Doug to tear his eyes away. When the man sent a penetrating glare back at him, Doug quickly, guiltily got it together and averted his eyes.

Who were these guys? The man with the ravaged face, for example. What was his story? A disgruntled Vietnam vet? Someone who'd seen everything there was to see—and had seen right through it? Doug was thinking there was a good novel here when James Bond waved him over.

Who, me? Doug pantomimed.

Yes, you. The man pointed at the seat next to him.

The man's smile bordered on patronizing. But who cared? He couldn't hug the wall all night. He'd give it a few minutes, see what was up. If he still felt like the proverbial gorilla...well, nothing lost, nothing gained.

"Doug Goodwin," he said as he reached the table, but no one accepted his extended hand. Okay, then. Not the warm-and-fuzzy types.

Chubster spoke first. "I think we've got us a new one, Mr. Cufflinks."

"I tend to agree with you, Mr. Chemist," said the one called Mr. Cufflinks (007).

Cufflinks? Chemist?

Doug didn't like the sound of this. It was like a game—one where he didn't know the rules. And he didn't like being the butt of other men's jokes.

Vietnam Man offered his opinion matter-of-factly. "Too young," he grumbled.

"Nah, he seems okay to me, Mr. Fingers," said the guy they were calling "Mr. Chemist."

You can't be serious. Really? *Mr. Fingers?* "Excuse my ignorance, *gentlemen*, but if you have something to say I'd appreciate it if you just said it."

The men seemed positively gleeful at Doug's comment, which irritated him all the more. It was like he'd been beamed down into a play where he was playing a starring role but had no idea what the plot was and no script.

CUFFLINKS: "Oh, dear. A live wire, eh?"

FINGERS (emulating Cufflinks' diction; imaginary pipe in hand): "Quite right. I'm elated beyond words."

CUFFLINKS (with smile that doesn't reach his eyes): "As am I, Mr. Fingers, as am I. Far too long since we have seen a new face."

CHEMIST (nodding): "True, true."

That did it. Doug pushed off his chair.

CHEMIST: "Oh, dear, we've been terribly rude. But we don't mean to be. Please sit down, won't you, sir?"

Doug hesitated, but finally sat back in his chair. Why, he had no idea.

CUFFLINKS: "Joanne, we would very much like to introduce you to Mr.—ah, Mr. Doug...Gooden, wasn't it?"

Doug felt a presence at his side. The woman in the lavender dress had rematerialized and was standing close enough to rub noses. He took in her long legs and breathed in the smell of her perfume. "Ah, Goodwin, sir, it's Good*win*. It's a pleasure to meet you, ma'am."

"The pleasure is all mine, I'm sure," Joanne said with the broad vowels of the south. With a flick of her finger she maneuvered Doug back in his chair and made herself at home on his left leg. Her arms snaked around his neck. Her curves made contact with his body. Doug felt a rush of desire and fervently hoped the table concealed what was going on down below.

The only action he'd gotten for months was his fantasy life with Coffee Shop Girl. Joanne, if that was her real name, kissed him softly on the cheek and ran her hand through his hair. Hypnotized by her touch and scent, any second he'd be clucking like a damn chicken.

When Cufflinks spoke Doug took a second to resurface. And keep your hands off the woman, he told himself sternly. You'll only embarrass yourself.

"Allow me to introduce myself, Mr. Goodwin. I am who you will come to know as Mr. Cufflinks."

Okay, right. And Colonel Mustard's in the library committing murder with a candlestick. But they could play games all they wanted if the girl in his lap stayed put.

CUFFLINKS: "And this is Mr. Chemist and Mr. Fingers."

Doug cut him off with a short snort. "Yeah, yeah. I get it, I get it. When my buddy gets back here we gotta do this to him, too. He's the one who appreciates a good joke."

FINGERS (not smiling anymore): "Joke, huh? Here, I'll show you a good joke. I keep it around fer special occasions. You'll love it." He picked up a long black leather box on the floor next to his chair. He waited until he had Doug's undivided attention. "Great for laughs," he said. "A real party pleaser."

Doug's spidey senses were pinging off the charts. Finger's grin was more of a leer, the tortured skin stretching his face into unequal parts. Doug looked away, down at the box, and adjusted Joanne, who'd gone still, on his lap. What was in it? Drug paraphernalia? Contraband cigars? He waited, determined not to give the guy any play. Two could go at a game like this.

With a disgusted look, Fingers opened the box.

Doug reared back. The move unsettled Joanne, who flailed to regain her equilibrium.

Sick bastard.

Nothing could have prepared Doug for what actually lay inside the box. His stomach clenched. Thirteen human fingers, evenly spaced, lying on red felt, each with a small bronze nameplate beneath it. Doug could read the names quite clearly. Mr. Smiles, Mr. Cross, Mr. Notes, Mr. Question, Mr. Omega, Mr. Star, Mr. Brass, Mr. Orange, Mr. Cavity, Mr. Crisp, Mr. Damp, Mr. Legs, and Mr. Night. A few slots on the end were still empty. He went icy cold. He was going to heave. He bolted upright. This time Joanne was knocked on her ass. "Hey!" she wailed. He had to get out of there. He got to the wall and pushed on it. Nothing. There had to be a button or a latch somewhere. He was sweating. He was losing it.

"Let me out of here! Open this damn door now." He pounded on the hard wood. *Crazy mother—*

Again. And again. He pounded until his fist stung, but the wall remained a wall.

Finally he spun around. The women had vanished. Joanne was nowhere to be seen. Almost a dozen men had formed a semi-circle around him like sharks around blood. They backed Doug up to the wall and pinned him there.

007—Cufflinks—was in the center. "Calm yourself, son. You are safe here, in this room. You're among friends."

"Friends?" I don't think so. "Who the hell are you people? That guy's got fingers in a box, for God's sake!"

CUFFLINKS: "Calm down, Mr. Goodwin, calm down. We'll explain everything."

"Look, *Cufflinks*, or whoever you are, I don't want any trouble. I won't press charges if you let me leave now." Now he sounded like a bad Western. The threat was lame and he knew it.

"Just hear us out, boy. We mean you no harm."

"And I'm not your boy."

The look on Cufflinks' face was not one to write home about. There was no way Doug was going down without someone else getting hurt first. He drew back his fist and struck him square in the jaw. Cufflinks, caught off guard, stumbled backwards. Two of the men grabbed Doug's arms before he could go in for another blow. Another yanked his neck from behind. He was immobilized and spitting angry. "Perverts! Let me out of here, let me go!"

CUFFLINKS (rubbing his jaw thoughtfully): "Perverts? Not quite."

"Touch me and I'll kill you," Doug declared.

Cufflinks laughed heartily as he wiped the blood from his lip with a handkerchief. "Gentlemen, I do believe the boy thinks we're homosexuals." Full-throated chuckles erupted around the room, as if Doug's reaction were too funny for words. "We have no intention of *touching* you, young man."

It was probably true. That is, if all the women were any indication. But was he mollified? Definitely not. "Then what the hell do you want from me?"

All eyes turned to the back corner of the room. Doug strained his neck, but couldn't see what they were looking at. Wait. Was that a man with a cigar in the corner. Now what? Who the heck was he...the Godfather?

"Bring him here," the man beckoned. The three men dragged Doug, thrashing uselessly, to the smoking man's table. The rest followed, holding their formation around Doug.

"Welcome to the Circle," the man said. "I am Mr. Black."

Doug made another attempt to free himself. Black waved his hand. A pool cue was placed against Doug's neck choking him.

"Listen closely, boy. You will act like a gentleman or my associate here will squeeze the life out of you and enjoy doing it. Do you understand?"

After a few unbearable seconds Doug shook his head yes. Black motioned for the man with the pool cue to back off. "Good. Then have a seat."

Doug sat, coughing and sputtering. His neck felt bruised and painful. As the oxygen filled his lungs again a sharp tingle of fear ran through him. What did these guys want from him, Doug Goodwin, a nobody from a little town in Colorado? Not money, that's for sure. He had none.

"Are you comfortable? Can we get you something? A drink perhaps?" asked Black solicitously.

"Really? You're asking me if I want a drink? I don't *think* so, no. I want to know what the hell is going on!"

"Mr. Lion, get the boy a drink, would you?" ordered Black, pointedly ignoring Doug's response.

Mr. Lion? There's a Mr. Lion now? These guys were insane. Although this one actually lived up to his moniker, with a flowing head of salt-and-pepper hair, a massive upper body. His well-defined muscles stretched his shirt tightly across his chest.

Compared to his fairly average lower half it made for a comical mismatch. That is, if Doug felt like laughing.

"Look, *gentlemen*," Doug said, "I don't want any trouble. No harm done. If you let me go, I swear I won't press charges." He was pleased with how this came out. He was a reasonable man, after all, right? Willing to let bygones be bygones and all that.

"Oh, we will let you go, Mr. Goodwin. You are not a prisoner here. But before we do, let's you and I have…a conversation."

"A conversation? About what? What do we have to talk about?"

"Mr. Lion" returned with Doug's glass. Scotch, neat. Doug tossed it down. Scotch wasn't his drink, but he'd manage.

Lion took the seat opposite Doug's, next to Black. He said nothing, but Doug felt his silent assurance that it would be stupid to try anything.

Black continued. "Well, first I want to get to know you a little better, if you don't mind."

"'Better'? If I don't mind? Are you nuts? Look, first of all, you don't know anything about me. Second, you lock me in here and threaten me. And then you say you want to get to know me better? Excuse me if I decline the offer. By now my friend will be wondering what happened to me. He's waiting for me outside. So, if *you* don't mind…." Doug went to get up.

"Oh, yes, Mr. Matthews, isn't it? I wouldn't concern yourself with him. The ladies are keeping him…occupied."

Doug blanched. That clinched it. They knew Eric. They *all* knew Eric. But what did that mean? Plus, if he was "busy with the ladies" Doug's ship was sunk.

"Mr. Goodwin, I just need a moment of your time…if you will permit me."

Doug surveilled his options. Oh yeah, right. He had none. Resisting wasn't going to get him anywhere. There were too many of them. Fighting them all would get him killed.

Sighing, he sat back. Let the asshole have his way. He'd listen, then split.

"Excellent! I believe introductions are in order. As I mentioned, my name is Mr. Black. It is not my Christian name. It was given to me by my colleagues. Mr. Black is the name of distinction given to the oldest surviving member of this chapter of the Circle." He paused as if to gauge Doug's response.

Colleagues? The Circle? *What is this, a video game?* Doug could hold his own on many subjects—the NFL, woodworking, the museums of Paris—but this crap? The Circle thing was curious, though, sounded familiar, but Black had already moved on.

"Let me ask you a question," he was saying, "Why do you think people love action heroes, Mr. Goodwin?"

Yeah, not playing, dude. "You said you know about me."

Mr. Black sighed. He disliked being pushed. "Douglas Goodwin, Jr., age twenty-seven. Son of Douglas and Margaret Goodwin of Grover, Colorado. Valedictorian of your high school; first in a graduating class of seven, if I'm not mistaken. Attended Colorado University, double-major in paleontology and anthropology. Graduated *summa cum laude*. Currently working for the Museum of Natural History as a tour guide." He looked at Doug. "You see, Mr. Goodwin, I know everything there is to know about you."

Doug's hands tightened into fists again. The walls were closing in around him. What the hell was going on?

"I will ask you again, Mr. Goodwin, and this time I'd like an answer, please. Why do people love action heroes?"

Screw that. If they were playing a game, Doug was a conscientious objector. He kept his mouth shut.

"Mr. Goodwin, I assure you, things will go a lot more smoothly if you just answer my questions. No harm has ever come from answering a question before, now has it?"

Yeah? Really? A few thousand examples came to mind right off the bat. Times when "answering questions" had led to death and destruction. In this case, however, well, it might be the lesser of two evils. "I don't know why people love action heroes," he said grudgingly. "They're entertaining, I guess."

"Yes, but *why* are they entertaining?" Black insisted.

Doug didn't answer.

Black's voice hardened. "I'll ask you one more time, Mr. Goodwin. Why are action heroes and their movies entertaining?"

Was this guy really threatening him with action movies? "Look, I don't know what you want me to say."

"Say what you think. No one will judge you for your answer."

"Fine. I guess they're entertaining because people get to leave their boring lives behind for a couple of hours...you know, live vicariously."

"Yes!" said Black, smiling as if he had an apt pupil. "That's my opinion as well. Let me ask you another question, then. Why a tour guide?"

Doug stirred. "Look, I'm not here to be insulted."

"Stay, Mr. Goodwin, sit. It's just a simple career-related question. I didn't know it was such a sensitive subject."

"It's not." *It so is.* "I like my job." *I so don't.* "So what's your point?"

"I'm just curious as to how a man of your obvious intelligence and educational background finds himself giving tours in a museum? I mean, I have my own theories, but I'm still curious."

I could rip the smug right off the your face. Well, maybe not just yet. "You know so much about me, why don't you answer that yourself."

"I'd still like to hear your take on it, Mr. Goodwin."

Doug felt himself deflating. Would the truth get him out of there any sooner? "I'm biding my time as a tour guide so I can get myself into a career in paleontology."

"And how do you feel about having to start from the bottom to achieve your goals?" asked Black.

"What are you, a damn shrink? How do you think it feels? It's damn humiliating. So, like I said, what's your point?"

"Why?" Black asked pointedly.

"Why, *what*?"

"Why is it humiliating?"

"You know why, damn it. I have degrees in paleontology and archaeology, and I'm giving tours to school children! Every day I wake up and I feel less and less...worthy." He could never decide which was worse—the humiliation or the shame.

"You feel belittled?" asked Black.

"Yes."

"Degraded?"

"Yes, goddammit!"

"Angry?"

"Yeah, alright? And I'm not all that happy about it."

And now he was letting a complete stranger, albeit a stranger who knew more about him than most of his closest friends, push every button he had. That was so not good. His face felt as hot as kindling in a campfire.

"What if I could give you back your manhood, Mr. Goodwin?" said Black.

"Huh?"

"I said, what if I could give you back your manhood."

"What does that even mean? Besides, I'm not asking for your help."

"I'm aware of that, Mr. Goodwin. But look around you. The members here understand you. We have all been where you are. We have all lived meaningless lives. Some of us are wealthy, with fortunes spanning centuries, inherited wealth...not earned. You would be surprised how empty the life of a wealthy man can be."

Yeah, right. Doug was not moved to offer sympathy.

Cufflinks had a front row seat to Doug's interrogation.

"It's true. I am the inheritor of a fortune based in petroleum. I owned the company, but I was just a figurehead. I had no real power to make decisions. Now my boards run the entire operation."

"Indeed." Back to Black. "And some of us, Mr. Goodwin, are just like you. Ordinary men, fighting the good fight, working hard to achieve our dreams."

Some of *us*. Was he including himself? Add another question to the growing list.

Black leaned forward to close the gap between them. "Son, man was not put on this earth to live like that."

Suddenly Doug was tired. The adrenaline rush was over. Elvis had left the building. He wanted to go home. "Listen, whatever, this is all very...interesting, but what's the point? And what does it have to do with me?"

"I'm getting there, Mr. Goodwin. Patience, please. Let me explain. As the world began to industrialize and corporations gained momentum and power, a small group of men from around the world made an unusual and fascinating choice. They chose to surrender their fortunes and begin new lives. They were the first members of the Circle."

Again with the whole Circle thing. Doug's memory pinged again, but he was tired. He couldn't get a hold of the thought. "And what exactly is this 'Circle'?"

"Imagine, Mr. Goodwin, if you could live each day as if it were your last. Wouldn't that be exciting? To live each day to the fullest? It should be the only way to live."

Doug's hackles rose. He felt like a cornered animal that didn't yet know why it should be afraid.

"The men who founded the Circle were hunters too, just like you. They knew the meaning of the hunt, the chase, the kill.

The men in this room, Mr. Goodwin...we are all hunters. But what is the point of wasting our skills on game that cannot think, cannot reason, cannot fight back?" Black stopped for a moment and took a good long look at Doug.

Doug experienced a flutter of absolute and complete terror.

"That's right, Mr. Goodwin, we don't hunt deer or elephants or bears...we hunt each other."

Doug's gut roiled in protest. He wasn't hearing this. It wasn't happening.

"We are a brotherhood of blood, and the brotherhood has saved us all. We accept this life. We accept our rivals as friends, but also our friends as rivals. Each and every day we live to die— or to survive and hunt again. It is our life. And now it is your life too, Mr. Goodwin."

Doug was paralyzed by an onslaught of emotion. Fear, anger, rage. But the one that concerned him the most was the survival instinct that had kicked in. He attempted to rise from his chair yet again. "You're all crazy. You hear me? Certifiable! There's no way I'm going to join you lunatics in your screwed-up game."

Three men had Doug pinned down in a nanosecond. His breath came in short bursts and he was perspiring.

"This type of initiation is always hard. We all were resistant at first." Black looked around for confirmation from his friends.

"Screw you."

"You will come to appreciate this life."

"No way. This isn't happening. I don't want any part of it." Doug didn't know what combination of words or promises or actions he needed to get himself out of there, but he was running out of brilliant ideas. This was too real a conversation to be having. Way too real.

Mr. Black sighed again, one beleaguered soul trying to save another. "This is where I will have to take a more formal tone with you, Mr. Goodwin. I apologize for what I am about to say, but it has become necessary over the years to be firm with our new recruits."

Doug tensed. Black leaned in so close Doug could see the pores of the sonnovabitch's skin. Doug jerked his arm to release it from the hold of the man on his left, but he was locked in tight.

Black had been polite, despite the threats and forced restraints. This time when he spoke his voice was low and menacing. "We have existed clandestinely for over a century now, Mr. Goodwin, and we have no intention of seeing that status change in any way. You are now a part of the team, as it were. Frankly, and it may sound harsh—and I apologize if that's the case—you have no choice. Absolutely none. From the moment you leave this room until your last breath on this earth, you will be watched. You will not know by whom, but we will be there. If you try to expose us, the dire consequences you will face will not only extend to yourself, but to your friends and family."

These last words were said so matter-of-factly that Doug was stunned. He sat virtually speechless, trapped in his chair, in a nightmare beyond the scope of his imagination. "But, I don't want this. I didn't ask for it! Why me? I'm just some nobody who works in a museum. Find someone else."

"I'll tell you why you, Mr. Goodwin. You were chosen. You have been judged on your abilities and you have been selected. So you see, Mr. Goodwin, it has to be you."

He must be in shock. His body had gone numb. His mind was darting from pillar to post trying to find a place to land that made sense. Not have a choice? *There's always a choice. ...Isn't there?*

"Forgive me, Mr. Goodwin," said Black, the polite gentleman back in place. "I understand you're processing this bit of information. But there's still the small matter of the rules. Tomorrow you will receive an envelope. Show him the envelope, if you please Mr. Chemist."

Chemist withdrew a folded blue envelope from his jacket pocket and showed it to Doug. He did not hand it to Doug and he was careful to make sure it remained closed, covering the handwriting on the reverse side with his hand.

"Now pay attention, Mr. Goodwin, this is important. These envelopes are the primary form of communication on all Circle business. Contained within your first blue envelope will be the detailed information of your first target. "

He waited until Doug dragged his eyes upward.

"You will hunt this target, a member of the Circle, to...his... death. Do you understand, Mr. Goodwin? At the same time, you will also be hunted. And your hunter, he will be hunted as well. This is the Circle of death that represents all of us, that defines us, unites us, gives our lives...purpose. If you succeed, and if your target meets his timely demise, you will be given a month of 'holiday.' During that time, you will be free to do and go as you wish. No one will be hunting you and you will remain target-free. On the morning of the thirtieth day of your holiday you will receive another envelope. Should the member assigned to hunt *you* meet his death, you will be notified and you will automatically receive forty-eight hours of leave time. If at any time you wish to leave the city permanently, you will be assigned to a new branch of the Circle. And yes, Mr. Goodwin, there are branches all over the world."

Mr. Black sat back and waited. He was not totally without feeling. He knew that it took time to digest a life change of this magnitude. After all, the amount of information thrown at new members, especially those who were being, shall we say, encouraged to join, was considerable. "This establishment is your safe house, Mr. Goodwin. You may use it for sanctuary; no one will harm you here. Use the time you spend here wisely. It may prove invaluable to you."

"Um...no," said Doug.

"Excuse me?"

"I said *no*. I'm not interested."

"But I thought I made myself clear, Mr. Goodwin. You do not have a choice."

"Of course I have a choice. You're crazier than Vincent Van Gogh. You're *all* nuts. Hunting...killing other human beings? Besides, you have no right to keep me here."

"Of course you are free to go at any time, Mr. Goodwin, but you have been well informed of the rules." Black sat back and lit his cigar, which had gone out a while back. "Like it or not, accept it or not, you are now a member of the Circle. I am Mr. Black because I am the oldest surviving member of this chapter of the Circle organization. When you reach my age—if you survive that long, to the age of sixty—you will no longer be hunted and you will not be required to hunt. You may even become a 'Mr. Black' someday."

Mr. Black chuckled to himself at the thought. He had spent most of his adult life engaged in the hunt or in this very club. When he'd sat in Doug Goodwin's position he'd also resisted and ultimately acquiesced. They all did. He had killed many men and earned this honor. The idea that a museum tour guide with a misguided sense of self-righteousness could ever sit in this spot was laughable, one could even say insulting. He looked at the boy before him, assessing him, his potential. Even still, the game had its rules for a reason, to give the new ones hope. Without that hope the Circle would not be the Circle.

Doug slumped into his chair. Despite the lack of restraints, he couldn't move, couldn't speak. *This. Cannot. Be. Happening. This is not my life. I come from nowheresville, Colorado. I work in a museum for almost nothing. I am a normal fairly well functioning male living in New York City. I am not a killer.*

Mr. Cufflinks regarded the new member. What Goodwin felt or didn't feel, whether he wanted to join the Circle or not. None of it was his concern. However, for appearances sake, he proffered a bone. "Don't worry so much, Mr. Goodwin. You will come to accept Circle life, as we all have. You will likely come to enjoy it as well. But just remember, there will be dire consequences should you choose to expose our...little club."

There were murmurs of "yes," and "indeed," from the group around Doug's chair. The feeling in the pit of his stomach was so solid that he felt he would stay rooted to this seat for the rest of his life—however long—or short—that might be.

Mr. Black concluded his factual assault. "Go home now, Mr. Goodwin. Rest. Tomorrow morning you will wake up feeling more alive than ever. Oh, and Mr. Goodwin? Welcome to the Circle."

Doug staggered up from his chair. Immediately, the men came up one by one, but this time they were shaking his hand and patting him on the back. As if he'd won an award or his wife had had a baby. One manly man to another.

The members returned to their table games and civilized conversation, their speculations about the new member the new main topic of interest. Mr. Black lit another cigar, one of his few vices, and leaned back into the shadows.

He lifted his highball glass to the new member's back. *Here's to you, Mr. Goodwin. Enjoy your last few days on earth.*

He'd been dismissed. He couldn't believe it. He almost wished for the bodily restraint again so he could fight something. Dazed, Doug walked over to the wall. This time, silently, it slid open. Why not earlier? Why not before the nightmare had begun?

Then he was back in the bar amid the tinkling of glasses and of the melodious crooner singing Frankie-boy.

His eyes were burning from the cigar smoke, unshed tears, and the longest conversation of his life. If only he'd never seen that woman. If only he'd never gone in that room after her. Lust had driven him, pure and simple. It was his own fault.

Patrons of the bar drank and conversed as if nothing had changed. In the meantime, Doug's life had shifted off its axis.

Didn't they know what went on back there? That behind the wall a secret society of lunatics—of killers—were sitting and plotting each other's demise? He could stand on the bar and make a scene, tell them the truth, but he was under no illusion that he'd be seen as the sane one.

The bartender was helping another customer. Although the crooner was no longer crooning, the band continued to play soft jazz in the background. Doug spotted Eric in the corner with a cigarette talking to one of the women Doug recognized from the VIP parlor. You think she's interested in you, buddy boy, think again. She's just another patsy paid by this sick "Circle" to entertain its "clients."

Oh, no. Wait a minute. Wait just a doggone minute. Eric couldn't have known about this. He couldn't have known about the Circle or he wouldn't have brought Doug here. Right? Doug realized he didn't know what was real and what wasn't anymore. He wanted to pull Eric up by the collar and slam him against the wall and beat him senseless until he admitted why he'd brought his best friend to the altar for slaughter. He wanted to run into Eric's arms and beg him to take him away and protect him and tell him it was all a bad joke. A really, really bad joke. He wanted… he didn't know what he wanted. Or what he knew. The only thing that mattered was getting away.

Holding himself in check, just barely, he walked over. "We're out of here, Matthews."

"Hey! Where you been, Doug? This is Lauren. Lauren, I want you to meet my friend—"

"*Now!*"

The woman slid away from the table as if this kind of thing happened all the time. It probably did. She was gone in a flash, detaching her hand from Eric's grip. Doug assumed she was headed for the back room, but he didn't turn to look. He felt the bartender's eyes on his back. Or was that his imagination, too? Real pal he'd turned out to be.

"Babe, it's been a pleasure," Eric called out. "Perhaps next time we can spend a bit more time...." She was already gone. "Well, Dougie, I hope you're happy with yourself. I was making some real headway with sweet Lauren there. What's your hurry anyway?"

Doug didn't answer. Eric nervously gathered up his things under Doug's watchful eye.

They left Tasker's through the front door. Outside, Eric prattled on. Doug canvassed the area. He saw nothing that seemed cause for alarm, but he honestly wondered if he'd ever be able to trust anyone ever again. If the people inside Tasker's were for real, any one of the people on the street could be a killer—his killer. *I can't believe I'm even thinking like this.*

"What did I tell you? Great place, huh," Eric said.

That did it. Doug grabbed Eric by the lapels and threw him against the wall, lifting him straight off the ground.

"Hey, what the hell is going on, Goodwin? I mean—hey, you don't look so good."

"Really, ya think? What's going on? That's what I'd like to know. How did you find this place, Eric? And don't bullshit me or I swear to God I'll...I'll...."

"What? Why? A couple of guys at the firm recommended it to me. What's going on? You like jazz. I thought you'd like it."

After a moment, Doug released Eric reluctantly and backed away.

Eric smoothed down the fine wool of his suit. "What's going on, man? Are you crazy?"

"I'm gonna ask you a question and I want an honest answer, Eric. Are you a part of this thing?"

Eric brushed a bit of dirt off his jacket. "A part of what? What are you talking about?"

Down deep, Doug was afraid he knew the answer. It was the only one that made sense, too many things that added up. The only question was how long Matthews would keep up the lie. "Look me in the eyes, goddammit, and tell me this had nothing to do with you."

"Dougie, what are you talking about? What happened to you in there?" He put his arm on Doug's shoulder. "Are you okay? What can I do?"

This is your best friend. You've known him forever. He'd never do anything to hurt you. Yeah, he's a stupid shit sometimes, but this? No way. Doug shook his head to dislodge the doubt and heard Black's parting words. *Expose us and face dire consequences. You, your friends, and your family.* He couldn't say anything to Eric. If he did, and Eric really knew nothing about the Circle, his best friend's life could be in danger. And Matthews, wuss that he was, would be defenseless against whatever came his way.

Apparently it was true. Apparently, Doug had no choice.

"I...I have to go," he said, and headed down the street.

"What? Where? What's going on?"

Doug didn't answer. He ran. He ran from Eric Matthews. He ran from the Circle.

He ran for his life.

8

Night was falling in that slow end-of-summer sort of way as Doug ran through the streets of the city. Every person he passed merited a second look over his shoulder. As if he were living the life of an avatar, trapped in a virtual world. Except this world wasn't of his own design. By the time he got back to his apartment building his breathing was ragged and he had a stitch in his side. He put his hands on his knees and tried to catch his breath.

He looked up at the enormity of the skyscrapers. He'd never minded before how insignificant he felt by comparison, a mere mortal among titans. But now their presence was sinister. The world he knew had dissolved. His life, built over twenty-seven years. As he stood, dazed, the final natural rays of the sun were abruptly devoured by the night. Doug forced his body to take the last steps. He needed to be home. He needed to get out of the open. In the dark, it was easier for hunters to track their prey without their knowledge.

What am I saying? I'm *the goddammed prey.* In the dark it'd be easier for his hunters to track *him.* He took out his keys.

"Good evening, sir."

A man on a ladder was outside Doug's apartment changing a light bulb.

"Samuel, sir."

"What?"

"My name, sir. It's Samuel. I'm the new doorman-slash-fix-it guy. Just started today. Give me just a sec and I'll be out of your way."

Not good. Surprises are not good. Not today, anyway. He had no time for them. He'd been lucky to find a building in Manhattan with an apartment the size of a postage stamp that he could afford. He'd been told the building once had a doorman, although no doorman had graced the foyer since Doug signed the lease. A new guy showing up today? He didn't like it.

Samuel slowly climbed down from the ladder and folded it up. Doug watched him. He had to be in his fifties at least. The name tag on his uniform said "Samuel" in cursive letters. Doug's shoulders relaxed slightly. Ol' Samuel didn't look menacing, or too limber either.

"4B. Am I right?"

"Who hired you?"

Samuel raised his eyebrows. All the other tenants had been pleased to see the upgrade, a real person instead of the usual empty foyer. "Property manager, sir. Wanting to improve security, since the burglary last month, you know, up in 6D? I only work nights. Don't sleep too well. My wife, God bless her, can't stand me tossing and turning all night, told me to take the job. Between you and me, it means some spending money in my pocket, some of which she doesn't necessarily have to know about, if you catch my drift." Samuel winked.

Doug wasn't buying it. He took a minute to study this new installment—this doorman. Since he'd moved to the city and into this building, there had never been a doorman. Now, tonight, a guy in a uniform was stationed outside his door? Coincidence? *I don't think so.*

"Who sent you? Mr. Black? The Circle?"

Samuel's smile slid from his face. He moved quickly, his ladder under his arm, and started for the elevator. "What? What circle?" Wait 'til the wife heard about the Loony Toon in 4B. "I don't know no Mr. Black."

"Just stay away from me," Doug said. "You hear me? Stay the hell away from me." He sprinted up the four flights and jammed his key into the lock on his door. He entered his apartment, slammed the door behind him, and then double-locked it. He leaned against it, sagging in relief.

Safe. For the moment.

But who was that guy? And what if there was someone waiting in the hall. Or one of the apartments. Or the storage closet just past the elevator. Someone could be lying in wait for him to show himself. Waiting to kill him.

Sweating and nauseous, Doug picked up his baseball bat by the door and unlocked it again. He put his head out an inch at a time. *Get it over with already. Take a look. Then you can rest easy.* He walked the few feet to the closet with his bat at the ready. He looked through the glass pane on the door. Total darkness. He couldn't see a thing. He made himself take a deep breath and then took hold of the handle and wrenched the door open. The smell of cleaning supplies hit him like a wall. He turned on the light to make sure. Brooms, cleaning supplies, rags, mops, trash can liners. No killers that he could see. He let out the breath he'd been holding and backed out the way he'd come in.

He chided himself for being so stupid. *Great idea, Doug. Walk right in.* What if someone had actually been waiting with a gun or a knife? This time he took off his watch to use as a reflector. He unlocked the door to his apartment. He stood with his back to the wall and pushed it open without having to reveal himself. He could see the foyer of his apartment in the watch face. He heard nothing. He had automatically shifted into his hunting mentality, his instinct on alert. The apartment felt stale, but empty of any other living being.

Still, he took no chances and crawled in along the floor, first through the living room and then into the kitchen. Finally he reached the bedroom and bathroom. When no one attacked him, he came to the conclusion that he was alone and safe—if only for the time being. He walked back through the living room and shoved a chair under the front door handle for extra measure. Not that a chair or a couple of locks would stop someone dedicated to pursuit, but it made him feel a little better. He turned on a small lamp and looked around to check everything was in order. More exhausted than he ever remembered being in his life, Doug flopped onto the sofa in the darkness.

Was he crazy or had he just been inducted into a society of men who killed each other for the thrill of it?

Doug's apartment was small, but felt spacious—at least by New York City standards—due to its many windows. An elderly woman, Mona Dickinson, had lived there prior to Doug. Mona had been in the process of moving out to the Jersey shore to be closer to her family when Doug had wandered into the building to look at a vacant apartment with a FOR RENT sign in the window a few floors above. It was wayout of his price range, as he assumed it would be, but before he hit the pavement again he'd helped Mona carry some boxes down the several flights of stairs.

"So, chivalry isn't dead after all," she'd said with a smile. Taken with Doug and his manners, she then did something very un-New York-like. She took pity on him. She called him a "true gentlemen." "Why don't I just hold onto the place, sublet it to you for as long as you want it."

The setup worked for a few months until the landlord caught wind of the arrangement. Furious, he demanded Doug vacate the premises, citing the no sublet clause in Mona's contract. It was only through Eric's connections at the law firm that Doug was able to sign his own contract at only ten percent more rent than Mona had paid, for a limited period of time. After which he'd need a lot more money or have to find another place to live. The only other condition was that Doug improve upon the space for any future tenants. No problem. Instead of wallpapering, he'd painted. The walls were now a subtle yellow to reflect the light. He'd installed Pergo flooring instead of the usual cheap carpeting. Once he'd added his paintings and his moose head trophy mounted on a wooden plaque, he was happy as a pig in, well, happy as a pig.

Home. *No such thing anymore.*

He went into the bedroom, looked longingly at his king-size bed. Nope. No time to lose. He ripped off his shirt, made a quick pass under his arms, grabbed another one from the closet and pulled it on. He got a black bag from underneath his desk. At a feverish pace he filled it with clothes from a nearby armoire. Inside his closet was a standing safe, locked with a digital combination. He unlocked it to reveal his weapons store, retrieving a cross bow and arrows and a large knife. Zipping up the bag, he moved quickly to the door, then stopped short. He looked back at the moose's head mounted on the wall. That moose had never heard him coming; a perfect kill. Clear as day he now saw his own head mounted on the wall of his would-be killer. He saw one of his fingers lying in Mr. Fingers' "collection." He shuddered. His life may not be perfect—not by a long shot—but it was his life. He wanted to keep it.

Doug chose the stairs over the elevator. As he descended a sort of calm came over him. A second wave of adrenaline had kicked in and he fed off it. He wasn't looking for a fight, but if one found him there was no chance in hell he'd lie down. He reached the lobby at the bottom of the stairs. Empty, except for Samuel, the doorman, over by the doors, changing another light bulb.

He was being paranoid. Getting carried away. This Samuel guy was just some poor shlub trying to do his job.

"Good evening again, sir," Samuel said politely, his face blank.

How much had he freaked out the man with his rant about Mr. Black and the Circle? "Need any help?" Helping might mitigate the damage. On the other hand, if the guy said yes, he'd be stuck.

Samuel was already descending the ladder. "No, no, I'm just fine here, I'll be out of your way in just a—"

Samuel's foot caught on the rung of the ladder, which swayed dangerously. Doug dropped his bag and reached out to steady the metal steps. Samuel righted himself.

"You good?"

"Well, thank you, son. I might have wrenched my back a bit, that's all. I'll just sit down here for a spell."

Doug helped the man over to a chair by the mailboxes, sending darted glances out the door every few seconds.

"Now don't you worry none, son," Samuel said. "I've come through a lot worse before. These old bones seen a lot of action. Nam, you know."

"Oh?"

Please. Not war stories. Not now.

"Yup. That's right. Enlisted a few years after Korea. By the time I got to Nam, I had the privilege of leading some of America's finest young soldiers into battle. Yup, that was back in '68 and '69. Two full tours." Samuel rubbed his lower back and settled into the chair. "Choppers could only get us so close to the ground, ended up jumping with full packs and our weapon. But these knees and this back aren't up to that kind of thing anymore, now are they?"

Doug struggled against a lifetime of etiquette training. Being rude to a doorman was nothing compared to being rude to an old Vietnam vet. But he really had to go. He was wasting precious time, and he was a clear target here, like this.

"Listen," he said. "Doug Goodwin, apartment 4B." He extended his hand. "Sorry about earlier. I'm a little...stressed right now."

"No problem. Sergeant Major Samuel Murphy." The doorman shook Doug's hand.

"Nice to meet you, then, Sarge."

"Haven't been called Sarge in a long time...friends just call me Murph."

"Then Murph it is. Look, I have to get going, are you sure you don't need anything?"

"Nah, I'm fine," Murph said, cracking his joints. "Good as new."

"Well, okay then, take care of yourself, Murph." Doug got to his feet. He picked up his bag and pushed open the door.

The doorman got up and straightened out his cramped spine. Poor man from 4B was a mess. And so young to be so tense.

"See you tomorrow, then, Mr. Goodwin," he said quietly.

Doug grimaced. That was a matter of opinion.

9

Eric Matthews was drinking. Had been since the moment Doug stormed off and ran down the street. He'd done a one-eighty right back into Tasker's where he'd told the bartender to leave the bottle of Johnnie Walker Blue Label. He'd gulped the first one, then settled in with the next, and the next. Maybe if he drank enough he'd stop feeling the guilt. Right. Who was he kidding? He didn't deserve it. He'd just sacrificed his best goddammed friend in the whole world.

The next drink went down as smoothly as the last one. He held up the shot glass and looked through it. He sees them as kids, him and Doug, in school together, summers in Grover, college. At the funerals of his parents, when Dougie stood by him like a brother. They'd been through everything together—everything until now.

The bartender meandered over and wiped the already immaculate bar surface with a clean cloth. "Listen, Mr. Matthews.

Don't be so hard on yourself. It had to be this way. You said it yourself. It's your job. You weren't meeting the quota. This saves you. If your friend is as good as you say he is he'll be a natural."

His job...his *job*?

Eric had always loved to gamble. It brought him in contact with real players, men—and women—with money, significant money. And the women. The women were amazing. Willing to do anything. For a fee, of course; occasionally without. But paying for it felt powerful, heady. He was on top of the world, in his element. Or so he'd thought. Then he'd met his first Circle member.

Eric was in Atlantic City. His regular jaunts there from New York added spice to his humdrum life as an attorney. The thrill of the chase, the smell of money. He belonged there. One night he happened on a guy at one of the Black Jack tables. They sat and had a few drinks, played a few hands. After a few more Eric felt comfortable enough to confide some of the more intimate details of his life. The man was his instant pal, his buddy, more than willing to help Eric place "the bet of his life." A no-brainer, he said. Eric had drunkenly agreed. Fucking kickers. All he had to do was split the uprights that night in Seattle. But nooo. If he'd done what he was paid to do in the first place Eric wouldn't be in this mess. He'd only made it worse when he let the bet ride. There was just no way the underdog was going to shock the world and win the National Championship, right?

But the fix was in. And just like that he was into the Circle for two hundred fifty grand. And, much as he liked to pretend he was one of the elite, he wasn't. He didn't have that kind of money and he didn't have the contacts to get a loan. What little money he had he used to keep up appearances. Everyone knows it costs money to look like you have money.

He'd been in debt even before the member had approached him. The convertible, the condo overlooking central park. His parking space alone was more than some mortgages. The Florida bet was supposed to get him out of debt, not put him further in the hole. Shortly thereafter, he'd been "invited" to Tasker's to arrange "payment." When he got there he'd found himself in the midst of some poor schlepp's initiation, the same kind he assumed Dougie had been subjected to. They'd meant for him to be there, to see it. And once he'd seen what he'd seen, he was in for good. It was that old expression, in for a dollar, in for a pound. And he was in up to his ears.

How it came about he still wasn't clear, but before the night was over his debt was wiped clean and he'd become a "volunteer" for the Circle. A recruiter. He'd played right into their hands, bragging about the people he knew, the potential talent he could bring to their "game." But his word wasn't good enough, was it? They wanted proof. Proof in the form of a real human being, someone who would live up to the "raw talent" they expected. That's when the only person he'd ever called a brother had become nothing more than a bargaining chip.

As the months went by and Eric came up short, he was brought in front of Mr. Black. It was made clear to Eric that his scouting was no longer serving its purpose. That a deadline would be imposed. If he didn't find a recruit within two weeks he would face the consequences. There was no need to enunciate what those consequences would be. Eric had seen enough members come and go, never to return.

Eric stifled a sound part giggle, part sob, and poured another drink. Yeah, that was it. In for a pound. A pound of flesh. Shakespeare...or was it the Bible? Only this time it was the flesh of his best friend.

Doug was the logical choice. His only choice. And he could handle himself. Dougie was the best damn hunter in Grover, heck, in most of Colorado, by the time they'd left. Moose, elk, didn't matter. Dougie could track anything, anywhere. He could survive in the wilderness for weeks if he had to.

Johnnie Walker thudded through Eric's brain. He was conscious enough to know he was drunk, but at forty bucks a shot he got to relive his buddy's imminent death at the hands of the Circle and look at a bartender who always smiled. Smiled and told him he should be proud of a job well done. Proud? He was friggin' proud all right. Proud of destroying the only good thing he'd ever known.

Eric picked up the bottle and threw it against the wall. It shattered, spraying the little whiskey that was left in the bottle and shards of glass everywhere. He got up, felt woozy. Drunker than a skunk. He fell into his stool. "I wish I nev' got 'volved w' you people," he said to the room.

"But you did." The bartender got the mop from behind the counter and calmly began to clean up the mess. "You'll get no sympathy from me, Mr. Matthews, it was your call. But what do I know. I'm just a barkeep."

Just a barkeep. Eric's laugh was more of a moan. "What a crock of shit."

"Well, I do know the 12s make Seattle a hard place to play on the road. And I know there's no such thing as easy money."

Eric reached across the bar. He'd wipe that smug look off the fuck's face—

Eric felt pain in his left arm as it was suddenly bent back in a tight hold behind his back. "Let go of the bartender, son. He's not your enemy." Mr. Black preferred not to interfere in the goings-on in the bar, but neither did he appreciate his employees being attacked by drunken disgruntled members. In this case, a pathetic recruiter who didn't know his place.

He shoved Eric down onto a stool. "You have yourself under control now, Mr. Matthews? Shall I let go?"

Eric was in too much pain to answer, but he nodded his head. When Mr. Black let go of his arm Eric rubbed it and pouted. For an old dude the guy had a nasty grip.

"You proposed this solution, Mr. Matthews, not the Circle. I would suggest that someone so anxious to sell out a friend to save his own skin might not be so quick to point his finger. Furthermore, from now on you will act like a gentleman in this place. At all times. Is that clear?" Eric heard his father's voice for the first time in a long time in the admonition. Shamed, he dipped his head again, then got up and reached into his pocket. He withdrew his money clip, unfolded a couple of hundred dollar bills, and tossed them onto the bar. He weaved his way to the door and put his hand on the handle. He wanted to have the last word, but "You guys just don't give a shit about anyone, do you?" or "You make me sick" would be more about him than them.

Walking—stumbling—around the city for another hour, Eric tried to hold a conversation with the Eric Matthews of ten years ago. But that Eric was long gone. All that was left was the shell of the man he'd once thought he could be. The night was humid and in the warm breeze he heard the murmurings calling him *traitor, liar, traitor, liar.* If Eric were a religious man he might feel the breeze as the wrath of God Himself, making His presence known. He longed for forgiveness, but how to get it and from whom...well, that was outside his purview entirely.

It wasn't all that late for a mid-week night, but Eric hadn't seen a taxi for blocks. His legs were about to give out. At Central Park and 79th he spied the entrance to the subway. Waiting for a train on a bench felt like a much better alternative to staying on his feet. He lurched down the two flights of stairs to the platform. He swallowed back the bile in his throat. He dug his Metro-Card out of his pocket and swiped it through the turnstyle.

Eric aimed for an empty bench and collapsed onto it next to a pile of rags. Mumbling rags.

No way. The same homeless woman he'd seen with Doug earlier that night. Before...everything. Repulsed, he scooted away. But wait. This could be it. A chance for redemption. To make things right! Eric reached into his pocket for his money clip and removed the bills that were left. He bent down to put them in the woman's pocket.

"Aahh!"

Damn. The crazy lady was screaming.

"You keep away. Keep your hands off my things! They're mine!"

The woman was stronger than she looked. She came at Eric full force, her arms outstretched.

Thrown off balance and inebriated with Johnnie Walker, Eric's foot landed on a bit of greasy food wrapper. His legs flew out from under him and he found himself on his tailbone. He groaned at the assault, his body crushed against the cold concrete of the subway landing. He could hear the screeching of the local trains coming into the station beneath him.

"Terry'll be here any minute. He'll show you, you thievin' bastard."

Eric cringed. He inched toward the stairs.

When it looked like she was going to come after him, he inched farther and farther to the top step until there was nowhere else to go. He couldn't believe it. The vindictive bitch was coming to get him. Him. Eric Matthews, attorney at law.

Eric's vision was fuzzy, but wasn't that a hammer in her hand? He rolled away to avoid the blow.

The stairs came up to meet him. He crashed down the steps, the force as strong as a freight train. Each step he met was harder than the last. When he finally landed at the bottom he couldn't move. He thought he heard the rumble of the train as it rolled into the station, but he wasn't sure. Eric Matthews had reached rock bottom.

10

Grover, Colorado, Fifteen Years Earlier

Eric Matthews and Doug Goodwin are twelve years old. They're sitting in the bus station waiting for their bus to arrive. In their hands are tickets to Wyoming. Eric had had an argument with his parents and running away to the big city of Cheyenne was his "only option." Scared to go alone, he'd dragged Doug along with him. Eric is nervous, twitching in his seat, tapping his leg on the seat in front of him. Doug wishes he'd calm down, but Eric's nervous energy never seems to quit.

"Hey, you'd a done the same thing, right?"

Doug shrugs.

"Come on," says Eric, "this is so much better than staying in that dump of a town."

Doug wants to go home. He knows what Eric wants to hear, but even at twelve he knows Eric is being an idiot. So why does he feel so much responsibility to be an idiot along with him? "What are you going to do once we get out there?"

"I don't know. I can get a job. People say I look like I'm sixteen."

Yeah, right, and I'm Sly Stallone. No one they know would say such a thing. Eric doesn't look a day over ten—on a good day. Eric hasn't hit his growth spurt yet and is a good three to four inches shorter than the other kids. But arguing is futile when Eric is manic like this.

"Where are you going to live?" If Doug doesn't ask no one will. Eric won't have thought it through. He never does. He just jumps in with both feet and hangs on.

"Doesn't matter, as long as I'm away from *them*," Eric says. "I mean, come on, two months is, like, forever."

Doug can't argue with that. Two months is a long, long time. But the crime isn't exactly nothing either. Eric had come to Doug's window in the middle of the night for what he called "Operation Spaceman." He'd hatched the scheme weeks before. Doug really wanted to go along, but he was in the process of serving his own two-week sentence for taking their tractor for a spin on the main road. It was a totally unfair punishment, too, because he only did it to get the groceries his mom asked him to get. How did he know his bike would spring a flat and he'd need another set of wheels? Not that he was unaware of the consequences for sneaking out of the house and hijacking the most expensive piece of equipment they had on the farm.

That's why, when Eric came to his window, even though he'd wanted to go more than he wanted a kiss from Suzie Blake, in the end he backed out. That's why while Eric made his way down Chatoga Avenue to the Stoneman's farm, Doug was at home in bed. That's why, when Eric was arming himself with a long piece of two by four with rope affixed to each end, Doug was trying to keep his eyes open until Eric got back to tell him what happened. And that's why, while Eric was carving giant nine-foot initials in the Stoneman's field the way he'd seen on the Sci-Fi network in the program about crop circles, Doug was sleeping like a baby.

It had taken him all night, but Eric Matthews was determined even back then. Unfortunately, the Stoneman's corn crop was ruined, and since Eric had drawn his own initials in the field, it was pretty easy to guess the name of the idiot who'd done it. Eric's parents were obligated to pay the Stonemans for their son's dalliance, and a hefty sum it had cost, too. The sentence was handed down without mercy: two months of chores and schoolwork. No bike, no TV, no friends, no nothing.

But that's neither here nor there now because there they are, two twelve-year-olds in baseball caps, sitting in a bus station, about to start a new life in Wyoming. Who knows what Eric thinks Wyoming has to offer, but that's neither here nor there either. All Doug knows is that he has to be there for his friend.

"Bus 1626, nonstop to Cheyenne, now boarding. That's 1626, nonstop to Cheyenne, now boarding on platform three," the loudspeaker crackles.

Eric drops his Rockies cap on the filthy floor at the announcement. He sweeps it up, gets to his feet, and collects his backpack. "Let's go, Dougie-boy, it's now or never."

Doug's feet drag, but he collects his John Elway duffel bag and falls into line behind his friend. "Yeah, let's do this," he says with a whole lot more enthusiasm than he feels.

At platform three, the attendant checks their tickets. When the group in front of them boards the bus, he gives them the onceover. "You boys traveling alone?"

Eric speaks up first. "We're going to Cheyenne...you know, Wyoming."

The attendant squints his eyes at them.

"Um, our uncle lives there," says Doug, stumbling over the misguided words leaving his mouth against his better judgment.

Eric, fearless as ever, lying like a rug, picks up the thread. "He's meeting us at the bus station."

The attendant's face relaxes. "Okay, boys, you enjoy the ride, shouldn't be longer than about an hour."

They board the bus and take their seats. Doug takes the window seat and Eric the aisle. "I told you I was serious," Eric says.

Doug doesn't answer. He isn't feeling too well all of a sudden. But Eric's face is turning bright red. "Hey, you okay?"

"I gotta go to the bathroom," he says, pointing a thumb to the back of the bus.

"What are you telling me for? You want me to hold it for you?"

Eric picks up his stuff and walks quickly down the narrow aisle to the restroom in the back.

Charter bus bathrooms are nothing to write home about, but this one has all Eric needs. He takes one look at the makeshift sink and the small window above it and his decision is made. The window opens outward. He sticks his face up to the opening and sucks in the clean fresh air he'd miss if he left Grover. The bus's engine creates a puff of diesel exhaust that meets Eric's face. He recoils with a cough and a wave of nausea.

In a minute he's pushed his backpack out the window and shimmied through after it. For the first time in his short life he is happy to be a late bloomer, small enough to fit through the small space. He hits the ground running and runs straight home, not once looking back to wonder what his friend might think when he arrives in Cheyenne alone.

It takes Doug a few minutes. To miss Eric, that is. To start to worry. Was Eric sick? What if he needed his help? Finally, he weaves down the aisle of the rocking bus to find out. The restroom is empty. Eric is nowhere to be found. A Rockies cap is lying on the floor.

Several hours later Doug is still sitting in the bus station in Cheyenne. He'd had enough money to call his parents and buy a hot dog. The worst part was the way he feels, knowing that he'd been suckered by his best friend.

Eric was afraid to tell his own parents what he'd done. Instead, he'd befriended a woman, a Mrs. Hebbins, at the Grayhound station in Grover. Gave her a sob story about his friend who got on the bus to Cheyenne by mistake. Could she please, please, call and ask them to stop the bus before it got too far. It was too late, of course. Eric had walked home. When Doug's parents called to ask if Eric knew where Doug was, Eric lied and said the last time he'd seen his friend was earlier that day, after school.

Doug spent four hours after the call to his parents in the Cheyenne bus station waiting. His mother had to drive the sixty miles to pick him up. Doug didn't speak to Eric for weeks, though Eric had apologized many times and vowed to be a better friend.

Doug had bought it. Hook, line, and sinker.

II

Doug studied each of his fellow passengers as he waited on the platform for the D express train to take him to Grand Central Station where he'd catch a bus out of the city. He was attempting to be discreet, to use only his peripheral vision, not move his head in any particular direction that would give away his newly acquired nervous disorder, but soon he felt he was only doing the opposite—attracting attention, casting suspicion on himself.

After a few minutes, he was sure everyone on the platform was gunning for him. Where was the damn train already? He leaned over the platform to look down the tunnel as if it would make the train arrive sooner. It never did. Finally he heard a deep rumble beneath his feet and saw the light of an oncoming train as it rounded the corner to enter the station. The small crowd merged into an amoeba-like entity, people no longer concerned with fiercely guarding their personal space the way they'd been seconds before. They were subtly pushing with elbows and knees, so that they could—what?—find their favorite spot waiting for them? If they were lucky they might get a seat, though.

A Hispanic man with a stubbly chin crowded Doug's left side. The man didn't bother to say excuse me; that wasn't necessary subway etiquette.

"Hey, man, you okay?"

Was the man talking to him? "What?"

"I said, you okay? You don't look so good."

"I'm fine," Doug said, looking away pointedly.

The man held up his hands. "Okay, man, don't bite my head off. I was jus' askin'."

He moved off, and Doug breathed a sigh of relief.

The train pulled into the 81st Street station, bringing a whoosh of hot air and the smell of dirt. It stopped with a high-pitched squeal of brakes that hurt his head.

Doug was shocked by how nasty he had just been to someone who was probably only trying to be helpful. On the other hand, paranoid or not, the guy could easily have been Mr. Throw-The-Target-In-Front-of-a-Subway, a friend of Mr. Demented's back at the bar. At the last second Doug let the swarm of human bodies flow around him onto the train and then pushed his way out the doors as they were closing. He headed around the corner, checking back to see if he was being followed. Nothing. He'd wait for the next train and switch to the 7th Avenue train at 59th and Columbus, which would take him over to 42nd Street. Slow, but taxis were out.

On the #2 train, Doug stood alone by the door of the train holding his bag. His eyes darted around, acccssing the possibility of a threat. Still nothing. Nothing he could see, anyway. His shoulders relaxed just a bit. At this hour the local trains had fewer travelers than the expresses. Most of them looked dog tired from long work days; some holding onto the rungs above the seats and swaying with the movement of the train, eyelids heavy. Doug turned his back to the window and used it for support. He'd been clutching his black bag like it was a newborn child; he made himself unclench and flex his hand before he lost feeling in it altogether. From under lowered lids he studied the people around him. A couple of women who looked Eastern European were speaking in a language he assumed was Russian; three frat guys out looking for fun in the city; an old Hasidic Jew with long side curls, in all black, complete with brimmed hat, reading a Hebrew newspaper. Sitting to his right a girl in a varsity softball jacket from Hoboken was doing a Sudoku puzzle. Across from her was a family of five. The two boys, who'd been running up and down and shooting each other with toy guns, had fallen asleep in their parents' laps, toy guns in their hands, as soon as the train had begun its lullaby of motion.

Their parents were in for it. They'd see the error of their ways eventually, inevitably. Wonder why their precious sons had turned to a life of violence, never questioning their lack of foresight. Doug could enlighten them. "Hey there. Do you know what'll happen if you let your kids play with guns? I'll tell you. How do I know? First hand, that's how. I was just like them once...."

"I got you first." Doug called from behind the wood pile.

"Did not," said Eric, confident from his position in back of the feeding trough.

"Did too, got you in the arm."

"No, you didn't, I have a force field."

"You can't have a force field. That's not in the rules."

"I made up a new rule. It says that force fields are okay."

"You can't."

"Can to."

"Cannot."

And so it went. Endless days of cowboys and Indians, cops and robbers.

What if some stranger had gone up to Doug's parents and told them that he'd grow up to be a murderer, someone who'd become a target for sick men to lead their sick lives? What if someone had told them to get a handle on their son, that allowing him to play with guns, that teaching him to hunt, would lead him to die young—or become the victim of a sick psychopath who killed for kicks.

Doug's stomach was in knots, full of acid. He hadn't eaten since lunch almost twelve hours earlier and although the alcohol he'd had at Tasker's had long since left his system, the drinks were still burning a hole in his belly and he felt hung over. He turned back to the window and watched the steel beams fly by, the sparks on the tracks illuminating every few feet of tunnel.

The conductor's voice crackled into life. "Fooorty-second Street, Fooorty-second Street, Grand Central Station, Port Authority. This stop, Fooorty-second Street, Grand Central Station. Change here for the one, two, three, and Q train, and all trains and all buses. Next stop thirty-fourth Street, Thiiirty-fourth Street next."

Doug's instinct was to bolt through the door. *No. Stay calm. Do not draw undue attention to yourself.* He looked for signs to Grand Central Station and started the long, dreary walk through the gray tunnels. Tired-looking street musicians lined the walls, busking for spare change. Doug ignored the violin players and the panhandlers alike. In the past he would have stopped and listened and tossed a few coins into their cases or cups. He hit the bus station, a huge terminal, the biggest rail station in the world, which hosted a behemoth American flag that hung from the ceiling. People, like ants, swarmed across its floor.

Doug spotted the ticket counter and searched for the right window. He saw it down at the far end. Above the booth it said "UPSTATE NEW YORK - ALBANY AND BUFFALO." He handed another bored clerk all the money in his wallet and purchased a ticket.

12

Eric woke up to the bleeping of a heart monitor. With a start he realized he was hooked up to two other machines and an IV. His pale arms were covered in bruises and his head felt as if it had been run through a paper shredder. He raised the arm without the IV and gingerly felt his scalp. Sure enough, a lump the size of Staten Island on the back of his head. Even breathing hurt, like he'd cracked a couple of ribs.

He looked around, starting to remember. He was in the hospital. The TV on the wall was quiet, as was the ward. It must be night still. The last thing he remembered was trying to give his hard-earned money to the deranged homeless woman in the subway. Talk about ungrateful.

He looked around for his clothes, which he spotted in a plastic bag on the table on wheels next to the bed. Even though no one was around, he groped to gather the scant hospital gown and secure it. It was barely covering his private parts. He reached for the bag and into his pants pocket for his cell phone but came up empty. His clothes were torn and brownish. Blood. His blood.

"Good, you're awake." A young good-looking nurse, rubber soles squeaking on the shiny linoleum, entered the room.

Eric might have wished for a more flattering presentation if he'd had the energy.

The nurse set about checking the machines and tubes. "Do you remember your name?"

"Eric Matthews. How long have I been here?"

"You were brought in about three hours ago. You took a nasty fall in the subway, according to the EMS guy. If not for the conductor who happened to find you, you might still be down there."

Eric looked at the clock. After three in the morning. "How long do I have to stay here? What's wrong with me?"

"Well, you'll have to talk with the doctor, but you've got a pretty nasty contusion on your head. Another one on your left thigh. Plus, you have a few broken ribs. We're going to need to take an MRI and an x-ray of your chest. I'd say another day for observation, to make sure there's no internal bleeding. You can ask the doctor when he comes in to look you over."

Eric, weak from alcohol and the aching, felt his eyes glaze over.

"You're going to be fine," the nurse reassured him. "I'm one of your nurses. Heather. I'll be here until seven this morning, then Sandra or Bobbie'll be here."

Heather gave a gentle plump to Eric's pillow and pulled up his covers before leaving. "If you're looking for your things, they're in that drawer by your bed. Meanwhile, if you need anything, you go ahead and push that button over there. 'Night."

Eric watched Heather's fine ass as she left his room. Maybe he'd get her number before he left the hospital. He opened the drawer. His wallet, keys, and cell phone were all there. Upon closer inspection, however, his credit cards were missing. At first he missed all the big bills he'd had in there too and was ready to raise cane with the staff—until his rash moment of misguided philanthropy came rushing back.

He groaned. What an idiot. Getting sloshed and giving his money away.

Which wasn't the worst of it. He'd only been plastered out of shame. Shame for betraying his friend. He reached for the hospital phone. He'd call Doug and explain. He'd tell him that he didn't have any choice, that he'd do whatever it took to make it right. The call went straight to voicemail. He disconnected. Where would Doug go? He wasn't safe. The Circle could find him anywhere.

He dialed again. Again the phone went directly to voicemail. This time he left a message. "Dougie, it's me, Eric. I'm in the hospital. Um, look, man, I need your help. I think I was robbed. I have no money, no cards, no insurance info. Like I said, I could really use your help, man. Doctor says it's pretty serious, maybe internal bleeding...." Eric's voice took on the timbre of a man on the edge. "Mt. Sinai, Room..." Eric craned his head to read the number on the door "...room 266. Call me, man."

He knows Doug. Doug will never be able to ignore that kind of message. Never.

The bus was full, but no one paid any mind to the well-built guy with the duffle bag. He could have been a soldier on leave or just a guy going to visit his sweetheart.

He'd been on the bus all night. He dozed on and off, jerking awake when the bus made a sudden movement or the guy in the next seat snored. The moon was floating full and high in the night sky over New York State. Doug checked his watch. Almost seven hours on the road; they should be in Buffalo any minute.

There was a click and the sound of an electronic device switching on. Right on schedule. "Evenin', folks. Sorry to wake you all up, but we'll be in Lackawanna in just a few minutes. If this is your stop, you might want to think about getting your things together. Remember to check over and underneath your seats...you don't want to leave anything behind. If you need help I'll be glad to lend a hand once we reach the station. Next stop is Buffalo, Buffalo, New York. Please remain in your seats until we have reached the station and come to a complete stop. Thank you for traveling with Greyhound."

The passengers cleared their throats, shook out their stiff limbs, and began gathering their belongings. Doug sat up straight, readying himself to disembark. He elbowed the guy next to him who gave a couple of snorts and then woke up, looking embarrassed to have been caught drooling on a shoulder that didn't belong to his wife.

Doug knew Lackawanna from three of his coworkers at the museum who owned a little hunting cabin there. When they found out Doug was a hunter they'd invited him up a few times to hang out with the guys, drink beer, talk about women. Doug knew his coworkers rarely left the city at this time of year. In fact, he was bargaining on it. With his open invitation to the cabin it was the first place Doug thought of. Secluded and surrounded by woods, it would serve his purposes well.

Doug planned to reach the cabin before daylight. The bus left him by a streetlight and a bench—what passed for a bus station in the hamlet of Lackawanna. As soon as he stepped out of the light's halo the darkness swallowed him up. He pulled out a flashlight and began the mile-long trek to the cabin. In the quiet he heard the hoot of an owl and a distant bark of a dog. The only other sound was that of crickets and night frogs. Normal night sounds. Sounds Doug loved. Sounds comforting to a man on the run.

Pine trees rose a hundred feet into a sky full of stars. Doug soon veered off the road and took a deep breath of relief as he stepped into the forest. The path was nearly undetectable to anyone who didn't know it was there. Occasionally he heard the scurrying of a night animal, but for the most part he was completely alone. The walk was cathartic, and he felt the troubles of the city lift slightly as he marched a pathway to the cabin's door.

The cabin, one of half a dozen just like it, each about 400 feet from the others, ensured privacy. The last time Doug was here was two months ago; it looked untouched since then. The wood he'd cut still sat on the tiny porch in a plywood box. The lock on the door had been an investment, a thank you from Doug to his buddies after they'd found the remains of a vagrant's dinner in the cabin, for including him in their expeditions. A digital combination lock, virtually unbreakable. Again, looked untouched. Doug punched in the five-digit code and entered the cabin. Immediately a musty, woodsy smell filled his nostrils. Flipping off his flashlight and on the wall switch, Doug set down his bag and looked around. Everything as he'd left it on his last visit, only dustier.

The interior was Spartan. On one wall a small wood-burning stove and an old-fashioned icebox awaited fresh-caught fish. Two sets of bunk beds, handmade, sat flush against two of the other three walls. In the middle of the room two old matching plaid couches and a coffee table, marred by the condensation from many beer bottles, formed a square. The only other things in the cabin were a coat rack, a wooden cable reel that doubled as a table with two chairs, and a couple of stuffed trophies.

Reassured, Doug dropped the black bag on the floor and collapsed into one of the beds.

Doug's arm hung over the edge of the bed. He was sleeping deeply, breathing slow and steady, eyelids twitching in concert with his dreams. The bright morning sunlight, weakened slightly by the dirty panes of the single window next to the stove, had just entered the cabin and hit his face.

He woke with a start. Remembered where he was, why he was there. The last twenty-four hours had been a constant crazy assault. At least here he could gather his wits and think things through. Where he could figure out his next move.

There had to be a way out. He just hadn't thought of it yet. This thing with the Circle—if such a thing really existed. In the light of day Doug couldn't be sure he hadn't dreamed the whole thing. Why anyone would pull a joke like that was way beyond Doug's understanding and sense of decency, but what other explanation could there be? A group of men who hunted each other? It had to be a hoax, if an unconscionably cruel one.

Doug padded over to the stove and lit the wood to heat the kettle for coffee. Barefoot and in his T-shirt and boxer shorts, he opened wide the front door and stretched in the morning air. The city had been hot and humid; here he could already feel the advent of autumn settling in. How nice it would be to have a dog again. When he had his own place, somewhere the dog could run. Growing up his family had rescued a hound, a great hunting animal, by the unfortunate name of Marvin. Marvin the hound. Poor guy deserved better than that.

He turned back into the cabin when the kettle whistled. Coffee mugs stood ready in the one cabinet above the icebox, powdered creamer next to them. He poured himself a cup of instant and added plenty of creamer, took a sip, and grimaced.

Lousy, but it would do. He took his coffee in one hand and one of the chairs in another to sit on the porch and watch the day begin. As he crossed the threshold something blue caught his eye.

It looked like an envelope.

No way. Not here. It can't be.

His mug of hot coffee crashed to the floor. He leapt back to avoid a scalding. The envelope was sticking out from under the welcome mat of hard bristles, just enough so he could see "ODWIN" written in thick black letters.

They'd found him.

13

Eric was tired, but too wired to sleep anymore. He'd been flipping through the channels on the television for over an hour,
impatient to be discharged from the hospital but just as impatient to hear from Doug to whom he'd been sending telepathic
messages. He'd left voice mails with the hospital's name and his
room number, too, but the phone hadn't rung.

The remote only had a channel up/down button and a
volume dial. Eric worked the channel button so hard it got stuck.
Programs whizzed by. He fiddled with it until it popped back
out. Nothing held his interest. Finally he settled on ESPN and
SportsCenter in the middle of a story. Some bald sportscaster
was on screen and the logo for the Seattle Seahawks was in the
upper right hand corner. He felt a flicker of interest before he
was reminded how he'd gotten into this predicament in the first
place. Disgusted, he threw the remote at the TV, forgetting that
it was attached to his bed with a springy cord. When it recoiled

it struck him directly on the forehead, precisely as Heather and the day-shift nurse entered the room.

"You okay here, Mr. Matthews?" Heather asked, breaking off the report she was giving to the nurse who would take her place.

"Fine. I'm fine. The stupid remote...forget it. And didn't I tell you to call me Eric?" Even in bandages with an IV stuck in his arm, Eric's automatic flirtation delivery kicked in. It was second nature. Heather had that tantalizing *je ne sais quoi*, unflattering artificial light and all, especially compared to the other nurses he'd seen since his admission. A real diamond in the rough, and she'd fallen right into his lap. Maybe she'd missed the remote episode. Whatever. This was a golden opportunity and he was all over it.

"Yes...of course. This is Bobbie, your day-shift nurse."

Eric nodded. Heather came over to check the machines. She smelled great. "But I'll see you tonight, right?"

Heather rolled her eyes. "Not likely. The doctor says you're good to go." The guy was amazing. Lying in a hospital bed looking like a complete wreck and still he managed to flirt. "I have to finish my report. Have a good day."

Darn. Eric watched her move toward the door, again taking note of her posterior curves. As she left she tossed a little smile at him over her shoulder. More than enough encouragement. "Wait. Heather. I have a question."

"Yes?"

"Um," Eric began, scrambling for legitimacy. "Your name badge." He pointed to her hospital ID, which had flipped over. "What's that mean, what it says on the back?"

"'Doctors save lives; Nurses save Doctors'? That's just a little joke around here."

"Little joke, my ass!" Nurse Bobbie said out of the side of her mouth. "If it wasn't for us, these doctors would be in big trouble.

Why, just the other day we couldn't read Dr. Patel's handwriting and—

Heather elbowed Nurse Bobbie hard. She stopped talking.

"Um, who's my doctor again?" Eric said.

"Don't worry," said Heather. "Dr. Pacheco is one of the good ones. But I'm off." She took Bobbie's arm meaningfully. "Let's go, Bobbie, time to check the meds."

"Hey, Heather," Eric called, "what if I want to take you out for dinner—you know, for taking such exceptional care of me? Would you go?"

But they were gone. The room was quiet except for the beeping of the monitors. Eric swore under his breath.

The door opened a few inches a minute later. Heather stuck her head into the room. "I don't date patients," she said, "but thanks for the offer."

Eric moped for a while longer, bored and hurting, before Dr. Pacheco came in and told him he was free to go. All his tests were negative. He checked Eric's bandages and looked in his eyes. "You're a lucky man, Mr. Matthews," he said. "Cement doesn't give the way it used to."

So much for hospital humor. "Yeah, right, thanks, Doc."

He was about to gather his clothes when Heather walked in. "I thought you left."

Heather picked up the phone and handed it to Eric. "Here," she said. "Dial your phone number." Eric did as he was told. "Now give it to me," she said. He handed her the phone. He could hear it ringing and imagined the sound of it in his empty apartment.

"Eric, it's Heather," she said when the voicemail kicked in. "I'm calling to let you know that it's illegal to give you my phone number while you're still a patient here, but since you're home listening to this, that's no longer a concern. Call me sometime." She recited her phone number, hung up the phone, and walked out of the room.

Yes! That's what he was talking about. A date with a gorgeous woman after the worst night of his life. A flicker of doubt made him squirm as he again recalled why. But compared to Eric's pursuit of gratification, Doug's situation was rapidly fading into little more than an inconvenient truth.

Doug cleaned up the shattered coffee mug and pulled on his clothes. He caught the first bus out of Lackawanna and sat in the back like a schoolboy hiding from bullies. He held in his shaking hand the blue envelope with his name on it. He couldn't bring himself to open it. Once he opened it, it would be real. He'd been fooling himself. This thing was as real as the pain in his gut. Too damn real. If they could find him all the way up there at the cabin, they could find him anywhere. He had to defend himself!

After a couple of hours on the bus the envelope in Doug's lap was on fire. He had to know what was in it. They'd won—for the moment anyway. He tore the end off and slid out the contents. A photograph of a man he did not recognize, credit cards, and several documents containing some kind of schedule. It was a man's life on paper. Oh my God. *His target.* Doug swallowed hard. His target...the man he was supposed to kill. He gulped back the bile in his throat. He was coated with sweat. He covered his mouth with his hand, told himself to breathe. *In. Out. In. Out. Throwing up on the bus will only get you remembered.*

He waited until he'd regained some equilibrium to look at the papers again. Page after page of detailed information. Times. Places. Habits of his intended target. On one sheet there was a list of banks and a series of account numbers. Doug read the information over carefully, but couldn't find anything that told him what the account numbers were for. He looked up and saw a big bald guy reading a *USA Today* in the seat across the aisle. The headline read "STANTON DOWD MISSING." He knew that name. One of the senior partners at Eric's law firm. Eric had raved about him when Eric first joined up with Connors, Dowd, Rodgers, and Simon. Doug couldn't read the print and was about to ask to borrow the paper when the man was done and turned to Doug.

"You want it? I just read the sports section anyway. Frickin' Bills. They'll be lucky to win six games this season. Can you believe that?"

"No, I mean, yeah, thanks," Doug said, taking the paper.

"No problem," said the man, and settled in for a nap.

Doug unfolded the paper and turned the pages until he spotted the headline.

Stanton Dowd, a senior partner at the illustrious law firm Connors, Dowd, Rodgers, and Simon, was reported missing three nights ago. He was last seen leaving his penthouse suite at the Plaza Hotel. "We are operating under the assumption that Mr. Dowd is alive somewhere in the city and we intend to find him," Police Captain Allan McCabe said yesterday. Police insist that this is a missing person report, but some sources have suggested foul play.

Doug felt the already familiar grip of terror. Was it possible that Stanton Dowd had been a target of the Circle? He searched the paper to see if there was any more news, but that was the only story that had any relevance. Quickly and quietly he refolded the paper and pushed it down in between the seats. He looked around for the hundredth time. The bald guy was snoring and no one else had looked at him twice. The bus wasn't his preferred mode of travel, but it looked like the Circle could find him no matter what he did, where he went. Where he lived, worked, ate, heck, even his Wrangler would be a known factor. They already *were* a known factor to someone out there. Doug's capabilities as a tracker were not in question. He just never imagined he'd be using those skills to track other human beings. His only hope was if the members of the Circle weren't as skilled as he was.

The only reason Doug knew anything about tracking was thanks to his father, Douglas, Sr. There was a man who always knew what to do in any situation. Since he'd died three years ago Doug couldn't go hunting or fishing or even hiking in the woods without thinking about his father and the things he'd taught him. Like their last long hunting trip, back in Colorado.

It was the summer before his freshmen year at CU. His father said it would be their last trip together before Doug became a "real man." It was more about the trip than about the hunt, one last father-son experience, before Doug would be leaving home for good. Douglas, Sr. would never have said so in words, but he was going to miss his son more fiercely than he missed his own youth. Doug would be the first son in a long line of Goodwins to leave Grover and a life of farming to pursue a college education. The opportunities would be endless.

They'd driven up to a heavy wilderness area just north of Whitefish, Montana, almost a thousand miles from home, and had spent the better portion of a week living out of a tent, hunting game or catching fish for food, enjoying nature and each other's company. It was the next to last day of their trip. They were on the trail of some caribou, a real treat seeing as how caribou mainly dwelled in the boreal forests of British Columbia. Judging by how close they were from the border, though, Doug and his father weren't all that surprised to see the small herd of the magnificent animals. Among them was a sixteen-point stag, antlers erect and spreading with flattened brow tines that pointed forward and downward over his forehead. They watched, downwind to avoid detection, awed.

They settled in, Doug behind a boulder and his father up a tree, long bows at the ready. Unfortunately, in their singular focus on the caribou, they hadn't picked up on the fact that a grizzly bear had the same dinner plans. Suddenly ten feet and nine hundred pounds of bear was swiping at the branch where Douglas Senior was perched and struggling to maintain his balance.

Doug didn't stop to think. He came out from behind the rock to distract the bear. The grizzly took the bait. He swung around, located Doug, and let loose with a gutteral roar.

Run in a zigzag pattern. That's what he'd heard he was supposed to do. It was supposed to slow a bear down. But tell that to the bear. Quick and agile, this one had obviously never heard the old wive's tale. He was gaining on him. In a minute Doug'd be mincemeat.

"Don't run! Play dead!" he heard his father yell. He was running at Doug who was running from the bear and endeavoring to keep up.

Normally, running for your life would be the only possible way to have even a glimmer of hope to get out of a situation like this alive. This was a grizzly defending a kill site. They taught you how to deal with bears in Scouts, but no one really believed he'd find himself lying on the ground in a fetal position inviting a bear to check you out while you played dead. It was all he had. Doug hit the deck and played dead for all he was worth.

He'd never been very good at acting. The bear kept right on charging. Through the hands and arms covering his face, Doug watched the giant rear up and come down. Smelled his musky odor. Saw each individual hair on his massive torso. The bear swatted at him. Claws caught on his shirt and ripped open his chest. Doug felt the pain and heard himself scream, then watched as the bear reared up again to come in for another swipe. From Doug's position on the ground, he was a goner.

Only this time when the bear reared up there was a moment of stillness. As if the world had stopped in mid-revolution. Then its hulking mass came crashing down. Doug rolled out of the way just before he was crushed to a pulp.

The arrow had penetrated the animal through the back of the neck between the shoulders. The grizzly was flailing, making sounds unlike any Doug had ever heard.

"Doug, get out of there! Run!" his father yelled.

Doug ran, holding his arm across his bloody chest, and didn't stop until he'd reached a big log and had taken cover.

Doug's father was at his side in an instant. He pulled him close. "Oh my God. Doug. Are you okay? Let me look at that. We have to get you to a doctor. I thought you were dead. I've never been so scared in all my life."

The grizzly died where he'd fallen several minutes later. Doug's father reached into his shirt and pulled out the golden cross he had around his neck. He kissed it and said a silent prayer of thanks.

They drove to the nearest hospital. Doug was given a rabies shot, his wounds were cleansed, and his broken ribs bandaged. He'd live to see another day.

As the Greyhound bus raced back toward the city, Doug wished like he'd never wished before for the safety of his father's arms. He reached inside his own shirt and felt for his father's cross. Still there. A tiny bit of comfort amidst the chaos. His mother had insisted he take it and it had been around his neck since Douglas Sr. died, a constant reminder of a father's love for his son and a son's love for his father.

Eleven fifty-eight. Eric was discharged from the hospital at ten, happy to be out of there. Hospitals gave him the willies.

He took a cab home. He'd been sitting on his couch alone since. He looked like hell and didn't feel much better, but it was good to be home anyway. Eric had used his signing bonus from Connors, Dowd, Rogers and Simon as a down payment on his lavish condo. Vaulted ceilings, marble floor, the condo looked like wealth—unless of course you came from wealth. Then you wouldn't be fooled for a minute. He'd been on top of the world then, sure that nothing could come between him and the life he'd always dreamed about—money, women, status...power. He stared at the blackness of his plasma screen television. Three grand he'd paid for the thing. He looked to the left and right. Things everywhere. He liked saying he was an art collector, but had the eye of a newt. The interior decorator he'd hired was a knockout. Very grateful for the money he threw around. The paintings flanking the TV, a cool thirty-five hundred a piece, were her idea. They looked like identical coffee stains on a kitchen counter. What was he thinking at the time? Easy. Getting into her pants, that's what he'd been thinking. It was easy to convince him they were the height of sophistication then. All these years later, what did he have to show for it? A one-night stand he could hardly remember and two paintings of coffee-colored blobs.

Eric reached for the phone, checked there was a dial tone. The unrelenting beep sounded loud in the quiet room. Where the hell was Goodwin? He pushed the play button to hear Heather's message again. The sound of her voice soothed the edges. He wouldn't call her yet. He'd let her stew a while first.

What he needed was to hear from Doug. Doug always got back to him right away. No matter what. Where the hell was he?

What kind of a friend ignored his best buddy in his time of crisis?

A friend who was running for his life, that's what kind of friend. A friend who needed his best buddy to help him deal with the hand he'd been dealt.

Eric slumped, groaning at his aching sore ribs. What if Doug had put *him* in this position? Would he, Eric Matthews, be forgiving? Not a chance. Forgiveness would be the last thing on his mind. It would be revenge, first, last, and forever. Besides, they both knew what the Circle would do to them if they found out Doug had made contact with anyone, let alone the guy who'd recruited him.

Eric tried to put himself in Doug's shoes, to imagine the course of action Doug Goodwin, goody-goody-slash-hunter, would take. But Doug had always been an enigma to Eric with his honest-Abe approach to life and all his inconvenient morals. On the other hand, Eric had never known Doug to back down from anything in his life. Why would this time be any different?

Even in grade school Doug had watched out for the kid who always got picked on for being smaller and less agile, helped him out of fights he couldn't win, bailed him out of trouble. All the things a best friend was supposed to do. Not that Eric hadn't done plenty to help him, too. Fixed it so he could keep that apartment for next to nothing, for one thing. Stuff like that.

Eric sighed. Not even he could justify the two things being equal. He searched his memory for all the times he was there to help Doug out of trouble. Nothing in particular leapt to mind.

Eric again picked up his cell and pressed Doug's number. Again it went directly to voice mail. "Hi. This is Doug, leave a message and I'll return your call as soon as possible."

"Hey, Dougie. It's me." Eric laughed weakly and his voice cracked. "Look man, I have something I gotta tell ya. It's really important and it can't wait. I fucked up...big, and I don't...well, I don't really know what else to say. But if you still think of me as your friend, call me and I'll explain everything. Um, anyway, I'm sorry, man. I really am."

After a while Eric got up to fix a drink. Every movement hurt like hell. It might not be such a good idea to mix liquor with the pain pills, but hey, what the heck. His life sucked and his best friend was MIA.

Eric stayed up all night waiting for Doug to call, woozy with booze and pain killers. He watched infomercial after infomercial. He left voice mail after voice mail. At 4:00 AM he got an automated announcement telling him he had dialed incorrectly. At 5:00 AM it told him that the person's voice mailbox was full, to call back later. At 7:00 he was switching between reruns of *Oprah* and *Court TV* when the phone rang. Heart racing, he swiped open the phone. Finally, an opportunity to explain himself! Doug would understand how hard it was—

"Hello? Doug? Man, am I happy to hear—"

"Good morning, sir. Is this Mr. Eric Matthews? This is the American Society for the—"

"WHAAT? At 7:00 in the morning? Are you crazy?" Eric tossed the phone onto the table.

He turned back up the volume on the television.

He wanted to hear what Dr. Phil had to say.

At noon he thought about ordering Thai for lunch.

14

It's mid-day. Doug was outside Tasker's bar, staring into the lone, small, tinted window as though it was a vortex into another dimension. In a way it was. A dimension of sickness, deceit, and murder. He didn't know what else to do when the bus pulled into Grand Central Station, so he came back. To the scene of the crime, so to speak. Sounds of jazz were seeping through the cracks in the nondescript wooden door onto the street. The last time he was here was with Matthews, just two pals having a night on the town.

It was still early. A handful of people were in the club—the usual lunch crowd?—all immaculately dressed. They could have been there since the night before. Doug's world had disintegrated but in here nothing had changed. A jazz quintet was playing on the raised stage. A Thelonius Monk tune, *Round Midnight*.

Doug took a seat at the corner of the bar facing the VIP door and surveilled the room.

"Looks like you could use a drink," the bartender said.

"No, thanks."

"But I insist." He poured Doug a glass of single malt scotch.

Why bother arguing? Doug drank it down like a shot.

"It's always hard for the new recruits."

Mr. Empathy himself. "So, I guess you know all about what goes on here."

"It's my bar, son."

"And that's okay with you?"

"Let's just say I'm well compensated for any discomfort."

A window of opportunity? Doug leaned in close. "You gotta help me, man. This…this thing…it's not me. I'm not… Please, talk to them…tell them I can't…."

"No can do, son," said the bartender matter-of-factly. "I'm just the bartender. And to be honest with you, nothing I say would make a difference."

Just the bartender. Right. Doug sat back. He should have known better.

The bartender filled Doug's glass and went back to washing glasses behind the bar. Mellow jazz, murmured conversations… you'd think it was just another day. How could these people go about their business when a few feet away there was a room full of killers waiting for their next assignment?

Doug placed his unfinished drink on the bar and walked to the door to the lounge. He heard a soft click and the door whooshed open.

007—Cufflinks—and Bearded Man—Chemist—were right where he'd left them, sitting in high-backed leather chairs, smoking cigars. Two men toward the rear were shooting pool, another two casually tossing darts. Otherwise, the room was empty and quiet. Too damn weird. Maybe he really hadn't ever left.

CUFFLINKS (greeting Doug like a long lost relative): "Young Goodwin, sit down, my boy, sit down!" Sunlight bounced off his cufflinks.

How could it have been only yesterday that he was giving tours to thirteen-year-olds? It felt like a lifetime ago. Doug picked up a chair and moved it over to the table. Would he ever see the sunlight stream through the stained glass windows in the museum again? He pointed to the cufflinks. "I guess that's why they call you Mr. Cufflinks, huh?"

CUFFLINKS (smiling): "Something like that. Care for a Montecristo, my boy?"

"A what?"

"Cigar, my boy. Cuban, hand-rolled. Very smooth...an easy drawing cigar. I find they lack the boldness of a Lars or a Macanudo, but they were a gift from Mr. Fingers."

CHEMIST (with a chuckle): "And you don't refuse a gift from Mr. Fingers."

"Don't smoke," Doug said.

CHEMIST: "Don't smoke? You're gonna have to lose that nasty little habit if you're gonna fit in here."

CUFFLINKS: "Indeed, Mr. Chemist. Which brings us to the next question. How are you adjusting so far, young Goodwin?"

"How do you think I'm adjusting? I'll be straight with you, okay? There's been a big mistake here. A *big* mistake. I don't kill people and I don't belong here. Look, I don't mean to be insulting and I don't want to offend you. I respect what you guys have going on here, I really do. But it's just not for me. I...." he swallowed "...what I mean is, thank you for accepting me, but I've thought it over and I'm afraid I'm going to have to decline."

CUFFLINKS: "We understand."

"Really?" It was that easy?

CHEMIST: "Sure, why ever not?"

The last time Doug felt so much relief was when he'd found out he didn't have to play the part of the donkey in his third-grade school play. He collapsed against the back of his seat. "That's great. Wow. Thank you both so much. I swear to God I won't say a word to anyone about your club. I mean it, not one word."

CUFFLINKS: "We certainly hope not."

"Then...I can go?"

CHEMIST: "Indeed."

All at once Doug had the feeling the other shoe was about to drop. When it didn't, he got up and made himself reach over the table to shake their hands. "Well, thank you, gentlemen. It's been a...a pleasure talking to you."

He almost made it to the door.

CUFFLINKS (still chuckling): "Oh, by the way, Mr. Goodwin, good luck out there. May your hunt be fulfilling."

There it was. "My what? I thought—I mean, you just said—"

"No, Mr. Goodwin. We said we understand. And we do. But there is no leaving the Circle. We therefore wish you a fulfilling hunt. It's only good manners."

Doug's knees buckled. "I'm not out, am I?"

"There is no 'out,' my boy. This is your life now."

"But if you understand...."

"And we do, Mr. Goodwin. We have all endured the rite of passage you are experiencing now. But that doesn't change anything."

CHEMIST: "After a while, well, let's just say you'll get to appreciate it."

What a load of BS. Doug doesn't want a new life, he was happy with his old one. Well, happy enough.

He kicked the chair across the floor. "I'm telling you, you can't do this! It isn't right!"

In a minute Cufflinks and Chemist were up, expensive cigars on the floor, pushing a hysterical Doug against the wall.

CUFFLINKS (low and menacing, no longer the cultured sophisticate of a moment ago): "You listen to me, *boy*, because what I have to say *will* save your life. This may not be right, or fair, or moral, but it is very real. Somewhere there is a man with intentions to hunt you dead and this man is not squandering his time questioning the integrity of the Circle. This man may even be one of us. Now, you can be smart and use your time here to discover your enemy and strike first...or you can die with your principles intact. Either way you will conduct yourself like a gentleman when you are here. Are we one hundred percent clear?"

With Cufflinks' forearm up against Doug's throat, he managed a small nod of compliance.

"Good. Now compose yourself."

The men took a step back and waited while Doug adjusted his shirt. He was embarrassed and horrified at the same time.

CUFFLINKS (to the room): "Our apologies, gentlemen." He bent down, picked up his cigar, and brushed it off.

"But...what do I do now?"

CHEMIST (unhelpfully): "Whatever you want."

CUFFLINKS: "Talk to people, Mr. Goodwin. Every face you see in Tasker's is a member of the Circle. You'll be fine, boy. And you'll find it really is quite a thrill."

"But...how do I make a living? I'm not rich like you. I can't spend my days in here smoking cigars and flirting with beautiful women."

CHEMIST: "I guess Mr. Black forgot to mention a few things."

CUFFLINKS (deferring to Chemist): "He must have. Shall I tell him or would you like to?"

CHEMIST: "You go on ahead."

CUFFLINKS (nodding): "Certainly."

Unbelievable. Would someone just tell me already? Doug's patience was shot and these guys were word fencing. Like Laurel and damn Hardy, except he was the one stuck on third base.

"My dear boy, it's like this. Our fortune is your fortune now. When you're inducted into the Circle, everything you own becomes the Circle's. And vice versa...everything the Circle owns becomes yours."

"I'm not so sure I want anything from you." Doug said.

"Be that as it may, whether you want it or not, you are now worth billions, Mr. Goodwin. Best to take advantage of it."

The list of account numbers in the blue envelope. "So those numbers, the ones in the blue envelope I got, are...."

"That's correct. Yours. Ours. The petty concerns of life are inconsequential now, and for good reason. Now is the time for focus. You must train for the hunt. You will learn, Mr. Goodwin, that life in the Circle is more than the hunt. There are...certain advantages, one might say. Wouldn't you agree, Mr. Chemist?"

CHEMIST (laughing through his cigar as if it's the funniest thing he ever heard): "Absolutely. I'd probably go so far as to say it's considerably enhanced my quality of life."

Doug was still stuck on "billions." What would it be like to have access to that kind of money? Still, accepting it would mean accepting the life of a rat in an infinite maze.

CUFFLINKS (chiding): "Do cheer up, Mr. Goodwin. You know, Mr. Chemist, I think it's best for young Goodwin here to find out on his own."

Cufflinks offered a cigar again, and this time Doug hesitantly accepted. After one puff Doug's face turned red and his throat caught on fire. Hacking coughs kept him from catching his breath. Chemist offered a few smacks on the back. Eventually the coughing subsided and Doug forced himself to take another, much smaller, puff, and watched as the smoke mingled with that of all the other cigars in the room.

The man playing darts in the back of the room completed his game and methodically placed his darts back into a personalized leather case. He was one of the younger members, not much older than Doug, casually dressed, pale face. Familiar.

With a jolt of recognition, he knew why. It was the face of the man in the photo inside his blue envelope. It was *him*, his target. In the same room. Right in front of him. Doug looked away.

Suddenly the man was at the table. "New recruit giving you a hard time, boys?"

CUFFLINKS: "Mr. Dart, allow me to introduce you to Doug Goodwin, our newest member."

Dart extended his hand. "Welcome to the Circle."

"Thanks," Doug stammered, taking the proffered hand and giving it a quick shake. What do you say to the guy whose eyes were as dead as Doug might be.

DART: "Well, I'm sure you're still getting acclimated, Mr. Goodwin. I'll leave you to it." He turned to Mr. Cufflinks and Mr. Chemist. "Good day, gentlemen."

With a small bow Dart approached the door and was let out of the room.

CUFFLINKS: "Mr. Dart will make an excellent hunt, Mr. Goodwin," Mr. Cufflinks commented. "He is quite skilled."

Doug was appalled. "You know? How?"

"Your face, my boy, you gave it all away. You must cultivate more of a poker face if you want to be successful."

CHEMIST: "He's right. It's like poker. Don't let the other guy know your cards until it's too late for him to counter-attack."

"Oh, God...so you think he knows it's me—that he's my target?" Doug was having that all-too-familiar feeling in his gut again. Could he make it to the men's room before he hurled?

CUFFLINKS: "Hard to say. Mr. Dart was recruited several months before you; I imagine he still has a lot to learn. You don't have to worry about us, though, Mr. Goodwin. We won't say anything. That would be bad form. Besides, I think I speak for all of us when I say we're looking forward to seeing what you're capable of."

"But what if he knows?"

"Well, that's simple. As Mr. Black told you, he will be attempting to kill you before you can kill him."

Etiquette be damned. Doug walked to the parlor door and waited. Nothing. Why wasn't the damn door opening? He looked back at his cigar-smoking companions. Mr. Chemist pointed to a round button in the floor to the right of the door. "Push it," he said.

Doug pushed.

He had to get it together. He couldn't afford to walk around in a daze when someone could be trying to kill him as soon as he left Tasker's.

"Don't take it so bad, kid, it could be worse," a voice said. "Mr. Lion," sitting at the end of the bar, his back to the VIP door. The guy with the huge upper body Doug remembered from the other day.

"Really? I don't see how."

"You could be my age."

Was he trying to be funny?

"Your age, I'd be out of this mess."

"Hey, don't get so far ahead of me, kid, I still have three years of service to put in before I can retire and be a Mr. Black somewhere." Mr. Lion gestured for him to sit. "Join me in a drink, Mr. Goodwin? I'm buying." He waved to the bartender and pointed to his drink and then to Doug.

Drinking out of boredom seems stupid, but he accepts anyway, as he had earlier. Drinking was apparently part and parcel of the culture here. Maybe he'd get used to it. Maybe he'd die of cirrhosis before one of the members killed him.

"I was just like you, kid," Mr. Lion said. "I got sucked in when I was about your age—twenty-nine—thirty—am I right?"

"Twenty-seven. But at this point I might not live to see twenty-eight," Doug said morosely.

"I know how you feel."

Doug looked at the old guy with the mane of silvery blond hair and flat gray eyes. "No, really, I do. I wanted out bad, too. But as it turns out, I'm pretty good at it. My concern is losing a step or two in my old age." Lion took a swig of his refreshed martini.

"You look like you keep in pretty good shape," Doug said.

"Well, thank you, son, but having these," Lion flexed his biceps, "doesn't automatically make me any better at the hunt."

"Can't hurt, though." Doug considered the room of men. Most of them were older than he was. Every last woman was gorgeous and young—very young. At least half the age of the men on whose arms they were draped and in whose laps they sat. What was in it for them? Oh, yeah. Money.

"The perks," Lion said, seeing Doug looking. "Yeah, they're nice, but you get tired of them after a while. You realize there are more important things. Like survival."

"So what you're telling me is that everyone in this place is a murderer?"

"Everyone except you, but I'd try not to think of it as murder."

Right.

"No, really. We are consenting adults engaged in an elaborate hunt. Murder is the act of killing someone against his will," Lion defended.

Doug didn't bother to address how insane that sounded. That sentence alone gave him a crystal clear picture into the psyche of the people who were trying to call him a "fellow member." "So I guess I don't have to ask you where you stand on Dr. Kavorkian," he said.

Lion's lips tightened. "Let me give you a piece of advice, kid. Life's too short for judgment." He took a long drag of his cigar. "Especially in this place. Another piece of advice? Be a Boy Scout. You know, prepared for anything."

"Doesn't change the fact that I still don't want to kill anyone."

"You'll come around after your first. Everyone does. By the time you're my age you see the way things really are."

"Just one really big game, huh?"

"That's right, kid, a big game. Only there's no reset button if you lose, so I suggest you make smart choices. You'll come around."

Thanks bunches. Nice teaching moment, dude. What was that...smart advice for the Nintendo generation?

Doug got up and politely toasted "Mr. Lion" with his drink before finishing the contents. He put the empty glass down on the bar. He again headed for the door. He only made it a couple of feet before Lion called to him. "Oh, and one more thing, kid, be careful out there. You heard about the Fink, right?"

Really. The Fink? How could anything so pathetic be taken so seriously? "Who the hell is that?"

"You'd think after all this time Mr. Black would include the Fink in his initiation speech," said Mr. Lion. "But no matter. The Fink was one of the first recruits when I came on board. He had a real flare for this stuff, big on drownings. Loves 'em. The East River, a bathtub, even a toilet once. Doesn't waste time, goes in and out fast. Usually takes his mark in two days or less. Problem is that he didn't like our rules too much. Got bored."

"Bored? What do you mean, bored?"

"Killed his marks and killed his own killers faster than we could recruit them, at least locally. We had to apply pressure. Insisted he take a brief sabbatical so we could bring in more members. He didn't take to it all that well."

Doug sighed, refusing to be goaded into asking.

Lion gave in. "That's right. He defected. Flat out abandoned the rules of the Circle. He's hunting us down one by one. It's how he gets his kicks."

"So, let me get this straight. You all live by these rules the Circle has. Except, um, not. Because the rules don't apply to anyone who doesn't want to follow them. Like this Fink guy. Is that about the gist of it?"

Lion swirled his drink. "Afraid so."

"So not only do I have to worry about someone I know stabbing me in the back, but now you're telling me I have to worry about some renegade ex-member rogue assassin killing me because he's bored?"

"I'm only telling you this because he always manages to suss out our new recruits. In other words, he'll be looking for you. I suggest you be ready."

"Does anyone know who he is?"

"Used to be Gérard Finck. With a 'ck.'"

Doug rolled his eyes.

"Yeah, I know...but he's had so many aliases it's hard to keep track. Richard Osterman, Benjamin Sanders, Marcus Cobb, Leonardo La Strada, Thomas Brown, the list is probably endless. He's had a couple facial reconstructions along the way, too. God only knows what he even looks like anymore."

"And they chose not to share this piece of information with me, why? For that matter, why are *you* telling me?"

Lion held up his hands. "Hey, just trying to help you out here, kid. Word just hit the street that he took out Mr. Eclipse just a few days ago."

Eclipse? A few days ago? Could that have been Stanton Dowd? He'd been reported missing and no one Doug had met was wearing the gloat of a triumphant kill. But there was no time to solve that mystery now. "Is he as rich as the other members?"

"That's the one thing we have going for us. We cut him off early on. He no longer has access to the Circle's funds. It's not foolproof, but at least it helps control him. The down side is that no one ever knows when or how he's going to strike. It could be months, it could be days. No one knows."

"I can't deal with this now," Doug said.

"Well, you'd better start. Because he's undoubtedly started planning your personal demise."

Doug's heart began to race. "Does he ever come in here?"

Lion shook his head. "No. I don't know if it's out of respect—which I doubt—or out of fear of getting caught. But he's a cocky sonnovabitch. I wouldn't be surprised if he showed up here eventually."

PART II

15

Dart was gyrating with a woman in tight jeans on the dance floor. They were in a trendy midtown nightspot packed with sweaty bodies and music so loud it was impossible to tell that it was music at all. Hundreds dressed to impress, the women flaunting their breasts, the men showcasing tight abs and fat wallets, filling the three-tiered hall illuminated only by a series of colored lights that swirled in tandem with the beat. It was one of Dart's regular haunts among the beautiful people. He fit right in, too: clean-shaven, hair parted deliberately, smart slacks, Berluti loafers...the message understated, yet clear. *I am a person of influence and means. I can do what I want. I can have what—or whom—I want.*

Weeks had gone by since Doug's recruitment and his talk with "Mr. Lion." It was actually that talk that scared him into thinking about doing something he swore he would never do. Which is why he was here spying on Dart, the rich, successful, smart, newish member of the Circle. Does he want to do this? No. Can he do it? He'd find out.

Dart enticed a second woman to join him and his busty redheaded dance partner on the floor. Soon his hands were exploring the redhead's body as she pressed chest to thigh against him. They found their way from the top of her outstretched arms down through the curve of her waist and around to her ass. Doug drank his Jack and ginger, his eyes glued to the show. Not to be outdone, the woman in the short green shimmery thing who was at Dart's back began her own expedition of his physique. Doug felt his pants tighten uncomfortably in response. Talk about perks. The easy money. Accessibility to all the hottest clubs and sexiest women. At the moment, Dart's position didn't look all that bad.

Doug shifted his own position and watched the scene unfold, although the crowded dance floor made it difficult. When the strobe lights went on he strained to keep his target in sight. Then the woman in green pulled Dart away from the dance floor and over to a VIP area of booths and lounge chairs that had been cordoned off by a thick purple velvet rope. The redhead followed.

In their new location his vantage point had improved. A waitress appeared at their table with a tray, deposited small squares of paper, then left. Dart lounged between the two women on a chaise the size of a king-sized bed. As the women draped themselves around him, arms caressing his chest and thighs, Dart threw back his head and laughed.

The waitress returned with a full tray of drinks, four blue something-or-others in martini glasses, two that might be vodka tonics, and six shots that could be anything from Jägermeister to Dewar's. A second waitress arrived with a bottle of Grey Goose. You could drown in so much booze. Dart peeled off a wad of bills, which the waitress stuffed down her cleavage as if it was an every-day occurrence. Maybe it was.

The next few minutes were a blur of downed drinks, roving hands, and overt invitations. The redhead on Dart's left was practically in his lap, her leg across his thigh. The woman on his right was whispering in his ear, one arm around his neck, the other reaching over to stroke the redhead's breast.

Doug needed to hit the head. It has been too long since he's been with a woman and memories of hiding hard-ons in high school were making him flush with the same desire and shame. Dart's *menage à trois* wasn't going anywhere for the moment. He made his way past the bar, past the throng of bodies, and down the hall to the men's room, where he thought about base-ball until he could relieve himself.

He looked in the mirror.

He's shocked. It's the face of Douglas Goodwin, Jr., but the eyes are empty, as if everything that made him *him* had been sucked out, leaving only the husk. He urinated, leaning one hand against the wall, eyes now closed against the image in the mirror, feeling the heavy bass booming under his feet. In the relative quiet of the bathroom he could finally hear himself think. When he was done he flushed, washed his hands methodically, and tossed the paper towel in the bin by the door as he was leaving.

I can't do this. It goes against everything I believe in. I'm not a killer. Period.

There had to be a way out. Just because no one told him what it was didn't mean he should just give in and do what they say. Jesus, he was tired. He needed some time to think, to sort it all out. But that was the one thing he didn't have—time.

When he re-entered the club he was assaulted by all the sights and sounds. At 1:00 AM things were reaching a fevered pitch. But now, instead of being turned on by the beautiful bodies, the raw smell of sex in the air, Doug felt only revulsion. By what was in front of him or the memory of his own reflection, he wasn't sure. The scene had taken on the qualities of a horror show, grotesque in the extreme.

Doug returned to what used to be his table where a small cluster of young men were evidently game-planning their next move. Doug's target was leaving the VIP area with his companions. They weren't returning to the dance floor. They were moving directly toward the exit. Where were they going? What if he lost them?

Doug ran outside just as the two women were climbing into a 1966 Shelby convertible, navy blue with two white racing stripes. Dart turned back to hand the valet a couple of bills and Doug moved into the shadow of a massive potted plant. The valet shoved his tip into his pocket and Dart got into the driver's seat. The Shelby peeled out into the light traffic on 7th Avenue. Doug scavenged his pockets for his ticket and handed it to the valet. "Make it fast, there's an extra fifty in it for you," he said. The valet scurried off to find Doug's vehicle. He returned quickly with the 1994 silver Wrangler, looking suitably unimpressed by the doorless, muddied vehicle.

"Guess that's why guys like that get all the women," said Doug.

"You're telling me," mumbled the valet.

Doug pursued his target through the streets of Manhattan at a safe distance. When they arrived on the East Side, Dart pulled into a parking garage on Park and 81st. The gates clanged shut behind the convertible, verifying that the information in Doug's blue envelope was correct. He inched his Jeep to within a few hundred feet of the gate, then parked and shut off his engine.

He'd memorized the gate code, also provided in the envelope. He grabbed his hunting binoculars, only one of the items he was now keeping in his vehicle at all times, and slithered into the alley across the street. From there he could scan the side of the building, the comings and goings, get a lay of the land. The stately brick building had ten floors, small by New York standards, but a landmark, home to some of the wealthiest people in the City. When the penthouse lights went on Doug swung his binoculars upward. That had to be it. Since Doug had been watching, Dart and the women had been the only people to enter the building. The blinds were open, allowing Doug partial access into the apartment. The women seemed to like the view. Or, more likely, liked being seen. Inches from the glass, they danced together, slowly removing items of clothing.

Doug's binoculars stayed glued to his eyes. At the moment Dart entered his sights Doug heard something whistle by his head. Instinctively he dove for cover. Several more whistles whooshed by. His right thigh was on fire. *He'd been hit!* Fighting the biting pain, he crawled his way behind one in a series of huge metal storage containers and drew the pistol affixed to his leg, which would need to be tied off soon. Real soon.

A man in black camouflage was scouting the alley, carrying his new sniper rifle, an M40A1, similar to his prized but older Remington Model 700. He set it down and removed a silenced pistol from a holster on his back. "Yo, Doug. Douglas Goodwin. You in there? Come on out, Goodwin, have some fun with me."

Doug looked around desperately for somewhere else to hide. The storage container to his left, away from the alley's entrance, looked like it had rusted in the open position. He made a dash for it, dragging his leg behind him. He stumbled over something—a piece of metal—which clanged against the hollow container. He winced.

The man in black swung around.

The alley was dark but the streetlight at the end cast far too much illumination. No way Doug wouldn't be seen.

The man in black held his weapon close and made his way toward the sound coming from the alley. He sang quietly. *"For what is a man, what has he got? If not himself, then he has naught. To say the things he truly feels, and not the words of one who kneels."*

Doug's assailant was getting closer. The lunatic was singing, too, Frank Sinatra, of all things. He knew that voice....

The man turned the corner just as Doug slid, gasping from the pain in his leg, into the container's opening, but he'd been spotted. Doug drew the Type 64 semi-automatic he'd recently acquired and held it in front of him.

The man in black stepped closer, still singing.

The bastard's enjoying himself. Doug was cornered. Even if he got off a shot it'd probably ricochet off the container and hit him instead. Oh, what the hell. He squeezed off a shot anyway.

Nothing. Nothing happened! Not a damn thing! He pulled the trigger again. No good. He dropped the gun and scooted farther into the container along the floor covered with empty Mickie D's boxes and a pile of rags. Was this someone's home he had tumbled into? Were those rats he was hearing in the back?

Hysteria was on its way. He was about to be shot and he was worried about a couple of rats.

Hunting gave the man in black confidence. And why shouldn't it? He was good at it. *"The record shows I took the blows...and did it my way!"* he sang, this time *sotto voce.* "That song was for you, Douglas Goodwin. If I had known you wouldn't put up a respectable fight I'd have taken you out on the first shot. This has been the least challenging of all my kills. Fucking new recruits. You did it your way, okay, but now you'll have nothing."

Although the man liked to stretch out the process, which made for better reflection later, sometimes you had to go with the flow. The glint in his eye shifted from determined to deadly cold in a nanosecond. "It has been a pleasure hunting you, Douglas Goodwin," he said, and took aim.

Doug prayed.

A shot rang out. There was a thud. Then all was quiet.

Doug opened his eyes, felt the burn in his leg. He wasn't dead. What the—?

On the ground lay his singing predator. A second man in black was standing on top of the neighboring storage container. The man hopped down off the container with cat-like agility. He walked over to Doug with a sniper rifle at his side.

Doug backed into the container. He had the shakes—bad— and his thigh was bleeding out. Had he been saved only to be taken out a few seconds later—*now*?

"The guy's no chairman of the board, that's for sure. I did the Circle a favor."

No way. Cufflinks? "Cufflinks?"

Cufflinks removed his black mask. "Young Goodwin! So *you* were Mr. Crooner's target."

"Who?"

Cufflinks pulled up the ski mask from the dead man's face to reveal the crooner from Tasker's bar. "Terrible Sinatra, don't you think? And, if you don't mind me saying, a bit of a showboat for dragging this bit out."

Doug ignored the thought that Cufflinks was scoffing at the fact that Doug wasn't killed *faster*. "You saved my life!"

"Not at all, Mr. Goodwin. I merely killed my target. I believe congratulations are in order. You have just witnessed the Circle in action." Cufflinks moved to Mr. Crooner's body and inspected his sleeves. "Alas," he said. "I was hoping he'd be wearing his Jorge Adelers tonight. Apparently he opted for more comfortable attire in your pursuit."

Doug's brain was moving about as fast as a turtle on Quaaludes. Finally it synced up. Cufflinks was tracking Crooner while Crooner was tracking Doug and Doug had been tracking Dart. Four members of the Circle had been within striking distance of one another for a period of over an hour. And this guy was dissing the dude's clothing choices? "And this matters, why?"

"Not all of us collect fingers," said Cufflinks. "Here," he added, tossing Doug a bandage of gauze from a pouch on his back, "for the leg. And you might want to learn a bit about your weapon of choice," gesturing to Doug's discarded weapon.

Doug regarded the pistol on the ground with disgust. "The thing jammed."

"Jammed? I doubt it. The Chinese don't make a faulty pistol. In the future you might want to check the safety switch on the side."

Doug blanched. Sure enough, the safety was just where Cufflinks said it would be.

"And you might want to stick to weapons more your style," he suggested mildly.

"Um, yeah, good idea, I guess I'll do that." As good a hunter as he was, Doug wouldn't have done too well at the O.K. Corral.

"Well, cheerio, then, Mr. Goodwin," Cufflinks said with a wink. "See that you get that leg taken care of."

Doug bandaged his leg, relieved that it was only a flesh wound. He'd panicked, that's all, totally panicked. The bullet had gone straight through. He pulled himself up off the ground, collected his gun and binoculars, and began the painful hop back to his vehicle.

He put the key in the ignition, but before he turned on the car he quickly stashed the pistol to the floor on the passenger's side. Then he took one last look up at the penthouse apartment. The action had moved away from the windows and the lights had been turned down low.

Enjoy it, *Mr.* Dart.

Tomorrow you might not get so lucky.

Across the water, through a pair of Steiner Predator 12 x 50 binoculars and a long-range Bionic Ear microphone, the Fink's shoulders bobbed in amusement. It thrilled him to know that with three quick pulls of the trigger he could have killed three members of the Circle. Three for the price of one. What a coup that would be. But it was the challenge he lived for, and the chase. He took his time to disassemble his sniper rifle and pack up his belongings.

Tomorrow was another day.

16

Professor Ronald P. Balachi sat quietly at his computer in his study, a distinguished man at sixty-six despite the receding hairline and the slight beer gut from too many evenings at the campus pub. Notwithstanding his worsening arthritis, he had aged relatively well.

The professor considered himself down to earth and in touch with the youth of today, a perception that was not entirely inaccurate, evidenced by the fact that on his sixtieth birthday a few of his students took him to a place called Adrenaline to have his ear pierced. The picture of him surrounded by his students in the chair at the tattoo parlor was in a frame on his desk, in a place of honor next to his monitor.

The professor had next to him a half-eaten peanut butter sandwich and a tall glass of milk. Seeing as he spent more time in his study than he did anywhere else in his home, he had designed it to be a place of order, a place he enjoys for the casual chat with an old friend or a small study group before exams. Six shelves along the back wall house a virtual library of scientific text. A large oval area rug lies in the center of the room under a square coffee table around which several comfortable leather chairs were placed almost twenty years ago and have never moved an inch.

Framed black-and-white photographs, along with one vibrant colorful image of what the Big Bang might have looked like from a few hundred thousand light years away, cover the wall surfaces. Opposite his desk hang framed degrees: a Bachelor's of Science from Penn State, a Master's in Anthropology from Ohio State University, and a Double Doctorate from the University of Maryland, an Sc.D. in Science Education and a Ph.D. in Anthropology. A much younger—and thinner—version of the professor adorns a framed issue of *Popular Science* in which he holds a globe in an outstretched hand up over his head. The headline beneath the picture reads, "Can Doc Ron Balachi predict the next Big Bang? (Page 146)." This had always amused him for two reasons. One, because one hundred forty-six was exactly the number of globular clusters discovered in the halo, one of the three components of the Milky Way Galaxy, and two, because no one except for his closest friends had ever had the privilege of calling him "Doc," yet there it was for the world to see. His family and friends had congratulated him on his moment of fame, but none of them had an inkling of the nature of his work—nor did he expect them to.

The professor had always assumed he'd marry, but as the years went by his work had been all the partner he ever needed. His family, up until recently, had consisted of his parents and his two older sisters. Three years ago, his mother, at a ripe old age of ninety-two, had died from brain cancer. His father went soon after, presumably of a broken heart; they'd been high school sweethearts, married for almost seventy-five years. The photo of his family on the top shelf of his computer station was one of his favorites: the five Balachis almost fifty-five years prior. Ron sat on his father's shoulders, the twins, Patricia and Catherine (or Pat and Cat, as they were called) at his mother's feet. The last time he'd seen a relative, of whom there were few left and far between, was at his niece's wedding almost five years ago.

Pat and Cat were eight years older. Virtually inseparable and pioneers in their hometown for having the gumption to remain unmarried and devote themselves to education, they had doted on their baby brother and were influential in making sure he stayed on track all the way through school. Not that he'd been tempted to stray. From math to romance languages, he'd been hooked on learning from the start. The girls had attended Penn State first, creating a path for him to follow, and he'd been a Nittany Lion for as long as he could remember. Though he didn't see his sisters much because they still lived within a stone's throw of each other in the small town in South Carolina where they'd all been born, the professor felt he owed them everything. The small photo of the three of them was taped to the bottom of his monitor to remind him of how he got where he was today.

Professor Balachi logged onto *sciencedaily.com* and clicked on various articles of interest; one about a new extra-solar planet in the constellation Hercules, another about reversing the signs of Alzheimer's, and another about the evolution of a dolphin's fin to a limb of a human. In the middle of his reading, an icon appeared on his screen. "You have new urgent mail!" Always interested to see who was contacting him and, in this case, what the nature of the urgency could be, the professor clicked and was re-directed to his email.

Doc - I need your help! Don't try to contact me! I'll call you on the pay phone at 12:30 AM. Don't tell anyone! - Marty

There was only one student who'd ever called him "Doc" and the signature of "Marty" clinched it: Doug Goodwin. Ron had nicknamed him Marty after months of Doug's relentless use of "Doc" to address the professor. Professor Balachi had to admit that there was an uncanny resemblance between them—an older scatter-brained but brilliant professor and the younger wise-ass kid—to the characters in *Back to the Future*. The reference to the pay phone meant Doug didn't want their conversation to be overheard. While Doug was in school they'd used that mode of communication for all the things that were "unofficial," and better kept out of the computerized phone system records. He was surprised Doug still knew the number, but it must be important if he needed that kind of secrecy. He glanced at his watch, lying next to his keyboard. Already 11:50 PM. His office was about a ten-minute drive from the house. Less than enthusiastic, but deeply concerned, the professor quickly changed back into his clothes from earlier, grabbed the swipe card to his office, and jogged out the door.

Two thousand miles away at an internet café in the Big Apple Doug Goodwin logged off his computer. *Come on Doc, be there. I need you.*

Campus security had installed a lamp post over the phone and cast-iron bench that sat outside the Science Building to encourage students who were working late to contact the security office if they felt unsafe walking back to their dorms. The professor wasn't under the impression the phone got much use, but it was probably a deterrent, and he agreed that it was a gesture in the right direction. Now, sitting there himself in the mist, still breathing hard from the exertion of the short jog from his car's parking spot, the professor saw how a young girl—or an old man—might easily be the target of some ne'er-do-well, and sent a silent thanks to the administration for the lighting.

Professor Balachi was concerned. Never having married or fathered a child, he considered Douglas Goodwin, Jr. the closest thing to a son he would ever have. He'd tried to keep it from Doug how broken up he was when he and his ego-driven friend, Eric Matthews, moved to New York—for both their sakes— but tonight's call had brought back the old longing for Doug's company.

The pay phone rang shrill in the night.

"Marty?"

"Doc."

"You're okay! Thank God. What's going on, what's wrong? Where are you?"

"I'm at one of the only remaining pay phones in New York."

"Why are you calling me here, on this phone?"

"I don't think it's safe for us to talk on normal channels. They may be tapped."

"Tapped? Doug. That sounds— What's going on?"

"I need your help, Doc. I've gotten involved in something and I don't know how to get out."

"Anything, just tell me what I can do. What is it you've done?"

"It's best not to talk about it on the phone, Doc."

"But—"

"Listen, I can't explain now. It's not safe. Have you started classes yet? Can you get away for a few days?"

"Classes don't start until next week. Of course I'll come. You want me to fly to New York?"

"No, I've got a better idea," Doug said. "I've already called the airport in Denver. I've booked you three seats on three different airlines. I emailed you all the confirmation numbers a few minutes ago. Get on the flight that takes you to Kansas City, okay? I've done the same with three tickets in my name. There's no way they can track all three flights."

"But what's this about? Who's 'they'? How can you afford to buy all those—"

"Just do it, Doc, please. The flight is at 8:40 tomorrow morning. I'll see you in Missouri—and Doc?—thanks."

"Missouri!? What's in Kansas City? Hello?" But Doug was gone. The professor hung up the receiver in frustration, his only thought to hurry home and get some rest. He wasn't as young as he used to be.

17

Doug took a taxi home. The carefree Doug, the Doug who was frustrated with his job and with his love life, had been replaced with a Doug who scanned all perimeters for imminent attack and kept his eyes hooded and wary. If he only knew then what he knows now he might have been more grateful for the life of a love-starved underpaid tour guide.

"Evening, Mr. Goodwin," said the doorman.

"Don't you ever sleep?"

"Plenty of time to sleep when you're dead, sir."

Yeah, always a plus.

"Can I help you with that package? Looks heavy."

"No, thanks, Murph. I'm fine."

"Hey, are you limping? What happened to your leg there?"

Doug looked down. Blood was seeping through the bandage on his leg and spotting his pants.

"Oh, nothing much. Just a scratch…football with the guys… you know…."

"Sure, I remember those days. You want me to call the elevator for you?" He reached for a key in his pocket.

"No thanks, I think I'll take the stairs. Need to keep limber, you know. Take care, Murph."

Doug made it up the stairs, his leg throbbing and burning. He could have kissed the door to his apartment. That's when he saw the welcome mat on the floor had been moved—not much, but still. It was now at an angle to the door. Was the person who'd been there so confident that he didn't care if Doug noticed? He put down the brown bag he was holding and took out the gun from the small of his back under his shirt. He moved to the side of the door and examined the edges of the door for booby traps. That's when he saw a speck of blue jutting out from under the mat.

Oh. Another delivery.

The standard blue envelope had his name written in thick black letters, just like the last one. Inside, there was a single sheet of paper.

Mr. Goodwin, The member assigned to you has been reported dead at 2:17 AM. By the rules of the Circle, you have now been given 48 hours furlough while another member is assigned to you. - The Circle

Doug had forgotten that one very important rule. *Should the member assigned to hunt you meet his timely death, you will be notified and will receive forty-eight hours of leave.* He was safe until at least 2:16 tomorrow morning—and he'd wasted precious time dodging what wasn't there. Reaching into the bag he took out a new doorknob and dead bolt. He got a screwdriver and a pair of pliers from one of the drawers in the kitchen and went to work.

"Hey, man, where you been?"

Doug whirled around. "Eric?"

"Bingo!"

"What are you doing here? You scared the shit out of me. You know I don't like surprises like that."

"I need a reason to come by here now? I thought your door was always open."

"Whatever."

"Am I going to be getting a copy of that new key? Or are you trying to keep me out, too?" The best defense was a good offense. And why not? It had always worked before.

Doug hesitated. Kick Eric out—or tell him everything? That was the question. Sharing anything about the Circle would put him in immediate danger. And the guy couldn't keep his mouth shut. He was his own worst enemy. "Just taking precautions, dude. The guy upstairs was broken into. I'll make you a copy tomorrow."

"Sure you will...you know, since we're still such good friends and all."

Doug put down his tools. Eric was sitting in his favorite chair in the living room, the chair they fought over when they watched games together and ate nachos. "Just say what you have to say, buddy."

"Like you don't know. You check your voicemail lately?"

Doug hadn't used his phone in weeks for fear it was being traced. Then he saw the cane at Eric's feet. "What happened to you?"

"If you got my messages you'd know what happened to me."

"Fine, I didn't get your messages. Are you going to tell me what happened or not?"

"I was in the hospital."

Eric was whining. "Why? Are you okay?"

"Oh, I'm fine, now. But where were you? I could have used some help, man."

"I had stuff I needed to take care of."

"Stuff?"

A long beat went by. "Yeah, stuff. The kind I can't tell you about."

Another long beat.

"What, all of a sudden you can't trust me?"

Doug shook his head. He couldn't put his friend's life in jeopardy just because he wanted to cry on his shoulder. "Sorry, man, I just can't."

"I see," Eric said coldly. "Now we keep secrets from each other."

"It's not like that. You have to trust *me*, Eric. It's better if you don't know."

"How can I trust you when I leave you messages that I'm in the hospital and you don't have the decency to even call me back?"

"I didn't have service. I was up in Lackawanna."

"Suddenly you go on vacation—and don't tell me?"

"It wasn't a vacation!"

"Well, what was it, then?"

Doug combusted in a combination of fury and impatience. "It's none of your goddamm business, that's what it was. All of a sudden you want me to check in with you? You go days, weeks even, without calling me back and now I'm supposed to feel bad when you call me and I don't get back to you!?" Doug caught his breath. "Look, I'm sorry you got hurt, but I can see you're perfectly fine...."

"Perfectly fine? You call this perfectly fine?" Eric pushed himself out of the chair with his cane for support and then held it out in front of Doug's face. "I spent almost three days in the hospital for a concussion, two broken ribs and a broken leg... all because of your homeless girlfriend in the subway. Do you know what that psycho bitch did? She knocked me down a flight of stairs." He stopped. Doug was staring a hole through him the size of a Buick.

"Don't look at me like that. All I did was give her some money. Trying to be the good Samaritan, like my friend, the perfect Doug Goodwin. And this is what I got for it. Don't tell me I'm perfectly fine!"

Wait. Eric was beaten up by a homeless woman? In the subway? "Wait a minute," he started, hoping to God his instincts were wrong. "Was that the day we went to Tasker's? And, speaking of which, how did you hear of that place anyway?"

"Don't try to change the subject. Besides, what does that have to do with anything?"

"It's a simple question, Matthews. Who told you about the place? Was it some guy named Black from the office? You want to talk about trust, why can't you look me in the face and answer that question?"

Eric had convinced himself over the past two weeks, after the "accident," that when—if—Doug ever asked him these questions he would tell him the truth. But it was Doug's fault he was nowhere to be found when Eric had been ready to share. "This isn't about me, Dougie, it's about you. I left you messages two weeks ago and you didn't care enough to make the time to call me. I don't have to take this shit from you."

"Look, I told you. I was away upstate. If you can't answer the question then maybe you should get your crippled ass home." He'd been running for his life for two weeks. He needed rest and some time to think, not an argument with his self-absorbed best friend.

Eric began a slow limp toward the door.

Hobbling for Doug's benefit? That would be low, even for Eric. Wouldn't it?

Eric stopped a couple of feet from Doug, looked him square in the eye, and lied through his teeth. "Guys from the firm go to Tasker's all the time. I thought you'd get a kick out of seeing how the other half lives. Guess I was wrong."

In the hall Eric tossed Doug's spare key onto the credenza. "Go fuck yourself, Doug!"

The door slammed.

Doug felt the wetness on his leg. His hand-sewn stitches had come undone and the blood was now oozing through his pants. Funny how Eric hadn't noticed. He went into the bathroom, popped a few aspirin, and sewed himself up again. Ten stitches, not too bad. He picked up his tools and got back to changing the locks. In a way he was glad they'd argued. Now Eric didn't have a key to the apartment. What if he'd showed up one day and let himself in and found himself head to head with a killer from the Circle?

Doug made sure to destroy the spare key that came with the new lock set, breaking it in half with his pliers. Next, he moved to his bedroom and removed a small locked metal box from under his bed. He entered the five-digit code and it popped open. Inside were various papers, his birth certificate, social security information, and a few valuables. Nothing worth too much. A few sentimental things, though, like the antique watch that had become a Goodwin family heirloom, two gold rings, one that belonged to his father and one to his grandfather, and a sealed envelope marked "Emergency Fund." Doug pocketed the envelope along with his passport and relocked the safe, changing the code as per his habit.

It was time to go.

18

Kansas City International Airport was busy as usual with hundreds of people milling about killing time before their flight or rushing to get to their gate. Doug was feeling slightly ridiculous in dark sunglasses and a fake mustache that itched like crazy, but paranoia had won out over hubris. He slouched with a coffee cup by the coffee kiosk, pretending to read a newspaper. He looked up periodically as if searching for someone coming in on a flight. What he really wanted to know was if, despite the supposed forty-eight-hour hiatus, anyone was following him. He glanced at his watch. Nineteen hours left. He looked up at the flight board. The professor's plane should have been in by now. Doug started to worry. Then, not three feet from him, the professor walked by, oblivious to Doug in his disguise.

Unfortunately, the professor, a modified version of Albert Einstein, complete with white hair and absentminded air, couldn't help being conspicuous. Doug sighed and folded up the newspaper. He took his coffee and walked behind the professor for a hundred yards before he spoke. No one had moved any closer or taken an undue interest that he could see. "Excuse, me," he said. "Don't you teach at Colorado University?"

The professor stopped short. "Marty? Is that you? What are you wearing? I've been so worried."

The hug Doc gave him was enough to bring on the water-works, but there was no time for that. "Yes, it's me. I'm in disguise. Let's go into the bar over there so we can talk."

The professor followed Doug into a dimly lit airport lounge that was open 24-7. They took a seat in the back. Doug kept one eye on the door.

"What's going on, Marty?"

"Hey, no serve right now, closed for clean," shouted a heavily accented voice from the back.

So much for 24-7.

"It's okay, we don't want food, we just need a place to sit," the professor said, looking every bit the travel-weary old man.

"Well, I guess is okay. But don't make mess," said the employee, and went back to his mopping.

"Talk to me, Doug. What the heck is going on?" Doug's fingers were tapping non-stop on the laminate table and his eyes roamed constantly. Normally calm and self-possessed, this new behavior was off-putting. And what was Doug looking for? "Doug, you're scaring me."

There was no right way to say what was on his mind. Doug leaned in. "Doc, I know that what I'm about to tell you will seem unbelievable, but you've got to believe me, it's true. Not only that but it's dangerous. Do you understand what I'm saying?" He spelled it out. "Once I tell you, your life may be in danger. Now, are you still sure you want to know?"

The professor blinked. "Doug, of course I want to know, I want to help you."

The unconditional offer of help brought the tears back. "Okay, Doc, listen carefully. We don't have a lot of time. Somehow, and I don't know how, I have been forced into an organization called the Circle. They call it being 'recruited,' but it amounts to the same thing. This organization was founded decades ago by wealthy men who had so much money they suffered from terminal ennui. The only way they could think of to put a—and I quote here— 'love of life' back into their lives—and don't think I don't appreciate the irony—was to establish an elite men's club that kills for the excitement."

The professor's mouth fell open.

"Wait," said Doug. "There's more. These guys meet in the back of a bar in New York City, drink expensive drinks, smoke expensive cigars, and cavort with the most beautiful women you've ever seen until the time comes when it's their turn to kill again—to hunt their next target to the death."

"Doug, I've never known you to fantasize. What's this really about? What kind of trouble are you in?"

"I'm trying to tell you, Doc. It's exactly what I said. These rich guys hunt each other. To...the...death. They made me a member against my wishes, but now there's no way out. If I choose not to participate, I'll still be hunted."

"Doug, this is crazy, this has got to be a sick joke. It's impossible."

"I wish it were. I know it sounds incredible, but these guys aren't kidding around. A couple of days ago I found myself staring down the end of a pistol. I was the guy's 'target.' And I get assigned targets of my own. It's kill or be killed. The only reason I'm alive right now is because my would-be killer was being tracked by *his* killer and died before he could pull the trigger.

"I know, I know. I know how crazy it sounds. But you've got to believe me. Right from the beginning they knew everything about me—where I grew up, where I went to school, my job, my whole life…. Oh, my God. Doc, that means you, too. I can't believe I— This was so stupid. I've got to go. I've put you in terrible danger. They'll know about you, too. What have I done?" Doug got up from the table.

"Marty, sit down," said the professor, holding Doug's arm. "Please."

Against his better judgment Doug allowed himself to be pulled back down into his seat.

"Why would *I* be in any danger?" asked the professor.

"The Circle is a secret society, Doc. Emphasis on secret. They made it very clear that I would risk 'consequences' for my family if I told them about it. God, if anything happens to you and I'm responsible, I'll…."

The crash of a tray hitting the floor from the kitchen of the restaurant sent Doug under the table, pulling the professor with him. "Is it them?" the professor whispered, fear in his eyes.

Doug realized his mistake and pulled them both back up, giving the professor his arm for balance. He felt both guilt and relief. "It shouldn't be. The way it works is that you get thirty days in between each kill—if you kill your target. If someone else takes out the guy who was supposed to kill you, you get forty-eight hours of leave. I still have nineteen hours left. Come 2:16 tomorrow morning, I'll be someone's target again."

"Then we don't have any time to lose," the professor said. "Let's get you out of the country. We can buy a ticket right now."

"That won't work, Doc. They have eyes everywhere. They *are* everywhere. That's why I bought us each three tickets…so they wouldn't know which flights we were on."

"So, no matter where you are, in nineteen hours, you'll be a target for some killer? I can't—this is insane, Doug."

"Yeah."

"Well, if they're looking for you in New York, what if you let them chase you all around the country? Won't they get tired of it...give up?"

"I don't think so, Doc. These people are dedicated. And they have branches...like damn banks. The first night I took off for the cabin in Lackawanna...they even found me there, like they'd been on me every step of the way."

Doug looked at Doc, his beloved mentor. "What am I going to do? I don't want to kill anyone, Doc."

"Well, first, let's see what we can dig up on them. Maybe there's information out there that we can use."

That brought a slight smile to Doug's lips. Ever the professorial researcher.

Doc got up, looking determined.

"Where are we going?"

"You'll see."

In a minute they were both inside HiTech, a small chain of computer stores that tended toward real estate in malls and airports. Amidst the ipods and BlackBerries a laptop sat on a pedestal in the center of the room. The professor went straight for the Internet connection, opened up a search engine and typed in "The Circle." In seconds 49,600,000 results filled the screen. At the top of the list on page one was a link to a Native American news and arts paper called *The Circle*. Wikipedia was next with information about the shape and mathematical concept of a circle. A club operating out of Colby College with the acronym C.I.R.C.L.E. (The Collective for Insight, Refuge, and the Celebration of Life Experience) was after that. Subsequent pages revealed things like "Buy into the Circle," a Greater Des Moines Partnership's public awareness campaign, and a group in North Carolina of pagans, witches, and alternative seekers, whatever that meant.

"Shoot. Nothing," proclaimed the professor, "and we could look forever with that many results."

"It doesn't surprise me," said Doug. "Why would a secret society have a website for everyone to see?"

"Let's not give up yet." He clicked through a few more pages, but Doug was right. They found nothing useful or remotely connected that they could see. Still, the professor kept scrolling through the pages.

"Hey, try that one," Doug said finally, pointing to the last link on the bottom left of the seventh page of results.

Doc clicked on the link and the computer redirected to several different websites almost simultaneously, instantly filling the screen with pop-ups. The laptop emitted a frighteningly loud beeping for a few seconds and then shut down abruptly.

"Oops," said Doug. "That can't be good."

1,500 miles away, in an underground computer lab, alarms sounded and lights flashed. A computer technician ran into the room that housed the large mainframe and typed in an access code. The flashing ceased and the alarm turned off as suddenly as it had begun. On the screen the words "UNAUTHORIZED ACCESS ATTEMPTED" were encased in a red box. The woman turned to another computer and, after a few keystrokes, brought up the security camera from HiTech, the airport electronics store in Kansas City, and began recording. Then the woman turned to the telephone and dialed three numbers. After one ring, the phone was answered.

"Yes, sir," she said, "We got a hit in Kansas City."

"That might have been something." the professor said.

"Yeah, something that we just broke," said Doug. "Let's get out of here."

From behind the counter, a middle-aged Asian woman emerged. "You break laptop, you pay for it."

"Yeah, about that," said Doug. People were said to respond to soft voices with soft voices and loud, demanding voices with the same. "We were just using it, uh, ma'am," he said, keeping his voice as low as he could, "and it went a little bonkers."

He whispered to the professor, "Go on, get out of here, I'll handle this." The professor scrambled around the corner.

"You give me thirteen hundred dollars—or I call airport police," the woman said loudly.

So much for psychology. Doug took out his emergency envelope and counted out the bills for the computer, more money than he'd ever spent on a laptop—or most anything else—in one shot. Pacified, the woman went off to recount the bills. Finally Doug left the store and found the professor. "Well, the good news is that I think we may have stumbled onto something."

"And the bad news?"

"I think we may have stumbled onto something."

The professor groaned. "Here's what we're going to do, Doug. You get back to New York before they notice you're AWOL. I'll go home and try to hack into that site. Maybe the answers are there."

Doug pulled out the envelope of dwindling funds again. "Here, take this money—" the professor waved his palm *no*, but Doug insisted. "Take it! Get a flight back to Colorado as soon as you can. I'll call you on the pay phone tomorrow morning. 9:30."

"Got it," Doc said with a small salute. Then, "Listen, Marty, we're gonna figure this out, together. You mean too much to me to let this ruin your life."

"Thanks, Doc. I hope you're right." This time a couple of tears spilled over. Doug wiped them away with his sleeve.

When the professor spoke, his voice was gravelly. "Now get going, and be safe. I'll talk to you in the morning."

Doug didn't watch the professor leave. Instead he ran to the nearest ticket counter and purchased a ticket for JFK airport, a flight that would depart shortly. He boarded and took his seat, next to a gorgeous woman he didn't see, closed his eyes, and felt the gut-wrenching, sickening, mind-numbing fear take over.

The light in Professor Balachi's office was the only one on at this time of night on a Saturday. He was working diligently at his computer. A milk night it was not, and a glass of scotch sat beside him just beyond the mouse for easy access. It was almost midnight, and with the exception of the clicking of keys and the occasional grunt of frustration emanating from his office, the building was calm and quiet. Unfortunately, even with his extensive computer expertise, he has not been able to crack what he knows to be the gateway to the Circle. Each step he takes is met with another dead end. It is obvious to him that access to the site was through a built-in password keystroke that only certain ranking members know, implemented to keep everyone else out. Stumped, he picked up his phone and called Doug at home, quickly putting the call on speaker phone when Doug picked up.

"Hello?"

"Marty, it's Doc, were you sleeping?"

"Are you kidding? It's like my eyes are stapled open. What's up?"

"I have an idea. When you first got initiated, did they give you any type of password, code number, anything like that?"

"Let me think—wait, Doc, you shouldn't be calling me. Are you in the office? They could be listening!"

"Marty, don't worry, I know what I'm doing. Technology... you know...I've got a few tricks up my sleeve."

"Doc, we just went through the trouble of meeting in another state to avoid detection. How can it be alright now?"

"Let's just say I know a few things about how to confuse cell towers and satellites. Don't spread it around, but I haven't paid a phone bill in years."

"Doc, I'm shocked!" Doug said, but he still wasn't mollified. What if something went wrong? "You're sure they can't track you?"

"Marty, relax, my office line is encrypted. Took care of it myself. Now, aren't you going to ask me about my other tricks?"

"Yeah, sure, Doc. What other tricks?"

"I'm afraid I can't tell you," Doc said.

"Very funny. So, what did you find out?"

"I'm not sure yet. I had to dive into the dark web, but I need some information first. Read me some of the numbers on those papers they sent you." Cyberspace was not where he generally hung out, but he'd do anything to help Doug. Besides, this was the most excitement he'd had in years. He knew all about Tor, The Onion Router, the worldwide network of servers developed with the U.S. Navy that enabled people to browse the internet anonymously. He'd started with *circle.onion* with no success, and his searches on *Grams* had yielded nothing of value yet, either.

"Hang on, I'll get them." Doug located the original blue envelope left for him outside his hunting cabin. He took out the sheet with the lists of unexplained numbers and letters. He now knew some of them were the account numbers to access the Circle's funds. The others were still unrecognizable. "Hmm. I think maybe...." he said into the phone. "The Greek letter π is on these sheets. But that doesn't make sense. Wait. You don't think...."

"Way ahead of you, my boy," said Doc. He had already typed pi.onion and was waiting for the dark web to return a result.

A long minute passed without a web page result. "Shoot. Dead end. So much for *pi.onion.*"

"There's no reason for that symbol to be here, though," said Doug. "What about the decimals?"

"Marty, how many decimals should I go to? π is forever."

Doug studied the documents more astutely, looking for some sign that he overlooked. A number, a letter, another symbol...anything. Then, there it was. Right in front of him. It was brilliant, actually. The date and time on the printout—March 14, 2015 9:26:53—couldn't possibly be the date and time the documents had been printed.

"3.141592653.onion!" he shouted gleefully into the phone.

The professor dutifully typed in the code and in a flash his computer screen shifted from the internet browser to a black screen with a flaming blue circle on it. He took in a breath. "I think we're in, Marty! Great work."

An organization called the Circle using the greek letter π. You had to appreciate the poetry.

The assassin heard his mark through the dark halls of the University Science Building. It had been a long time since he'd set foot in the hallowed halls of higher education, but tonight he'd be teaching a lesson, not learning one.

His soft footfalls met the floor without a sound as he approached the office door and crouched low beneath the glass pane. He could hear the conversation echoing through the halls as if the speaker were right next to him. Stupid, stupid man. Did he not understand the risk he was taking?

The professor gazed at the three drop down menus; *Country of Initiation*; *Current Chapter*; *Years of Service.* Underneath those dropdowns was a box requesting a member ID. "Okay, Doug,

Country of Initiation is America." he said. "Current Chapter?" He clicked the box dozens of locations appeared in alphabetical order: Ahemedabad, Alexandria, Ankara, Atlanta, Baghdad, Bangalore, Bangkok, Barcelona, Beijing, Bogota, Boston...the list went on for pages. A whispered "Jesus," was all the professor could muster.

"I guess New York," said Doug. "That makes the most sense to me."

"So, years of service we can confidently select zero...and now your ID. Should I just try *Last Name / First Initial* like everywhere else?"

"Worth a shot."

"Access Denied. Invalid Login. Two Attempts Remaining," read Doc. "We've got to do better than that."

"Shoot. Well at least we know it's three strikes and we're out."

"Is there another set of numbers, Doug? A password, a login name, anything that looks like it might let us in?"

Doug scanned the papers one more time. In the lower left-hand corner of every page was the same alpha-numeric sequence, his member ID. "Try NYC—all caps—2931." Was that the number of members who'd already died at the hands of the Circle?

"Nope. Same thing. One attempt left."

"What if—?"

"Wait. I can't believe it. I typed 2391 by mistake."

"Christ, Doc. Please be careful."

"I'm sorry! N-Y-C-2-9-3-1..." Doc carefully checked back to each dropdown to make sure there were no errors. Pressing the "Return" key felt like pushing the button on a nuclear football. The hourglass turned on his desktop and the two men waited in limbo.

"We're in," Doc said.

The professor was sitting behind his desk facing away from the door and focused on the three computer monitors in front of him. Poor planning at best. Careless. Pathetic. But from the killer's perspective? Perfectly convenient.

"I'm staring at a picture of you," said Doc. "It says, 'Welcome, Mr. Goodwin' across the top. Now your picture is shrinking…now it's in a blue circle—like a circle of fire—in the top left corner of the page. Underneath is another picture. It's a man in a green circle. In the green circle it says 'Mr. Dart.' On the right is a box that scrolls—it's full of information, I guess it's this Mr. Dart's… his last known whereabouts, an address, phone number, parents' names and addresses, siblings, friends, former co-workers, bank information. It's like a personnel file, but much more extensive. Even what he likes to drink. Doug, this is incredible. Who *are* these people?"

"Doc, you don't want to know, trust me." The keys keep clicking.

"Marty, I gotta tell you, son. I think we're in trouble here. You need to get yourself connected and check this out."

"Why, what do you see?"

"It's incredible, like nothing I've ever—"

"Doc, you there? What do you see?"

Silence.

"Doc?"

Doug had a feeling. A bad, bad feeling.

Forgive me, God, for I have sinned, recited the killer as he did after every kill. The professor had fallen without a peep, locked in the killer's tight grip, which maintained the necessary pressure without breaking the neck until the job was done. With any luck it would look like the heart attack of a feeble old man, although it wouldn't much matter either way.

"Doc, are you there?"

Had the connection failed? Had the professor hung up for some reason? Maybe Doug should hang up and wait for him to call back. But there was no dial tone. Only dead air. "Professor! Talk to me. Please."

No. He refused to believe that—

The professor wouldn't—

But the odds were—

The professor. His friend. His mentor.

Doug couldn't face it.

That he'd heard the slightest intake of breath. The slightest creak of a chair. Right before Doc had suddenly gone MIA.

That if it meant what Doug suspected it meant, someone had found the professor. *They'd* found the professor. And if they'd found him, he was already dead.

They'd killed him. The Circle had killed Doc. The man he loved like a father. Doug stared at the phone as if it were some kind of beast he'd never seen before. He wanted to tear its head off.

The man delicately moved the professor's lifeless body to the floor. It needed to remain free of bruising in order for his tactics to prove effective. He sat down in the professor's desk chair. He held down the escape key on the keyboard in the middle of the desk and typed in a series of keys. The Circle's database disappeared. Then he accessed the computer's hard drive and deleted every shred of memory related to the Circle's website and the browser's history. When he was satisfied, he picked up the phone.

"Hello, Mr. Goodwin."

A tinny voice was coming from the phone. Doug crammed it onto his ear. "Who is this," he demanded, "where is he? What did you do to him?"

"You were warned, Mr. Goodwin. You were told unequivocally not to discuss the Circle with anyone," the man said. "Perhaps from now on, you will respect our rules; they are in place for a reason."

"I want to talk to the professor. Put him on. Now!" Terror reached into Doug's chest and pulled out his heart.

"I'm afraid, Mr. Goodwin, that Professor Balachi has become a casualty of the Circle."

The click of the receiver was like a coffin being nailed shut. "No!" Doug screamed, and threw his phone against the wall. It shattered and left a large crack in the plaster. The man who had guided him, laughed with him, stood by him…gone. Collateral damage of a fight he'd never asked for. A fight Doug had brought to his doorstep.

Doug took another giant step into the deep hole of darkness that had become his life.

The next day was the loneliest Doug had ever known. He'd barely slept through the night, waking every half hour to the image of his friend and mentor dead in his office, surrounded by a lifetime of work. He imagined Doc's throat cut or a blade in his chest, but it was more likely the sound he'd heard was a gasp for air. How the hell had they gotten there so fast? Of course now the question was hardly worth asking. As he'd told the professor himself, they were everywhere.

Doug's life was like a runaway roller coaster, and he had no way of slowing it down. Numb with shock, he sat on his couch, a blanket draped over his body, racked with chills for hours, watching television. 2:16 AM had come and gone. He was now officially back on the map for anyone from the Circle to find him. He recalled learning about the five stages of responding to death. Guilt was one of them for sure.

When the sun shined through the window of his apartment, he moved robotically, for the thousandth time, to his door to check that his new lock was holding. The morning paper, *USA Today*, was on the mat as always, delivered by the paperboy who lived in 6F, Tommy somebody-or-other. The president was making some speech about a new healthcare bill and the financial markets were struggling, both stories on page one. Below the fold on page five were the words he'd dreaded, but knew he'd see.

Award-winning Professor Dead. Denver, CO. Professor Ronald Balachi, 66, was found dead on Thursday, August 14 after an uncharacteristic absence from his scheduled pre-semester departmental meeting by Dean Alfred Richards, who said, "I was shocked, but we knew something was wrong when he didn't show up. Ron would never miss the first meeting of the year." Unconfirmed reports have ruled this a death by natural causes but a formal autopsy has been ordered as the professor has had no serious medical issues in the past. The professor, a highly respected cosmologist and a much-beloved academic, had been in talks to become the new host of 'Cosmos' in a revival of the Carl Sagan docuseries of the same name from the late '70s. Professor Balachi

is survived by his two sisters who, through a
family friend, have thanked the global community
for their thoughts and prayers and have requested
that the media continue to respect their family's
privacy during this difficult time....

The paper fell to the ground. An autopsy would never lead anywhere. Even if it did turn up irregularities they would only lead investigators in circles. Christ, now he was making puns?

Tears fill Doug's eyes again, but he has no time to mourn. It was easy to blame the Circle, they'd pulled the trigger, but he couldn't pass the responsibility onto someone else. If he hadn't contacted Doc, he'd still be alive today.

19

The rules declared Tasker's a safe-house, but outside the bar the hunted were fair game. Doug therefore approached with extreme caution. How so many men came and went from the place without losing life and limb was an unanswered question. At the door he took a deep breath, rubbed his eyes on his sleeve for the umpteenth time, and stepped inside. The scene was the same as the last time he was here—and the time before that. Mostly older men with attractive women half their age. This time, however, the stage was empty with only the remnants of the band from the night before. Doug sat at his usual seat at the bar. Pathetic. He already thought of it as "his seat."

The bartender materialized.

"Jack, leave the bottle," Doug said.

"Whoa, cowboy, you sure you want to do that?"

"I didn't ask for your opinion."

"If you say so. But why so glum?"

"Glum? You're kidding, right? This...place has made me a killer. Just killed one of my closest friends. And it's the only place I can be to feel 'safe.' It's wrong. Any way you look at it, it's just plain wrong." Doug downed the contents of his shot glass.

"Oh, so you were a big fan of Mr. Crooner?"

For a minute Doug had to work to place the name. The killing of a couple of nights ago had retreated far into the past with the professor's death. He looked at the stage. Empty.

"Not Crooner. My *friend*. They killed one of my closest friends. He wasn't even a member. Just a friend trying to help me."

The bartender shrugged. "Well, you probably shouldn't have asked him for help. You know the rules."

"Yeah," Doug said, "the 'rules.' Well, the rules suck. The Circle murdered him pure and simple."

"Really? Or did your professor die because you neglected to follow the rules you say you know?"

He knows about all of it. The guy who'd offered him his first "free" drink, who'd led him by the nose into the "distinguished" back room. Even the damn bartender was in on the Circle's game of death.

"My condolences, Mr. Goodwin."

"Yeah, thanks, but with all due respect, screw you. Just open the damn door."

The paneled door swung open. Cufflinks and Fingers were playing a hand of poker with two other men at the table. If he hadn't just witnessed Cufflinks kill a man in cold blood, Doug might have easily believed that he was a warmhearted, debonair gentleman with an affinity for cards.

CUFFLINKS (motioning for Doug to join them): "Mr. Goodwin, come, sit. We will deal you in."

The only empty seat was between the two men he'd never seen before. Doug placed his glass on the table, then the bottle. The men at the table looked at one another but said nothing.

CUFFLINKS: "Let me introduce you. This is Mr. Stahl from Germany and Mr. Kvele from Norway, here to see the big city. Of course you know Mr. Fingers. Doug Goodwin."

Fingers managed a grunt in acknowledgment. The others nodded.

Doug didn't care one iota about Kvele and Stahl. If he'd expressed interest he might have learned a couple of interesting tidbits, however. About how Mr. Stahl, a short stout man wearing a derby and a three-button suit and vest, got his name, which meant "a strong type of metal," from bludgeoning his victims with a lead pipe, for instance, and how *kvele*, meant "to choke" in Norwegian, based on Mr. Kvele's predilection for death by strangulation.

Doug nodded a brief hello.

CUFFLINKS (smiling, dealing cards): "A man of few words."

FINGERS: "Giddy after a kill. Reminds me a me."

CUFFLINKS: "Hogwash. I'm in good spirits today, that's all."

STAHL (barking in Doug's direction): "And you have been a member how long, Mr. Goodwin?"

"A few weeks."

STAHL: "And you still don't have a name? *Wie lästige!* How embarrassing!"

CUFFLINKS: "Young Mr. Goodwin currently suffers from an aversion to killing. He will learn quickly, of course, one way or another."

STAHL: "You disgrace yourself by not striking first. *Hat Sie keine Ehre?*"

Stahl was living up to his reputation for being plainspoken.

"Self-respect? You don't know me," Doug said with a snarl. "So I suggest you mind your own damn business."

STAHL (rising up from his seat, shouting, making a move for Doug's throat):. *"Wie könnt ihr es wagen!"*

"How dare I?" said Doug. *"How dare I?"* He defended the German's attack easily, brushing his hand aside and allowing his own momentum to force him to the ground. He held Stahl's arm behind his back. "As you see, *Mr.* Stahl, I am perfectly capable of defending myself," he said tightly. "As far as the Circle goes, rest assured that if I need to kill to maintain that defense, I won't hesitate." He gave Stahl's arm another twist. "Do...we...have...a problem...*Mr.* Stahl?"

Stahl's face was dripping with perspiration. He shook his head no.

KVELE (speaking up for the first time): "Herr Goodwin, if I may. My associate is rather hot-tempered. My apologies on his behalf. I assure you, many of us do admire your approach to the Circle; in my country we would call you *Fredvakt*, or peace-keeper. Naturally, we wish you all the luck."

Kvele extended his hand, but his foray into etiquette just pissed Doug off. He let Stahl up and got to his feet. Stahl pulled himself up on the arm of the chair and sat down. He adjusted his vest, his collar, his jacket, looking daggers at Doug.

Doug took his seat and picked up his glass. He hadn't broken a sweat.

FINGERS: "Well, the kid has a little spunk in 'im after all."

STAHL (rubbing his shoulder): "Yes. My apologies, gentlemen, for disrespecting the Circle."

CUFFLINKS: "Please don't concern yourself, Mr. Stahl. Our Mr. Goodwin has been known to put on quite a show."

Doug didn't like being talked about as if he weren't there, as if he were there for their amusement. But now probably wasn't the time to make the point. He poured another drink.

KVELE (diplomatically): "Mr. Cufflinks, how long were you a member before you received your name?"

"Oh, my, that was ages ago. Let me think. Three weeks, I believe."

FINGERS: "Five days f' me."

CUFFLINKS (drily): "Well, some might say your taste for blood goes beyond the spirit of the hunt."

FINGERS (with a snort): "Some *would* say...an' lose their fingers."

"Call."

The five men turned down their hands. Fingers had won. He scooped the proceeds to him. "Lady luck on my side, fellas."

Doug was bored with the interplay and looked around. He didn't know how he'd missed it before—his altercation with Stahl notwithstanding—but there was a woman playing darts with two men. It was the first time he'd seen a woman in the room who appeared to be on equal footing with the others. Doug whispered to Cufflinks, who had begun shuffling the cards for another game. "Who are they? I've never seen them before."

"Introductions will have to wait for a more appropriate time, but their names are Mr. Spear, Mr. Necktie, and Ms. Mantis, our first female recruit."

"I didn't know women were allowed. When did she start?"

"I would say she's been with us for almost eight years now. Be careful of that one, Mr. Goodwin. As her name implies, she is cunning and ruthless."

Doug still felt the whole name thing was juvenile, but like everything else in this organization, the choice was not of his making, and despite himself he was adapting Circle speak. "So, let me get this straight. None of you knows who the top dog is around here—who pulls the strings?" He directs this to the group. He doesn't really expect an answer, or at least not an honest one.

FINGERS: "It's none a ya goddamm business who runs this organization."

CUFFLINKS: "I think what Mr. Fingers is trying to say is that you are correct. We don't know."

"How long have you been in?" Doug asked Cufflinks.

"Seventeen years now?"

"How did you become a member?"

"Like everyone else, I would imagine."

"And how's that exactly?"

STAHL (assertively, groping for the English translation): "Someone must, how you say, *Verbürgen Sie sich.*"

KVELE: "Someone must vouch for you."

STAHL: "Ah, yes, thank you, Mr. Kvele."

"Vouch for you? How do you mean?"

KVELE: "When you reach your fifth year, Mr. Goodwin, the Watchers will approach you. They will ask you to vouch for someone."

"The Watchers?"

CUFFLINKS: "They are the ones who deliver the envelopes and track your movements. You see, if members were also responsible for bringing in new recruits, we would never have time for the hunt. The Watchers were organized not long after the Circle was created. The Watchers are the people who want to be a part of the Circle, but...."

FINGERS: "Don't have the balls."

CUFFLINKS (nodding, pained): "Well, yes, quite right."

"But if you don't know who runs everything, how are you supposed to 'vouch' for someone?"

STAHL: "You report this to the Mr. Black in your chapter. He takes care of the rest."

CUFFLINKS: "Indeed, and then the Watchers evaluate the potential recruit's abilities to see if he is worthy."

The words "evaluate your abilities" flashed like a beacon in Doug's mind. The three camouflaged men in the forest. The way Mr. Black referred to Eric as "Mr. Matthews." Eric's sexy new Lexus. Doug got up. "Gentlemen, if you'll excuse me."

CUFFLINKS: "Of course. Take care, young Goodwin. Good hunting."

KVELE: "Yes, *Vellykket jakt.*"

STAHL (begrugingly): "*Ya, Erfolgreiche Jagd.*"

For killers, they were awfully damn polite. And Mr. Black was right again. It wasn't by chance Doug had walked through the Circle's door for the first time.

20

Among the hundreds of skyscrapers that decorate the skyline of New York City looms the office building of Connors, Dowd, Rodgers, & Simon. Its prime location, the corner of W35th and Broadway, implies the power the firm has at its disposal. Reaching only sixty-five stories high, it is not one of the tallest buildings in the city, but structurally speaking it is one of the more magnificent, if also the least attractive. Situated on a corner lot, it has a lobby like the hub and spokes of a gigantic wheel, with the other sixty-four stories rising straight up from the center. Thousands of glass windows cast long glaring rectangles a full block long. At its base four carved stone entry ways connect the spokes to the wheel, some architect's not so brilliant idea of mingling the old and the new, and creating instead the sense of being locked in a bizarre time warp. In order to enter, one has to walk down a slight decline and then through several revolving doors. The landscaping around the structure is well maintained, complete with topiaries of what appear to be African safari animals—although what African safari animals have to do with ancient stoned archways Doug has never been able to fathom. In fact, Doug has always found the whole setup pretentious and over-the-top. But, hey, he doesn't have to work there.

As he parked his Wrangler at the curb in front of the building, he looked around for meter maids. He'd probably get a ticket. Oh, well. He got out and descended the long ramp to the lobby.

The main vestibule was massive, a spouting fountain in its center, in front of which sat the security desk. Behind the desk was a bank of at least ten elevators that lined the wall. He didn't bother to sign in.

Right on cue, a security guard moved to intercept. "Excuse me, sir, you can't park there."

Doug kept on going.

"Sir, you need to move your car and sign in. Sir?!"

Doug didn't break stride. He moved quickly into an elevator and let the door close in the security guard's unhappy face. The panel buttons inside the elevator to the right were sectioned into two separate groups: black for floors two through sixty-one, red for floors sixty-two through sixty-five, each button with the initials "CDR&S" in the center in white print. If you don't know what it means, you're not invited.

Doug pushed the button for the lowest floor of the group, sixty-two. The high-speed elevator climbed the stories with stomach-plunging efficiency and the door opened to a crafted oak sign with gold letters, listing the associates whose offices are on the floor. Toward the bottom with the other M's was the name he knew so well.

Doug didn't have much time before the rest of security would be alerted to his presence. He hadn't been here all that often, and sometimes after office hours, but he knew exactly where he was going. He made a right at the receptionist, who must have been new because he didn't recognize her. She was yapping on the phone, but when she saw Doug she told the person on the other end to hold on.

"Excuse me, sir, can I help you?"

Doug kept going.

"Sir?" she tried again, but Doug continued on his path past one office cubicle and then another. A seemingly endless stream of cubicles. Working here would be worse than in the bowels of the museum. Shit, the museum. Doug hadn't thought about the place in days. He set the topic aside for later.

He finally spotted Eric Matthews' secretary who sat outside his door, a woman much plainer and with a much less developed sense of fashion than the high-profile receptionist out front, typing at her computer. What was her name again? Oh, yeah, Mary Ann.

Mary Ann looked up at Doug's arrival. "Oh, hello, Mr. Goodwin. Nice to see you again. Was Mr. Matthews expecting you?"

Doug sidestepped the secretary altogether and put his hand on the doorknob to Eric's office.

"Excuse me, Mr. Goodwin, sir? You can't go in there. Mr. Matthews is on a conference call—"

Doug closed the door behind him. A full-length conference table sat in the center of the room. A huge black-and-white photograph of Eric Matthews, Esquire in a contemplative posture adorned the whitewashed wall behind his desk. Eric was pacing back and forth with a file in his hand. His limp had noticeably diminished since the last time Doug had seen him.

"Bob, you know there's no way I can file a complaint like that in twenty-four hours. It's just not going to happen," he was saying.

Doug waited until Eric made a U-turn and saw him by the door. "Bob. Wait. Bob. Yeah, hold on a second, okay?"

Eric put on what he hoped was a mask of pleased, yet skeptical, surprise. After all, he and Dougie hadn't been on the best of terms the last time they'd seen each other. He held up a finger.

Mary Ann had followed Doug in through the door and was protesting in a loud whisper, "Mr. Goodwin. Please. Mr. Matthews is on a conference call!"

"Hang it up, Eric," Doug said quietly.

Eric cupped his hand over the Bluetooth receiver on his ear. "Doug, I'm on a very important call here."

"I said, hang it up!"

Eric looked shocked. An act?

Eric spoke into the phone again. "Yeah. Bobby? Yeah. I'm gonna have to call back. Yeah. Yeah. Around three. Talk to you then." He arranged his face and turned back to Doug. "Happy?"

"Sir, I tried to tell him you were on a call," Mary Ann pleaded. She'd been on the receiving end of Mr. Matthews' bad temper too many times before.

Eric looked at Doug, who was obviously fuming. He went with polite. "It's okay, Mary Ann. I was expecting Mr. Goodwin, it just slipped my mind."

"Yes, sir, but security is already on their way. Shall I call them and—"

"That's fine, Mary Ann. I'll take care of it. Please close the door behind you."

Unconvinced, Mary Ann slowly moved to the door. After one more look over her shoulder, she did as she was told.

Doug looked at Eric, who had suddenly gone quiet.

Seconds later three security officers blasted through the doorway. "Gentlemen, thank you for coming," said Eric, cool and collected. "But everything's under control. You can stand down."

Stand down? Who did he think he was, General Patton? Eric's resilience was impressive, yet repulsive. It was like watching a PBS special on a new kind of species that devoured its mate and licked its lips afterwards.

"In the future you might want to let us know if you're having guests, Mr. Matthews," said hulk number one. "Yeah, we got procedures to follow," said number two.

"My apologies, gentlemen," Eric said unapologetically. "Now, if I can be left alone with my associate...?" He called to his secretary. "Mary Ann, would you see these gentlemen out? Thank you."

Eric gave Doug a long patronizing look before he turned and moved back to his desk, reaching for a fat cigar from the humidor in the corner. He tapped the cigar on the desk's surface and made a show of clipping off the end before inserting it into his mouth. Since smoking was forbidden in all New York City buildings these days it was an obvious ploy, a stay for time.

"What exactly do you want, Doug? I'm working here, and I don't appreciate your barging in and making a scene in front of my employees."

To anyone else Eric Matthews might look like the picture of ease, the gentry at home in his milieu, but he never could hide the twitch in his eye that started up when he was nervous. Or lying. Probably both.

There was no reason to beat around the bush. "You're a member, aren't you, Eric?"

"That again?" Eric said, waving his cigar dismissively. "The scene in your apartment wasn't enough? You had to come all the way to my office to insult me?"

"Enough bullshit, Eric. I know you're involved. I just want to know how."

Doug wasn't bluffing. Eric bought some more time straightening up some paperwork.

"Eric, please don't make me come over there. You know what'll happen if I do."

All at once the hot air that was Eric seemed to deflate. For a minute Doug saw the Eric he'd known as a brother and a friend.

"Fine. What difference does it make now? I'm...I'm a Watcher."

No. Doug knew it was true. But hearing it blew his world apart.

Eric couldn't look Doug in the eye. "I was into them for two hundred fifty thou."

This was so much worse than the time Eric had left him on the bus. "You sold me out, Eric? For some damn *money*?"

"I had no choice. They made me join. They were gonna kill me, Doug, I swear."

"I am your friend, Eric. I could have helped you. But you chose to sell my life to save your own ass."

"Oh, now you're my friend again?" The lip-licking insect was back. "Suddenly you have the time to 'deal with me'?"

Doug recognized the pathetic attempt to turn the tables. They both did.

"Don't change the subject. You're a fraud. And we're no longer friends. How could you do this to me?"

"I tried, man. I recommended other people, at least three of them, but nobody made the cut. I went through everybody I could before I told them about you. Everybody. You were the only one I knew who had any real talent. C'mon, man! Look at what they give you. I can do anything now. I'm rich! I'm powerful! Do you think I could have made this kind of money in New York City with a law degree from the fucking University of Colorado that I barely scraped by to get? I was going nowhere, Doug. These people gave me a way out of some crappy existence." He waved his arm toward the view which overlooked the city, Staten Island, and New Jersey. "Look at me now."

Unbelievable. Matthews was making this about *him.* "Yeah, just look at you now, Matthews. You've got it all. I guess it doesn't mean much that my life is over—that I'm as good as dead—now that you've got all that money and power now, right?

"We're through, Eric. Not that it matters. Because thanks to you I may not survive long enough to follow through on that decision."

"We were through a long time ago, Dougie...or don't you remember how your best friend was in the hospital, the important phone calls you never returned? You're a selfish sonnovabitch. I was going to tell you everything. I was going to help you."

Could it get any worse? Doug shook his head. Talk about repackaging the truth. "Bullshit, Eric. It's all bullshit. Every last word. We're through. Over. Done. From now on, stay away from me. I never want to see your slimy face again."

"Yeah, like Mr. High and Mighty wouldn't have done the same thing in my position."

Doug stepped toward the desk, his fists itching to make contact with the smooth, underdeveloped jaw of the snake behind it. "You were the closest thing I had to a brother, Matthews," he said through clenched teeth. "I loved you. They would've had to kill me before I'd ever sell you out."

"Well, I guess you're a better man than I am. Besides, judging by the looks of things, you weren't the friend I thought you were anyway."

"Really, Matthews? Really?" Doug's restraint went out the window. He punched Eric in the jaw. Eric fell with a thud. His Bluetooth went flying. His eyes rolled back in his head. He was out like a light.

Doug rubbed his sore knuckles. Man, that felt good. He opened the drawers of Eric's mahogany desk. There must be something there that could help him. The reality of what the blue envelopes he found implied gave him a jolt in the pit of his stomach. He opened each one quickly, assuming his time in Eric's office was limited. Schedules, photos of numerous Circle members, lists of numbers like the ones he'd received. A small vial with a single pill inside, hexagonal in shape and resembling a pill he once read about, the one that astronauts took up into space with them for a quick painless death in case of emergency. He placed the pill on Eric's desk next to his phone. If he had to stare death in the face, so should Matthews. He looked over. Still down for the count.

In the last envelope he saw his own name carefully printed on the outside. His heart beat harder. He slid his finger under the flap and withdrew his own photo. He remembered when this particular picture was taken, months ago. Eric had "surprised him," a visit from a friend at the museum.

Doug crumpled the picture in his hands and dropped it to the ground next to Eric's motionless body.

Let the games begin.

Mary Ann Hall was vacillating. She'd heard the scuffle and the raised voices, but Mr. Matthews was always extremely particular about not having his privacy disturbed. She was about to ask Mark, the paralegal down the hall, for his opinion, when Mr. Goodwin stepped out of the office. He looked okay, not disheveled or anything. Maybe they were just fooling around or something. No. It sounded too real for that. She could try to stop him from leaving, but she wasn't paid enough to get in the way of *that.*

She waited until she could see that he'd stepped into the elevator and the door had fully closed before she got up from her desk and went into her boss's office, patting her hair into place. That's when she saw him on the floor.

"Oh, my God. Mr. Matthews! Are you okay?"

Eric groaned and felt his jaw. That Doug packed a punch. He shook off Mary Ann's offer of help and sat up. "Leave me be, Mary Ann. I'm fine."

"But you're hurt—"

"I said, I'm fine! Hold all my calls. And if a Mr. Black calls, I'm away on business until Monday. Is that understood?"

"Yes, sir, but are you sure you're—"

"I'm sure. Now get out of here, I need to think."

"But you were attacked—"

"I said, leave...me...alone. Please."

When his busy-body administrative assistant finally left, shutting the door a little too forcefully for his taste, Eric reviewed the scene with Doug. Quickly he opened the drawer to his desk. Shit. Gone. Doug got them all. No, way back there, there was one more envelope...empty, too. Then he saw the capsule on his desk. He picked it up and stared at it long and hard.

The phone on his desk rang. "Damn it, Mary Ann, I told you to hold my calls," he said, but picked it up anyway. "Eric Matthews."

"Mr. Matthews. Having an interesting afternoon?"

Mr. Black.

Eric disconnected and tore the receiver from its base. Seconds later, his cell phone rang. Eric pushed the "ignore call" button, powered down his phone. He heard the phone ring outside his office door on Mary Ann's desk, then the annoying ring of the fax machine. He bolted from his office. The fax was a few feet away in an alcove. He had to get there before anyone else did. A new fax was just sliding out onto the tray.

Good day, Mr. Matthews. Mr. Goodwin has identified you. The rules are clear. Watchers are everywhere. You know what you have to do.

Eric stared blankly at the sheet of paper in his shaking hands. There was no mention of the Circle, no mention of anything incriminating. He had to think. This was SO not how things were supposed to be. He moved past Mary Ann who was watching him as if she'd never seen him before—and, in essence, she hadn't. She hadn't seen this Eric Matthews, the one who had betrayed his best friend to access money and power. The one who had nothing else to screw up. Eric locked himself into his office. He looked around for his Bluetooth and spotted it on the floor by the window. He put it on and dialed Doug's number, rubbing his sore jaw as he did. Maybe if he could....

No. There were no more maybes.

He took off his headset and set it down on the desk, swung around his chair, and looked out at the expansive—and expensive—view. He'd miss it.

His shoulders slumped. He swung back around, took out a piece of paper and a pen, and wrote. *Doug - Please forgive me. - Eric*

The pill went down easily. It was done.

21

The elevator doors opened at the lobby. No commotion, no police, no company security to detain him. Considering he'd just attacked a junior partner of one of the biggest law firms in the city, he'd expected to have to at least fight his way through some kind of resistance. Not that he knew what he would have done had reality supported his anticipation. Truth was, for once in his life, he was the one looking for a good fight.

He jumped into his Jeep just as a meter maid was sticking a ticket on his window and a tow truck was pulling in behind him. One more minute and his vehicle would have been impounded. Doug jumped behind the wheel. "Hey," yelled the tow truck driver, a massive pit bull of a guy in striped overalls. Doug peeled out in a cloud of smoke, burning rubber.

It wasn't the tow truck that concerned him. A jet-black Dodge Charger was following him, and not bothering to be discrete about it. He shifted his Jeep into high gear and accelerated around the corner, heading north on Broadway, daring the Charger to pursue him. It didn't disappoint.

As Doug's eyes stayed fixed on the car close on his ass the blocks flew by in a blur.

39th Street.

40th Street.

41st Street.

Doug took a sharp left turn onto 42nd and jetted toward 9th Avenue and Hell's Kitchen, a maneuver that could turn the tables in his favor. The Charger, with two men in the front seat, was unrelenting, however. It continued to follow him through the busy streets. They wove through traffic. Doug, driving more erratically than his pursuers, skimmed the corner of the side-walk to make a sharp turn down 39th Street toward the Lincoln Tunnel.

The line of traffic in front of him was typical. The tunnel was always packed, no matter the time of day or night. He pulled behind a soccer mom's minivan and waved to the kids in the back window who were sticking their tongues out at him. Would the Charger get aggressive? Would the guys get out and accost him? Apparently not. It was idling in traffic as he was. Traffic was traffic. Nothing you could do about it.

Think, Goodwin, think. They wouldn't do anything with all these people around. How could he get the upper hand? Crash through the gate? Big headache. All he needed was the New York and New Jersey police after him, too.

Think, think. There. An opening. He wasn't the only one who'd seen it. A dozen cars were attempting to maneuver into the tiny opening on the right in the hopes of beating the traffic. Doug put on his tough I-don't-see-you face and pushed on in. Aggressive drivers in New York were the only ones who got anywhere. The Wrangler's size made it easier for him to squeeze by the other larger SUVs and into the tunnel. In his rearview mirror, the Charger attempted the same maneuver, but without the same success.

Doug barreled through the tunnel, knowing the men in the Charger wouldn't give up their pursuit so easily. He pressed on, the dimming yellow lights above rushing past in a blur. He remembered the first time he'd ever driven through the long tunnel, the distinct feeling that it was going to rupture. This time a different set of walls was closing in on him.

He saw daylight at the end of the tunnel. He exited in Weehawken and took the jug handle around onto 495. Knowing his predators were still trapped inside the tunnel, he found the first turn-off, 31st Street, and waited. Before long the Charger would emerge, hopefully unaware of his own change in tactics.

There they were. Trapped behind a HazMat truck. Unable to see around it, the Charger drove right by 31st Street where Doug had turned around and was idling on the corner.

Now! Go!

Turning the tables was good, being the hunter instead of the hunted, but Doug was tiring of the game. He stayed close, gaining on the Charger until he was within a few feet, then accelerating into the Charger's rear fender. The Charger veered sharply to the right, then shot across several lanes of traffic and then into a parking lot behind a factory that overlooked 495 and the junction to Route 9. The turning radius of Doug's jeep allowed him to easily match the move. He followed the Charger through the lot. He accelerated into them once again. This time they went into a tailspin that landed them smack up against a parked loading truck.

Doug stopped the Jeep with a squeal of the brakes and leapt out. The passenger's head was propped against the window, blood dripping down the side of his face. Doug rounded the front of the car. The driver appeared dazed but was reaching for something, presumably a gun.

With his jacket over his fist, Doug punched through the cracked glass, pulled the now visible gun out of the driver's hand, and pointed it. The passenger was coming to. "Get out of the car. Now. This way."

The driver opened the door and got out, his hands raised high above his head. The passenger slid with some effort over the seat and out the door and also put his hands in the air. Done this before, thought Doug. They both wore jeans, expensive leather jackets. Their features were nondescript features, one blond, one dark. Both scowling.

"You! Throw the gun over there. Now!" Doug said to the one with the blond hair, the driver. The gun skittered over to Doug's feet.

"Who the hell are you?"

"You know who we are," said Dark Hair.

Of course. Watchers.

"And now you've seen our faces," said Blondie.

Simultaneously, the men made a move to reach into their pockets.

"Keep your hands up! I'll shoot you both, I swear!"

Sirens in the distance were growing louder. Cops. On their way to supervise the scene of the "accident." Passersby on 495 were slowing up to rubberneck. It was a pastime Doug had never understood. Time to go.

Still, he hesitated. The men's hands had produced vials identical to the one Eric had in his desk. Doug didn't need to be told what was inside. What was he supposed to do? Shoot them both? Not there. Not now. Not ever. And not with so many people watching.

"We have rules, Mr. Goodwin," said Dark Hair.

Doug almost felt sorry for the guys.

The Watchers looked at each other—saying goodbye?—and tossed the pills into their mouths. Within seconds they were slumped on the ground. Spittle trailed from their lips. Doug stood motionless until the blare of the sirens were too loud—and too close.

No time to think. The gun he'd taken from Blondie down at his side, Doug ran back to his Jeep, his mind a jumble. He had to get back to Eric's office. Warn him. Matthews was a Watcher. The Circle would be after him. Doug pictures the pill he'd left on Eric's desk. The guy was an A-number-one asshole who had forced Doug into a life of primal survival. He deserved to see how it felt to stare death in the face. But to kill himself? He wouldn't. Would he? Eric was no John Wayne, but would he be stupid enough to take that pill?

He hurried back to the Jeep, praying no one had been smart enough to record his license plate. So much for his beloved Jeep.

It was at least half an hour's drive back into the city at a more conservative speed. Doug put the gun on the seat beside him. At 39th and 8th he realized he was talking to himself. At least nowadays he'd look like just another cell phone-addicted driver.

The drive took forever. Doug swore, hit the steering wheel, and implored the gods and goddesses everywhere, but the sea of vehicles wasn't listening.

Back at Connors, Dowd, Rodgers, & Simon, he lucked out, pulling into an iffy but usable space about a hundred feet from the building just as a Mercedes SUV was embarking with its passenger. He stuck the gun in his waistband and held his breath as he tore past the nicotine-crazed office workers hanging by the side door in a cloud of cigarette smoke. The side door of the building's spoke to the right brought him closer to the elevators, but he still had to pass the security desk. Security didn't come cheap at Connors, Dowd, Rodgers, & Simon. The same guard who was here earlier, a burly guy with a buzz cut, was no slouch. He was already picking up the phone and pushing buttons. Doug pointed the gun at him. "Put the phone down," he said quietly.

The security guard dropped the phone and put up his hands. Doug continued toward the bank of elevators, still training the gun in the guard's direction. People were running from him. He'd have only seconds before the guard—or a concerned citizen— called the police.

What was he doing there anyway—trying to save Eric's life? Why should he bother?

The display above the elevators told him that most of the cars were on high floors. It was either wait or take the stairs— and sixty-two flights was daunting even in the kind of shape he was in. Out of the corner of his eye he saw some activity going on—the police already?—just as the elevator closest to him opened. He pushed past the block of people getting off, several of whom made remarks about his rudeness, and smacked the "close door" button. *Come on, come on. Close already.* He was in luck. It was a little after five. More people were exiting than arriving. No one else got on and he hit sixty-two.

The sixty-two flights went by in an agonizing blur of fear and adrenaline. The cops would be there any minute, no question. You couldn't go around waving a gun and expect no one would care. Probably thought he was a terrorist.

Act normal. Act normal. Not like the madman you are.

When the doors opened, he stepped out, gun back in his waistband, and fast-walked past the rows and rows of cubicles. Mary Ann's computer was covered. One less obstacle.

He burst through the door of Eric's office, half expecting it to be locked, but it opened soundlessly. The office looked the same as when he'd left, but Eric was no longer sprawled on the floor by the conference table. He was seated in his chair, slumped over, his face planted on the old-fashioned desk blotter he had loved so much for its air of eccentricity and wealth. "Looks like the old bank gentry, right Dougie-boy?" he'd said to Doug when he bought it. At the time Doug had only shaken his head in amused despair.

Eric must have told the secretary to leave him alone, or else certainly she would have discovered him like this. Doug couldn't bear to look at the body of the closest friend he'd ever had. The same whitish drool was on his lips as the Watchers from the Charger. Under his hand was a sheet of paper with Doug's name on it. It was short, only a few words.

Doug pocketed the note, turned, and left the office, closing and locking the door behind him.

He'd take the stairs through the basement. It was his only chance.

The police were there when Mary Ann returned to the office to retrieve a folder with some paperwork that needed dropping off at the courthouse first thing in the morning. When she saw the policemen and the two security guards from downstairs she knew something was very wrong.

She threw down her purse. "What happened?"

Officer Williams, by the name on his badge, held out his arm. "And you are—?"

"Mary Ann Hall. I'm Mr. Matthews' assistant. Did something happen?"

"You tell us, ma'am."

"I don't know. I just came back for a file I forgot. What's going on."

"We don't know yet, ma'am," said the officer with the scar on his face, an Officer Johnson. "Do you have the key to the office?"

"Yes, but Mr. Matthews hates to be disturbed. He told me not to disturb him under any circumstances, to hold all his calls. And I know better than to go in there when he says that." She shouldn't need to justify her position, but no one was going to tell her how to do her job.

"What time was that, ma'am?"

"Oh, around three or so. Oh, no, could—? No—forget it."

"What's that, ma'am?"

"Mr. Matthews' best friend, a Mr. Goodwin, came to see him today. They had a fight. Mr. Matthews was hurt, but he wouldn't let me call security. He said they'd worked it out. Are...are you going in there? Do you think he's okay?"

"Did this Mr. Goodwin say anything to you when he left?" Officer Johnson asked.

"No, but he was acting crazy."

They were wasting time with this charade. "Officer Johnson" knew that every single minute was critical in cases like this. They needed to get into that office, resolve the matter fast, get out. Before the real cops showed up. He looked at the security guards, gave them an indulgent smile to include them in the action. "Guys, would you please escort Ms. Hall here to the conference room and stay with her until we get there? She looks like she could use a glass of water. Thanks."

"But don't you want a description of Mr. Goodwin?" asked Mary Ann.

Officer Johnson tensed. "Plenty of time for that later, ma'am. Right now we need to find out what happened in there. Besides, the security cameras will have picked up everything we need."

Mary Ann allowed herself to be taken by the elbows down the hall. Why—how—did the police know something was wrong? Why were they here? She was curious, but to be honest, she was on the low end of the caring scale. Eric Matthews was the most arrogant boss she'd ever had, a real creep. If something happened to him, maybe she'd get a new position up on the sixty-fourth floor with that cute new guy, Chad something-or-other, in real estate. Maybe she'd even get a raise.

Inside Eric's office, "Officers" Smith, Johnson, and Williams were efficient and quick. They put on gloves and then erased all remnants of Eric Matthews' earlier struggle with Mr. Goodwin. They repositioned the conference table and washed the specks of blood out of the carpet. Luckily it was a dark Oriental and showed very little. The lighter shades always made their job much harder. Johnson went directly to the desk and found the empty vial, which he put in his pocket. Then the three men lifted the body and placed it on a piece of thin, strong plastic on the floor. Williams and Smith got to work wrapping it.

Johnson returned to the laptop, clicked open a new document, and typed. *Mary Ann - There's been a family emergency. I will be in Colorado indefinitely. Transfer all my calls directly to my voicemail, and give my current files to John Simon. He knows about this and will take care of everything. I'll call you when I have some news. - Eric*

Johnson hit the print button and a perfect copy of the note spit out of the HP Deskjet in the corner of the room. He placed the note on the desk, dead center, and nodded, pleased with his handiwork. He spoke to his coworkers. "After a few days, Ms. Hall will be let go...something about missing files...legal papers stolen, something like that.... Her credibility will be shot and she'll have too much on her mind to think about our Mr. Goodwin ever again."

His companions nodded in silent agreement. They were ready to go, the body in a dark bag with handles. With a final look around to make sure everything was as it should be,

Johnson checked the outer office and then gestured for Williams and Smith to take the bag to the service elevator. They would leave the same way Doug did, through the basement, and then out the lowest level of the parking garage. In the elevator they exchanged their police uniforms for janitorial gear. In another ninety seconds the Ace Janitorial Service van was on its way to the East River.

22

The soft strains of Count Basie's *Basie at Birdland* echoed through Doug's apartment. He was physically and emotionally drained, a seemingly permanent state nowadays. The shock of seeing the lifeless body of his childhood friend had set in, as had the gravity of the entire situation. In a matter of days, he's lost the two closest people in his life.

He had no appetite, but eating was important. He had to keep up his strength. Funny how often his parents told him that when he was a boy. He started with an orange, the last from the ceramic bowl on his kitchen counter, and began peeling it apathetically. When was the last time he'd gone shopping? Bought a cup of coffee? Done anything normal.

Those days are over. Deal with it.

He shot a curl of rind at the trash can but missed by a mile and it fell to the floor. With a groan he bent down to pick it up, making the shot the second time. He moved listlessly to the sofa and lowered himself down. He was so damn tired. With each section of orange, he thought of a new way he might have saved his friends. If he'd been smarter, less impulsive, quicker. When he sat back the gun in his waistband jabbed into his back, reminding him of the dead Watchers in the Charger. And trading in his Jeep? That was really gonna hurt.

He placed the rest of the orange on the coffee table, wincing as the Nighthawk Custom Lady Hawk pressed into his back. Doug despised guns, but this guy knew his. Sleek, light. Easily carried. Only a problem when you went to sit down, like now. He twisted around to pull it out and set it by the orange.

As he did, a high-pitched whistle zipped by his left ear. A bullet burrowed into the wall at his back, and then another buried itself into the orange and then down through the table, creating a monsoon of orange pulp. Doug grabbed for the pistol and dove behind the sofa.

Safety, off.

He rolled into the adjacent dining room where he opened the fuse box. With the power off in the apartment the only light would be from the city outside. That had taken Doug a while to get used to, too—that lack of complete darkness. Even in the middle of the blackest night, the lights of New York managed to cast a glow inside his apartment walls. That also meant he wouldn't have long before the darkness would dissipate entirely and leave him exposed.

He got his bearings. From this vantage point he could see the whole apartment except for the bedroom and inside the bathroom. There was a movement from the hall. Doug breathed in. He reminded himself to stay fluid, relaxed, ready.

The door of the foyer closet creaked open. A masked man emerged. In the near absolute darkness, he moved cautiously toward the living room.

Doug only had brief seconds before the hunter's eyes adjusted to the increasing grayness. He fired a misguided shot in the direction of the foyer. He had to get to the bedroom, more specifically to his weapons closet, light years away. Cufflinks was right, he should stick to the weapons he knows. Putting safety first was a hard lesson to unlearn.

Doug rolled over on the rug without a sound. Because the wood flooring around it was sure to creak, he waited until the right moment. When the masked man collided with the coffee table and let out a muted curse of annoyance, Doug took his chance.

Before he could regain his footing, the man in the mask became aware that he was being charged by a moose.

Doug heard a mumbled expletive before the guy panicked, tried to turn and run. His shin smashed against the coffee table again and he lost his balance. His weapon, knocked loose from his hand, discharged with a flash. The smell of cordite filled the air.

Doug's ears were on alert after the discharge of the silenced gun. He wielded the trophy-moose-head-turned-battering-ram again and this time toppled the hunter into the coffee table, glass shards landing everywhere. He heard a loud "uumph," but didn't wait to check his work. He ran for the bedroom, dropping the moose head as he spun around.

In the closet, he considered the best weapon for the job. Too late. A shot came whizzing through the wooden door. His ear was on fire. He checked it. Bleeding, but he'd survive. He grabbed his loaded crossbow from its hanging post. In one motion he dove out of the closet into a roll, turned and instinctively fired out and upward in the direction of the bullet. For a second there was a suspended silence.

Then, *thud.*

He crawled to the bedroom door to investigate, keeping the crossbow loaded and pointed. A body lay prostrate and limp at the threshold. The arrow had gone through the man's Adam's apple and was protruding out the back of his neck. There was no doubt that he was dead. Shaking, sweating, Doug moved away from the body again, horrified at the sight of the fourth dead human being he'd seen that day. He crawled around the bedside table and picked up the phone.

"Nine-one-one, what is your emergency?"

"Someone's in my house. He tried to kill me."

"Are you in the house now, sir?"

"Yes, but I think I killed him."

"Is your attacker still in the house?"

"Yes, I told you. I shot him."

"Sir, please remain calm. Give me your name and address. We'll send a car right away."

"It's Goodwin, Doug Goodwin. 2110...."

"Mr. Goodwin."

"Yes?"

"I don't think there is anything I can do for you at this time. Please go directly to Tasker's and inform them of your successful kill."

What? "What?"

"Congratulations, Mr. Goodwin. Welcome to the Circle."

The phone line went dead after the "operator's" pronouncement. Doug screamed a torrent of obscenities and went to hurl his phone to the ground.

Stop. Stay calm. Regroup. You have just killed a man. A man who was trying to kill you. A member of the Circle.

Until he got a new one, an untapped one, this phone was his link to the world. Resigned and shaking, he left his apartment, ran down to the garage and climbed into his Jeep.

Pulling out into the street, he took stock.

Let's see...there's a dead man in my apartment, I have no job, no best friend, no Doc. In fact, I have no life anymore. Perfect.

The treads of the car ker-thumping down 6th Avenue threatened to put him to sleep. He was that tired. He hadn't really slept since the night in the cabin, before the delivery of his first blue Circle envelope. He'd always liked long drives, exploring open spaces for possible hunting, enjoying the seasons, but this was not a pleasure jaunt and eastern New Jersey was not known for its green spaces. At least not where he was going.

He sped down Route 78 toward Maplewood. Michelle, his tour-guide office mate, and her husband John lived a mile or two off the exit. Only about fifteen miles from New York City, Maplewood was a typical suburb of about twenty-four thousand and surprisingly little crime. Michelle took the train to the City every day. It would drive Doug crazy to have such a long commute, but she used the time on the train to catch up on her reading.

He still can't believe he's just killed a man. And now he was supposed to go back to Tasker's and "celebrate." Celebrate the taking of another life? Even in self-defense, the element of pride for a job well-done, the element of humility in the face of life's greatness was conspicuously absent.

He was walking a fine line. When he talked to Michelle he would have to say very little. Nothing about the Circle, not even an inference, or she and her husband could become more collateral damage. He can't ask for advice and he can't ask for any help. But he still needs to talk to someone unconnected to the madness, even for a few minutes. He recites what he is going to say in his head, the words that cannot cross his lips: *Circle, kill, dead, hunt, secret club, Tasker's....* Anything that might lead the Watchers to believe she knew anything.

Exit 124 was up ahead. He peeled off and merged with the main road. At this time of night in suburbia there were few vehicles. He checked the clock on the dashboard. Almost midnight. He took his third left onto Bertha Avenue, an easy street to remember because he'd played golf with a club called the Big Bertha a long time ago. Another lifetime ago. He pulled into the fourth driveway on the left and turned off the motor.

Doug positioned himself to get out of the Jeep, but found he was frozen in the driver's seat listening to the clicking of the cooling engine. Fear, paranoia, and concern for his friends swarmed like flies in his head. Coming here was a big mistake. If another close friend died because of his mistakes, because of his inability to cope with his own problems—

Well, that wasn't going to happen. He'd rather spend his life alone than be responsible for something like that.

Resolute, he turned the key and started the engine again. He put the car into reverse to back out of the driveway.

"Nice night for a drive?"

Doug stomped down on the brakes. "Shit, you scared the shit out of me."

Michelle was standing by the passenger door. "I thought you'd be coming in, but I guess I was wrong."

She was wearing a nightshirt and a pair of run-down flip-flops. Her long, smooth legs were illuminated by the motion-sensor light over the garage.

"Oh, yeah, well, it's late."

"You think? What brings you all the way out here? It's midnight. And where have you been? You didn't show up for work for days and then Jenkins says something about a sabbatical. I didn't know tour guides could get sabbaticals. I wouldn't be surprised if your ass is grass."

Just seeing her reminded him of how much he'd left behind, the normalcy of things he'd never have again. What he'd give to be back in that tiny office complaining about that promotion he'd never get. He cleared his throat. "Where's John? Shouldn't he be the one out here in the middle of the night?"

"John sleeps like the dead, snores so loudly I can't sleep half the time. You know I'm a night owl. And I'd know the sound of that Jeep anywhere. And I gotta be honest here, Doug, it sure looks like you need some company."

"I guess you could say that."

"Come in, I'll make us some coffee," she said. "It's not from the Bread Basket, but I can charge you seven bucks if it'll make you feel more comfortable."

Doug forced a laugh and followed her inside.

The living room was simply decorated. Michelle had great taste in art, but even though John made a good salary she still couldn't afford the kind of art she wanted. A few cheap black frames encased some of her own black-and-white photographs, landscapes mostly. Not that Doug was an expert or anything, but he thought she was pretty good. A couple of wedding pictures sat on the mantle. When they'd first moved in, she and John were only going to stay here until they found something better. That was two years ago, and unpacked boxes labeled with the word "stuff" still sat along the walls. Right now it was the most comfortable living room in the world.

"I'll be right back with that coffee," Michelle said.

"Don't skimp on the caffeine."

Doug sank into an old La-Z-Boy and moaned with relief. He was lightly snoring when Michelle returned with two coffee mugs, a jug of milk, and a sugar bowl on a tray. She placed it on the coffee table and sat on their futon, which was more uncomfortable than a park bench.

"Always stealing the most comfortable seat in the house, huh?" she said loudly.

Doug roused. "Well, I know what's what around here."

"Tell me about it." She handed Doug a mug and he added milk and a teaspoon of sugar. "Not that I don't like seeing you, Doug, but what the heck are you doing here?"

Michelle's forthrightness was also comfortable. He'd grown up in a single-child household. His family was loving, but not all that demonstrative, and pretty much talked to him like an adult. They were of the belief that love didn't need to be expressed verbally or physically; you knew that you were loved and that was that. He had, too. Known that he was loved, that is. Michelle's direct way, her easy banter, gave him the same feeling, like she was kind of like a sister. He hadn't known her very long, but he felt he could tell her anything.

In the past. He could tell her anything in the past.

This honest, loving woman, who had a husband, a house, and two cats could no longer be his confidante. He heard the voice of bumbling Sergeant Schultz from the old TV show *Hogan's Heroes.* "I say nothing, *nothing!*"

Michelle was looking at him. Doug was a big mouth. Why was he so subdued?

Doug stifled Sergeant Schultz and said the words he'd practiced in the car. "I needed to get out of the city. Too much cement and all that…I guess the Jeep just drove itself here."

"Bullshit, Douglas Goodwin. Absolute Bullshit. I know you. What's really wrong?"

Stupid to think she'd buy such a lame excuse. Should he tell her he'd fought with Eric? She'd never liked Eric, always calling him "the fancy dude with the wise-ass mouth." But Eric was part of the whole Circle thing. Eric was off limits.

He made a big deal about pouring another cup of coffee and took his time adding more milk and sugar. He could sense Michelle's frustration. He stirred the coffee and then put down the spoon. He'd stick to the truth as much as he could. "I didn't want to say anything. But someone was killed in my apartment building tonight."

"Oh my God!" said Michelle. "It wasn't on your floor, was it?"

"Actually, it was," he improvised, "the police were all over the place when I got home today."

"Doug, that's crazy. Listen, stay here tonight, this futon unfolds, you know that. You don't have to go back there tonight—it's too creepy."

"Nah, I just needed to get out for a while."

"No. I mean, are you sure, because—"

"Hey, Michelle—" he started.

She stopped. "What?"

Doug searched his soul for the right question to ask, the one that would provide him with an answer to his problem. "When you were in college, did you ever feel like you were trapped? Like you had no way out?"

"What's that got to do with— Okay, fine. Sometimes, I guess, like maybe when I was writing all those papers. But I knew I had to get through it, that school was a gateway for me. I knew I'd never get anywhere in my field unless I got my degree. Why?"

"But what exactly got you through it?"

"I don't know. I really didn't think I was as smart as everyone else, that I could produce anything worthwhile. And I hated the competition. I almost quit. I could be the world's most brilliant waitress—I actually tried it. But I really, really suck at waitressing. I don't know what happened. I took some time off. Hung out by myself. I guess I came to my senses. Realized I'm not that stupid. I'm pretty sure my pushy personality helped, too. I'm too stubborn to give up." Michelle looked at him. "But what's this got to do with—hey, you're not thinking of moving back to Colorado? To *Grover*?"

"No. Maybe. Who knows?"

At least they weren't talking about murder anymore. "I just don't think I have the energy or the courage—or the resilience—to keep it up here."

"Really? 'Cause that just doesn't sound like you, Doug, and I don't buy it. So, listen up. I know you. And I like you. And I know you never run away from anything. The second you do, you'll regret it, and you'll carry that with you forever."

Bull's eye. If she only knew that forever might be sooner than she thinks. "You're probably right."

"I know I'm right. Besides, you work in a museum, I mean how much pressure is there being a tour guide?" Doug had to laugh. Michelle got up. "Which reminds me, how's this sabbatical thing going?"

What Sabbatical?

"Sabbatical?"

"Yeah, sabbatical. *Hello.* Jenkins sent around this memo saying you were doing some kind of study program somewhere. I've got to tell you I was pretty miffed that you didn't tell me anything about it and then suddenly you were gone."

Michelle was hurt, which made Doug feel even worse.

She went over to her briefcase, which was already positioned next to the front door for the next morning, and handed him an official museum memorandum. "Here, see for yourself."

Sure enough, it was a very short formal notice addressed to all museum tour guide personnel.

Due to Doug Goodwin's sabbatical of an indefinite time period, overtime opportunities are now available until a suitable replacement can be found. All those interested should report to Mr. Jenkins, Room B39.

The Circle. It had to be. He'd never told the museum he was taking any time off. They'd fixed it so no one would suspect foul play when he didn't show up. These guys' damn tentacles had tentacles.

"Um, yeah, about that...I'm sorry, Michelle. It all happened so fast. I applied months ago—I almost forgot about it. And then they called and I had to get ready to go."

"Where are you going?"

Not again. He hated this lying. He never used to lie. "Um, Egypt...then maybe China...."

"Well, I want to hear all about it. Come on in before you go, okay? You know, it's going to be the pits not having you around, bitching and moaning, carrying on about Coffee Shop Girl."

Doug snorted. "I'll try, I really will. I'll, um, miss you too."

Too serious.

"And Jenkins and all those thirteen-year-olds and don't forget the circulars...."

Michelle's laugh turned into a yawn. He looked at his watch. Time to go. He had to get to Tasker's and she had work the next day.

"Listen, thanks for the coffee. I gotta get going, and you should get to bed."

She didn't argue. At the door she turned to him. "Hey, Doug—"

"Michelle, I—"

"You first this time," said Doug.

"Well, I just want you to know that I appreciate you, Doug. And I'm your friend, if you ever need anything."

He almost reached out and grabbed her. Instead, he patted her shoulder. "Thanks. Thanks for everything."

"Anytime, Sabbatical Man. You know our door is always open."

Just before he slipped out, Michelle managed to give him a hug, short, but long enough that he had to break it off before he fell apart and spilled the beans. Every last one of them.

"Hey, what's that on your shirt?"

Doug looked down. "What? Oh, it's nothing. Cut myself when I was fixing the car."

"Here. Come back in. I've got Band-Aids and—"

"No, no, I'm sure."

"Well, okay, if you're sure. Take care, Doug, okay?"

"You too, Michelle. Best to John, and thanks again."

Outside Doug's apartment building three cleaning service employees approach the front door, dressed in grey overalls and wearing painter's caps, goggles, and surgical masks. On the right side of each set of overalls the name of the company is printed in black ink on a white patch: Ace Janitorial. Under that are their names: Smith, Johnson, and Williams. Though the names are the same, these are not the same three men who serviced the body removal at Connors, Dowd, Rodgers, & Simon. This Mr. Johnson is pushing a hand truck full of cleaning supplies. This Mr. Smith carries a large duffel bag.

Samuel Murphy had dozed off at his post. He awakened to the sound of banging on the door. He rose slowly to his feet and unlocked it using one of the keys on the huge key ring attached to his belt. "Can I help you gentlemen with something?"

"We have an emergency work order here for Mr. Douglas Goodwin's apartment..." Williams, the spokesperson, looked down at the paper he holds in his hand, "...4B."

"At this hour? I'll just call Mr. Goodwin first."

"No need for that, sir, I have a signed work order here. He just came by about a half hour ago. He told us you would let us in. You're..." he looked back down at the paper again "...Samuel Murphy, aren'tcha?"

Murph scanned the work order. It wasn't the regular course of events, but here in the City anything—and everything—happened in the course of a day. Sure enough, Goodwin's signature was on the order, plain as day. "Well, then, I guess if Mr. Goodwin wants you in the apartment, I'm gonna have t' let you in," he said. "I'll take you up."

"Um, you might wanna wait here, sir. From what he tells us, the smell is awful," said Johnson.

Murph weighed his options. It was irregular, but if they let themselves in and out he could get back to doing what he did so well—taking a long-needed rest. He disconnected 4B's key from the giant ring. "Have fun up there, boys. Don't forget to bring that key back down here when you're done, you hear?"

The men took the elevator to the apartment and let themselves in. They went to work like a well-greased machine. Williams focused on the living room, tackling the bits of blood on the floor, sofa, and wall, and then the table, which would have to be replaced with the one they had in the van. Smith headed for the bedroom. He started with the weapons closet, checked for any blood spatters, and applied stain remover and elbow grease. Johnson was in charge of removing the gun slugs from the wall and floor—along with the bits of orange fruit, which had splattered everywhere.

When the peripheral work had been accomplished, the men tackled the biggest job—the body still in the bedroom with the arrow through its neck.

"More blood than I would have thought," Johnson commented. "Almost as bad as cleaning up after Mr. Fingers."

In silent agreement, they set to work. It took some maneuvering, what with the arrow and all, but they lifted the body and placed it on the large tarp they laid out a few feet away. They scrubbed without talking for at least another ten minutes. The rug looked like new when they were done. With a grunt of satisfaction, Williams directed Johnson and Smith to wrap and secure the body in the tarp after he trimmed the arrow at each end. They folded the masked man in half first, for convenience's sake, and inserted him into the hand-truck where the cleaning supplies had been stored. They put the supplies into the duffle bag along with the trash, the broken glass and pieces of wood from the coffee table. Before they left they ran a thorough check of each room, including the kitchen. Nothing seemed to have happened in there, but mistakes weren't tolerated in their business.

Finally, they made their way toward the door. It was almost 1:00 AM. They'd get the new table up there and be gone. They'd made good time. Mr. Black would be pleased.

Samuel Murphy had always been a light sleeper; it was something you learned during the war. When the three big men came down the elevator, the creaking and cranking of the old cables woke him up.

He made a half-hearted attempt to get up. "Everything go alright, boys?"

"Don't get up on our account," said Williams. "We got everything under control."

"That sure is a big bag you got there. What happened in 4B anyway?"

Nosy bastard. If they weren't on a time table he might think about ending this here and now. "Oh, just some plumbing problems...you know, made the whole place smell like sh—well, you know, awful. Had to install some new parts."

"But I coulda told the super. That's his job," said Murph.

Williams was losing his patience. "Mr. Goodwin wanted it fixed right away. Didn't want to wait." He turned to leave before the meddlesome doorman could ask another question.

"Well, la-de-dah," said Murph. "You have a good night then, boys. I'll be sure to tell Mr. Goodwin what a great job you did."

"Precisely," said Williams. "Like nothing ever happened."

"Exactly," said Johnson.

Smith, a man of few words, just grunted.

23

The drive back to the city from Maplewood was too short, given Doug's inevitable destination. It was 1:56 AM. Never having been at Tasker's at this time of night—or rather, day—he doesn't even know if the tavern, let alone the back room, will be open. Yet there seemed to be very little life outside Tasker's for members of the Circle. The thought made him unbearably, overwhelmingly, sad.

He parked the Jeep. The thump of a bass was vibrating through the heavy wood. That answered that question. It was like stepping into a permanent *Twilight Zone*, where nothing ever changed. Except for the ghosts of the hunted and dead.

Doug bypassed the bar altogether. He didn't want a drink. In the back room he found Cufflinks playing cards with Chemist and Mantis. Doug had always believed that women were more sensible than men and found this woman's involvement with the Circle off-putting. Maybe he just didn't like to think of women as killers. Either way, if she'd been recruited the way he was, she probably had no choice. As he sat down a drop or two of blood from his ear wound splattered on the table, leaving bright red stains on the discarded ace and eight of hearts. It seemed his recent wound had reopened.

CUFFLINKS: "Mr. Goodwin. You certainly know how to make an entrance. But you're here at a late hour. Did something happen?"

"The hunter was in my house. Waiting for me."

MANTIS: "By the looks of things, Mr. Silence is either quite upset with himself or quite dead. Which is it then, Mr. Goodwin?"

Doug took a moment to consider the woman across the table. The crow's feet probably meant she was no spring chicken, maybe in her early fifties, but it was the coarse, leathery skin and short graying hair that made her look so tough, so hard. Her accent said UK. Bulging arm muscles strained the material of her white shirt. No arm-wrestling here.

Doug can't make himself say the words *I killed him.* Or even *He's dead.* "It was self-defense."

CUFFLINKS (exclaiming): "Nonetheless, congratulations are in order, Mr. Goodwin. You have, what's the expression Mr. Fingers enjoys using so much…busted your cherry."

"I still don't want any part of it. I don't *want* to hurt anyone."

Dude. Listen to yourself. Whining like a kid.

CUFFLINKS: "That certainly isn't the tune you sang for us and our European guests not too long ago. I highly doubt Mr. Stahl will underestimate Americans ever again after that encounter."

"It's not the same," said Doug. "And I didn't think it was going to happen so soon."

CUFFLINKS: "Ah. But it has, Mr. Goodwin. But then, it can't be Mr. Goodwin anymore, now can it? Tell us the details."

Defeated, Doug told them how he'd managed to avoid getting shot and accessed his crossbow. He is sickened by the memory. "I've never killed a man before."

MANTIS: "Felt good, though, didn't it?"

Good?

"Are you crazy? And who do you think you are? None of you know anything about me." The room fell quiet, but only briefly this time, before the hum of activity picked up again. Doug's outbursts were nothing more than punctuation marks.

Fingers joined them. "So, the kid here made the first cut, huh?" He turns to Doug. "You mean to tell me that knowing you got the best of someone—someone who was trying to kill you—doesn't make you feel accomplished...even proud? That you didn't feel the excitement of the win? This one's starting to worry me."

CHEMIST: "Mr. Fingers, a little more class, please."

FINGERS: "Bloody good, Mr. Chemist. So sorry to offend."

Why didn't anyone else notice the way he mocked Cufflinks' demeanor and tone?

CUFFLINKS (to Doug): "It's about time for your naming, then."

"Naming?"

"Your new Circle name must reflect some facet of your first kill. You say you killed Mr. Silence with your crossbow?"

Doug nodded reluctantly. He turned to Chemist. "So, what, you killed someone with your chemistry set?"

No one spoke for a moment. Had he stepped over the line again? Although a room of murderers adhering to a code of conduct was surely oxymoronic.

CHEMIST (unamused, hissing his disappointment at Doug's comportment): "No, you disrespectful little shit. But like you I learned to kill my prey the best way I knew how. Now it's what I do. What I am. A hunter. Just. Like. You."

Mark Ainsworth had been no older than Douglas Goodwin at the time. The ladies found him attractive, like a young Paul Newman, and he learned to heighten that perception through his dress and mannerisms. He was the maitre d' of a newly established restaurant in the City, Bellotti's Eatery, a new place, classy. Real good tips, the right clientele. Six nights a week he smiled from his podium and greeted the patrons at the City's newest hot spot. His plan was to own the place within two years.

When he was recruited to the Circle, his first blue envelope was waiting for him on the shelf inside the podium beneath the seating chart. His first kill was a well-dressed middle-aged man with a much younger woman with perky full breasts and long legs. In other words, a typical pair. The man had slipped Mark a hundred, and Mark had led them to the last table by the large picture window on the street side where he could best parade his wealth and his arm candy. "Victor will be serving you this evening," he'd said. "Enjoy your meal." This was the standard line they had been taught to parrot. Tonight it held a special meaning.

Back at his pedestal, one more glance at the photo in the blue envelope told him what he already knew: that the man he had just seated was indeed the man in the photograph. He looked around and located Victor. "New table?" Victor asked.

"Yeah, good tippers, too. Let me know what wine they order. I'd like to serve it personally."

Victor told the maitre d' that the man had ordered a bottle of Modra Frankinja, a full-bodied wine of great character.

Ainsworth's trip to the wine cellar had to be quick. His hovering manager would not be pleased if he weren't in place to seat people as they arrived. He only had one chance to make this happen. One. He wouldn't let his nerves get the best of him. His first kill would only be his first if he succeeded. Ainsworth was a survivor; he'd simply adjusted to the circumstances. There was nothing left to reconcile.

He removed a bottle of Modra Frankinja from the shelf. Murder She Wrote might have you believe that injecting poison into a wine bottle was something everyone knew how to do, but it took time and the right paraphernalia. Instead he'd decided to use the old-fashioned approach, straight into the glass from the cleverly concealed compartment in his wrist watch. He checked the mechanism one last time. Satisfied and aware of time's passage, he returned from the wine cellar with a tray, the bottle, and two red wine glasses.

"Sir, madam, your wine."

The woman nodded absently. Ainsworth removed the foil wrapping and twisted the corkscrew. He used to feel uncomfortable when conversation ceased while he opened and poured. But the rich fell into two classes: those who acted as if servers didn't exist and those who acted as if their existence was an inconvenience. Ainsworth's first mark was of the second variety.

Ainsworth presented the cork to the man, who smelled it and waved his approval. Ainsworth poured a small taste of the wine into the man's glass.

The man sipped and nodded again. Ainsworth poured a full glass for the woman, making sure to lift the glass high up off the table, and angle it with a flair. He'd practiced this maneuver many time. The rich liked a show—as long as it was done tastefully and on their behalf.

He picked up the man's wine glass in his left hand. The man was ogling his dinner companion as she swirled the wine in her mouth. Mark tilted his right wrist inward just so and a bit of red *powder floated down into the glass to join the fine red wine. A perfect execution.*

"Enjoy," he said. He loathed the expression they were told to use. After tonight he'd never utter it again.

Back at the podium, Ainsworth watched the gentleman swallow his wine, then begin to cough. After a moment, his companion squealed, "Help, he's choking." Ainsworth took advantage of the ensuing panic to leave through the back door. His fake name badge, fake mustache and goatee, bow tie, and green-tinted contacts were tossed into a dumpster six blocks away.

And then Mark Ainsworth danced a little jig at the thrill of the kill.

When Chemist finished his story Cufflinks was the first to speak. "So you see, Mr. Goodwin, Mr. Chemist exists first because he had to, but now because he chooses to."

Yeah? I choose to be unimpressed.

CHEMIST: "Our fellow members gave me my name, and that's how you'll get yours."

"I don't want a name," insisted Doug.

MANTIS: "Why on earth not?"

"I take a name, I'm one of you."

CUFFLINKS (drily): "Too late for that now. ...What do you think of 'Mr. Archer'?"

There were nods of approval around the room. "Excellent choice, Mr. Cufflinks," one of the men says.

"I can't do this," Doug says again.

CUFFLINKS (coldly): "You can and you will. Do you honestly think, Mr. Archer, that you, one mere man, has the ability to change anything? You have killed a distinguished member of the Circle. You are one of us now, like it or not. You killed your hunter, Mr. Archer. You have earned forty-eight hours to enjoy some freedom. It is up to you how you want to spend them, but I suggest you celebrate your continued life. Because then a new hunter will be appointed to you and—well, by now even *you* are aware of the rules."

CUFFLINKS (turning to one of the women hovering by the table for the next request that came her way): "Won't you bring us some cigars, my dear?"

"Certainly, sir." She sashayed out of the room. Her fine behind elicited no response from Doug, who'd never felt so trapped, so helpless.

The woman returned with a box of cigars. She handed them around and offered a light to each of them, Ms. Mantis included.

MANTIS: "Here's to Mr. Archer. Welcome home."

CUFFLINKS, et al. "Here, here."

Doug excused himself to the men's room where he was sick as a dog.

He still felt a little green when he got back to the table. He could go home—but where was that? Was Tasker's his new residence too?

Suddenly Doug remembered that he'd left a dead man in his apartment. "Oh, my God, there's a dead body in my apartment. If anyone finds it—"

"No one will find it, Mr. Archer," said an unfamiliar voice.

"Who are you?"

A tall dark man with a bright yellow tie is extending his hand. Doug declines to take it.

"Forgive my bad manners...Mr. Spear, pleasure to meet you.... As I was saying, the body is likely gone and the space... fully sanitized by now."

"What? How is that possible?"

"Cleaners."

"You've got to be kidding me."

"Not about this, Mr. Archer."

Doug winced as his new identity is forced down his throat.

"There's nothing to kid about. Just as a Watcher recommended you..."

Yeah, that's not exactly the way I'd put it.

"...there are Cleaners who clean up after the fact. They work with the Watchers to find out when an...attempt has been made, or is about to be made. After the event the scene is closed and the body is disposed of appropriately. Like I said, by the Cleaners."

FINGERS (enjoying Doug's discomfort and waving his cigar in the air): "Mr. Spear's right. The body's prob'ly gone by now."

"But what about the police?"

The members in the room laughed heartily, all a big joke.

CUFFLINKS: "How shall I put this, Mr. Archer? The police are not a threat to us."

"So you're telling me that the body in my apartment has already been disposed of?"

CUFFLINKS (looking at his watch): "Quite right."

"And that the apartment has been 'cleaned'?"

"They *are* efficient, aren't they, boys?"

FINGERS (disdainfully): "Sometimes a little too efficient."

Yeah, not going to touch that one.

"But how? I mean, if people see who they are, they can't be Watchers anymore."

MANTIS: "An excellent observation, Mr. Archer, but there are hundreds of Watcher teams assigned to each branch of the Circle. Each team has a Mr. Smith, a Mr. Johnson, and a Mr. Williams, the three most common last names in the United States. Names so ordinary that they are easily dismissed by the masses. It remains each Watchers' own business how he keeps himself—or herself—from being identified. Suffice it to say, Watchers have been watching for decades. They are quite skilled and very seldom caught by those who matter."

Just then, the doors to the VIP parlor opened. A young man dressed in tight jeans and a blue T-shirt with a number thirty-three on it walked in carrying a pint glass of dark beer. The room took a collective breath and then returned to business as usual. The new face looked around the room with an expression that says he'd hit the jackpot. The chair next to Cufflinks is empty.

CHEMIST: (smiling, sucking in his stomach to accommodate the new addition): "Welcome."

The man was all muscle. Standing well over six feet tall, he had the build of a pro football player. His pointy boots actually had heel spurs on them. "Thanks. Nice place y'all have back here. Much nicer than out front." He spoke in a thick Texas drawl.

CUFFLINKS: "Quite. A lovely place for gentlemen to enjoy some sophisticated company."

"Y'all ever have music 'round here? The right talent'd make a killing," the cowboy said.

The men at the table chuckled at the Texan's unintended double entendre.

Get out! Get out now before it's too late! Doug screams in his head. *You're dead if you stay. Run for your life!* But the words stayed where they were. What use would it be? If the guy was here, he'd already been recruited. His life was over, he just didn't know it yet.

The Texan's naiveté made him almost despicable in Doug's eyes, horrible as that was to admit. As the chuckling continued, the man's good-natured demeanor shifted a bit. He was catching on. They weren't laughing with him, they were laughing at him.

He stiffened. The smile on his lips stayed, but his eyes shut down. *Fuck with me and you'll regret it* was written all over his face.

MANTIS: "I believe Mr.—ah—Mr. —" She looked at the Texan.

"Randall, Randall Webb," the Texan said tightly.

"—Mr. Webb here is on to something. A singer would make a killing indeed. Wouldn't he, Mr. Cufflinks?"

Smoke was coming out from the new guy's ears. Doug watched with fascination a replay of his own—what?—enlistment, induction, indictment?

CUFFLINKS (standing up and bowing): "Certainly, Ms. Mantis, but I'm afraid this entertainer won't be making a killing anymore. Sorry, gentlemen—" then "—ladies."

MANTIS (nodding): "Thank you."

Doug's disgust rose. They were practically rubbing their hands together, like the Wicked Witch of the West setting fire to the scarecrow.

FINGERS (grumbling): "He's too young."

"Too young for what?" demanded Webb. "What the hell is going on here?"

CUFFLINKS: "Mr. Fingers, why so negative? He is simply new. Personally, I'm ecstatic. This will be our first new recruit since Mr. Archer."

"Recruit? Recruit for what?"

"Forgive us, Mr. Webb. Please indulge us a moment longer and allow us to introduce ourselves. I am who you will come to know as Mr. Cufflinks. To your right is Ms. Mantis, to your left, Mr. Chemist, and this is Mr. Spear, Mr. Fingers, and Mr. Archer."

"What is this? We playin' 'Clue' or somethin'?" The Texan had lost a little of his swagger. Something was going on, but he didn't know what. His discomfort was as obvious as the sweat on his brow.

"This isn't a game, Webb," Doug finally said, "you should probably pay attention to what they have to say."

"You're kidding, right?"

Doug shook his head sadly.

FINGERS (As if on cue, gets up and takes out his leather case): "Let me show you how much we kid around in here, pal." Outside, Doug took deep breaths of fresh, or not so fresh, city air in a weak attempt to dispel the horror he'd just witnessed inside Tasker's. And he was a part of it, the initiation of another human being into a circle of killers. The unsuspecting Webb—*age 32; son of Craig and Jolene Webb of Keller, Texas, about 30 miles outside of Dallas. Dropped out of high school at the age of 16. Went to night school and earned diploma at age 19. Attended Texas A&M for 5 semesters, leaving abruptly when an accident left father paralyzed from the waist down. Father died 3 years later from complications during experimental surgery. Two sisters: the oldest, Skylar, married to Harrison Woods in 2001, lives in River Oaks, Texas with their 2 children Jack and Nancy. The youngest, Holly, married to Brody Young in 2003, lives in Argyle, Texas. One brother, Shane, 10 years senior, lives in Oregon with his wife, Claire, on a sheep and horse ranch*—as so eloquently spelled out by Mr. Black—had looked every bit as ill and as irate as Doug had felt—still feels—at the unfairness, the incredible invasion, the vulnerability.

With only forty-six hours or so left of his reprieve, and dread in the pit of his stomach, Doug sets off for the place he used to call home.

A full city block behind him, the Fink was busy tracking Doug's movements. The rooftops of Manhattan are more of a home to him than most people's condos and McMansions, so familiar is he with his territory.

He took out a small spiral notebook and neatly inscribed a few words, *Douglas Goodwin = Mr. Archer*, threw his head back, and laughed.

With only precious hours left to kill—he can't quite manage to laugh at the number of death-related puns that are constantly making their way into his thoughts—Doug queued up for the ATM on 79th and Broadway. Day or night, the ATM machines in New York City always had people waiting to use them—yet another aspect of city living Doug thought he'd never get used to. Now they were a commonplace convenience. The card in his hand had come in his first blue envelope. He'd sworn never to use the Circle's money, but without a job, without income, and without any point to getting one that he could see, Doug was between a rock and a hard place. He had to eat and he had to pay his rent, it was as simple as that. Plus, all the members of the Circle, along with any of the witnesses to the Charger incident in Weehawken, likely knew about his silver Jeep Wrangler, still stashed in his building's garage. Time to get rid of it. Today.

Cufflinks was right about one thing. Now that Doug had killed someone, railing against the Circle's hold over him was useless. Figuring out a way to live within the system—at least until he could figure a way out of it—was paramount.

He punched in the pin number supplied with the card and waited for the screen to come up with his options. He pressed "Checking Account" and waited again. Then "Account Balance." He held his breath. When the balance appeared on the screen Doug was so shocked he nearly turned to the guy a couple of feet in back of him to ask if he saw the same thing. Ten figures. Billions of dollars. All accessible at the touch of his finger. Doug withdrew the maximum amount, five thousand, with a shaky hand, and grinned maniacally when the machine asked if he'd accept the $2.75 processing fee. He reinserted the card and repeated the process three more times.

Suddenly Doug realized what an easy target he made, standing at an ATM in plain sight with bill after bill shooting out of the machine. *I am such an idiot.*

He pressed against the money slot and slid the money out. Twenty grand landed in the palm of his hand.

He stuffed the bills in his pocket and tried to look poor as he took to the streets. He picked up an *Auto Shopper* at the next newsstand. A dealership wouldn't work. Cash might turn heads. The perfect solution was in the used-car section, not far from where Michelle and John lived, in Irvington, New Jersey, some guy selling a fairly new Ford F-150. Not exactly NYC practical, but not a Wrangler either. Besides, F-150s were good off-roaders. He called the number and announced he'd be there within the hour.

The relatively light traffic allowed him some speed. Who cared if he got a ticket or his insurance went up? Guilty liberation you might say. He'd never see the inside of a jail cell, not with the Circle parked so snugly blanketed on the police force.

Before he knew it, he was a few blocks from the truck seller's address. He parked his Jeep in back of a local Walmart and walked the rest of the way to a neat little ranch, one of many in this typical urban sprawl. Small, neat lawns, fencing. Not much in the way of kids playing; a real working community. The navy-blue truck in the driveway of number 1133 confirmed the address. He spent a minute looking over the tires and the truck's general condition before ringing the doorbell. Except for a tiny scratch in the rear bed, the ride was in pristine condition.

He didn't waste any time, and didn't bother to haggle too much. The ad said fifteen thousand or best offer; he offered thirteen five. "Thirteen eight," the fiftyish beady-eyed guy countered, but it was more of a real-men-don't-give-in-right-away thing. Doug took it. The seller would have no reason to speak ill of him—or brag he'd gotten away with something—if someone asked questions about the transaction.

When Doug had the paperwork he drove the truck back to his Jeep in the Walmart lot, where he immediately removed any trace of his identity, including license plates and vin number from the dashboard. Next he emptied the glove box and the trunk and then removed the fuse panel and all identifying marks and numbers. He was thorough, checking under the car and in the engine and under the seats for any personal items. He took the key off the key ring and placed it in the ignition. He wrote the word "FREE" in big block letters on a piece of cardboard and stuck it on the dash. The Wrangler wouldn't last long on the streets of New Jersey where chop shops were second only to junk yards in some places. He tried not to think about the blue envelope with his name inside, the one that was in someone else's hands at that very moment. Then he climbed back into his new F-150 and returned home. Potential threat one: averted.

The drive back into the City was slow, but he had a lot to think about. How he only had a few precious hours left on his leave time. How he'd grown so fond of thc words, even knowing that in order to earn it someone had to die.

24

Doug had always worked, always kept busy, with school, hunting, sports. Having whole days—or a month—free feels like the vacation he's never had. Oh, yeah, except for the fact that when it's over he'll be back in the nightmare again. He gives himself a mental slap. *Prioritize! Hold on to your sanity. Get out of the apartment. Stay away from Tasker's. Do what you have to do. Don't think about it, just do it.*

He deposited his new vehicle in his assigned space and hit the streets, overwhelmed by the need to get out, to take advantage of his so-called "free time." He was disturbed by the parade of people accessing his apartment. Mr. Silence, the Watchers... they'd all gotten in somehow. It was safer, at least for the moment, on the streets of New York.

Doug had been eating and sleeping and walking and talking, but if you asked him what he'd eaten or said, he couldn't tell you. It was as if he'd been in a bubble. Now the sounds and sights of the city penetrate in a way they haven't since his last day at the museum. Tires squeal and a taxi driver breaks and swears out the window at the car in front of him. A garbage truck on its last run of the day, stopping at every building to load up, is resolutely and uncaringly blocking anyone stupid enough to find himself behind it. The crowds of people, the conversations, the peanut and hotdog vendors, they're all out in full force. Doug walks among them, feeling slightly more human and less like the alien he's become.

Then it hit him, the reason for his renewed vigor.

I'm alive.

That's what Cufflinks and the others meant. About how facing death made them feel so alive, how nothing could compare. Doug was both repulsed and fascinated by his reaction. He'd lost so much *joie de vivre* lately. Resignation was at the foundation of this resurgence, he knew that, but it felt too good to berate himself for it.

Doug took another hour to stroll through Central Park. The days were getting shorter, but they were still warm. Kids were everywhere. For a minute his mind went blank. He counted forward from the day he and Eric had met at the museum to go for a drink. That would make this Saturday. The weekend.

His first weekend as a killer of men.

He crossed Central Park West at 85th Street. The rumble of a subway train beneath his feet traveled up through his shoes. He could turn left and go home, but what was there? An empty, super clean apartment. No, thanks.

An open door to the sidewalk beckoned him in with a big four-leaf clover on the glass of the window. Perfect. A good 'ol Irish Pub. Lots of drinkers. No one to notice a single guy off the street who comes in for a drink.

Inside the pub was dark. Doug's nose wrinkled up at the smells of beer and Pine Sol. New York City's ban on smoking in bars and restaurants could not deter the lingering scent of smoke would remain in the walls and floors forever. The sign above the bar said "O'Leary's Irish Pub" in big letters with a bowing leprechaun under the words.

It was late afternoon. Small crowd. You had your early drinkers and your newer arrivals gearing up for Saturday night partying. A place where you could blend in as a regular guy. In the corner adjacent to the doorway three guys were playing a game of Cricket. Two others were in a video bowling competition next to the dart board.

No, thank you.

The bar, situated just off center, left room for a few high tables and chairs for waitress service. The close end of the bar made a "V" shape and turned a sharp corner to the far side of the bar, about five feet from the wall. Along the back wall at a big table seven or eight women were toasting the bride-to-be at a bachelorette party. Doug did a double-take at her inflatable hat in the shape of a penis with a button that flashed "Another One Bites the Dust." Periodically, one of the guys from the bar would go over and attempt to pick up one of the women. They smiled and flirted, but were having too much fun without the company of men. U2 was playing on the jukebox. At no point did Doug get the feeling that a secret door would open and invite unsuspecting victims inside. His kind of place.

There was an open spot at the bar. "Excuse me," Doug yelled over *Beautiful Day*, hoping to catch the eye of one of the two bartenders, the dark-haired, blue-eyed one. No luck. A waitress walked past him with several drinks in her hands. She nodded distractedly, but didn't stop. "Excuse me," he yelled again. The waitress—Chelsea—pointed her chin up to a carved wooden sign. "Do not stand here, waitresses only!" Rejected and thirsty from all his walking, Doug sidestepped to let her go by. "What's a guy got to do to get a drink around here," he muttered.

At the end of the bar, a woman sitting on a stool was playing some kind of video game on her phone. "Hey, Arlene, get this poor guy a drink, will ya already? He looks like he's ready to collapse."

Her accent was pure New England, the "r" dragging into oblivion until Arlene had become Ah-lene. A minute later Doug had his drink. He raised his glass in her direction and mouthed a thank you. She nodded back, grinning.

Doug blinked twice to make sure.

No. Yes. It couldn't be. But it was! Coffee Shop Girl. The one he'd lusted after—stalked would be much too harsh a word—for months. He'd never forget that face. She couldn't possibly be alone. Someone who looked the way she did was never alone. He assessed the local talent and proximity. No likely candidates close by. His eyes traveled back to the bar. He'd only seen her dressed in business attire and high heels, her hair tied up away from her face. Tonight her long reddish-blonde hair flowed past her shoulders. Their eyes met and Doug was lost in a sea of dark green he could write poetry about.

He raised his glass to her and then took a quick swallow of beer for courage. He cleared his throat. "I was starting to think I was invisible."

"No problem. I've seen you someplace before, haven't I?"

"I've heard that line before. Wait, I think I've used it. If you're trying to pick me up, I'll have you know it'll take more than just one beer."

She laughed. "Then I guess you'll never know."

"Damn, I knew it couldn't be that easy."

She studied his face. "Really, though, you look familiar to me. Wait, I know," she announced with a snap of her fingers. "The Bread Basket. Early mornings. Am I right?"

She remembered him? "Yeah, that's me." The one who sat there day after day drinking coffee he couldn't afford just to see you walk by. "I think I remember seeing you a few times, too." As if every single solitary thing about her wasn't indelibly imprinted. "I'm Doug," he said.

"Liz," she said, taking his hand in a nice, strong grip. "Nice to meet you, finally."

"The pleasure is all mine."

Liz took back her hand. Two spots of red dotted her cheeks. "So what brings you to O'Leary's—I've never seen you here before."

"Oh, well, changing it up, you know...."

"Well, it's a great place for finding yourself," she said. "Welcome to my world—my sanctuary."

Doug's eyes were glued to the sight of her full lips taking the last sip of her drink through the straw. "I'm going to have to buy you another one of those, you know."

"Well, if you insist," she said, and touched his upper arm lightly.

The zing of her fingers startled Doug into action. He happily reached into his pocket for a couple of bills he'd set apart from all the cash he'd gotten at the ATM. "Think I can get Arlene's attention this time?"

"Definitely not. You'll need my help for sure."

"Care to bet on it?"

"You're on."

"Name the stakes."

"I'll give you three—no, wait—two minutes. If we don't have new drinks, you have to send those guys over there a couple of Shirley Temples." She nodded across the bar in the direction of two large men in white t-shirts, black leather vests, and full complements of tattooed arms and necks. One had a full beard and ponytail, the other a handlebar mustache that could challenge Hulk Hogan's.

"Wow. You must really want me to get my ass kicked. And what if I win?"

"Your call."

"Okay, let's see. I know, if I get the drinks, you have to let me buy you dinner."

Liz let a few beats go by, agonizing seconds. "You're on," she finally said, taking his hand to seal the deal. "It's pretty much a win-win for me."

"How's that?"

"Well, I either get to see you embarrass yourself or I get a free dinner."

"I'll take my chances. But I hope you like a good steak."

Liz laughed and the sound set Doug's spine tingling. She looked down at her watch. "Your two minutes start...now!"

Doug disappeared from Liz's view, almost immediately swallowed up by the abyss of bodies jockeying for position at the bar. She searched for him for a few seconds before she looked back at her watch. Half a minute gone. Where was he? He wasn't her typical type, but she liked him enough to have dinner with him. She was rooting for him to win the bet when he reappeared. This time from behind the bar. Serving her a Shirley Temple.

She popped one of the maraschino cherries from her drink into her mouth. "How did you pull that off? Arlene never lets anyone back there." His eyes were following her mouth as it moved around the cherry. He was right where she wanted him.

"I have my ways." he managed. A thousand bucks to pay off the bartender and another for Chelsea. Worth every penny. "They promised me we won't go thirsty tonight."

Her lips turned up at the corners.

"So," he said, "about that dinner."

25

During the long flight back to Norway Mr. Kvele confidently concluded that he was being tailed from New York. Not by that abrasive Mr. Fingers, but perhaps the member with the strength of an ox—no, a lion. Mr. Lion. In truth, it could even be that new recruit with the attitude. Ah, well. High alert was a state with which he was imminently familiar.

In his office on the top floor of the Equinor building, Kvele contemplated the inevitable. How would it manifest, the attack on his life? Would he feel it coming? Would he feel a sweet relief from the long burden of hiding his diagnosis and physical symptoms?

He opened his laptop. The Doctors Without Borders website came up, taking only moments to load. He clicked on the "Make a Donation" page. It asked what he wanted to donate, $25, $50, $100, or a "custom" amount. Kvele clicked on "custom" and put $10,000,000 in the box. A moment later he modified it to $20,000,000. It was only money; you only lived once.

He closed the laptop with a satisfied sigh and leaned back in his chair with his feet on his oak desk. The Circle had been his life for so long he couldn't remember exactly when his focus had shifted. From reluctant recruit to enthusiastic hunter to believer that the means justified the ends. Who could have foreseen his predilection for caring? For philanthropy?

Money in his pocket, the Circle's money, meant money for schools and medicines and food and politics. Money meant he'd leave a legacy he could be proud of. A legacy as the man who gave back, who created change with dollars and cents, not words. His own personal fortune would have merely scratched that surface.

It was the ALS that would bring it to an end sooner than he'd expected. Amyotrophic Lateral Sclerosis. Such a benign term for such a turbulent, ugly disease. He was on borrowed time now. Either by the hands of The Circle or the rapidly turning hands of time, death was a *fait accompli*. What better way to go out than as a humanitarian who'd made the world a better place for his fellow humankind?

He glanced at his watch. Precisely 6:20 PM. Time for his Kokekaffe. A time-consuming process, normally eleven minutes, but a worthwhile ritual that brought him pleasure. Four minutes to bring the water to a boil, five to steep the coffee and two extra minutes of anticipation before pouring it into his cup.

"Anders?" Goran Larssen, his assistant, was in the door. An underling, but an underling with whom Anders had a long-standing friendship.

"The party's about to start. Don't tell me you're not coming. Work can wait this once."

"I don't think anyone wants their boss at a party. You go on. I'll stay here, drink my coffee in peace."

"Forget it. It's late. We're all going to Utopia for a couple of drinks. You can toast me on my birthday. You don't have to stay long."

The bar would be crowded and Kvele didn't drink anymore. Goran knew that. Still, he was a good friend, invaluable to the team.

"Okay, okay. I'll give up my coffee for you. But don't think it'll happen again. I'll finish up here and meet you at the club."

"I'm holding you to it," Goran said. "I'm coming," he called to the people in the hall. He waved to Anders and was off.

"Anders Husby" was the name on the gold plated plaque on his desk. It was the name everyone knew him by. It would be the name etched on his headstone. Kvele straightened the papers on his desk then went into the adjoining restroom to wash up. The earlier he got to Utopia, the earlier he could leave. In a minute he returned to his desk, where he'd forgotten his coffee mug.

The figure hovering in his office by the window was not the size of a monster. Not the size Kvele assumed Death would be, nor the menace. He was slightly hunched over, as if the weight of the world were on his shoulders. As if killing Kvele was in some way merciful.

The two shared an awkward moment with an elasticity to it, as if it might spring back on them at any moment. Glued to each other like a bull and a matador. No way to tell who was which. Why would this man, this man who must be his hunter, stand silent, do nothing?

The door to Kvele's office was closed. Everyone had left. The man must have arrived only a moment before.

The mug of hot coffee was within arm's reach. He toasted the man—*"Jubel"*—and aimed the java at his face.

The hit was not a bull's eye, but Kvele had the advantage, and some of the hot liquid contacted the man's eyes. Kvele landed on his attacker with his full body weight. They landed on the floor and thrashed about in the narrow space between the wall and the desk. The man grappled for purchase. The legs of the chair, the side of the desk. Kvele had other plans. He dragged the man by his legs into the corner. On the shelf behind him was one of his numerous philanthropic awards, a heavy glass orb. With it he struck his attacker's head and face. Blood sprayed them both. Was he really going to bludgeon this man to death with his *Faces of Philanthropy* award? *Irony...or poetic justice?*

But it wasn't over yet.

The man caught Kvele's arm in an armbar and squeezed until Kvele dropped his weapon. Then raised his knee into Kvele's groin. With a heavy *oomph* Kvele collapsed. The man got to his knees and slammed the orb down on Kvele's head. More blood. Head wounds bleed a lot.

Kvele was woozy. He'd gone from attacker to attacked in the blink of an eye. The strength born of adrenaline was dissipating. The dreaded ALS had made him weak.

But wasn't this what he'd been waiting for? The final scene, the completion of the circle—the circle of life?

He looked at the man. The man looked back.

The outcome was clear.

Kvele nodded.

The attacker took Kvele by the head and slammed it into the side of the desk. The dense thud echoed in the room. A blade had somehow appeared in the man's hand. With it, he made his move, plunging it into Mr. Kvele's neck.

A muffled gurgling. Another. Then quiet.

Mr. Dart caught his breath and wiped his brow. The subclavian artery was a good choice. For a sick guy the Norwegian had put up a darn good fight.

Williams, Johnson, and Smith—or the Norwegian equivalents thereof—would be there soon to clean up the aftermath.

Scandinavia was always nice this time of year. Maybe his furlough would include a visit to the fjords.

26

The Colorado History Museum is nothing compared to places like the Natural History Museum in New York. Still, Doug is glad to be working there. Through his connections at the University, specifically Professor Balachi, he'd been granted an internship for his junior year, a rare opportunity for someone so young, only twenty. Twice a week he climbed on his mountain bike and headed down Broadway toward the museum for his ten-to-six shift to do research in the Stephen H. Hart Library for brilliant minds like Dr. Miles Anchack and Dr. Stanley Cosgrove. He loves the job; if it weren't for his classes, he'd do it full time. He likes to think of the Colorado Historical Society as his pet project—he does the majority of grunt work—but it's Dr. Cosgrove's baby. He was the one spearheading the project way back before Doug had even graduated high school.

One particular Friday afternoon in December, about two weeks before his second semester was over, Doug is let go early to study for his exams. The two-mile walk back to the apartment he shares with his girlfriend Sarah is an easy one. The clean air fills his head with thoughts of freedom and the future. The sun, just about setting, is casting a grand shadow from the Capital building over a block away. The white granite building with large pillars and carved stone statues depicting early life in Denver draws him in as the bright orange slowly turns to a dark blue and he feels the calm of the anticipated long weekend ahead.

On the steps he took a seat and removed the remnants of lunch from his backpack, a peanut butter-and-banana sandwich that Sarah made for him. He'd told her a thousand times that he hated the combination, but she had a lot on her plate, too, and, well, here it was again. She was studying poly-sci at the University, struggling with her senior thesis. Doug would ask her to marry him as soon as she passed her exams.

He patiently removed the bananas first, then ate the rest of his sandwich with the great view as incentive. To either side of him two cannons pointed north and south. On the grass median separating Lincoln and Broadway, the Colorado Veterans Monument, similar in shape to the Washington Monument, rose into the sky. He could see clear across Lincoln Street and Broadway to the magnificent architecture of the Denver County Building. From the air they'd probably seem designed as a pair.

He walked the rest of the way home to 19th Street in the dark, the street illuminated by the bright green lights of the dome of the Capital Building above him. As he ascended the outside staircase to his second-floor dorm-style apartment, he heard sounds of a struggle from inside. He placed his backpack quietly on the ground and withdrew the hunting blade that he always carried. Pulse racing, he leaned over the railing and peered into the window. The filmy curtains fogged his vision, but he saw enough to know that Sarah was being attacked. She was tied to the bed, twisting and kicking her legs, flailing at her attacker. Doug froze for a second, horrified, then locked the blade into position, opened the door, and raised his arm.

Then the attacker turned around.

"Sarah?"

 Sarah's eyes opened wide. "Doug?"

As Doug processed the clichéd scene in front of him, he felt as if he were slipping under water in a strange world that held no semblance of reality. Sarah, his friend and lover, the woman he'd planned to marry, was bending over a strange man who had both arms tied to a corner of the bed.

"Hi, honey, I'm home," he said.

He woke up covered in a cold sheen of perspiration. He hadn't thought about Sarah or the "incident" in well over five years. The guy in the bed was just a guy Sarah had met at school the day before. Doug had packed and left within the hour.

Why on earth would he be dreaming about her now? He got out of bed, naked, feeling ashamed and afraid and totally undone. He pulled on a pair of boxers and went into the kitchen for a drink of water. He threw some on his face first, then cupped his hands to fill them and bring them to his mouth. When he turned off the water, unfamiliar sounds were coming from the open bathroom. A shadow flitted across the door sill.

No! His leave time wasn't up yet!

He dive-rolled back into the bedroom, swiping the bath-room door farther open on the way. He tore across to his weapons closet. In seconds he'd locked and loaded his shotgun and stood perched on his bed, gun aimed at the bathroom door. "Just try it," he said.

The door slowly opened. Liz, wearing his old, faded University of Colorado T-shirt, face white, took a tentative step into the room. "D—Doug? What's wrong? What are you doing?"

"Liz?" Oh, my God. Liz. He'd just aimed a gun at Liz. He dropped it to his side. "Liz, I can explain."

"Really?" Liz took a step, one hand on the towel she'd turbaned around her head. "I'd like to know how. What the hell is wrong with you? I go into the bathroom to take a shower and I come out and Rambo is here? Pointing a gun at me?"

How was he going to talk his way out of this one? "Liz, look, I'm sorry. I know how it looks. I had this nightmare, I thought it was real. And I had a break-in a few days ago, a guy with a gun." True, if fundamentally inaccurate.

"Really? *Really*? Doug. You have a shotgun in your hand! And here I thought you were a nice, decent guy. Normal, even. Jeez, I meet a guy in a bar, give the guy a break, go home with him…. I can't believe I'm that stupid…."

"Liz, please."

"Don't *Liz please* me. We're done here."

Liz picked up her clothes and jammed them onto her arms and legs over Doug's shirt. "Damn psycho. Can't I ever find a regular guy?" She bent down to retrieve a shoe from under the bed.

"Please, don't go, Liz," Doug pleaded. "I am normal. *Well, I'm trying to be.* "Please…I'll prove it to you." Doug rummaged through his trash and found the plastic casing from his new doorknob and dead bolt and his old lock. "See, new locks. The old one was trashed in the break-in. Please, don't go. I'm sorry." He positioned himself in front of his door and got down on his knees.

Liz studied the man in front of her, the toned body, the well-defined abs, the sculpted chest. No one had ever begged her to do anything. Normally they couldn't wait to split the next morning. She sighed. The Rambo-with-the-gun thing didn't hurt either.

"Wow, you're really desperate, huh?"

"If you only knew. So, you'll stay?"

Liz was taking a moment to think, inclining her head to the moose head on the wall. Doug had put him back in his place of honor after the break-in, scuffed antlers and all.

"Promise I won't turn into one of those?"

Doug held up his right hand, put his pinky to his thumb. "Scout's honor, cross my heart and hope to die."

"One more chance, then," she said. "And only one. I don't take kindly to terror tactics."

She moved into the living room and kicked her beautiful legs over the arm of the sofa. Doug could look at them forever. "Do you have to work today?"

"It's Saturday, remember?" She clicked on the television. ESPN came on. She clicked the TV off again.

The countless back-and-forth between his apartment and Tasker's had led each day to merge with the next. If Liz said it was Tuesday he would have believed her. At least with a nine-to-five job there were weekends and off-time. Not with the Circle. The Circle was 24/7/365.

"Plus, as I said, I'm an art buyer. I have a flexible schedule." She got up from the couch and moved toward him.

The eroticism of her every move, her skin, her smell. Doug had never been so turned on. Liz put one finger in the elastic of his boxer shorts and pulled him closer. Her lips tasted like mint toothpaste, seductive and chaste all at once. He was drowning in her touch, her lips. When she pulled back, he swam to the surface.

"I'm all yours if you want me, Rambo," she said, and slid her hands into his shorts.

An hour or so later, Doug looked at the clock. 10:18 a.m. Somehow along the line they'd gone from the living room back to the bedroom. The woman at his side was dozing, her magnificent chest rising and falling.

Barefoot, Doug quietly padded into the kitchen. On top of the fridge was a case of water bottles. Between the booze and the night that followed, he needed at least one. As he gulped down the half liter he checked the perimeter, his movements automatic as he again inspected the front door. Still locked. Dead bolt secure. Nothing amiss. The sweep of his apartment might be unnecessary, but habits mattered. Getting careless got you killed.

He opened the front door to retrieve his morning newspaper. A blue envelope was lying next to it. He stepped into the hall to open it.

Mr. Archer, Your intended target was successful in eliminating his assigned member at 9:44 PM. You are to refrain from all Circle-related aggressions for the next 30 days. See to it that all attempts are made to honor this sacred rule. - The Circle.

Doug was willing to bet there were members who would be devastated by that news. Members who had been planning the perfect time to strike. Not him. One less threat to worry about once his clock ran out on his forty-eight hours. He felt lighter for a brief moment. There was a goddess sleeping in his bed. He'd enjoy her company as long as he could. He softly closed and relocked the door and eased back under the sheets. Liz moaned slightly at the jostling.

"Hey," Doug whispered. "Hey, you up?"

"I wasn't, you jerk. Now I am."

"Listen, I never thought I'd say this to you, but get dressed. There's someplace I want to take you."

"If I'm going to get dressed I need another shower first." Languidly, she rose and walked naked across the room. He'd never met anyone so uninhibited. She wasn't showing off; she just liked being in her own skin. And the sight made the blood in his veins pulse up into his throat. Her long hair flowing down to the center of her back, her round, supple breasts gently touched by sunlight, the curve of her slender waist accenting the perfect contour of her firmly toned buttocks. She was perfect.

She turned back to him and cocked her finger. "I'd hate to have to shower alone."

Liz turned on the shower faucet. She kissed him again, and he wrapped his arms around her, ran his hands down over her back. He pulled away to kiss her from her neck all the way down her body, stopping along the way to nibble at her breasts, her stomach, her thighs. With each caress he felt a rush of something so heady, so powerful, that he wasn't sure he wouldn't collapse from its intensity. More than physical desire, it was almost like the grip of pain.

Doug let himself be led. As steam filled the room she sat him down on the edge of the bathtub and straddled him, wrapping her legs round his waist and running her fingers through his hair.

Was she feeling it, too? Was she feeling what he was feeling? It would be nice, but for now, it really didn't matter.

By the time they arrived at the American Museum of Natural History, it was 1:15. They'd grabbed coffee and croissants from a bakery near his apartment and had just purchased tickets for a full tour. It had only been weeks since he'd worked in the bowels of the institution, had been the one giving the tours. "This is my world," he said to Liz. "Can't find artifacts like these anywhere else in the country—maybe the world. What if I take you through the prehistoric section, then we head across Central Park to the Met and you can give me an advanced tutorial on art?"

"Why not?" Liz said, "not a bad idea for a second date—or should I say the date that never ended?"

Doug smiled and squeezed her hand. The next tour group to leave was being led by Raúl, probably Doug's replacement, who looked fresh out of college. Doug knew the museum inside and out. Every tour started with the dinosaurs, but after that they'd be able to break off from the pack.

"Good afternoon, ladies and gentlemen, I am Raúl, and I will be taking you on a tour of the greatest museum in the world today," the guide enthused. "We're going to take you on a tour through time, starting with the beginning: prehistory... dinosaurs!"

Raúl led the group to the first dinosaur on display, Stegosaurus. "The Stegosaurus lived during the late Jurassic period and had seventeen bony plates embedded in its back. Since the Stegosaurus was a peaceful animal and an herbivore, or plant-eater, its strong bony plates were its only protection from its many predators which included the Marshosaurus, Torvosaurus, and even packs of smaller carnivores, or meat-eaters, such as the Ornitholestes."

Poor guy. Same old, same old. But compared to what he was doing now? Doug would take it. Wouldn't he?

The Circle was instantly back, front and center. He looked over at the woman at his side. She felt his eyes and turned, grinned, and a flush that began in his crotch traveled up to his face. Liz's smile got bigger and she moved a step closer.

"If I could direct your attention to the hip region of the spinal column," Raúl continued, "there are theories that suggest this large canal here could have accommodated a structure almost twenty times the size of the Stegosaurus' brain. This discovery has led doctors to believe that this animal may have had a second brain which controlled its reflexes and, quite possibly, its tail." Several of the tour group took pictures of the skeleton. "Two brains, not a bad deal," Raúl added, and chuckled at his contrived joke.

Doug leaned in to Liz and whispered, "None of that has been scientifically proven, it's all theory still. Most of the studies done to see if creatures can exist with two brains have come back negative, although one has come back inconclusive."

Liz mimed taking notes at Doug's professorial delivery and turned her attention back to the guide. "Next, the largest of all the plant-eaters, the Titanosaur, weighing up to one hundred tons. Titanosaurs are named after the mythological 'Titans,' the deities of Greece. Up until ten years ago, this type of dinosaur was not even believed to have existed; once they were discovered, they were found to be far larger than the Brachiosaurus. They had two protective devices: A, their massive size, but also, B, their skin was found to be armored with a small mosaic of small, bead-like scales around a larger scale. One species has even been discovered with bony plates."

Doug leaned in again. "Most of these were average size, but there were also some that were an island-dwelling dwarf species, the result of allopatric—that's geographic—speciation."

Liz giggled, her hand in front of her mouth. "Okay, okay. College boy here has nothing on you. What else do you have to show me?"

Doug led Liz away from the tour through a couple more rooms, the African mammals and then the sharks, one of his favorites. "Now it's my turn," she said.

The Metropolitan Museum of Art, or the Met, was only a mile away by foot. Their welcoming committee, a group of employees on their smoking break, waved Doug over.

"Hey, Dougie, where you been, man?" shouted one of them.

"You know me," Doug said vaguely, "Around. Anything new in there we should see?"

"Got a great Kandinsky exhibit up on the third floor," said a small woman in a huge straw hat. Liz's eyes sparkled like a kid's on her first bicycle ride. "Let's go," she said, and took his arm.

They were waved past the ticket counter by yet another friend and moved past several works of art on the way to the elevator. Liz looked at him. "What are you, the mayor around here?"

"Nah, not quite. I've helped them out here from time to time. Filled in for a few people in emergencies. I don't mind, it's a great place to work. Too bad I don't know what I'm looking at half the time."

Up on the third floor Liz launched into a lecture, mimicking Doug's own prior professorial tone. "Wassily Kandinsky, died in 1944, one of the most important innovators of modern and abstract art. His works combine the qualities of Art Nouveau with the strong folk art of northern Russia." She walked Doug up to a painting called *Colour Circle and Square*, painted in 1913. The colors and shapes were so vibrant they leapt off the canvas. "Take a look at this piece," she said, "and then look how he enhances this style into a more elegant, complex approach—" she gestured to the wall on their left"—that resulted in beautifully balanced, jewel-like pictures. He's a genius."

Liz was awed by the artwork, but Doug was awed by Liz. Not only was Liz the single most smoking-hot woman he'd ever seen, but her capacity for intelligent conversation seemed limitless. Sapiosexually speaking, she'd keep him on his toes.

He watched as she paused to soak in the beauty of each painting. "Take this one, for example," she said. "*Rond et Pointu*, 1939. Look at the contrasting geometric shapes, the way he uses blues and purples, quite brilliant. So innovative, so many subtle nuances. Purple is such a powerful color, don't you think? Far more powerful than red. When used in this way, he's sending a real message. Kandinsky set the table for abstract art."

Doug was captivated, not by the artwork as she was clearly hoping he'd be, but by Liz and her passion for it. It had been a long time since he'd been around someone so happy with her life's work.

An hour later, sated with art and talk, they left the museum. "I should be getting home, Doug," Liz said. "I've had a really wonderful time."

"So soon?"

"I haven't been home since I left for the bar last night. That's almost twenty-four hours ago. I need to change my clothes, get ready for work...."

Doug raised his hand to signal a cab. "I understand. I'll ride with you."

"Oh, you don't have to do that. I have some things to do at home, and I have some work to do before I go in tomorrow. It's probably better that I...."

Was this a brush-off? After almost a whole day together? He nodded, going for casual indifference. *When will I see you again?* was what he really wanted to know.

"Here's my card," Liz said as a yellow taxi pulled up. She hastily scribbled her home number on the back and handed it to him, but didn't release it when he took hold. "I had better be hearing from you soon."

"Trust me, you will." He leaned down to kiss her. The taxi driver leered appreciatively. Doug couldn't help it, he preened.

27

With Liz gone, there was no way to keep the darkness at bay, and Doug's world crashed. He'd been resigned—well, at least he was working on being resigned—to the bleak existence of Circle membership. Now the only thing on his mind was what he'd be giving up. Just like the dinosaurs. Fighting to survive; nowhere to hide.

Then there was his laxness, his stupidity. He could have been killed. During all that time with Liz he'd been living on expired time. So busy thinking with his other brain he'd forgotten the only thing that should have mattered—staying alive. He desperately wanted to see her again. An hour felt like weeks. But he had more important things to worry about, like being someone's target.

At Tasker's, Randall Webb, the new recruit, was sitting alone at the bar. The room was quieter than Doug had seen it. Did killers rest on the Sabbath or keep it holy? Nah.

Webb's ashen look of stunned confusion and anger looked a lot like the same one Doug saw in the mirror most of the time. He took the next seat. "How was your night?"

"Rough. I kept thinking I dreamed it. But I knew I didn't." Webb's eyes were bright with exhaustion and a plea for absolution.

"Sorry, man, can't help you. I've been there...I'm still there."

"But what am I supposed to do? How do I get out? What about my life—my family?" Webb's words echoed Doug's own almost verbatim from the recent past.

"I hate to say it, man, but you're stuck, just like the rest of us."

"What do you mean 'stuck'? I thought all y'all guys agreed to it."

"Not all of us...I mean, did you?"

Webb's shoulders slumped even more.

The bar phone, a replica from the early 1900s with a handset and a stationary microphone, rang. The bartender moved to answer it. "Tasker's. Yes, I can put you in touch with Mr. Williams. One moment please." He depressed the receiver three times in succession and hung up.

Williams...why was that name so familiar?

"But how are these people supposed to know where I am?" Webb was saying.

"Have you gotten your envelope yet?"

"Yeah. But I was afraid to open it." He reached for his back pocket.

Doug held up his hands. "Keep that to yourself. But open it soon. It has all the information you need—who it is you're supposed to kill, addresses, bank accounts, work schedules, everything. Your hunters will all have the same workup on you. You'd be surprised how thorough they are."

"Who's *they*?"

"The Watchers. They...well...watch everything—and clean up after the fact. You know, afterwards."

That's it. Williams, one of the Watchers. That's where he'd heard the name. The bartender must be the conduit.

Webb blanched. "How did you do it?"

"Do what?"

"How did y'all kill your first...Mr. Archer?"

Doug hates that name, hates that a killer's moniker has become his own. He shouldn't but....

"You can call me Doug. But keep that between us, too. Listen, Webb, you seem like a good guy. If I find my way out of this, I'll do my best to help you out, too."

"Thanks, Mr.—Doug. But it sure seems hopeless."

Doug left Webb as he'd found him, staring morosely into his drink.

Traffic was heavy in all directions. He'd had an idea, a brilliant idea, sitting at the bar, but he needed help to pull it off. The first— the only—person that came to mind was Michelle's husband, John. Doug turned onto Bertha Avenue in his new F-150. How would he word his request? He'd have to wing it.

John came to the door in a pair of cargo shorts, a button-down Hawaiian shirt and flip-flops. Michelle complained that John generally worked Sundays, so today must be one of his rare days off. Their social networks rarely overlapped outside the office, but the three of them had checked out new movies and restaurants in the City from time to time. By now they knew the intricate details of each other's lives the way only close coworkers or a spouse could. John and Michelle were always arguing over whose friend Doug really was. John was pretty much a worka-holic and he never wanted to be far from the office.

The last time Doug was there Michelle said that John's ad agency mandated that he use some of his many vacation days. Basically, he was being forced to take three-day weekends for most of the summer. It was hard for Doug to imagine having to be forced to take off from work. Even work you liked.

"Doug E. Doug! What're you doing here? Come on in!"

"John Boy. What's happening?"

"Not much, taking another darn day off."

"Um, I think most people take off on Sunday."

"Standing in the way of progress," John said sadly.

Doug went straight for the La-Z-Boy.

"Michelle told me you came by the other night. I can't believe she didn't wake me up. What brings you all the way to Joisey again so soon?"

"I need to ask you a favor."

"Whatever you need. Michelle said you were kind of, well, out of sorts. That you'd taken a sabbatical. You okay?"

"Yeah, yeah, I'm fine."

John gave Doug a sharp look, but said nothing.

"Grab your wallet, dude," said Doug. "You're coming with me."

John had about a minute and a half to collect his wallet and keys before he was hanging on for dear life in Doug's truck, on the way to the City.

"Whoa, where's the Jeep?"

"I had to get rid of it. Alternator was shot." John knew nothing about cars. "Timing belt, too."

"Bummer," said John. "Well, truck's cool. Here." He turned around and tossed some spare change onto the floor of the back seat. "Italian tradition, brings good luck."

"Okay. But you're not Italian."

"Yeah, but I love their food."

Doug grimaced and went back to concentrating on the road, and his plan. More importantly, what he'd do if it didn't work, or if John didn't come through.

Jersey traffic was bumper-to-bumper and the ride was grueling. "All you have to do is call the number I give you and ask for a Mr. Williams," he told John. "If they ask for a name, give them a fake one, like John Lennon—well, maybe not so obvious. When you get connected, tell him you want to be a member, and that you want to meet him somewhere. That's it."

"And why do we have to go all the way into the City?"

"I don't want them to be able to trace this call back to you or Michelle."

"Doug, I don't get it. This actually sounds dangerous."

"It might be."

"Not the words I wanted to hear. What's going on with you, man? Michelle's worried, too."

"I can't tell you," Doug said, paying the toll for the Lincoln Tunnel back into Manhattan. "But this could be what saves me. If you're not comfortable, now's the time to bail."

John sat back. "Wow. I gotta be honest here, man. I'm not. He sighed. "But that doesn't mean I won't help you."

Doug pulled the truck over a block away from a phone booth with cracked glass and littered with fast food wrappers on the corner of 33rd and 8th Ave. He handed John a slip of paper with a phone number written on it. "See that pay phone? Call this number. I'm going to go around the block so no one sees us together. Just say exactly what I told you to say, then hang up. I'll be watching you. If they start asking questions you don't think you can answer, just hang up." Suddenly Doug had doubts. "Are you sure you're okay with this?"

"I don't know what *it* is, but I guess so," said John unconvincingly.

No time to argue the point. "I owe you one."

Doug drove down 33rd to 9th Ave and over to 34th Street. He parked in the middle of the block, out of range of traffic cameras. He watched from a distance with his binoculars. John walked up to the pay phone and reached his hand into his pocket for some change. Good thing the tri-state area still had a few phone booths left. They'd be joining the phone booth graveyard in the sky any day now. John was flipping a quarter in the air. He looked as nervous as....as John doing something he didn't really want to do.

Hang in there, dude. Stay calm.

John placed his right hand on the phone, but immediately pulled back as if it were burning hot. He looked at the phone number in his hand one more time. This time he actually picked up the receiver, but the paper in his hand was swept up in a gust of wind. John chased after it. Doug groaned. All the guy had to do was make a phone call and he was running around after a little piece of paper. Maybe this wasn't such a good idea after all. Maybe he should take John back to Jersey, forget the whole thing.

The Watchers could be anywhere. What if they were watching right now? Taking all this time to make a phone call wasn't normal. Doug was about to run after the damn paper himself and stuff John back into the car when John stomped on it. He held it up for Doug to see and pumped his fist in the air. *Got it!* he mouthed.

Doug took in a long breath and prayed.

John's hands were clammy and he was slightly out of breath. What was all this fuss about a phone call anyway? And why would Doug drag him all the way into New York to do it? What the hell had Doug gotten himself into anyway? It was craz—

"Tasker's," a man's voice said.

John promptly forgot his lines. "Um, hi, how are you?"

"Just fine, sir. Can I help you?"

"Oh, uh, yes, I was told I could find a Mr. Williams there."

"I can put you in touch with Mr. Williams. One moment please." The voice disappeared. Three short clicks of the phone, then a different ringing sound. A moment or two later, a new voice on the other end. "Williams."

"Um, yeah, I'd like to become a member," John said, remembering Doug's coaching.

"Who are you? How did you hear about us?"

"Um, name's Jason. I don't want to go into details on the phone," he ad-libbed.

"Understood," responded the voice. "I'll need to evaluate you. Today, if possible."

Okay. "Today is fine. Where?" Sweat poured down John's face, but it wasn't time for a handkerchief break. Mr. Williams was talking again.

"Go to the New York City Animal Shelter in Brooklyn. Ask to see a Dr. Williams. Tell them you have a ferret that won't eat. I'll be waiting for you." The phone went dead.

All the cloak-and-dagger stuff had him jumpy as hell. John ran to Doug's truck, trying not to forget his instructions. "New York Animal Shelter, Brooklyn, tell Dr. Williams you have a ferret that won't eat."

"Is that all? What else did he say?"

John gulped for air. "Well, for one, he asked me my name and how I heard about this 'club.'"

"Oh. What did you say?"

"I said I was Jason and I didn't want to go into details now. He bought it."

"Anything else?"

"That's it, just go to the Animal Shelter, ask for Dr. Williams, say you have a ferret that stopped eating."

"That's great, John. Thanks."

"You're welcome. But truthfully, this stuff makes me very, very nervous, and now I just want to go home."

"How about I take you to your wife instead?"

The ride uptown was virtually silent, neither man divulging what was going on in his mind, both figuring correctly that the other probably didn't want to know. Doug pulled up in front of the Natural History Museum. John gave Doug his hand as if to wish him luck and turned toward the main steps.

"Hey, John Boy," Doug called.

John leaned into the passenger side window.

"Thanks again, you don't know how important that was."

"Well, I just wish I knew what was going on, Doug. I mean, you're obviously in some kind of trouble and I hate the fact that we can't help—or you won't let us."

"I get that, I really do. But I can't talk about it right now. You're going to have to trust me on this one. Just don't mention any of this to anyone, not even Michelle, okay? You didn't see me today."

A limousine had pulled up behind Doug's vehicle and the guy was leaning on the horn.

John looked unhappy. Keeping this whopper a secret from his wife was asking a lot. "Don't worry," he finally said. "It never happened."

Doug put the car in drive before the limo driver lost his cool. John would be okay. He knew nothing about the Circle. They were just two guys, one of whom had to stop and make a phone call, right? It was time to head for Brooklyn with his poor sick ferret.

Doug took the Queens Midtown tunnel toward Brooklyn. He'd done more city driving in the past few weeks than he'd done in all the time he'd been living in New York. Most people didn't even keep cars in the City, but the whopping fee Doug paid for his space was now paying off in spades. Of course, now that money was no object...well, he'd be making some changes.

The tunnel was a strobe of dark and light, dark and light. He felt like a mole wishing for sight. How far was he willing to take this thing? He'd have to figure it out as he went along. Deal with the consequences. Not a comforting thought when the consequences could be death. He looked around for a hardware store. Saw only Starbucks and Taco Bells and Mickey D's. Out of the tunnel he consulted the Garmin that had come installed in the F-150. He located a hardware store along 495 next to a Walmart.

Brooklyn was pretty much uncharted territory for this Colorado transplant. He tracked his progress down 495, looking for the exit for Woodhaven Blvd. After he got off, it should only be a few minutes to Cross Bay Blvd. Then, at least according to the map, only a couple of miles to the New York Animal Shelter. Five minutes later he was parked in front of a large brick building with a parking garage connected by ramps. Prime real estate close to the city only meant one thing: money.

Doug slung his new duffel bag over his shoulder and entered the professional-looking building. The main counter was protected by two-inch-thick glass. The shelters he'd known had dirt paths and the sights and smells of too many animals in too small a space. This one was spotless and if all the animals in the waiting room were any indication, a veterinary hospital as well. At his entrance, a couple of the dogs growled and were pulled back by their owners. One was cleaning up the floor where his dog had had an accident; the rest were seated quietly, holding tightly to their animals or carrier boxes. Muted sounds of more barking dogs and chirping birds rose and fell in the background.

A receptionist with teased red hair a mile high spoke from around a big wad of gum. "Can I help you?"

"Yes, I'm here to see Dr. Williams. My ferret won't eat."

The receptionist looked pointedly at his hands, which clearly did not hold any kind of a ferret, let alone one that refused to eat, but got up from her seat. "Just a moment," she said and exited through a door that said "Employees Only."

"Ferret won't eat, huh?"

The elderly man in long brown slacks, a white button-down shirt, a sweater vest, bow tie, and hat looked as if he were going to teach a lecture or attend some important legal meeting. Fifty years ago. Someone Doc would have shared space with. Doug shrugged. Doc didn't even like animals.

"You know what I used to do," the man offered helpfully. "Crush up a banana and hand-feed it. Of course this was sixty years ago, when I was a kid. ...Where's yours?"

"Um, what?"

"Your ferret. Where is he?"

"Oh. Um, in the car. He freaks out around other animals."

The old man nodded sagely. "Know just what you mean. Skittish little guys."

The wait was taking much too long. Where was the woman? His sense of unease grew. One more minute. Then he was outta there.

The gray metal door opened with a swoosh. "You can go through, now," the woman said. She pointed to her right. "Through that door there, then left down the stairs."

It didn't feel right, but he followed the woman's instructions, having to flatten himself against it to avoid sideswiping her chest, and took a left down the stairs as instructed. A man at the bottom stood silently with a lab coat on. "Williams?"

The man shook his head no. "Go out through that emergency exit," he said, and went back up the stairs.

So much intrigue. But how secret would a secret society stay if it didn't take precautions. *Yeah, and now you're at the bottom of a staircase in a building you know nothing about in the middle of Brooklyn. How do you spell T—R—A—P?*

He pushed open the emergency exit, half expecting an alarm to go off. Nothing. His tension fell maybe a decimal, but the adrenaline kicked in big time. He felt the familiar rush of the hunt, blood pumping, heart beating faster. His hands were steady and dry; no shakes, no clammy sensation. He stuck a hand in his duffel bag, took hold of his knife, and stashed it in his back pocket.

The back door opened onto an alley. A big green dumpster sat against the back wall. A guy in a blue surgical gown and scrub mask was leaning against it.

"Dr. Williams? I'm here about my ferret. He won't eat."

The "doctor's" eyes slit and then got wide. Then he swung around and took off down the alley.

Doug gave chase down Essex Street, throwing his bag over his shoulder, closing in. He'd been made. The guy had to be a member, a Watcher probably.

The blue gown tore around the corner of the parking garage, but Doug lost sight of it in the time it took him to make it around the same corner. Rows and rows of cars as far as he could see. He stood motionless, slowing his breathing. Guy had to be there somewhere. Doug heard the sound of papery scrubs brushing against a car. He crept behind the first row of vehicles to his right and ducked down to look underneath. He caught a glimpse of blue three cars up—and then it was gone.

He got down on his hands and knees and scuttled through cigarette butts and oil slicks until he reached the spot where he'd seen the speck of color. There it was again. Another three cars up. Doug put on a burst of speed, tough from his low-lying stance. In a few seconds he was almost on top of the guy, who was checking the other side of the vehicles. When he settled back thinking he was clear, Doug made his move, jumping out from behind the last car, a hideous pink Cadillac with a Mary Kay sign in the window. He launched himself at the form in the blue scrubs.

The guy fought hard, you had to give him that. Doug fought harder. He strong-armed Williams to his feet, drew the knife from his pocket, and held it up to his throat, dragged him into the parking garage elevator, and pushed the button for the roof. They slowly rose to the top level of the parking structure. When the doors opened Doug shoved him into the far corner and onto the ground on his knees. He took some rope out of the duffle bag and used it to bind the guy's arms behind his back. The guy hadn't uttered a word since they'd met in the alley.

Doug unlocked his hunting knife and placed it on the ground within reach. "I'm going to make this simple," he said. He reached into the bag and pulled out his pliers, then sandpaper, and finally a hammer. "So listen carefully. I want out. I don't want to have to use these, but have no doubt that I will. And if they don't work, I'm going to remove that mask of yours so I can see your face. And we both know what that means." The man was sweating, but didn't seem unduly alarmed.

Doug punched him in the nose and heard the crack. "Do you think I'm joking?!"

Blood dripped from "Williams'" nose and mouth.

"Say something, you sick asshole!"

The guy laughed. A sickening sound.

"Something funny, Doc?"

"Mr. Matthews was right. You're perfect for the Circle."

"Perfect, huh?" Doug closed the pliers around Williams' ear and squeezed. Hard. The guy sucked in his breath, which was now ragged. "Yeah, perfect. I mean, look at you. You hunted me down and you're ready to kill me, to torture me. You tell me how that isn't perfect."

"The difference is I'm going to kill you because I want to, not because I have to."

So not true. Not true if he lived for a million years.

"Really, Mr. Archer? I have not attacked you. Rumor has it that you said you'd only kill in self-defense."

His own words. Thrown back in his face. "That's only because you—the Circle—all of you—are attacking my way of life." Doug raised his fist and punched the guy's nose. "And I'll defend that..." punch "...until the day..." punch "...I die. ...You hear me? I want OUT!"

"But I can't," the man managed, spitting blood. "It's not a decision I can make. The Circle has accepted you. There's no... way...out."

"Wrong answer."

"But Mr. Archer, I can't—"

Doug punched him hard in the stomach. "Stop calling me that!"

"Kill me," the man said, panting, "or I kill myself. Tomorrow... there'll be another Watcher t' take...my place. It's futile. The Circle's far bigger...than you an' me. I can't let you out, 'cause there is no 'out'...for either of us. The sooner you accept that... the better."

Doug heard the words. They were meaningless.

"I've been doin' this...for a long time," the guy continued, spitting more blood, "...never seen anyone so insistent...to be released. Admirable...really...but...changes nothing."

Sick of all the talk, Doug picked up the hunting knife and pressed it across the man's jugular. "Last chance, Doc."

The man pushed his throat closer to the blade. "I am a Watcher of the Circle," he said. He lurched forward and sliced open his own throat on the blade.

Doug recoiled. Blood turned the man's blue gown a dark shade of purple. Doug's mind flashed back to his conversation with Liz about the power of color, the power of purple. What would she have to say about this?

The only way out of the Circle had just slipped through his fingers. The Watcher was dead.

Doug used the bottom of the blue surgical gown to clean the blood off his blade and locked it closed. He picked up the hammer, the pliers, and the sandpaper he hadn't used—stupid to think he could have—and took the ropes off Williams' hands. If the Watchers were as good as billed it would be as if he'd never existed. Doug bowed his head for a moment and left the scene.

28

The table was set for two, but only one place-setting had been used. By the second sat a single white rose in full bloom. Liz raised her glass to the rose and then took a final swig of the full-bodied red wine and got up from the table. Toasting her father once a year like this is all she has left of the man she loved—and misses—so much.

Silently she went about the task of cleaning up her dishes and putting on some coffee. On the day she set aside to remember she let the staff go home early, cooked her own meal, and drank wine alone.

Finished in the kitchen, she settled in the living room. On the way she nabbed a new bottle and a cork screw from the small wine room off the dining area. She curled up into the plush sofa, setting down her cut-crystal glass only long enough to open and pour from the new bottle. It hadn't breathed properly—her father would be horrified.

The paintings on the walls are the only things she chooses to see, the only things that can pull her out of herself when she is in this state. The townhouse has many of them, some replicas, but most authentic Van Goghs, a Monet, a Renoir, and of course, a Kandinsky. Orson Hughes was a serious collector—and now they were hers. She adored them, but she'd rather have her father back.

She picked up the fourteen-karat-gold picture frame that held the last picture of Orson Hughes and his daughter ever taken on the night he died. They'd gone to the theatre first and then to The Four G's for dinner. It was his favorite restaurant. They'd ordered that super-expensive wine.

The bullet had found its mark precisely, almost artistically, before they'd even ordered their meals. During the bedlam that followed, Orson Hughes was carted off by the EMTs to the hospital.

The thing that had made the whole thing so bizarre was that by the time she, his only daughter Elizabeth, had arrived at Mount Sinai Hospital and made her way to the emergency room, his body had gone missing. She'd hounded the police for an entire year, banking on her father's close relationship with both the mayor of New York and the police chief, but they'd come up empty. Supposedly. At first, she'd been their prime suspect. They'd put surveillance teams on her house, taps on her phone, both at home and at work, and constant unmarked tails followed her around the city. They wanted to know what she planned on doing with all the money. Every new clue, every dead end, all led back to her. "I don't want the money," she always said. "I just want my father back." Thanks to Orson Hughes' meticulous foresight, she already had plenty of her own.

Then suddenly they'd dropped the investigation. One day they were hounding her; the next day they were gone. They had nothing to tell her. No answer for how a body could disappear from an ambulance, never arrive in the emergency room or the morgue or the crime lab. She'd never been able to say goodbye.

For years she and her father hadn't known of each other's existence. For most of her life, Liz's mother maintained that her father had died long before, an ultimately futile attempt at trying to protect Liz from the evil man her mother had convinced herself that Orson Hughes had become. As he'd gone about amassing his billions, her mother had watched his journey, as the rest of the city did, through newspaper headlines and television interviews. As his power and wealth grew, Liz's mother grew more certain that the temptations of money would only corrupt her innocent little girl—even as that innocent little girl became a woman. It was only when Liz's mother died that Liz began a search, piecing together one detail after another from old papers, letters, and innuendos. When she finally established her father was Orson Hughes, with the help of a very good, very expensive, private eye, it was like winning the lottery.

Enough procrastination. Enough fear. Liz picked up the phone to call Orson Hughes. What did she have to lose? His office assistant Colleen answered. Liz haltingly explained the situation to her. Was it possible to speak to him? Colleen had been surprisingly polite, helpful even. "I'll hand this message to him personally," she had assured Liz, "He'll be thrilled to meet you, Ms. Reynolds, I'm sure."

A week passed, then another and another. Even if her father's assistant gave him the message, he hadn't taken it seriously. Either that or he didn't want anything to do with her. Her mother had probably been right. "You have a daughter," could scare even one—perhaps especially one—of the wealthiest, most powerful men in the country.

She wasn't done yet, though. She'd go for a more direct approach. The next day she made it all the way to the floor of his office by blending in with the crowd of coffee-chugging office-workers. His inner sanctum would be impenetrable. She'd wait in the hall outside the carved mahogany double doors, just outside the range of the receptionist's vision, and hope her milling about would go unnoticed in the business of the day. For hours she alternated pacing outside the doors with brief visits to the ladies' room, afraid to leave her stakeout for too long, afraid she'd miss him altogether. If that happened, she might lose her nerve as well.

Lunch time came and went. Liz bemoaned her lack of foresight in bringing a snack. He had to come out some time, though, didn't he? Her blood sugar was reaching a dangerously low level when a security guard rounded the corner. Liz prepared herself to be removed by force, but he continued on to open a locked door farther down the hall. A man stepped out and headed for the elevator, the one on the end that needed a key to access.

Orson Hughes. Her father.

A sharply dressed confident man in a million-dollar suit. A man who "shook the very ground beneath his competitors," or so the Wall Street Journal *said. Liz would have one shot and one shot only. She'd better make it good.*

"Mr. Hughes. Mr. Hughes, I have to speak with you, It's very important."

Hughes didn't look up from his phone. The guard stepped between them. "Make an appointment with my assistant. I'm afraid I'm late for a meeting."

"But...I'm your daughter," Liz blurted.

The guard froze, one hand ready to unlock the private elevator, the other on his walkie-talkie.

"Impossible," Orson Hughes said after one short beat. "I don't have a daughter. You shouldn't be here. You want money, is that it?"

"Sir, would you like me to remove this woman?" asked the guard.

"I don't want money, I just want to get to know you," Liz said. "It's taken me a long time to find out who you were, but now that I know I can't just—"

"Young lady," Hughes interrupted, "you are not the first to try something like this—I dare say you won't be the last. I'll say to you what I say to all of them. Prove it."

Liz swallowed the lump in her throat. "My mother was Amanda Reynolds."

The words echoed off the marble floors. Hughes stopped walking.

"Excuse me?"

"Amanda Reynolds. She was my mother."

"Was?"

"She died two years ago. Leukemia."

"Mandy's dead?"

"Yes, sir. I'm her daughter, Elizabeth."

There wasn't too much left in the world that still surprised Orson Hughes, but the things that did required his attention. This might be one of them. "Perhaps we should continue this conversation behind closed doors," he said, and gestured to his office.

He and Liz's mother had met in 1976 at a bicentennial party, Hughes told her. They were poor, but in love. She got pregnant. He wanted to marry her. "But as time went on, Mandy wasn't happy. With what I was doing. With what she called my pursuit of the dollar—my dogged pursuit of the dollar. She left me. And I let her go."

A letter had finally come after months of silence. She said she'd miscarried and that he wasn't to try to find her or contact her. He'd complied.

"When is your birthday, Ms. Reynolds?"

"August 21, 1978."

"Mandy told me she'd miscarried after four months...it was the end of March, that same year," he said. "I suppose it's possible....

A week later the results were in, the blood samples an undeniable match.

They'd both been lonely. When her father asked her to move to New York from Hoboken, she didn't hesitate. He'd bought her the townhouse she lived in now, paid off the mortgage, then told her to furnish it however it pleased her. In college she'd put up posters of her favorite paintings, never dreaming that the genuine articles would be gracing her walls.

She told him she didn't need his money, just his time and love, but he'd doted on her, and she'd lived in grace and gratitude. Three years after they'd officially found each other, she legally changed her name from Reynolds to Hughes, but used her old name at work. No one there needed to know who she was. He told her it was the first gift anyone had given him in thirty years that he couldn't get on his own.

A year later Liz's promise to herself to find his murderer had been mercilessly unsuccessful. She'd spent a small fortune on investigations, the only money she'd spent from her inheritance, but nothing had surfaced. Until now.

She picked up the phone and dialed the number on the plain white business card in her hand. "Yes," she said, "I'm looking for Mr. Williams."

PART III

29

None of the people Doug had killed were prey, and not all of them were intentional, but six human beings had died because of him. The professor, Eric, the two Watchers in the Charger, Mr. Silence—the guy he'd hit with the crossbow and who'd earned him his new name—and, of course "Dr. Williams." No word from anyone in the Circle about the incident in Brooklyn. Why not? If they had eyes everywhere, why hadn't he been spoken to, reprimanded...something? Was it a good thing or a bad thing?

"I'm grabbing another one. You thirsty?"

He and Randall were in Tasker's back room, playing an intense game of cricket. "No, thanks, I'm okay."

"Suit yourself. I'll be right back."

The room was nearly empty. What were all the other members of the Circle out doing? Oh, yeah. That's right. Killing each other.

"If I'm not intruding, Mr. Archer?" Stahl had been reading the *Wall Street Journal* at another table.

Doug gave a small nod. He still didn't like the guy.

"A little piece of advice, if you don't mind."

"Why not? You wouldn't be the first. I'm sure you won't be the last."

STAHL (cocking his head): "I see you are becoming rather friendly with Mr. Webb. But it may not, shall we say, be in your best interest to become too close. You never know what can happen. As we say in my country, *freundlich sein, nicht freunde.* You understand me?"

Doug shrugged. The overall gist was clear enough.

STAHL: "Be friendly, but not friends. Makes sense?"

"Unfortunately," said Doug, "it does."

STAHL (returning to his paper): *"Gŭt."*

Moments later Webb returned with a new beer.

"Let's go sit out at the bar," Doug said.

The two men left the parlor and sat down at two stools away from all the others at the bar. Doug pulled his stool closer to Webb's and placed his arms on the polished wood.

"So, Randall, that way out I thought I found. It fell through. I'm sorry."

"I figured it would. I figure we got about a snowball's chance in hell to get out of this place.

"Listen, I've been meaning to ask you," said Randall. "Did y'all find it hard to leave? The safe house, I mean."

"Yeah. I still do. It's hard to adjust. But we have to rely on our instincts—that's why they chose us anyway. In my case, I think they saw some kind of potential for enjoyment—like if they were wrong they win 'cause they get to kill me, but if they're right about me then they get entertained by watching me kill others. I've been brought here for their viewing pleasure."

"Well, I'll tell you what, when I walk home, I'm afraid of things I never noticed before. I'm hearing strange noises, lookin' around bushes and trees. It's pathetic."

"Yeah, well, welcome to the f-ing Circle."

"But, how did y'all deal with it? I mean, obviously I want to survive, but...."

"Let me ask you something, Webb. How did you end up in New York anyway?"

"Company got relocated. It was either pack up and move or unemployment. I wasn't tied down back in Texas, so here I am."

"What did you do?"

"Middle management stuff. Worked my ass off to get there, too. I started off as an electrician. Then one day I was in an office building fixing a fuse panel. I happened to mention something to the boss, a way I thought the company could save money. Bingo, got promoted."

The guy looked more like a rodeo rider than an electrician. "Well, I'm sorry you got caught up in all this. But I can tell you one thing, as much as I can help you, I will."

"Well, thanks, man. Some of it's not so bad anymore... it's like I got this big promotion and now I can have just about anything I want. All that money...and the women are hotter 'n two goats in a pepper patch."

Doug laughed so hard beer nearly sprayed out of his nose. "You sure don't look much like a killer, Webb," he said.

"Only when my country needs me." Webb rolled up his sleeve to reveal a Marine Corps tattoo.

"You served? When?"

"Did two tours of the Gulf, helped liberate Iraq. Now that's some crazy shit. I hoped my killing days were over, but I guess, in a really sad way, it kinda prepared me for all this."

Randall Webb, Lance Corporal in the Marine Corps, in charge of a small fire team just outside Baghdad, was under evaluation for his leadership skills. His team of five, along with other small teams, had responded to the bombing of the Canal Hotel. As they'd maneuvered through the smoke of the wreckage, gunfire had broken out. The sky rained bullets. They were sitting ducks down on the ground. Lance Corporal Randall Webb ordered his men to take cover. They obeyed. Webb gave another order, "Return fire," and again they obeyed. In the near-zero visibility they shot blind into the rubble.

Flashes of muzzle fire could be seen through the dust from the rooftops surrounding the hotel. Webb ordered his men to stand by, but his command was drowned out by the sounds of the firefight. A bullet struck PFC Walters, entering his left shoulder and penetrating through to the chest cavity. When Walters fell, the remaining members of his team dragged him to the safest place they could find amidst the debris. Webb turned and fired, spraying the neighboring rooftop with bullets. A body fell.

Webb ordered his men to tend to their injured brother, while he wove his way around the burning flesh and electrical wires to investigate with PFC Jacobsen, his best and most talented soldier.

The firing had ceased. The two men, eyes stinging, searched for the fallen terrorist. With Jacobsen monitoring the rooftops, Webb found what he was looking for: a soldier's dead body. But it turned out this was the body of a young boy. He was still holding onto an assault rifle, strapped across each shoulder with a bandoleer. He'd been shot three times through the stomach and once through the head. He couldn't have been more than ten or eleven. His blood was everywhere, his stomach torn open, organs spilling onto the ground.

Webb led Jacobsen back to the team. The bullet that had punctured Walters' shoulder had done some serious damage to his lungs; he was struggling to breathe. Webb gave the order to move out, get medical attention. Back at the base, PFC Walters was pronounced dead after three hours of surgery to repair the damage to his lungs and liver.

Randall Webb had turned down every leadership position he was offered from that day forward. When his time was up he went back home to Texas and tried his best to forget.

"Sorry, man," Doug said. It wasn't much, but all he could come up with. What do you say to something like that?

"It's all in the past," Webb said. It was the first time he'd ever shared his story with anyone. Must be the bizarre camaraderie the Circle inspired.

"I was cleared by the Military Review Board. They said I made all the right tactical decisions, that it was a justifiable kill. But a little boy died, a little boy who'd killed one of my men. I couldn't make sense of it." He looked at Doug. "I just don't know how I can be a killer again."

"I can't help you there," said Doug. "The best thing I can tell you is what some of the other members told me. Be aware of everything that's happening around you. Don't leave anything to chance. Surveil everything, notice everything, don't be surprised by anything. But you can probably give me better advice than I can give you."

"Well, I appreciate it anyway. I know one thing, though, I won't pull a trigger ever again."

Doug nodded. To each his own.

"If you need anything, Webb, let me know....unless I'm your target. Then you're on your own." It wasn't meant to be funny and they both knew it.

"Thanks, man, I'll keep that in mind."

Webb hummed the theme song to James Bond as he made his way to the door, his back and arms spread up against the wall as if hugging it, and then ducked under the windows.

Doug raised his glass one more time and laughed, this time for real.

Webb left Tasker's and all semblance of humor left his face. The picture in his pocket was of Mr. Stahl, a prominent member of the Circle both here and in Europe. Webb had met him a few times in the back room, but had never engaged him in conversation or a game of cards. The guy's coldness could put out a fire. And if he was as calculating as he looked, it might put out Webb's flame forever.

The house in which Mr. Stahl chose to live while in the States did not quite fit with the others in this diverse Queens neighborhood. His lawn was a bit larger than his neighbors' almost non-existent ones; his house was three prominent stories compared to the two-stories surrounding it. Most of the members preferred to live in New York City proper, but Mr. Stahl liked to get out when he could, where it was quiet and where no one knew him—or cared. The cab fares were costly, but money was nothing, not when it could be replenished at the—what was that expression?—oh, yes, at the drop of a hat. Mr. Stahl likes learning American colloquialisms.

The cab driver pulled over to let him out, said a pleasant good day, and drove off. Mr. Stahl took in the details, checked for discrepancies in the norm. Nothing appeared altered. No one had trampled the flower beds, the garage door was closed (and locked), the newspaper was where the boy always left it on his stairs. Even the ant hills appeared to have remained constant.

There was a stillness in the air and the chirping of the morning birds mingled with the grinding of the garbage truck making its rounds. The sights and sounds of his own country were far more compelling, but this would do very nicely for now.

Mr. Stahl was a careful man. Of course that was the nature of his existence and if he weren't he'd most certainly be dead by now. He checked that the trip wires he'd affixed the night before were still in place at the back and front doors and at all the windows. Only then did he reach into his pocket for his keys. A nice quiet cup of coffee out on the enclosed porch would do nicely right now, and then perhaps an hour with the newspaper. Other than Tasker's, here in New York his house was his sanctuary.

It hadn't taken much to get into Stahl's house—in fact, he'd been surprised by the target's lack of tight security. Where were all the fancy precautionary measures? Where was the top-of-the-line security system? Who didn't know that overconfidence could get you killed? All it took was a simple know-how of electrical wiring in order to rewire the doorknob to the fuse box by bypassing the electrical outlet directly inside the door. Every ounce of power from the house was now channeled into the metal lock plate. Easy as taking candy from a baby.

Mr. Stahl put his right hand around the door handle and with the other eased the key into the lock. As soon as his hand touched the doorknob he knew something was wrong.

He had no time to react, even to think about how or why. As the shock reverberated, his hand contracted around the metal, refusing to let go. He gyrated violently for several seconds. Even if he could have pried his hand from the door physically, the signal from his brain couldn't make it down into his hand, which was sending the sizzling pulse of electricity throughout his body.

Mr. Stahl's body convulsed for a moment or two after his passing. The birds never stopped their twittering.

The Fink was impressed. Mr. Webb had made it through Mr. Stahl's complex system of booby-traps without a hitch. Naturally, he would rather have had the pleasure of making the kill himself, but watching was entertaining as well.

The garbage truck had provided a nice cover. No one looks twice at the things they see every day; they become complacent and, hence, easy targets. Look at Mr. Stahl, a perfect example.

The Fink drove to the end of the block and took out his list of names. The dead body of the trash collector on the seat next to him had begun to stink. It was time to return to the car he'd parked a block away. He reconsidered his list: ~~Stahl~~, Dart, ~~Goodwin~~ Archer, Webb. It was time to have a little fun.

30

The Rainbow Room at Thirty Rockefeller Plaza boasted, arguably, the most breathtaking view of the city. The restaurant revolved a few degrees every few minutes, typically accomplishing one complete revolution throughout the course of a relaxed, exorbitantly priced meal. Doug, Liz, Michelle, and John were sitting at one of the tables closest to the window listening to dessert options on a wheeled cart presented by a heaveyset woman with a too-black beehive after a three-course dinner that shouted Michelin.

"We'll have one each of those," Doug said, pointing to a slice of pecan pie, a bowl of blueberry crumble, a piece of cherry cheesecake, and the chocolate mousse cake. Oh, and a piece of the zabaglione, of course. And don't forget the Fonseca, 1997, please." He smiled magnanimously, relishing the look on his friends' faces. "Relax, I told you, dinner is on me."

"You know we can't let you do that," said Michelle.

"Why not?" asked John.

Michelle elbowed John in the ribs. "Because, you jerk, it's a lot of money and Doug is a lowly tour guide on sabbatical."

Sarcasm. Good. Keep it light.

It was painfully obvious he hadn't gone to any of the locales he'd claimed to be visiting for his now clearly fraudulent sabbatical.

"He can pay for me," Liz said with a grin.

"Shut up, everyone, it's on me, no questions asked. I told you. I came into some money. Some great uncle I never heard of left my mom and me a boatload." It wasn't a bad lie and it came easily. Which reminded him. He had to go to the bank. He planned to set up an account with the Circle's money for his mother. Before the inevitable happened. He'd been calling her frequently, which had her half thrilled and half anxious.

The waitress arrived with the wine bottle and four small liqueur glasses.

"Cheers, Doug." John raised his glass. Thanks for being the nephew of a rich guy."

"My pleasure."

"Hey, I meant to ask you. How's your ferret?"

Doug swallowed wrong and choked.

Liz slapped him on the back a couple of times. "Are you okay?"

"F—fine."

"You don't have a ferret."

"Yeah, when did you get a ferret?" Michelle asked. "Those things are nasty—nothing more than giant rats."

Doug scrambled. "John's crazy. I told him I was *thinking* of getting a ferret. A friend was giving one away. But I had to take it to the vet first."

"Okay, this makes no sense," said Michelle. John, copping to his mistake, blanched.

"Yeah, well, it turns out it was sick anyway. Too sick to save. They had to put it down."

"Aaww," the two women said in unison.

"I guess I didn't get a chance to tell you about it. Hey, look, here's dessert," said Doug. "Who wants to share what?"

Doug put his arm around Liz who was shivering in the cold night air despite her wool coat and scarf. It had been a practically snowless winter so far, but they were predicting a whopper of a storm in the next few days and the cold was biting. Doug let go of Liz to bend down. He pretended to retie his shoe. He checked the perimeter. A man smoking a cigarette was leaning against a building across the street a couple of hundred yards behind them. It was damn chilly to be lounging about. Doug made a mental note, then stood back up and resettled his arm back around Liz. "Would you like to catch a cab instead? It's cold."

Liz took out her gloves. One slipped to the ground. Doug went to pick it up. "No, I'd like to walk, especially after an amazing dinner like that, and all the booze. You know, Doug, you can let me pay for dinner once in a while. I *am* rich."

Doug laughed and handed her the glove. "True, but the way I was brought up men paid for dinner when they took a lady out." Liz shook her head at him. "Fine," he said. "Next time dinner's on you."

As he rose he cast another sidelong look to see if the smoking man was gone. Nope. Still there. Now leaning against a light post, keeping a constant distance between them.

Don't panic. Stick to the plan. The guy could be a Watcher or a hunter...but more likely just a guy who likes to lean against things and smoke.

Not that he wanted to find out. If anything happened to Liz....

He raised his arm to hail a cab. "You know what, it's really cold. Let's take a cab the rest of the way, okay? Taxi!" he yelled at the first cab he saw. Liz gave her address. As they pulled away the dark figure moved to the other side of the road. Doug would probably never know his story.

The game was always on, though. As much as he enjoyed being with Liz, the game never stopped, never slowed. The game was always on.

Doug paid the driver at the townhouse. "Wait here," he said. He walked Liz to the base of the stairs and took her in his arms.

"You're not coming in?"

"Not tonight. I forgot to take care of something, and it's either tonight or early tomorrow morning."

"You sure I can't change your mind?" Liz said, nuzzling his neck.

His instant response was as predictable as one of Pavlov's dogs. "Sorry, I'd really, really like to, but not this time. I can't." He kissed her on the forehead, "I have to go. But I'll talk to you soon." He waited until Liz had ascended the stairs and unlocked her door before he went back to the cab.

Liz stayed on the stoop long enough to wave goodbye. As soon as the taxi was out of sight, she bent down and picked up the blue envelope with her name on it, HUGHES, in big black block letters. Finally! She was really in. She was lucky Doug had something else to do. How could she have explained *this*? *Oh, don't mind that, it's just my initiation packet for this club of assassins I joined recently.*

Inside, Liz took off her winter coat, her black thigh-high boots, her gloves, and scarf. The townhouse was kept at a constant seventy degrees, perfect for walking around barefoot.

She opened the envelope. Schedules, account numbers, addresses, flight itineraries, everything she could hope for in one place. Lastly, she found a note:

Ms. Hughes - Despite your lack of experience, the Circle is allowing your membership due to your relentless inquiries, obvious dedication to learning the necessary skills, and passion for the hunt. We remind you, however, that once you have your revenge, your life will continue to belong to us. Enjoy the hunt, Ms. Hughes. - The Circle

Liz wasn't cold anymore, but a chill ran up her spine and reached her neck and she involuntarily shuddered. She knew the rules, probably better than some of the members. She had willingly accepted them. It was a deadly game she was playing, one where the odds were not in her favor, but there was nothing—*nothing*—that would stand in her way. Finally she could put into motion the plan she had been designing since the night Mr. Cufflinks had taken her father from her side.

31

Without knowing it at the time, Randall Webb had taken a page out of Mr. Stahl's book when he'd chose this tranquil spot outside Hoboken, New Jersey for his home. Now it feels like he has something in common with the man he's just killed, that it has bonded them somehow, albeit in a perverse sort of way.

Webb often missed his Texas life, the space, the bigness of everything. Here everyone was all packed together, like steers in a packing plant instead of on the open range. It made him feel desperate for the open sky. Maybe he'd take his furlough and go home for a while, camp out under the stars, get him some good old fashioned R&R.

His walls were covered with reminders of that life. Him and his sisters on Lake Travis in Austin. A glossy wooden clock in the shape of his beloved state of Texas, the one he'd bought at the Dallas airport. A picture of his fire team, taken in Iraq. On the mantel sat a framed newspaper headline: "Indians Set

Team Record," and under that was a picture of Randall sacking the Burleson QB with the caption "Keller holds Burleson to 55 total yards." Webb's old navy blue-and-gold football helmet, covered with stickers signifying the various accomplishments of his high-school career, sat on his desk. A potted cactus held his Marine Corps dog-tags and more pictures of him and his family filled a bookshelf. Webb carried his beer over to his recliner, and toasted his father. "What the hell else am I supposed to do, Pop?"

His father had always told him that if he did what was in his heart he would never go wrong. But he didn't think Pop could have imagined this particular scenario. And now his heart was filled with doubt. He'd sworn he'd never kill again, and that was what he was doing—and would have to keep doing over and over and over again to stay earth bound—not under it. He'd rented this house for its tranquility, but there was precious little of that now that he'd become a hunter of men.

"I don't think you have an answer for this one, huh, Pop?" In a moment of self-pity, Webb swept his arm across the shelf. Picture glass and pottery shattered on the floor. A slip of yellow paper he'd never seen before had loosened from behind the picture of his parents. Curious, he unfolded it, breathing heavily. It was his father's handwriting, dated a year before his death.

Randall, I don't know if I'll ever be able to tell you how proud I am of you today. There were some bumps in the road but you got here. It means so much to your mother and me that you went back to school and that you're going to college! Remember, son, your family loves you very much and will always be here for you. Best of luck, study hard, and if you get lost, follow your heart...it's sure to lead you in the right direction. Love, Pop

Randall felt a pinch in his right upper chest. Blood splattered on the letter he was holding in his hands. No! He still had time off. Weeks even. He dropped to his knees. The next shot came through the window, this one missing him by a hair. He rolled to the table and grabbed his pistol.

Outside, the Fink cut the electricity to the house. Instantly it went dark. He kicked open the front door and headed for the living room where he'd last sighted Webb. His night-vision goggles revealed furniture in stark contrast. "Come out, come out, wherever you are," he called.

Webb's wound had almost put him out of commission. From behind the sofa he held the pistol in his left hand, but he was a weak shot on that side, so it was less than ideal. He had other weapons stashed. He dragged himself around the sofa, wincing at the loud crunch of the broken glass.

The Fink came up from behind him and Tasered him in the neck. "Mr. Webb," he said, "you've turned out to be yet another disappointment. Not half the fight I was hoping for."

Webb's upper body was only partially numb. He'd play it up. His gaping at the stranger in black was no act.

The Fink prodded the photo of Webb's family with his foot. "Too bad your family here won't have the pleasure of your company ever again."

The words hit him like a bomb going off. Webb's foot shot out and chopped his attacker's kneecap. The Fink went down with a loud crunch. The Taser went flying. Weaponless, Webb used his fists to punch the Fink in the stomach and kidneys.

The Fink realized his miscalculation. Webb had a lot of body mass. A higher Taser setting would have done the trick. He crumpled to the floor, his knee on fire, taking the punches, planning his next move. When Webb reared up to strike again, this time with a football helmet in his hand, the Fink took a small blade from his boot and pressed the latch to open the six-inch serrated blade that could cut through a tree trunk. He held it down by his side, poised and ready.

Webb felt the man weakening beneath him. He raised his left arm high and swung. The helmet hit the Fink's jaw just as the Fink plunged his blade into Webb's abdomen, where it lodged deep in his gut. He screamed.

The Fink twisted the blade, feeling the hot blood of his opponent flowing onto his clothes, his skin.

In a minute it was over. Webb lay motionless. The Fink rolled him off like so much debris. "Quite the disappointment, indeed," he whispered and yanked out the blade, which unsettled with a satisfying slurping sound. He wiped it on Webb's sleeve and stashed it back in its sheath.

The Fink tied a piece of his own shirt around his knee to stabilize it for the ride back. He was used to pain. He searched for a small memento of the kill, settled for the newspaper article from Randall's high school football career, and left the house the way he'd entered. Back in his vehicle he took out his ring of photos. He stopped at Randall Webb's. With a red marker he drew an "X" through his face.

32

Doug had come to think of Tasker's as his second home. Each time he came through the door he did so with a sigh of relief. The cab ride over tonight was a thoughtful one. About the tour at the museum he'd taken with Liz the morning after they'd met. It was the dinosaur, the Stegosaurus, that stayed with him. Herbivores that fought, not because they wanted to, necessarily, but when they had to.

Mr. Dart and Mr. Lion were sitting at the bar, talking with the bartender. "I figured it out," Doug said. "I figured out what we are."

MR. DART: "And?"

"Dinosaurs."

MR. LION: "I hope you're not directing that at me."

"Not at all, Mr. Lion."

When had he started referring to the members of the Circle as "Mr." and "Ms." in his own mind? He couldn't remember, and this scares him even more than thinking of Tasker's as his home away from home.

MR. DART: "I can't wait to hear this logic."

"It breaks down like this. Way back before anything human, life was simple. The carnivores killed the herbivores. But it was too easy. So Mother Nature decided to give the herbivores a way to defend themselves. So now, dinosaurs are killing other dinosaurs and it's not even for food, but for survival. And now that's all we are. The Circle is nothing more than a bunch of prehistoric creatures, only we don't have the common sense to see it. It's not like we have peanut-sized brains either. We're smart. Smart enough to found billion-dollar companies. Smart enough to go to the moon. So, my question is this. Why aren't we smart enough to see our own animalistic behavior? I mean, we're not starving, we're not in need of shelter. I've never heard of an animal killing another just for the fun of it. Even animals have reasons."

Silence.

"No? Nothing? I'll give it to you, then," Doug said. "I think we've evolved to a point—a sick point—where we don't need reasons anymore. We just do whatever it is we want to do."

MR. DART: "What a bunch of crap!"

"Don't hold back," said Doug.

"Dinosaurs only had to hunt other stupid dinosaurs. They never had to hunt anything intelligent, anything that had the ability to reason. Nice try. But I'm not buyin' it." He got up and went into the parlor.

The bartender was more philosophic. "You know, Mr. Archer, I grew up in this place. My family bought it back in 1917. I've been working here for as long as I can remember—speaking of dinosaurs. I've seen great ones come and go. I've seen some not-so-great ones make it further than they might have expected. And do you know what I think? It's instinct. It's all about instinct.

You mock the existence of the Circle, Mr. Archer, but let me tell you something. Instincts can't be taught. The ones who survive have just one or two more of these so-called killer instincts than the next guy. You call yourself a dinosaur, well, fine, so be it. But you're forgetting one important thing. For some, to kill is a choice, for some it's an instinct, but the people within these walls exercise control over both. And that's what separates us from the animals."

This was more than Doug had ever heard from the bartender before. Was he done?

The bartender poured a beer and handed it to him. "I guess we're gonna have to agree to disagree on this one."

MR. LION (clapping): "A fine debate by the both of you. I've been watching you, Mr. Archer. We may not be on the same page, but you have strong beliefs. And you're starting to develop quite the poker face."

"Thanks. I think. Because I don't think I'll ever get over it, the senseless killing. How do you do it? Every few weeks...taking another life...."

"The same way you do, Mr. Archer..."

Point taken.

"...I'm not going to lie to you. I do feel for some of the people I'm assigned. Some of them I have even considered friends. But you have to understand something. Outside these walls, we have no friends. You can only rely on yourself and the integrity of the Circle. Everyone and everything else is just an obstacle."

"Let me ask you this, then," said Doug. "If you weren't a member, would you believe it if someone told you what went on in here?"

"It doesn't matter. As long as we believe it—as long as *you* believe it. Any one of your friends in here could very well be your hunter out there. Remember what I told you, Mr. Archer. Be a Boy Scout. Be prepared for anything."

"That's why I'm here. I think I was being tracked."

"You see? You're developing the skills, and already outlasting everyone's expectations."

"Well, that wasn't my goal," Doug said, taking a long drink of cold beer. "But I guess it could be worse. I could be dead already."

"Touché."

The men picked up their drinks and moved into the VIP parlor. On the way there, Mr. Lion placed his arm around Doug's shoulders. The gesture, innocent enough, made Doug so instantly homesick that his head spun. He misses his father and the professor. What would either of them say if they knew what he was involved in now?

"Side pocket." Mr. Necktie was playing a game of Cutthroat pool with Mr. Cufflinks and Mr. Fingers. Mr. Necktie made his shot and squared for the next. "Far corner pocket," he said, and banked the shot off the close wall and sunk another.

Doug and Mr. Lion sat down in leather chairs and placed their drinks on a nearby table. Mr. Dart went over to start up a game of darts with Mr. Spear in the corner, as usual. Their actions within the parlor were predictable. The women held no interest for him anymore. He'd grown fairly immune to their allure, what with Liz in his life. They couldn't hold a candle to her.

MR. FINGERS: "Hey, maybe ya shoulda been called Mr. Billiard instead. I'm outta here and I ain't even shot yet."

MR. NECKTIE: "Sorry about that, Mr. Fingers. It's all in the way the balls lie."

Mr. Fingers tossed down his cue stick and walked over to Doug and Mr. Lion. He was about to speak when the door swept open. Mr. Chemist came bursting in. "Hell of a day, isn't it, boys?"

MR. LION: "Well, now, what do we have here? Another victim, I presume?"

MR. CHEMIST (his eyes to the ceiling): "That's right, and the dearly departed Ms. Mantis will be sorely missed."

MR. LION: "You do realize you killed the only woman in our chapter."

MR. CHEMIST: "Still of a segregated mentality, Mr. Lion? She was as much an adversary as you or any other member of the Circle. If she weren't, she never would have lasted this long."

MR. LION: "Fair enough."

The others gathered around the paunchy, excited Mr. Chemist. Hearing about the kill was part of the pageantry, part of the ritual.

MR. CHEMIST (laughing crudely): "I'm proud to say that Ms. Mantis' seductions didn't work on me."

Was that how she got her name? "So, let me get this straight," said Doug. "Ms. Mantis slept with her targets and then killed them? How stupid does that make the rest of us—not to realize that anyone who sleeps with her dies?"

MR. CHEMIST (coldly): "No, Mr. Archer. That's how she got her name the first time. After that, she took to using the women—the ones that...uh...."

MR. LION: "Cavort?"

MR. CHEMIST: "Yes, exactly. The ones that enjoy the company of our fellow members, the ones here every day. All she had to do was follow her targets and their lovely companions until they were, uh, compromised. It was clever, but I caught on a while ago."

MR. DART: "How did she suffer her demise?"

MR. CHEMIST: "Well, let's just say mercury is used for more than just thermometers. I can't give away all my secrets, can I, gentlemen?"

The room laughed at this joke far less nervously than Doug liked. Was he crazy or were they laughing at the fact that someone in their midst was probably planning to poison them in their sleep one day?

Generally Mr. Black said very little. From his corner he watched with a hawk's eyes all that happened in his domain. Today was no exception. He waited until Mr. Chemist had gotten his pats on the back from the other members and then stood up.

"Gentlemen," he said. Either no one had heard him, or they had chosen to ignore him. "Gentlemen!" he said, more insistently this time. The men stopped what they were doing to listen. He hesitated for only a moment. "I have news. The Fink has struck again."

A low murmur started. Doug stepped forward to address Mr. Black. "Who was it? Who did he get?"

"The recently initiated Mr. Lightning."

"Mr. Lightning?"

"I believe you knew him as Mr. Webb. He was to be given his name upon his next arrival."

The room was silent for a few moments. For the first time Doug thought he saw fear on the faces of the men.

Doug turned to Mr. Lion. "This can't be happening. He was just here a few days ago. We played darts."

MR LION: "I know it's hard, kid, but likely he was going to die anyway. Everyone in this room knows he is potentially looking at his last day on earth. Webb knew that coming in."

"But he was like me. He didn't know anything 'coming in.' He didn't want any part of it either. You forced him in and now he's dead. And the kill wasn't even by the damn rules!" Doug was heating up, his anger bubbling to the surface. "You, all of you, should be ashamed of yourselves."

MR. BLACK: "Mr. Archer, please control yourself. We are all saddened by this news. Please do not point fingers at people in this room. If there is a finger to point, it should be pointed at the Fink. He is, after all, the man who orchestrated this atrocity."

Doug was shaking. It hurt more than he thought it would to lose a friend, even a not-so-close "inside" friend like Webb. "He has to be stopped. This can't be allowed to happen."

MR. LION: "Frankly, there is no way to do that. We just have to wait for him to strike again—and hope the next person is up for the challenge. Maybe he's going for the newest members."

Yeah, and Mr. Dart and I are the two newest. Awesome.

MR. DART: "That would be Mr. Archer and me."

Like I said.

MR. BLACK: "Time served doesn't matter. It's quite possible that Mr. Lion's theory is wrong and that the Fink is working randomly. The truth is, there is no way of knowing. So be prepared out there, everyone."

Be prepared, everyone? Was that supposed to be some kind of motivating pre-game speech? *Let's kill this one for the Gipper!* The sandwich Doug had for lunch turned over in his stomach. It wasn't so much the idea of Webb's death—that was bad enough—but the raw fear he saw around him. He turned to Mr. Lion. "I take it that this is what you meant by the integrity of the Circle."

33

Stalking his prey was a carefully orchestrated dance of wits, sometimes a tango, sometimes a jig, but always a kick. Today Mr. Fingers had his trusty police baton and a battery-powered circular saw stowed away in a small travel bag on his shoulder.

Mr. Necktie was sitting alone across the street in a leather reclining chair, reading the *New York Times*, and attempting the crossword puzzle. The blinds were pulled almost down to the bottom for dual protection from the sun and from prying eyes. He put down the newspaper and picked up the phone.

Next in the box, thought Mr. Fingers gleefully. The remote camera device he'd installed on the windowsill had flawless resolution. Then, suddenly, Mr. Necktie jumped up and opened a drawer from which he drew a pistol. He then grabbed his keys and sped out the door. In a minute his car was backing out of the garage and peeling rubber down the street.

What the hell?

Mr. Fingers climbed back into his car. He'd just wasted an entire afternoon getting ready for a kill that hadn't gone off. He'd done his frickin' homework, too, set his schedule, had everything prepped. There went his upcoming flight to Venice. Would his buddies in Italy hold the yacht for him? Nah. He wouldn't do it for them. He flopped dejectedly into his car and let go with a string of satisfying expletives. He tossed his tools into the back seat.

"Looks like something must have spooked him."

Mr. Fingers turned at the voice coming from his back seat. *Stike first, ask questions later.* He twisted to pound the guy's face, whoever he was, but was stopped by a fierce burning shock on his neck. He slumped down against the seat.

The man in the back pulled back the cattle prod. "You know something, Mr. Fingers? It's quite a shame, really. In another time and place, we may have made a good pair. You remind me, well, frankly, of...me."

Mr. Fingers' eyes were wide with shock. The cattle prod had left his entire right side useless, his whole body in agony. He was nauseous as well, concerned about passing out before he could fight back. But what was more f-ed up? The hunter's face. It was unmasked. Mr. Fingers had now seen his face. Not good. Not good at all.

"Who...are...you?" he managed between clenched teeth.

"Names," said the man, "well, you know what Shakespeare said...."

Mr. Fingers' feebly attempted to work his useless hand into a fist.

"Now, now, Mr. Fingers," the hunter tsked, savagely prodding him again with the high-voltage electroshock tool. "We'll have none of that. I have to say, though, you're one sick bastard.

That's what I've always liked about you." The man's voice went hard. "You can't kill enough. Neither can I."

Awareness hit Fingers like a brick. "Fink," he croaked, "you sneaky fucking bastard."

"No, Mr. Fingers, I'm afraid it's you who let your guard down. You made it too easy." He leaned forward. "It's been fun, Mr. Fingers, truly, but it's time for me to go." The Fink covered the immobilized killer's mouth and nose with a heavy cloth. Asphyxiation, like drowning, was so personal. So intimate. A preferred method when given the opportunity, one he had been saving for Mr. Fingers.

Mr. Fingers made a halfhearted attempt to rally his neuro-logical system, but it was too late. His last thought was how much he'd miss the holiday on his friend's 80-foot yacht.

The Fink watched with the interest of a scientist as the life slowly drained from Mr. Fingers' toned body. When the twitching and spasming finally drew to a close and all signs of life had been erased, the Fink removed the cloth and stored it away appro-priately. He pulled the body from the vehicle and smiled again. What better way to honor the dead than to use Mr. Fingers' own tools of the trade?

He withdrew the conveniently small circular saw, admiring Mr. Fingers' choice. The pitch of the whisper-quiet machine only increased slightly when he cut through his prey's fingers one at a time. The sound of saw cutting through bone and the resul-tant spray of blood on the ground were exhilarating, so much so that it was difficult for the Fink to stop at the fingers. He had to remind himself of the point of the message, the irony that was sure to reach the other Circle members. As Mr. Fingers always did, so would the Fink. When he was done, each of Mr. Fingers' hands was left only with a thumb.

Back at his SUV, the Fink removed his photo ring, shuffled through it until he found Mr. Fingers' picture, and drew a big red "X" through it.

34

After lunch in the museum café with Michelle, Doug returned to his office for the first time since his "sabbatical," only now it was Michelle's office and she shared it with someone else. From the Spanish poster on the wall and the cup on the desk that said Raúl on it, he guessed it was the guy from the tour he'd taken with Liz. Doug had treated Michelle to a mixed-greens salad with goat cheese, pecans, and a raspberry vinaigrette. Generally employees didn't eat at the café, which was known for its exorbitant prices, and Michelle had ordered her favorite meal and her favorite dessert, the chocolate mousse cake. She was such a foodie. It was fun to watch.

Back in the office, Michelle told Doug she had to run to a meeting downtown, something about tour guides and museum publicity. Doug assured her that she should go, that he'd sort through the box of personal belongings that were still sitting there since she'd packed them up. He agreed to lock up the office when he left. Michelle blew him a kiss and was out the door.

"Say hi to John for me," he called to her back.

Doug looked around. He wouldn't have long. Jenkins was likely to be on the prowl and technically Doug wasn't supposed to be there. But he missed the place. He'd always loved museums, especially their basements, where the real work took place. Even the stack of new circulars on Michelle's desk was bringing on a bout of nostalgia. Absentmindedly, Doug picked one up. His life had changed radically since his years in the museum. And so had he. There was little of the old Doug left since the Circle had usurped every aspect of his free will. His freedom. He straightened a few of the piles of papers. He had nothing to do here, but didn't want to leave. It was as close as he was going to get to his old life ever again.

There was a knock at the door. Was it locked? Michelle was usually pretty obsessive about it, but…. "Yes?"

"It's Stew. Here to clean the room."

Doug didn't recognize the voice, but that didn't really mean anything considering he hadn't been around for ages. On the other hand, unless there was some new policy, the offices were never cleaned before the museum office staff left for the day. He looked at the time. Only two.

Doug took out his hunting knife. "Sure buddy, give me a second," he said, stalling. He moved to the door where the shadow of two feet could be seen just as the door crashed open and a knife whizzed by his head to land in the wall behind his old desk. Note for later: Remind Michelle to lock her door.

Another knife sailed past Doug and into the wall behind him. Doug yanked it out and ducked, poised for the next attack. It never came. Instead, he heard footsteps retreating.

Doug took off down the hallway of the Natural History Museum after "Stew" as if it were a sports track. At any moment any number of staff might enter the hall and the line of fire.

Someone unrelated to the madness might get hurt. Doug picked up his pace. His attacker, up ahead in green pants and shirt and a cap was pulling out yet another knife from his belt. He flew over a shipment of boxes waiting for delivery and took cover. Doug was so close he could hear the man's uneven breathing.

The knife caught Doug's shirt and nicked his left biceps. A few inches to the right....

His assailant's cap hovered above the boxes. He was moving, about to take off again. Doug waited. No reason to waste a perfectly good knife while the guy was behind a bunch of boxes. He didn't wait long. The killer made his move, rolling from behind the cardboard fortress and surging onto his feet. He had two knives now, one in each hand. How many knives can one man have?

Doug was ready for him. He neatly side-stepped the attack, getting in a kick to the guy's ribs. The man was solid, though, strong. He swiped at Doug and connected with a nasty cut to the cheek. Doug staggered back. A door closed and voices came from around the corner down in the hall. The man ran in the opposite direction. Doug positioned himself, then aimed his knife and released it with a satisfyingly direct hit to the back of the man's thigh. He moved in silently, quickly. They'd be discovered any second. The man was on the floor, attempting to remove the blade from his bleeding thigh. There was something familiar about him....

The voices were getting closer, two museum workers debating the authenticity of some archeological find. Funny. Even here, now, Doug found the subject alluring. He wanted to go out and join the conversation. He reached the powerfully built man. He almost felt sorry for the guy. So many tries, so little connection.

He had just seconds to finish this and get the heck away from there. He took careful aim. The "janitor's" face went still. An awareness passed between them. A knowing that things hadn't quite worked out in his favor.

The knife sliced cleanly into the man's chest. He made a last feeble attempt to reach for it, but expired before his hand reached the hilt.

The footsteps were just feet from where Doug stood over the body. He put his hands under the dead man's armpits and dragged him over to an office door. Locked. Sweating heavily, he checked another door before he saw the door across the hall marked "Janitorial Staff Only." With a speed born of desperation, he dragged the body the remaining few feet through the closet door just as the museum workers turned the corner.

Doug watched through a crack in the door as they walked by him, oblivious to the streak of blood on the floor and the sound of Doug's torn breathing on the other side.

Doug shook his head. Thank God for intellectuals with their amazing ability to see and hear only what they wanted to.

Back to business. Cautiously Doug checked for the capped man's pulse. Nothing. He removed the knife still clenched in "Stew's" hand and then peeled off the black ski mask to identify his hunter. Mr. Spear. Doug wiped the blood from the blade onto Mr. Spear's shirt. The act felt offensively pedestrian.

A moment later Doug caught a glimpse of something, a new sensation. If he had to put a name to it he'd have to call it... serenity. He rocked back on his heels, revolted. How could killing someone cause him to feel serene? A sociopath maybe, but not him. Then he remembered what Mr. Fingers said, that it was about getting the best of someone who was trying to kill you.

But Doug wasn't Mr. Fingers. He doesn't get any sick enjoyment out of it. *You might not enjoy it buddy boy*, his alter ego Mr. Archer sniped, *but you're here and he's dead. Get over it.*

That night a package was delivered to Tasker's bar, addressed to Mr. Black. The bartender signed for it and personally delivered it to the table in the back room.

"Thank you, you may go," Mr. Black said. He looked at the package for a moment. There was no return address, just like the other ones. He could almost smell the bad news.

Slowly he ripped off the tape, dreading what he'd find. Inside was a black case. It looked like the one in which Mr. Fingers kept his "trophies." No, it *was* Mr. Fingers' case. That could mean only one thing.

Mr. Black took a deep breath, steeled himself, and opened the box. Eight of Mr. Fingers' digits were staring at him from the plush velvet lining. Eight digits with congealed blood on the ends.

The Fink had struck again.

35

April in the Appalachian Mountains is as beautiful a sight as one can hope to behold, the sun just warm enough to counter the cool winds from the high altitude. The bright green of new forest growth and the dark blue of a cloudless sky is the perfect backdrop for a perfect weekend getaway.

It was just after noon. Doug and Liz had started up the relatively high mountain a couple of hours ago and were now breathing heavily from the exertion. At the top, the trail forked and Liz led the way down a short path beaten down by years of foot traffic. The sound of rushing water increased as they approached the source. Liz pushed away a large branch to reveal a smallish, but still impressive, waterfall. She removed her backpack and set it down on the ground.

"Surprise."

"Wow, it's gorgeous out here," said Doug. "Now I know why we spent seven hours in the car."

"Well, Virginia isn't exactly Lackawanna."

"Very funny. But really, this place is great, how did you find it?"

"My dad had some partners who lived around here. One weekend we took the jet down and went for a hike." Liz began peeling off her clothes to reveal a bikini barely worthy of the name. "We ended up here."

"Nice," he said. He wasn't referring to the surroundings.

Liz grinned. "Now watch closely," she said. Turning, she ran full speed to the edge of the cliff above the waterfall, gathering velocity, then jumped, screaming as she plummeted down into the water. Terrified, Doug ran to the edge to look for her. His heart was pounding harder than a drum. He called out, panicking when he didn't see her.

Oh my God. Liz. A few more seconds ticked by with no sign of her. "Liz!" He can't believe she'd do such a stupid thing. It had to be fifty feet down. What the hell was she thinking?

There was a splash from the pool of water below. Liz emerged from the water, the grin on her face so huge that he could see it from up there.

"You're out of your mind!" he said. "Are you okay?! You nearly gave me a heart attack."

"I'm fine. Get down here, the water's great," she yelled, treading water.

Doug stepped back a few steps to remove his clothing, with the exception of his suit trunks, and then walked back to the edge. "You sure about this?"

"Why, you scared?"

He assessed the depth of the plunge into the swirling waters below. "Um, yeah."

"It's a cinch," Liz called up. "Just make sure you jump out, not up."

Yeah, right. He was certifiable even to think about it.

Then he was backing up to get a running start. He was up here and she was down there. No contest. Doug stopped thinking and ran fast and hard. He remembered to jump out from the cliff. At the last second he tucked his legs up under his torso. No sense chancing an encounter with the canyon walls. Then he was falling, flying through the air. It was like nothing he'd ever felt before. He was falling so fast he could hardly absorb the beauty around him. Adrenaline was speeding through his veins. His body tumbled forward. The water came up to meet him.

He tried to correct his position, but hit the water with a hard slap, almost face first, and sank.

The Goodwins rented a rustic cabin near Lake Ogallala in Nebraska for two weeks the summer before Doug entered high school. It was his father's idea, the man who loved nature more than almost anything else, other than his wife and son. Doug had the same passion and was happiest in the wilderness at his father's side.

The Goodwins had been enjoying themselves for days, swimming in the lake, fishing, hunting, and eating what they caught. Doug was fourteen. He'd made quick friends with the other kids on vacation at Lake Ogallala and spent hours each day in tests of strength and competitions of skill that they cooked up. Two days before the end of their vacation, the oldest of the bunch, Billy Jack Bell, organized the final contest to establish the season's winner. Doug and Billy Jack were neck and neck and this was the contest that would break their tie. Doug was a strong swimmer, but Billy Jack practically had fins. Seeing which of them could swim to the other side of the lake first was an unprecedented challenge and Doug was psyched.

All fourteen of the kids catapulted off the dock into the water. Doug was easily out to an early lead, but it wasn't long before his arms began to tire and then cramp up. The lake looked a lot bigger than it had from the dock. Halfway across, his muscles were so tight it was all he could do to keep bobbing up and down in the water. Even his ability to tread water left him, and he began to sink. Panicking, he willed himself to the surface for air, but opened his lungs too soon and swallowed a mouthful of water. Choking, his arms and legs in agony, he managed to flail about, but moments later his legs lost feeling. From far away he thought he heard his mother's voice calling for him. That was the last thing he remembered.

When Doug woke up in the hospital, it was to his mother's tears and his father's hand on his. Billy Jack had gone farther than Doug by about ten yards. When he saw Doug's distress, he turned around and pulled him back from the depths of the lake. By then a few of the other kids had come out to help and together dragged Doug into shore. An ambulance took him to the tiny local facility and he spent the night, exhausted.

He'd never gone into the water again.

Liz was watching expectantly until Doug hit the water. When he didn't come up she dove under the surface at the spot where she'd seen him go under. There he was, motionless. Kicking down, she reached him in seconds and took hold of him. She hauled him to the surface. No burst of air expelled from his lungs; there was no movement from his limbs.

Doug was big and heavy, but Liz was a strong swimmer, her muscles well developed. She towed him to shore and laid him on his back. She administered CPR, pressing on his chest, breathing life into his mouth, outwardly calm, as if she'd done this many times before. Press, breathe, press, breathe. *Please God, don't let him die.*

A loud cough and a burst of water spurted from Doug's mouth.

"Thank God," Liz said and collapsed backwards. "I thought you were a goner. No more cliff diving for you."

Doug gasped for air. Finally he caught his breath. "Maybe I should have mentioned that I'm not the best of swimmers."

"Ya think?" Liz punched his arm. "You scared the hell out of me, Doug. What were you thinking?"

"Um. Let's see. I'm a macho idiot who didn't want to admit to this obvious failing?"

Liz shook her head at him and sighed.

The long walk back to their belongings was not as tranquil as the hike in. Doug was wet, cold, and barefoot, although he was well enough to admire Liz as she walked ahead of him, dripping wet and luscious. The hike was difficult. When they reached the campsite they toweled off. He wanted to make love that instant, but he was too tired and too hungry. Reading his mind, Liz opened her backpack and unpacked their lunch, crusty French bread, softened brie cheese, fruit, and red wine. They fell asleep in each other's arms and woke up to the heat of each other's bodies. They made passionate love under the red glow of the sun to the counterpoint of a smaller waterfall nearby. Doug snapped a mental picture of the moment, the most sensual experience of his life.

In the morning, satiated after a night of more pleasure and a breakfast of dry cereal and fruit, Doug and Liz packed up. It was time to go home.

For some reason Doug couldn't put his finger on, the car ride back to the city was unnervingly quiet bordering on uncomfortable. Something was on Liz's mind, but he was hesitant to push her to talk about anything she might not want to share. After almost an hour, however, he gave up. He wasn't secure enough to deal with the thick air of tension. "What's going on?"

"What do you mean?"

"I mean, it seems like something's wrong."

"Oh, it's nothing."

Nothing? Right. When a woman says the word nothing what they really mean is something—with a capital "S."

"Are you sure? Because— Really, Liz, you can talk to me."

"It's just something I have to do tomorrow," she said.

Okay. After a weekend of deliriously passionate love she was telling him to back off. He wouldn't take it personally.

The hell he wouldn't.

"Big auction tomorrow, a show...what?"

"It's my dad's company," she said. In a round-about sort of way, she supposed it was. "I'm just getting nervous."

Okay. Her answer felt all wrong. He was *so* taking it personally. "You're amazing, Liz. I'm sure you'll knock 'em dead."

"Thanks, that means a lot," said Liz, adjusting in her seat to put her head on his arm, which was resting on the middle console. "We really did have a perfect weekend, didn't we?"

He kissed her forehead. "The best," he said. "Now, why don't you get some rest, you seem like you need it."

"Okay," she said, and kissed him on the cheek.

"Sweet dreams."

Doug didn't want to move. He drove slowly, mulling over their last conversation, avoiding lane changes and use of the brakes. He avoided bumps in the road. He could have driven all night, as long as her head was nestled on him, where it belonged.

36

"Mr. Archer, I must say, you seem to have taken to this life rather well."

Startled, Doug shook himself at Mr. Cufflink's pronouncement. "What makes you say that?"

"Well, we haven't seen Mr. Spear in almost two weeks now."

Doug was playing Thirty-one with Mr. Cufflinks, Mr. Chemist, and Mr. Necktie. Each had a bet on the table of up to three arbitrary chips. All but Mr. Necktie were missing between one and two.

Doug didn't answer.

MR. CUFFLINKS (breaking the strategic silence): "Care to enlighten us as to why?"

"Fine. He came after me at the museum, and let's just say I don't think he'll be in to play cards anytime soon."

MR. CUFFLINKS: "Just as I said, adapting beautifully."

MR. CHEMIST: "How long have you been here now?"

"Going on nine months. Eight months, fourteen days to be exact."

"You make it sound like a prison sentence."

"It is."

"Still, Mr. Archer, I bet you're surprising even yourself. Not that there haven't been some close calls...least that's what I've heard."

"I don't know about that. But I guess I'm starting to see the wisdom of what Mr. Fingers said to me once."

The men bowed their heads for a respectful moment of silence. News about Mr. Fingers' death hadn't taken long to circulate. It had hit the chapter hard, two members gone at the hands of the Fink in a matter of weeks. And say what you want about Mr. Fingers, and despite his clear appetites and sometimes crude demeanor, he was a dedicated member of the Circle who had not once violated the rules.

MR. NECKTIE: "Here's to you, Mr. Fingers."

MR. CUFFLINKS: "Indeed. A cunning and ruthless member of the Circle. His presence will be missed. But go on, Mr. Archer, you were saying?"

"He told me that feeling good about getting the best of someone—those are his words—who tries to kill you is the right way to feel. And now I suppose I see what he meant."

MR. CHEMIST (chuckling): "Go figure, Mr. Fingers the philosopher." The others chuckled along with him.

"I told you! I'm not called Mr. Dart for nothing." The men looked up. Mr. Dart and a new recruit, Mr. Combustion, were playing a game of Cricket. Mr. Dart wasn't attempting to hide his lack of hubris.

MR. COMBUSTION: "Shut your damn mouth!"

Mr. Combustion hadn't learned yet that members acted with decorum at all times. "One more game."

Mr. Dart complied, unperturbed.

MR. CUFFLINKS: "I say, that Mr. Combustion has a bit of a temper."

The men returned to their card game.

MR. CHEMIST: "Indeed. Someone might think about explaining the definition of the word *gentleman* to him." The men nodded agreement. "Although, admittedly, he does have us checking under our cars these days, doesn't he now?"

MR. NECKTIE (drawing a new card): "Enough about Mr. Combustion. What's the deal with Mr. Dart? He's been here for more than a year now and he never seems the slightest bit anxious. Never a story about a close call...nothing. In my estimation he's nothing more than a punk. When I get his file I'll make short work of him."

His rant discomforted the members.

"Looking to take Mr. Fingers' place already, are we Mr. Necktie?" Doug chimed in to dispel any further thoughts about Mr. Dart's "luck" in the Circle.

MR. NECKTIE: "It's not like that, Mr. Archer. But I'll be damned if I'm going to sit here and let some punk walk all over the Circle."

Nobody said anything. Mr. Necktie was taking Mr. Fingers' death hard. Everyone knew Fingers had been a kind of mentor to him—at least as much one member could mentor another in an organization like the Circle. Tacitly they chose to give Mr. Necktie his space until he'd had a chance to regroup.

Suddenly Mr. Necktie threw down his hand. "Thirty-one! And now, if you'll excuse me, gentlemen, I have an appointment with my old war buddy, Captain Morgan. I wouldn't want to keep him waiting."

The members at the table each pushed a chip into the center pot as Mr. Necktie exited the parlor.

MR. CUFFLINKS (shuffling the deck): "Mr. Necktie does make a good point, Mr. Archer. Mr. Dart seems to be experiencing a fascinating kind of, shall we say, immunity. It would do the lot of us a great service if you would simply kill him so all of us might enjoy some time off."

What? He couldn't have heard that right. Was he serious? Did Cufflinks just ask him to off another member to get it out of the way? It bothers him that he can't tell. "I don't hunt innocent men and I don't hunt for sport. I never have and never will. This may be your game, but I'm playing it my way."

MR. CUFFLINKS: "I find your use of the word *innocent* interesting, Mr. Archer. I would venture to say that not a man among us could claim innocence. We have all killed before, most of us more than once—or even dozens of times. Frankly, I suggest you purchase yourself another dictionary. And, furthermore, might I inquire what makes you think you are any more innocent than the rest of us?"

Shoot. Doug had tripped himself up. To his knowledge no one inside the Circle was aware about his role in the torture and killing of Dr. Williams. He really *was* a hypocrite, but no one knew how much of one. His holier-than-thou presentation still served him, though, at least for a while longer. "I've killed, you're right. But I did it to protect myself, to preserve one of my inalienable rights...the right to life."

MR. CUFFLINKS: "A bit self-righteous, but I won't argue the point. I will ask this, though. What about our rights, the right to the pursuit of happiness?"

Doug blinked. *Happiness?* That confirmed it. The dude was nuts.

"This club, for example. Whether you like it or not, this club makes its members happy. And we endanger no one other than those within our own walls."

Doug felt the sick bite of bile again. He wasn't about to argue the Declaration of Independence with these people. He's pretty sure a number of his rights are being violated by the sheer fact that he is being forced to participate to kill against his will. Not to mention, if all the Circle's members were so happy, what about him—*his* happiness? What about "recruits" like him who had no choice in their membership? What about all the Watchers, hooked in before they knew what they were in for? The argument was as futile as it was definitive.

Doug did the only thing possible to avoid further confrontation. He conceded. "Look, I don't want to get into this argument again. I've heard the speech before. I'm just not quite there yet. I'd prefer to hold on to my illusions—if you don't mind."

Mr. Cufflinks nodded graciously. He'd made his point.

MR. CHEMIST: "Comfortable or not, Mr. Archer, you put the rest of us at a big disadvantage. This Mr. Dart isn't feeling much competition from the rest of us members, that's pretty clear. He's free to kill with immunity. That means he's either damn skilled—or not too smart. It looks like he doesn't have a clue that you're the guy assigned to him, so that rules out the possibility that it's due to his skill. In my opinion, you'd better strike while he's still in the dark."

Doug sat quietly.

MR. CUFFLINKS: "Just remember, Mr. Archer, illusions can be dangerous in this business."

How could he possibly forget?

37

Mr. Ambrose had been a faithful customer of the Metamorphosis Day Spa for many years. When the Spa began to go under, it was his purchase of fifty-one percent of the business that had kept it afloat. He enjoyed the clout of being a much-valued "client" whose weekly appointments now spanned over twelve, going on thirteen, years. Mr. Ambrose has a strict ritual for his relaxation: twenty-five minutes in the steam room, followed by a strong cup of Adams Peak White Tea with lemon, imported from Sri Lanka specifically for him, capped off by a deep-tissue massage. In twelve-plus years, Mr. Ambrose has never deviated from this schedule, nor has he ever missed a session. Today would be no different.

"Good afternoon, ladies."

"Good afternoon, Mr. Ambrose," came the sing-song response.

Mr. Ambrose walked in the door of the fifth-floor health spa and greeted the ladies with a warm smile. He relished the stir his entrance always caused, looked forward to it almost as much as the attention to his body that followed. The women at Metamorphosis often argued over who would have the privilege of fawning over Mr. Ambrose. And why not? He was rich, good-looking, distinguished, charming, and, as far as they knew, single. Not to mention a great tipper...when he was pleased.

Mr. Ambrose bent to kiss the receptionist on the cheek. "Tracy, you look beautiful."

"Why, thank you, Mr. Ambrose," Tracy blushed.

Mr. Ambrose worked the room, making sure to address each woman personally and with a kiss. "Anna, I've missed you, dear, how's the family?"

"They're great, my son made honor roll."

"Wonderful, wonderful. Grace, love the new hair style, really accentuates your cheekbones."

"Thank you, Mr. Ambrose."

As he made his way through the attendants, it was almost as if Beatlemania had gripped the office. The women stopped what they were doing to greet him. With their livelihood at stake it would be downright idiotic not to stake a claim.

"Jackie, you look great, did you lose more weight?"

"A little," replied Jackie, flushing at the compliment.

"Dana, when are you going to ditch that husband of yours and run away with me?"

"I'm working on it," Dana joked back.

"And now, who do we have here," Mr. Ambrose asked, stopping at a new face.

"That's Beth, she started here about two weeks ago," said Tracy from behind the counter. "She's been training with Grace... it's her first day on her own."

"Well, then, I'll be delighted to help break her in," chuckled Mr. Ambrose, ever the picture of bonhomie.

"Thank you, sir, it's an honor," Beth replied, well-versed in spa etiquette.

"The pleasure is all mine, my dear. If you come with me, young lady, I will show you how I like my steam. And while I'm stewing, you can prepare my tea." He started down the narrow hallway to the locker room.

Beth attempted to follow.

"I think I can handle this part alone," Mr. Ambrose said, suddenly cold, eyebrows raised. No one was allowed into the locker room when he was there. No one.

"Oh, I'm so sorry, sir," Beth said, stepping back quickly. "I'm a little nervous, sir, first day and all. I didn't mean to—"

"No worries, dear," said Mr. Ambrose, but with a bit less enthusiasm. "You wait here. I'll be out in a moment."

A plush terry-cloth robe and a pair of slippers sat on a white marble bench. Mr. Ambrose quickly changed and showered, eager to be under the hands of this new girl, Beth. She may not have too much in the brains department, but she had the body of a goddess.

He let the water cleanse him of the day's concerns, then toweled off and shrugged into the thick white robe.

Beth was waiting for him with a fresh towel, warm from the dryer.

"Thank you, my dear. I'll teach you how I like my steam this time. Next time I come in, I expect you'll be able to handle it on your own." Mr. Ambrose has always appreciated the concept of the teaching moment, and uses it often to benefit those of lesser stature. "Never too hot, yes? 105 degrees, not a degree over. After my steam, I will require a cold shower and then my tea. Nice and hot, please, Adams Peak White, with lemon—just the right amount. Quite delicious, really. You know it?"

"No, sir, I've never tried it."

"Exquisite, picked near Adam's Peak, in Sri Lanka. Only thirty kilos produced each week because only the freshest shoots are selected, then withered and sun-dried."

Beth widened her eyes to show she was impressed with Mr. Ambrose's vast worldliness and held open the door to the steam room.

"Twenty-five minutes, dear," said Mr. Ambrose, "not a moment sooner, not a moment later."

"Yes, sir. I understand, sir. Enjoy your steam, Mr. Ambrose." Beth pulled the door shut and set the timer.

Back in the front office she put her hand on Grace's arm. "Why didn't you tell me about this guy? Who is he?"

Tracy butted in. "Are you kidding? That's Mr. Ambrose."

"I got that. But who is he? What's all the fuss about?"

Grace placed an arm around her shoulders. "Girls, girls, girls," she started, "Beth doesn't know about Mr. Ambrose!" The women cleared a path and Grace walked Beth back down the hall to the window of the steam room. "Take a look," she said, "but brace yourself first, honey."

Beth was confused. Afraid she'd be seen spying on her first big solo client, she put her face up to the edge of the glass, but quickly ducked down as she saw him move around the room. Grace gave her a little encouraging shove and a wink. "It's okay," she said, "You'll miss the best part."

Beth wasn't sure what to expect, but did what she was told and looked inside. She saw Mr. Ambrose looking at her, his eyes replete with innuendo. His hands went to the belt of his robe. She instantly felt the heat of shame, but fascination, too—and Grace's arm, which kept her glued to the spot.

Mr. Ambrose began to disrobe, slowly and confidently, for his adoring fans. The rest of the women gathered behind Beth and proceeded to swoon at the sight of his naked body. He knew they were watching—and they knew he knew. But that was why he was doing it! Appalled, Beth couldn't tear her eyes away.

"You know he knows we're watching," said Jackie.

"Really?" Beth said. Who did he think he was, God's gift to womankind?

"What man wouldn't want a bunch of women looking at him—at *it*? Especially one that big! He could run a three-legged race all by himself!" The women, reduced to schoolgirls looking at their first porno magazine, let loose with high-pitched squeals.

"Jackie, you're so bad," Dana teased.

"Better than my husband and his Irish curse," Anna chimed in. "All I get is the Dublin roller coaster."

"What's that?" Beth asked. This was an education she hadn't expected at the most exclusive spa in all of Manhattan.

"You know, short and over before you know it," Jackie said. The girls laughed some more as Grace patted Anna on the shoulder, consoling her. Jackie was enjoying the spotlight now, but all eyes were still glued to Mr. Ambrose. "Forget about your husband, Anna. Check that thing out, Beth. It's so big, it affects the weather." More giggles from the crowd. "It's so big, he probably has to check it as luggage when he flies." "It should have its own zip code." The giggles turned into uproarious laughter.

Beth was mortified, but the camaraderie was nice. Thank God the steam room was airtight—and soundproof.

Grace saw the look on Beth's face. "Okay girls. Show's over for today. Time to reign in the party. There's work to do." She herded the group back to the front. "We have new clients coming today. Three Japanese businessmen. Who wants 'em? Okay, Anna, Jackie, and I will take them." She turned back to Beth. "Just remember what I taught you and you'll be fine. Just try not to stare at it."

"Thanks," said Beth. Yeah, like not looking at the elephant in the room. She looked at her watch. Only seventeen more minutes 'til Mr. Ambrose's rubdown. Perhaps he'd like something a little different today. Grace was always telling her to take some initiative.

She entered the alcove connected to the steam room and pressed the intercom button. "Excuse me, Mr. Ambrose, is everything okay?" The steam room was state of the art and automatically maintained a constant level of steam. "Shall I adjust the level?" When he nodded, Beth turned a dial on the machine until it reached almost half way. She stopped when she saw him give her a thumbs-up, and set the timer for fifteen more minutes.

Beth's watch beeped seven minutes later. She moved to the alcove and pressed the intercom button again. "Mr. Ambrose?"

"Yes?" The voice sounded annoyed. "Is it twenty-five minutes already?"

"Not yet, sir. I, uh, I was wondering if you would like me to add an herbal relaxant into your steam for the remaining few minutes."

"I have a very specific routine here young lady. Surely you've been informed," Mr. Ambrose answered with an irritated sigh.

"Yes, sir. I'm so sorry, Mr. Ambrose, sir. I just thought a hint of jasmine would enhance your experience. I read that the scent has very soothing and calming effects."

Was the tension in the air that Beth felt real or perceived? Had she overstepped her place? After ten or twenty excruciating seconds, she figured she'd lost her job. Then Mr. Ambrose said, "Actually, now that you mention it, jasmine sounds lovely. Thank you, my dear."

Elated that she hadn't enraged the highest high-roller at the spa, Beth put on a pair of heat-resistant gloves and opened the steam contraption to allow more steam to rush out of the little door. It filled the small room in under a minute. She tapped a few flakes of a dried flower essence into the canister fitted to the top of the device, closed and locked it, and left the room.

Seven minutes later, the steam shut itself off. Mr. Ambrose let himself out of the room and into another shower back in the locker room. He took his time, making sure he rinsed well to close his open pores. The cold water usually woke him up, but today for some reason he was feeling a bit more lethargic than usual. Must be the late night and the two women he'd taken home for fun and games. He recalled the event with a sudden hardening. He stepped out of the shower, dried off, and put his robe back on. Before he exited, he took an extra minute to make sure his member was as it should be.

Outside, Beth was waiting with his cup of tea on a saucer, a lemon wedge in place. "Excellent, my dear, thank you," Mr. Ambrose said, taking a dainty sip. "How long did you steep this tea?" he asked, the chill suddenly back in his voice.

"Four minutes, Mr. Ambrose, as it said on the package."

"Four minutes is much too long, you idiot. It's bitter." Mr. Ambrose rammed the one-of-a-kind china cup back on the tray so hard the cup cracked in two.

"I'm so sorry, sir. I'll go get Grace," Beth said through tears.

He'd take pity on her this time. Maybe she could make it up to him in a more creative way. He purposefully softened his voice. "Now, now, no need for that, dear, all is forgiven. Perhaps you can make it up to me during our massage, yes?"

"Oh, yes, sir. Certainly, sir."

"Well, then, it is time. Show me what you're made of."

Beth managed a small smile. She didn't want to put her employment in jeopardy. Not just yet.

Mr. Ambrose felt another surge beneath his robe in anticipation. He allowed the lovely creature to walk him into the massage room. He felt deliciously relaxed, to the point where he almost stumbled before reaching the table.

Beth took his arm. "Oh, those darn slippers," she said of the padded paper shoes all the clients wore. She wouldn't want Mr. Ambrose to feel clumsy. "Here. The table is all ready for you. You can disrobe whenever you're ready."

Mr. Ambrose lowered himself onto the table. He could use a good resting massage. He heard the door lock behind him, but suddenly he was too tired to move.

In the recesses of his mind a switch went on.

"Hello, Mr. Cufflinks," Beth said, coming around the table so the client could see her face.

Mr. Cufflinks' eyes widened in shock. He went to get up but he couldn't move. His limbs were paralyzed.

"Oh, you'll be moving soon enough," said Beth. "As soon as the seizures start."

Sure enough, in moments Mr. Cufflinks' body began to convulse. The table shook at its foundation.

In another minute he was vomiting. He had no control. She'd given him something! Who was this person...this girl? Why was she doing this to him?

"Ah, vomiting," said Beth, as if she were a doctor diagnosing his symptoms. "Yes, it's going wonderfully, exactly according to plan."

But who are you? Mr. Cufflinks asked, the words not leaving his lips. He couldn't speak; he was gasping for air.

"I bet you're wondering who I am. Well, I'll tell you, Mr. Cufflinks, since you don't have much time left." Mr. Cufflinks eyes dilated. "Listen carefully. My name is Elizabeth Hughes. You killed my father, Orson Hughes." Nothing. "Mr. Cecchino to you." Liz waited. She watched for the reaction she'd been envisioning

for as long as she could remember. When it came, she felt immediate vindication.

"It's taken me years to track you down. But now you're
mine. What you're feeling right now are the effects of the Giant
Hogweed plant. Inhaling the pollen results in severe seizures—
obviously—and eventual death. All in under fifteen minutes. A
really accommodating poison, wouldn't you say, Mr. Cufflinks?
And it makes such a nice, relaxing steam." His eyes rolled back
into his head. The end was near for the man who had killed her
father.

"Oh, and that gasping for air thing you're doing? That was a
special addition of my own, Autumn Crocus, and a little Oleander.
Hang on, let me read this to you." Liz pulled a printout from her
pocket. "I got this off the internet. You can learn so much from
surfing the web these days, don't you think? For example, 'All
parts of the Autumn Crocus contain alkaloid colchicine, which
causes cramping, vomiting, diarrhea, increased blood pressure,
irregular and weak pulse, and respiratory failure.'" She looked
over at Mr. Cufflinks' flailing body. "Yup, working perfectly."

Mr. Cufflinks lost control of his bowels and defecated on the
massage table.

"Lovely," said Liz. "But wait, don't go yet, you have to hear
what it says about the Oleander. According to the International
Oleander Society, 'The leaves and stems contain a milky, sticky
sap that has a bitter flavor, somewhat like a rotten lemon.' Liz
smiled and continued reading. 'The toxic sap, containing a
mixture of cardenolide glycosides, causes symptoms similar to
that of digitalis poisoning.' What is digitalis poisoning? Why, I
don't really know, but a dose of more than ten milligrams is fatal,
and I gave you twenty-five in your special Adams Peak white
tea—with just the right amount of lemon, of course."

Liz stood over him, leaned down close to whisper in his ear.

Mr. Cufflinks was hardly aware of her presence, so caught up was he in his own demise.

"Just one last thing, Mr. Cufflinks, and then we'll part company forever." Liz paused for a moment, enjoying every nuance, every movement, every syllable. "Welcome to the Circle."

Liz placed an Oleander on Mr. Cufflinks' body as he drew his last breath. She had chosen the calling card for its perfect irony, the most innocent of the flowers used in her toxic cocktail.

In the men's changing room Liz opened Mr. "Ambrose's" locker. She removed her father's diamond cufflinks from the specially constructed pocket of Mr. Cufflinks' Armani suit and pocketed them. On the way out through the emergency exit stairwell Liz took the heavy dark wig from her head and removed the fake wire-rimmed glasses. She'd always known who she was. Now she knew she was a killer.

38

"Hey asshole, what's the matter, you can't fuckin' read!?"

Doug jerked into consciousness. He looked at the man in the hard hat in front of him and then at the sign that clearly said, "WET CEMENT." Disgusted, he pulled up his feet from the thick gray muck. They came up with a loud sucking sound. "Sorry," he said.

The man muttered something about muthafuckin' rich idiots who didn't know their ass from their elbow in a thick New York accent and repositioned himself to rework the section Doug had just ruined. Doug reached in his pocket and pulled out a few hundreds. "I'm sorry," he said again. "Here, this should cover it."

"Sorry don't cut it, man," said the cement worker. "Fuckers think they can fuckin' buy their way out of anything...." A point of view that didn't stop him from snatching the money from Doug's hand, however.

Doug had left Tasker's immersed in thought, as he so often did, going over and over in his mind the scope of the things he'd witnessed in his short time with the Circle. To feel even a shred of gratefulness seemed wrong, but if it were not for the abundance of money they provided he never would have been able to set up a nest egg for his mother back home or, possibly of equal importance, to meet and eventually win over the girl of his dreams. Or be so quick to reach into his pocket to pay off a street worker.

"I said I was sorry," said Doug again.

"Yeah, but I don't like your attitude," said the guy.

"My—my attitude?" stuttered Doug. "Are you crazy?"

"Crazy, yeah, I'm crazy alright," said the man and gave Doug a shove with one of his beefy arms.

Doug fell back, stumbling over the wooden forms used for laying the cement. He tried to regain his balance before he ended up in the wet concrete again, this time on his ass. Was this really happening?

He heard a pop, and suddenly the beefy street worker's eyes went big and round. He fell forward, flattening Doug to the ground.

The guy's head was in smithereens. He'd been shot. Doug was covered in human yuk.

That shot was meant for me. Still trapped under the big guy's weight, Doug couldn't breathe. He had to weigh two fifty at least. With a grunt, Doug rolled the body off his chest just as a second shot penetrated the worker's back.

Doug tried to trace the trajectory of the bullets. They were coming from the rooftop across the street. He cut his eyes to peer into the darkness. A dark figure was running across the tops of the buildings. If it weren't for the insane encounter with the crazed guy in the hard hat and the cement, Doug would be dead.

He was on his feet and moving. He watched as the figure jumped off a roof and onto a fire escape, which probably ended up in the alley about fifty feet away. Doug followed, clueless about what he'd find.

He ran down the dark narrow space, trying to pick out any obvious discrepancies, hiding places, but the alley was clean of everything but the debris that had found its way into the corners and against the walls. There was a tall chain-link fence at the end. Doug got a running start and catapulted himself over the top, catching his jacket on the rough wires and shredding the right front. As he took a second to tear the jacket off and continued down the other side, he heard another pop. This time it was his blood he saw. He'd been shot in the right shoulder and it burned like hell.

Doug lowered himself to the ground with his good arm. Now he was on the same side of the fence as his hunter and there was no way out. No way he could climb over the fence again with only one arm.

The hunter was dressed in black. He was big, walked with a swagger. Doug took an instant dislike to him—ridiculous, but even if the guy wasn't trying to kill him, Doug knew he wouldn't like him. The thought would be funny if it weren't so irrelevant.

From his injured position, Doug looked up as the figure came closer, gun pointed at Doug's chest. His face was hidden by a black ski mask, but Doug sensed a smile on the other side. His assailant knew the game was over. He knew he'd won.

Doug feigned weakness. The hunter came in closer, taking aim with his silenced pistol. Doug lurched forward and plunged his knife deep into the hunter's left calf. The man screamed. The gun went off above them.

Doug wrapped his good arm around the man's legs and forced him to the ground. He punched him in the face, hard, again and again. The man's head rolled on his neck.

Doug kicked the gun away across the alley and pulled out the blade from the man's leg. He moaned out a long wail of pain.

Doug jumped to his side and held the knife to his throat, then ripped off his mask.

No way. It couldn't be. "Who the hell *are* you?"

The man didn't speak, but raised his chin to give Doug an easier cut across his jugular.

No way he'd give him the satisfaction. "I swear to God, old man," Doug said, "tell me who you are!"

The man just raised his chin another inch. "Poor Douglas Goodwin, always looking for answers."

Doug was furious with himself. He should have known. God, how clueless could he get? Clueless. Clueless. Clueless.

"Just kill me Goodwin. Be a man for once," said the man disgustedly.

Doug shook his head. He still hoped that he was somehow mistaken, that the man in front of him wasn't someone he'd trusted—or at least someone he had decided was no threat. "Why, Murph, why?"

"It's my business—just like it's yours. Not that I haven't enjoyed my work." This came out a little wistfully. "Frankly, I was getting tired of holding the door and changing light bulbs anyway. So go ahead, get it over with."

Doug pressed the blade closer. A drop of blood appeared. "Does the name Randall Webb mean anything to you?"

"Not anymore."

The pieces of the puzzle snapped into place. Murph was a member of the Circle, but Doug had never seen him at Tasker's. "Murph...you're the one they told me about?"

The man on the ground shuddered. "Please, don't call me that. It's so...blue collar."

Doug can't believe it. The man was dying and he was worried about his social status. "I guess you'd prefer the Fink."

"They're still calling me that? How pathetically predictable."

Doug should kill the bastard and be done with it. He'd heard the stories. He knew what the guy was capable of. He'd just experienced it. But this was his one chance at some answers. He'd never have this opportunity again. "Tell me why. I want to know."

"I don't have to answer to you. And I couldn't care less about your delicate psychological state. Killing is easy. Now finish me off—that is, if you've got the balls."

Doug reeled from the ramifications of what he saw before him. Even the Circle, an organization that thrived and survived on a sort of cannibalistic annihilation, had rules. This man preyed on the hunters without regard for even a modicum of fair play. Once again, Doug's sense of all he held decent had been pummeled into chopped liver. His pressure on the knife lightened. He doesn't have the stomach for this. And besides, the guy was an old man....

The Fink's eyes gleamed. Time for some more fun. He threw a handful of gravel he'd scraped up from the ground into Doug's face.

Doug dropped the knife to protect his eyes.

The Fink swung his fist and connected with Doug's jaw. Doug staggered and fell to his knees. The Fink packed a punch, nothing like the wounded war veteran Doug had come to know. His own shoulder was useless and he was losing a lot of blood.

The Fink laughed. "Pathetic. I don't know how you've lasted this long, *Mr. Archer.*" His eyes skirted the alley for his gun.

Doug rolled away toward the wall. His jaw felt as if a sledgehammer had reconfigured it. He must have cut himself on something too, because blood was dripping in his eye, making it hard to see. His knife was gone, skittered away somewhere in the darkness. He had nothing.

In the near darkness, the Fink spent only a moment searching for his gun. Bare hands were fine too, he decided. A good fist fight to the death might be just the ticket. He dragged his bleeding leg over to Doug's position.

Doug's shoulder wound was a gaping hole; hot blood was coursing down his chest. Was this it?

The Fink took hold of what was left of Doug's collar and pulled him up to his knees. A slam to the face and Doug was swooning. The Fink pounded his fist into Doug's stomach, his chest, his kidneys. They danced together in an awkward bear hug.

Doug's strength left him with a whoosh.

The Fink let him fall to the ground in a heap.

Somewhere in the recesses of Doug's mushy brain he computed that he was a few inches from a brick wall. If he had the energy he'd laugh at the irony. His back was up against the wall, where it had been for months.

He blacked out. Frankly, it was a relief.

When he came to, Doug remembered the wall. He felt comforted by the idea of this wall, only inches away. It was his savior, a solid, loving, warm place to rest. A place where he could let go. If he could only get a little closer, lean back against it, he'd be able to rest, relieve his body of the burden of its own weight.

His hand inched back, looking for leverage. He needed assurance that the wall was there to support him. But instead he connected with a hard, rough object. Cement. Something that felt like thick cables protruding from the end. Like a piece of a crumbling wall...his wall? Doug panicked. He needed that wall. That wall was his only hope.

He blacked out again. Who knew for how long. He dragged himself back. He heard something...the sound of his own breathing...frayed, croupy hiccups. The sound of a dying man. Him.

But there were other sounds as well, different sounds. Out of sync. Nearby, but not too near. Finally it penetrated. They weren't his! Doug blinked and saw...the Fink. Hurt, but still alive. Still somewhere close by in the dark.

He had to do something. If the Fink was alive, he'd be coming for him.

Doug's hand clutched around the cement, his love affair with the wall a thing of the past. What had be been thinking? He wanted to live, if only long enough to smash the block of concrete into the Fink's face. But even if he got the opportunity, he was in no position to wield it. He was as weak as a baby.

He talked to himself. *Don't pass out. Don't pass out. You can do this. You can do this. You HAVE to do this.*

Doug tightened his grip around the rough weapon and waited. He waited some more. Would he die of waiting?

Finally, he heard the sound of his hunter moving in. A moment later he felt the brush of the Fink's legs as they straddled his prone body. *Play dead, play dead!* his head screamed. But his raspy breathing was giving him away. How long...how long should he wait before opening his eyes? Any second might be his last.

Now. He had to see the attack he knew was coming. He felt a lightening above him, an opening, a chance. *This is it. Do it now or you're done for. The Fink will have won.*

In the darkness Doug opened his swollen bloody right eye. The Fink reared back, readying for the thrust.

The Fink hurt in a way he hadn't hurt in a long time. This Mr. Archer, this Douglas Goodwin, apartment 4B, had been a worthy adversary. But this one last thrust will finish him off and in the end Mr. Archer will be nothing more than a dead amateur like the rest of them. The smell of blood called to him, enticed him, comforted him, seduced him. The Fink forgot everything. The pain in his leg was gone. He floated back to gain the momentum he needed.

Doug watched as the man he'd thought of as good ol' Murph threw his head back with a guttural sound of pure animalistic appetite, his arm raised against the sky. He felt the raw thrill that pulsed from the killer as he reveled in his power, in the bloodlust.

His eyes were thick with blood, but Doug knew the Fink's body would soon crash down to smother Doug's in its final furver for the kill. There is no misinterpreting the sound of the velocity, the fury, the compulsion.

Doug prayed for strength and brought up his cement weapon with all the speed and impetus he had left. He connected with the right side of the Fink's head.

The Fink did not have time to be surprised. His face, frozen in motion, sunk into the thick cables. His eyes were bloody masses of pulp. His knife fell away. He covered his head with his hands and fell away with agonized screams.

This time Doug didn't hesitate. He crawled over and picked up the knife. He plunged it into the Fink's neck.

The screams stopped.

Doug collapsed into nothingness.

When Doug came to, his first thought was that he was dead. When the stab of pain asserted itself and he realized this wasn't the case, his next thought was that if he didn't get to a doctor soon, he really would be. But first he had to know.

The Fink was lying next to him, dead. Doug snaked his hand into first his left pocket, then his right. No wallet, no money. Just a key ring—no keys, just a bunch of photos. Doug crawled to the light of a streetlamp. He saw his own picture, and those of several other Circle members. Doug put the key ring away to think about later. He had to get back to Tasker's before the rest of his blood ended up on the ground.

Bleeding and filthy, he showed up at the door. The bartender ran out and put one arm around Doug's shoulders and one under his elbow and supported him into the lounge. "I could use some help over here!" he shouted.

Mr. Necktie was first on the scene. "What happened?"

"I don't know. He collapsed when he got in the door. Here, help me get him to a chair. He's bleeding like a stuck pig."

Mr. Dart helped the bartender get Doug to a seat. "Get the medical kit," he said.

The bartender raised his eyebrows, but ran back to the bar for the emergency first aid kit.

"He's been shot in the shoulder. Quick, I need a knife. A *sharp* knife," Dart reiterated. The bartender left, returned with his sharpest paring knife, and handed it to Mr. Dart.

"We don't have much time. He's lost a lot of blood. I need to cut around the wound and remove the bullet. Do what I tell you to do and everything will be fine."

Unfazed, the bartender ripped away Doug's shirt, sticky with blood, from his skin. He was unconscious. Mr. Dart and the bartender swept the cards off the nearest table and lay Doug on its surface.

Mr. Dart put on latex gloves and washed the wound. As he made the first cut he kept up a stream of directions. "Hold open the wound, Mr. Necktie. Bartender, get a needle and thread ready. He'll need stitches. There, there, yes, keep it open for me. ...Hold it ...Hold it... Another few seconds... I've almost got it...yes! Mr. Necktie, put pressure on the wound. Yes, like that. Bartender! Where's the nee—good. Give it to me."

Two minutes later Doug was stitched up and resting fitfully. Mr. Dart went to wash up.

Mr. Combustion joined the group. "That was unbelievable. That Mr. Dart operated like a fucking surgeon."

It was another twenty minutes before Doug stirred. His eyes opened to a slit.

"He's waking up," announced Mr. Chemist, who had also come over to the table. "Mr. Archer? Mr. Archer can you hear me?"

"W...Where am I?"

"You're at Tasker's."

MR. NECKTIE: "What happened?"

"F...Fink." It was all Doug could say.

Mr. Black had been watching since the bartender brought Doug in. Now he made his way to the table. The other members backed away.

"Did he say 'Fink'? Mr. Archer, are you telling me you've seen the Fink's face—that you know for sure that's who it was?"

Doug blinked his eyes. He was too tired and in too much pain to move his head.

MR. BLACK (turning to Mr. Necktie): "Is he going to make it?"

"Mr. Dart seems to think so."

MR. BLACK: "He can't die now. He's our only link to the Fink—he's the only one who's come in direct contact with him—and lived." Mr. Black looked hard at the others. "Take care of him."

Doug struggled to tell them about the key ring in his pocket, but speaking was too hard. His left hand moved down to his side.

MR. CHEMIST: "Look. I think he's trying to tell us something."

MR. NECKTIE (excitedly): "Yes. There's something in his pocket."

MR. BLACK: "What is it? Take it out, Mr. Necktie."

Mr. Necktie reached in to bring out the metal ring that had come part way out of Doug's pocket. "It's a key ring. But look, no keys...just photos." It took a second to sink in. "They're photos of—of us! Circle members...with X's through the faces. All except for Mr. Archer's here. There's no X."

MR. BLACK: "I...I believe Mr. Archer has defeated the Fink."

The members were silent. For such a new member to have killed the Fink, the hunter who had eluded all of them for so long...well, it was incredible.

Mr. Dart returned. "Everyone, get away from him. He needs medical attention, not conversation. Bring him over here."

Mr. Chemist and Mr. Necktie carried Doug over to the blankets that had been laid on the floor.

MR. DART: "Careful, gently. Don't open the stitches...over here. Lay him down here. That's right."

MR. BLACK (surprising the others): "What can I do?"

"We need to get some antibiotics in him, fast. And you can help me clean up these other wounds. How he made it back here I'll never know."

MR. BLACK took out his cell phone and made a brief call. "Antibiotics are on their way—along with painkillers."

MR. DART: "Good."

MR. COMBUSTION: "You wanna explain how you did that?"

MR. DART: "I was a trauma surgeon—in my other life. Some things just never leave you. Kind of funny, though, if you ask me."

MR. COMBUSTION: "What's so funny about it?"

MR. DART: "My job used to be to *save* lives. You might call it doing a career one-eighty, eh?"

MR. BLACK: "We thank you for your swift action, Mr. Dart. I think you may have saved the life of the man who has saved us all."

MR. DART: "What do you mean?"

"It appears Mr. Archer here has ended the threat of the Fink."

MR. DART (going still): "Mr. Archer killed The Fink?"

"Yes, I believe he has. And, thanks to you, he'll be able to tell us about it."

MR. NECKTIE (raising his glass): "A toast."

The men reached for the drinks they had been enjoying prior to the interruption. "To Mr. Dart—and to Mr. Archer."

"Cheers!"

The room echoed the sentiment. "Here, here!" They toasted the mostly unconscious Mr. Archer, drank, put down their glasses, and applauded Mr. Dart. Mr. Dart nodded his head and took a slight bow.

Doug is in the alley, bleeding. He's going to die. He'll never see his mother again. "Nooo...no—"

"Mr. Archer. *Mr. Archer.* Wake up. You are alright. You are in Tasker's lounge. You've been shot."

"Whaa—what time is it?"

"Six."

"AM or PM?"

"PM. You've been asleep all day."

"Dart? What're you doing here? What happened? I need to—"

Mr. Dart touched Doug on the arm to get him to lie back down onto the cot the bartender had dragged in from the back of the bar. "You don't need to do anything right now, Mr. Archer, except rest."

"What happened?" Mr. Dart was right, he was as weak as a baby.

"We were hoping you could fill us in on that, Mr. Archer. But not now. It will have to wait. You need your rest."

When Doug woke up again Mr. Dart was still there. "What time is it?"

"10:30. AM. You've slept 'round the clock. How do you feel, Mr. Archer?"

Like he'd been run over by a train, but other than that, not bad. "Hungry."

"That's good, very good. Let's see if you can sit up." Mr. Dart put his arm around Doug and lifted him to a sitting position. Doug winced with the pain, but was happy to see he had all his parts. He took the glass of water Mr. Dart offered him and drank deeply.

MR. BLACK: "Mr. Archer, I see you're awake. How are you feeling?"

"Lousy, but okay, I guess, considering."

MR. DART: "He may not be able to remember much just yet. He's suffered some serious head trauma."

In his prior life, Mr. Dart had had these conversations with police officers, detectives, and investigators of all kinds when he was working in the ER. Mr. Black was like all of them, insistent, but somehow more impatient. Police have training on how to deal with situations such as these. They tended to be more... human about it. Mr. Black, on the other hand, had waited decades to get the answers he wanted.

"Can you remember what happened, Mr. Archer?"

"All I can remember is that when I left he was out there. He followed me, shot at me from the roof of the building across the street. I chased him down." Doug stopped to take a breath.

MR. BLACK: "Yes? Then what happened?"

"We fought. I killed him. End of story."

"Dammit, this is no time to be coy. Who was it?"

He figured they knew. "The Fink."

"You know this for sure?"

Doug nodded.

"Are you certain he's dead?"

"Um, yeah. I smashed a piece of concrete reinforced rebar through his skull and then stabbed him through the neck with his own knife. So, yeah, I'm sure. Happy now?" Annoyance combined with pain. "I doubt he's still there, but I'm willing to bet that the alley across the way will provide you all the evidence you need."

There was a long silence. Mr. Black didn't get spoken to that way, but such circumstances had never presented themselves before either.

Doug lay his head back down on to the pillow and winced. "The Fink was the doorman at my apartment building. I walked past him every day. We talked, for Christ sake, even played checkers a few times. Just a nice old man. The guy was always smiling."

"He was playing a part, Mr. Archer. Luring you into his trust, playing with you."

"Did a damn good job of it, too," Doug said weakly. "He could have killed me every day for the past nine months. What was he waiting for?"

"He enjoyed knowing that fact more than he would have enjoyed killing you all this time. He thrived on the power."

Doug remembered the key ring. He reached into his pocket, but it was gone. "The pictures. I had pictures—from his pocket. Where are they—?"

MR. BLACK (taking the pictures out): "Don't worry, Mr. Archer. Are you looking for these?"

Doug relaxed. "He had my picture, Webb's, and Mr. Fingers'. Stanton Dowd—my friend's old boss—he was there, too. There were lots of them. I didn't get a chance to look."

"And no wonder, Mr. Archer. You were otherwise occupied, shall we say. But they were all good men. Many before your time, but honest men, skilled men. Taken by a man with no sense of sport, no sense of morality or fair play. In essence, a fink. A contemptible man, a miscreant, a renegade. But thanks to you, Mr. Archer, he is out of the picture. The Circle is in your debt. How can we repay you?"

Doug heard the words he had waited almost a year to hear. His way out. As simple as killing the Fink and he was out of the Circle forever? "You know what I want," he said. "I want out."

It felt like the air had been sucked out of the room.

MR. BLACK: "I'll take it up with the Council, but I already know their answer. This is the one thing we cannot do. Still, there are extenuating circumstances here. You never know."

Doug has learned that hope is dangerous, especially the hope that his life would ever be given back to him. He knows so much about the Circle, how could they ever let him go?

"My life has been nothing but shit since I stepped into Tasker's almost a year ago. I've been running for my life. I've been shot twice, attacked in my home, on the streets. Not to mention the fact that I've killed eight people. I don't want to be here, Mr. Black. I never did. Please. Let me out of this world you live in."

MR. BLACK: "I'll let you know their decision when I have it."

Even a long shot comes in once in a while, doesn't it? A slim chance is still a chance, isn't it?

Doug's faith held out until Mr. Black returned only eleven or twelve minutes later. An eternity. Doug knew the answer from the look on Black's stoic face. He couldn't look Doug in the eye as he walked to the patient's makeshift recovery room bed.

"Mr. Archer, I am sorry."

It took every ounce of willpower he had for Doug to keep from sobbing.

"Is there anything else we can do for you, Mr. Archer?"

"I want a furlough. I need some time to myself. Far away."

"How much time would you like?"

"How's thirty years sound?"

Mr. Black allowed himself a small smile. "How's thirty days?"

"A year."

"Sixty days."

"Six months."

"I've been authorized to offer no more than 90 days. I assume you'll take it."

Doug nodded in agreement. Jerk couldn't have led with that?

"The clock will begin after your recovery, so take your time to rest up while you're here. You will be informed in the usual way when the hunt has again begun. Enjoy your time, Mr. Archer. You deserve it."

Members come and go. Days fade into nights and back again. Too weak to leave after his "operation," Doug alternates sitting at the bar with traversing the bar's perimeter while he works up the strength to go home. They've given him space with a cot where he sleeps and reads. Once he leaves he'll have a whole ninety days off and yet he's too damn weak to leave and get them started. He always wondered what would happen if he never left, and now he's starting to see. Members greet him by name, people he's never seen before; it seems everyone knows who he is now. They thank him for his "service," his great deed done in the name of the Circle. Doug cringes at the words, but thanks them. Manners and all. The bartender serves him expensive organic juices and Perrier. No liquor, not with the antibiotics and painkillers he's on.

39

Mr. Dart has been monitoring his progress. Hospitals are out—gunshot wounds are legally required to be reported by doctors to the authorities. Granted, Doug has been led to believe that the Circle owned the police, but he assumes it stops short of owning the entire world's supply of ER docs. He has to believe that kind of bribe would put a crimp in the Circle's anonymity factor.

Mr. Dart sat down at the bar next to him. "Can you lift your arm yet?"

Doug lifted his arm to the point of pain, about to chest level. "Not past here."

"That's better than I would have thought. It's only been a few days. It'll probably take a few weeks before you gain total use of the arm again."

Doug nodded, resigned. "Hey, I have a question for you." Since the moment he'd regained consciousness, Doug hadn't been able to let it go. "Why did you help me?" What bigger irony could there be than having the very man who saved his life be the same man he is supposed to kill. If these were ordinary circumstances, he'd owe him a debt of gratitude. But in these circumstances....

"You needed help," Mr. Dart said, "It's that simple."

"It's anything but simple."

"Touché," conceded Mr. Dart. He searched for a more complete answer. "You are a member of the Circle, Mr. Archer, and you came to the safe house. You deserved to find the safety you sought. Besides, before I became a member I took an oath. Couldn't let you die on my watch, now could I?" The irony cut deep.

"I guess you could say I owe you one, then," said Doug.

"Don't mention it. I'm sure you would do the same for me."

Doug dredged up a half-smile. Could the guy be so blind? Didn't he know Doug would be hunting him as soon as he recovered? But now he owed Dart. Didn't he? That was the insanity of it all. How do you tell your friend, the man who saved your life, that you're going to try to kill him? The irony was unbearable this time.

Doug was feeling lightheaded. He'd been up too long. His bed in the back room off the bar was calling to him.

"In fact, I think it is I who owe you *one," said Mr. Dart.*

"How do you mean?" asked Doug carefully.

"Well, don't you think it's a little odd that while you have been fighting to leave the Circle, I myself have not been in any danger."

Doug flushed. He knew! He'd known the whole time!

"Please, Mr. Archer. You didn't think I was that naïve, did you?"

"How long have you known?" Doug asked.

"For a while now," Mr. Dart admitted. *"That's why I'm extending you the same courtesy. You refuse to hunt, so I refuse to strike first."*

"But they say there's no way out."

"That may be so, but I see you as an honorable man, Mr. Archer. And honorable men aren't the ones who stab you in the back."

"But that means that eventually...one of us is going to kill the other."

"Makes you feel alive, doesn't it?"

"Not really. Makes me want to throw up. How can I take the life of the man who has saved mine? For that matter, how can I kill someone who hasn't tried to hurt me?"

"Life is full of these little tests, isn't it?" said Mr. Dart. *"How can I sleep with my friend's wife? How can I steal my partner's money? But people do."*

Philosophy aside, it didn't help much. *"I guess you could say that."*

"I hope you don't think this will change what we have to do."

"Don't you think it should?"

"No, I don't. When the Army captures enemy soldiers, don't they make sure they stay relatively healthy and fed? It's the same here."

"So that makes us enemies then?"

"Not right now. Not in here. One day, though...out there...it'll have to."

"But I don't want to kill you."

"I don't particularly want to kill you either, Mr. Archer, but when the time comes, if it comes down to you or me, I will do what I have to do."

"Unless we both take a stand and stop it," Doug said, taking a big risk.

But all Mr. Dart said was, "Why would we want to do that?"

"Mr. Archer? Can you hear me?"

Doug got a whiff of the smelling salts Mr. Dart was holding under his nose and shuddered. He was on the floor in the bar, people huddled around him, curious. "You back with us, Mr. Archer?"

Had he imagined the whole conversation? He couldn't have. "What do you mean?"

"You passed out, fell down," said the bartender. "You were out for a few minutes. You were mumbling, too. Something about taking a stand...."

Mr. Dart shot the bartender a look. The bartender cleared his throat and stepped back behind the bar to clean glassware.

"Mr. Archer," Mr. Dart said, "I'm going to have to address that wound. It's bleeding again. It needs cleaning and possibly re-stitching."

"Whatever you say," Doug said, as he was helped to his feet. Mr. Dart placed Doug's arm around his shoulder for support.

"Hey," said Doug. "What's your real name?"

"Why?"

"Because it doesn't feel right to thank someone named Mr. Dart for saving my life."

Mr. Dart paused for so long that Doug figured that was his answer.

"Nolan, Kevin Nolan," he finally said, "from Pittsburgh."

"Well, then, thank you, Dr. Nolan, for saving my life."

"You're welcome," said Dr. Nolan/Mr. Dart gruffly. "Now, let's get you fixed up."

40

Liz held her father's cufflinks in her hand. She could not look away from them. On leave for thirty days from the Circle, she hadn't left her bed for the first three of them except to eat and use the bathroom. Her body was screaming for activity. She got up and placed the cufflinks in front of a gold-framed picture of her father that was leaning against the mirror on her bureau. Her period of mourning had to come to a close, but it was painful nonetheless. She fingered the frame and moved it a few inches to the right, then considered the stack of printouts next to it outlining the uses and hazards of poisonous flowers. The research that had set the framework for her successful hunt and elimination of Mr. Cufflinks. She wasn't ready to throw it all away.

She was still at odds with the sting, too—not with the hunt, the killing, or the tactile presentation of the death of another human being—but by the man's unadulterated display of ego in the steam room. When she was young she and her friends used to scrunch up their noses when something "grossed them out." That's exactly the way she felt when she'd seen Mr. Cufflinks, like a kid who was witnessing something unbearably disgusting. That's how she feels now, remembering. Dirty from the depravity of it. She has absolutely no remorse for having ridded the planet of such a man.

She picked up the pile of papers and filed it next to a large blue folder with her name, "Hughes," on it in big block letters. The conversation the day before the envelope had landed on her doorstep was one she'd never forget.

"I was told to contact you about becoming a member."

"You were told correctly. How did you hear about us?"

"That's not important, Mr. Williams," she said. "What is important is how much money I can bring to the table. My name is Elizabeth Hughes. I'm worth over three billion dollars."

"You know what the rules are, Ms. Hughes? You're willing to donate your entire fortune to the Circle and give yourself over to it completely?"

"Yes. On one condition."

"You don't have the right to ask for anything."

His affront was meaningless. "I should think three billion would give me that right." Liz waited for that to sink in.

When there was hesitation, she continued. "I want Mr. Cufflinks to be my first assignment."

"Joining the Circle for vengeance is frowned upon, Ms. Hughes."

Liz was prepared for this response. "I'm joining for my own reasons, Mr. Williams. Frankly, they are none of your business. I'm willing to give the Circle my life and the fortune my father left me. The part you didn't get your hands on. Now, are you going to work with me or not?"

"I'll see what I can do, Ms. Hughes."

"See that you do."

Liz locked the folder in her fireproof safe under the bed. When she emerged, she reorganized the top of her dresser, repositioning the photo of her father a few more times until she decided on front and center, and placed one cufflink on either side. Finally satisfied, she then found a picture of herself and Doug taken months before. She was sitting on his shoulders and he was flexing his biceps, hamming it up for the camera. A smile came to her face as she remembered being there on the edge of the mountain, setting the timer on the camera, and then feverishly running back into position. Had she ever been so happy? The answer was easy: no, never. Doug had been the best thing in her life. It was her fault they'd fallen out of contact after that weekend. Of her own design.

The car ride home had been distressingly difficult, knowing that she would have to curb her need for his company, her desire for their intimacy, in order to devote herself to her search for—and extermination of—Mr. Cufflinks. His caring questions had torn at her. But she could no more have shared that she was a member of an elite organization of killers than she could the fact that she'd been lying to Doug all along about who she really was.

Suddenly she missed Doug so acutely that the ache physically assaulted her. She was helpless to resist. She needed to see him. But what would she say? What would she tell him about where she's been, and why? She didn't know. Before she chickened out she picked up the phone, scrolled down to his number and hit send. One ring...two....

She hung up before he could answer. Why would he forgive her? She'd disappeared for weeks. She had no right to ask for anything. But she had to talk to him. She dialed again, waited. But what if he—

"Yeah."

"Doug?"

"Liz?"

"Yeah, it's me. Um, how are you?"

Silence.

He wasn't going to forgive her, then. It was over. She should never have called.

"I'm sorry, Doug, I thought maybe...I understand, I'll just...." She went to disconnect.

"No, wait. I'm just surprised, that's all. To what do I owe this honor?"

The bite in his voice stung, but beneath the acidity was something else. Fatigue? Pain? Had he been ill?

"Um, I wanted to talk to you, Doug. I feel like it's been forever," she said.

"That's because it has. I wondered if I'd ever hear from you again. You pretty much vanished off the planet."

The hurt in his voice was devastating. "I know, I...I can't really explain it just now. But I wanted to apologize. I'm sorry for—"

"Well, now you've apologized. Thanks. You don't have to worry about it anymore."

"No! No, that's not what I meant. Please, Doug. Just listen."

Dead air. Well, at least he was still there.

She made her pitch. "Doug, I'm really, *really* sorry. I had some important things to take care of, over in Europe, things to do with my inheritance...I was up to my eyeballs in meetings and lawyers and...my old life... I just couldn't think about anything personal. I'm sorry, I should have....

"Doug? Are you still there?"

"Yeah, I'm still here."

"Please forgive me, Doug. I've missed you so, so much. Please, can you come over for dinner tonight? I promise things will be different."

Of course she couldn't promise that at all, not with her life in the hands of the Circle. But she needed Doug more than she had ever needed anything—with the exception of killing Mr. Cufflinks, and that was done. She crossed her fingers and said a prayer.

"I'd like that," Doug finally said.

"Great," she said. "Can you be here around 7:00?"

"Sure. I'll pick up a bottle of wine. You still like that white merlot we found that day in the country?"

"Nothing would be better," she said quietly, her heart beating a little faster. "I'll see you tonight, then."

Liz hummed as she dressed and made her shopping list. Maybe a duck with all the trimmings, pecan pie for dessert. Nothing was too good for Douglas Goodwin.

The atmosphere at Tasker's shifted as soon as she stepped in the door. Since this was her first time, Liz wasn't really sure why until she took a good look around. She was sticking out like a sore thumb. She was the only woman in the bar not hanging all over a male patron. She would have preferred to leave, but then again, she was there for a reason. She took a seat at a stool and beckoned for the bartender.

"Well, now, what can I get you, little lady?"

Little lady? She should tell him to piss off. Instead she went with the plainest words she could. "I'm here for an audience with Mr. Black." The general commotion of the room didn't exactly let up, but the decibel of sound decreased almost imperceptibly. Liz shifted uncomfortably.

"Mr. Black," repeated the bartender, "I'm afraid I don't know a Mr. Black."

She motioned for him to lean closer. "Look. I need to see the man in charge of the Circle. Are you telling me he isn't here?"

To her right, a door silently opened in the paneling. The bartender gestured in its direction.

"Thank you," said Liz. Someone must have been listening, or watching—or both.

Inside, she took in her surroundings, more of the same. Gentlemen dressed to the nines with a select group of women seeing to their needs. Liz didn't know, nor did she wish to find out, exactly what those needs were. The men were playing cards, darts...it was basically a game room, an elite men's club—from the women to the cigars. In the past, Liz would never have been caught dead in such a place, not that she'd ever be invited. The thought struck her as funny. This might well be the only place where she *wouldn't* be caught dead. Black humor. She almost laughed again at that.

Keeping any hint of a smile from her lips, she glided into the room. She knew the effect she had on men and didn't hesitate to use it when she needed to. She'd chosen a creamy lightweight woolen suit with a short skirt and a red Gucci scarf around her neck. Her red Manolo Blahniks had four-inch heels. Her mother always told her that it was all about the entrance—even when you didn't have the money to back it up.

A man with the torso of a bear and a mane of silvery hair cleared his throat. "Can I help you?"

"Yes, I'm here to see Mr. Black."

From his seat in the dark corner, Mr. Black had been watching his computer screen. As soon as the woman walked into the bar he'd been put on notice.

"I see. Won't you have a seat, my dear."

It was not a request.

"Sure," said Liz, taking the seat. "But I don't have all day." Of course she did, but she would not be intimidated.

"Of course not, no, can we get you something to drink? A Perrier perhaps?"

"Vodka on the rocks," Liz said. She'd rather a nice IPA and didn't like vodka, but it came to mind as a good drink to order when you wanted to impress people.

"Monica," Mr. Lion called to one of the women. "Please fetch Miss...our guest...a vodka on the rocks."

Monica sashayed out to the bar, her perfume leaving a wake of sexual promise. Liz almost gagged.

"By the way," said Mr. Lion, putting his hand out, "I am Mr. Lion."

Liz was supposed to reciprocate with her name, but she was unwilling to part with even an iota of information until she saw Mr. Black. She shook Mr. Lion's hand, but kept her mouth shut.

Mr. Black was impressed with the woman's style. He made sure his jacket was buttoned and that his face remained in the shadows. "I'm Mr. Black," he said from the dark corner.

Liz stood up, ready to move to him, but suddenly, as if on cue, the ten or so men in the room converged around her, blocking her progress.

"Mr. Cufflinks is dead," Liz said loudly, making sure everyone heard. "I'm the one who killed him."

Ah, not a new recruit at all. Rather, the industrious self-initiated member who'd managed to kill one of their most seasoned, Mr. Cufflinks. Intimidation certainly wouldn't be necessary. She'd have been versed in most of the rules as well.

"Congratulations on your first kill, Ms. Hughes," said Mr. Black, "and welcome to the Circle. I was expecting you, perhaps not this soon, however."

"Mmm," Liz said noncommittally. "And were you planning on sharing the rules at some point? Like the fact that I will be a target in another, oh, twenty-six days?"

"It appears that you already know our rules," Mr. Black said, "but, if you'll forgive me, it's twenty-seven days actually."

"Ah," Liz said, "A stickler for detail." She let a beat go by. "So, this is the safe house. No one can kill inside these walls, is that correct? And after a kill I have thirty days off?"

"Technically that is correct," said Mr. Black.

"Ah...'technically.' I've heard there's a renegade out there somewhere as well, ready and able to kill us all. Name of the Fink. I'd like to hear more about that, too. Oh, and I'm stuck here until I'm sixty, is that right? Unless I'm killed before then.... Of course, that would suck for me."

Mr. Black was not amused. "Ms. Hughes," he said coldly. "There is a certain level of etiquette we maintain at Tasker's. If you are incapable of that level then I'm afraid you won't be welcome here. Is that understood?"

Liz looked at him. She was not put off. She'd pushed the limits and now knew what she wanted to find out: how the game was played. She was a woman in a man's world—a world of nothing but killers; she needed to know.

Mr. Black took her silence as acquiescence. "It is now time for your naming, Ms. Hughes. From now on you are no longer Ms. Hughes—or anything else you wish to call yourself. As far as the Circle is concerned, you will now be referred to and addressed with your new name. Is that clear?"

Liz nodded. *Whatever. What's in a name anyway?*

Mr. Black continued. "Since I am the only one who knows the details of your kill, I will do the honors. I have chosen Madame de la Fleur. It's French for—"

"I get it," said Liz. "Lady of the Flowers. I don't hate it."

"Well, well, a Francophile," said Mr. Black. "A simple thank you will do."

Liz was beginning to understand that she was dealing with someone with at least a modicum of brains. Dissing the boss may not be the best idea she'd ever had. "Thank you."

"I'm afraid you are misinformed about one thing, however, Madame de la Fleur. Our Mr. Archer has eliminated the threat of the Fink once and for all."

"Well, I don't mind being wrong about that. I'd like to thank Mr. Archer personally. Is he here?"

"No, for his service to the Circle Mr. Archer has been given a ninety-day furlough. I believe he is only six days into it, so you will be unlikely to meet him in person for some time.

"Let me ask you a question, madame," he continued, "Why did you seek me out?"

"To make myself known, Mr. Black. I believe in putting my cards on the table."

"Noted, Madame de la Fleur. Enjoy your remaining holiday."

"Thank you, Mr. Black, I'm sure I will."

Liz rose to her feet. She'd been dismissed. Instead of leaving the room directly, she walked over to Mr. Black's table to shake his hand. "It's been a...pleasure, Mr. Black."

Mr. Black reciprocated warily and nodded goodbye.

Liz strode from the room and the door swooshed closed.

"She'll add quite the spark around here," said Mr. Chemist. "I wouldn't half mind the pleasure of that hunt, know what I mean?"

"That's not the only thing I'd enjoy the pleasure of," started Mr. Combustion. "A good f—"

Mr. Black was up and across the room before Mr. Combustion could finish his sentence. He grabbed the member by the throat and levied him against the wall.

As he struggled to free himself, Mr. Combustion knew he could die there and then, even in the supposed safety zone of the walls of the Circle's safe house.

"Remarks like those are not the sign of a gentleman, Mr. Combustion," Mr. Black said. "If I were you, I would bear that in mind from now on."

Mr. Combustion could only nod.

Mr. Black let him go, dusted off his jacket.

The room was quiet except for Mr. Combustion's hacking.

"Pick him up," said Mr. Black. Mr. Chemist and Mr. Necktie put Mr. Combustion into a chair and handed him a glass of water.

"This woman killed Mr. Cufflinks without setting foot inside the safe house even once. She is far more dangerous an adversary than you ever will be, Mr. Combustion. You will show her the same respect as you did Ms. Mantis or any other member of the Circle. As for the tenor of your remark, if I find out anything discourteous is said about her—or done to her—I will personally remove your safe house privileges—or kill you myself. Is that clear?"

"Yes, sir," said Mr. Combustion, anger shooting out his eyes.

"Very well," Mr. Black said. "Take him away."

Mr. Combustion disappeared.

41

Using the password and keystrokes he'd learned from Professor Balachi, Doug accessed the Circle's online database. He'd come close to using it once before but was too much of a chicken. The dark web was a dangerous place and he wasn't comfortable navigating it. That, and the fact that he was afraid that utilizing it, would mean he'd totally given in. At this point, what could it hurt to give it a good look? He had plenty of R&R left. What better opportunity could possibly present itself? Immediately his own picture came up, then the picture of Mr. Dart. Doug looked at the likeness of the man who'd saved his life only a few weeks ago. How could he hunt and kill someone who'd just saved his ass? Yet, Mr. Lion was right. "Any one of your friends in here could very well be your hunter out there."

Doug clicked on Mr. Dart's picture and was taken to a Website that listed all of the information that had been included in his packet upon his initiation, addresses, schedules, and so forth. What interested him was the icon in the right corner of the box that looked like a globe. Clicking the icon brought up an interactive map of the planet. As the world became focused, it zoomed into the island of Manhattan, limiting the search to inside the five boroughs, creating a circular border.

The program was a lot more sophisticated than the one he'd used before. This one, unlike the traditional version, was a live satellite feed. Doug stared at the little blue dots, constantly in motion. He hit his head in awe and disbelief. The blue dots were moving because they were part of a GPS system! He clicked on one of the dots. Instantly he was two hundred feet above his target, Mr. Dart. He clicked on another. He was two hundred feet above Mr. Chemist. Above a third, he now knew exactly where he could find Mr. Black. They were all there. Every single member. They weren't identified as hunter or target, but all of them were accounted for.

Doug zoomed out, back to the aerial view of Manhattan, and discovered that there were at least sixty different dots, all in motion, all of which he could click to review. He clicked on Mr. Dart again and followed as his blue dot walked down West 49th Street and made a left onto Broadway. He zoomed out. Next he found his own apartment on the map, and sure enough, there was a dot over the building, only his dot was red. He clicked on it and the name "Mr. Archer" appeared, but, unlike the others, his had the number "84" underneath it. He didn't have to do the math to know that a red dot meant he was not to be touched for, in this case, eighty-four more days. Several other red dots were out there too, moving around...members going about their business, living their lives—for now. Doug sat back. He was blown away, and an idiot for not using this program before. It was the perfect way to locate your target.

Of course that meant it was the perfect way for your target to locate you as well.

He withdrew money from the Circle's seemingly endless supply, increased by more than three billion dollars since he'd last checked, and made his way to an electronics store. In the past if he'd wanted to purchase something electronic he'd take the subway down to the very bottom of Manhattan to Canal Street where the best deals could be made. Now, it made no difference where he shopped. With the cash, he purchased an expensive smart phone with a huge amount of capacity and data. Suddenly he felt more secure. Now he could be logged onto the tracking system while he moved around the city. It was interesting. Despite being on furlough, he could still monitor all the other members. As they could him. If he saw a blue dot in his area, he could presumably prepare for it, or maneuver away from it. The app was customizable, too. He could program the system to beep whenever a blue dot approached within one thousand yards of him, twice if within five hundred. Since he's on furlough, he set the device's alarm to start after the eighty-second day was over to give him an extra day to work out the kinks.

He's still surprised by the call from Liz that afternoon. For weeks, aside from his injury and the date his next hunt would begin, he'd thought about nothing else. He'd been desolate at the loss of her presence. He'd called and left messages at home and on her cell, but she'd never answered. It was as if she never existed, as if the weekend in the mountains had been a figment of his imagination. He'd been ready to say he loved her. Then, out of nowhere, she was gone. Hearing from her had knocked the wind out of him, just as not hearing from her had taken the wind out of his sails.

He's not sure he's doing the right thing in going to see her. But he has no choice; he's drawn to her like the proverbial moth to a flame. It's that simple.

The first wine shop he checked didn't have the one he wanted, and it took him two more stops before he found it and made his purchase. Whitewater Hill White merlot, made in Colorado, was what she liked and that's what she'd get. The closest subway stop to Liz's townhouse was 1st Ave and 60th; he'd walk from there.

The platform at 72nd Street was packed with bodies. Liz lived on Sutton Place, one of the glitziest, yet sedate, New York neighborhoods. Regardless of the fact that he now had access to all the money in the world, he still thought of it that way, as somewhere he could never afford, never live. Her inheritance must have been mighty steep for her to maintain that kind of lifestyle.

Doug stayed back away from the tracks. Even on furlough, even with the Fink out of commission, standing too close to the tracks was asking for trouble. He parked himself next to a bench behind which someone had dumped a pile of trash. You had to love the city.

The trash moved. Doug peered down into the dim space between the wall and the bench. It wasn't a bag of garbage, just some poor sad schmuck of a homeless person. "I'm sorry," he said automatically. Had he disturbed the person somehow? An arm snaked out of the rag pile, then two, and then a head with a knit cap on it. Male or female, he couldn't tell.

Now would be a really good time for the train to arrive. Doug thought about staking a claim farther down the platform, but he felt perversely fascinated by the form at his feet, which was slowly taking shape. Like a turtle poking his head out of his shell to take an exploratory look out at his surroundings, a wrinkled face revealed itself. There was something familiar about the face, the hat, this spot. But that was crazy. He didn't know any homeless people.

Doug snapped his fingers. *Yes, I do.* Of course. It was that woman—the same woman he and Eric had "met" on the way to Tasker's on the very first night of his Circle recruitment. Since his best buddy had taken his own life to avoid the Circle's retribution and Doug had become a hunter of men. He looked at the woman, old way beyond her years, he was sure, her face cracked and weathered, her eyes fearful and crazed.

Doug spotted an ATM machine not far from the turnstiles. So what if he missed the next train, the one that was already entering the station. He'd get the next one. He withdrew ten thousand dollars easy as pie. The woman's cardboard box was a few feet back now, over a heated grate. The homeless in New York City staked out the best grates in the best places for safety and warmth in the cold months. This woman's box was lined with newspaper, probably to provide a layer of insulation.

The woman could be sick or crazy, neither, or both. He bent down to talk to her. She scurried back as far as she could go into her box, maybe three feet. She actually growled at him. Doug reassessed the situation. He really doesn't want to get bitten—or worse—stabbed or assaulted. Maybe this wasn't such a good idea. On the other hand, curiosity was working on him. On the third hand, curiosity killed the cat. Oh, well.

"Ma'am, do you need some help?"

"Son? Terry?" The voice was raspy from disuse.

"No, ma'am, I'm not your son. I'm not Terry, I'm, um, one of his friends." Doug recalled how the woman had mistaken Eric for Terry, too.

"My son's coming to pick me up soon."

She might be crazy, but she was semi-coherent. "Terry can't come right now, ma'am."

Her eyes filled with tears.

"No, don't cry, ma'am. Terry sent me instead. He'll, um, he'll be here soon. Look," he took out the money from his pocket, "he asked me to give you this."

Her eyes lit up. "That's from my Terry?"

"Yes, Terry said for you to hide it away carefully, to use it to buy the things you need. Do you understand?"

Was any of this making it through to the woman's brain? She could fling the money into the river or burn it for warmth, for all he knew. The woman looked left and right, then snatched the money from his hands. Before you could say Houdini, it was gone, deep into her cardboard capsule.

"Ma'am," Doug asked again. "Are you sure you're okay? I could take you to the hospital."

"No!" She spoke from the back of her cardboard home. "No hospital."

"Okay, okay, no hospital."

The woman reached into her many layers of clothing and brought out a blue envelope, much creased and stained.

Doug's forehead knotted. It looked like a....

"Give this to my Terry," she said, and held out the envelope.

The morning after my recruitment. The blue envelope under the doormat in Lackawanna. The blue envelopes that appeared at the doorstep of every member. This was no ordinary blue envelope. It was from the Circle.

"Where did you get that?" asked Doug. His intensity must have frightened her because again she scooted back into her box with the envelope. "I'm sorry, ma'am, really. It's okay," he said, coaxing her out again. "I'll give it to Terry." He put out his hand. *Give it to me, lady, it's okay, just put it in my hands. Come on, now. Right here....*

The envelope sailed out and landed at Doug's feet. He picked it up and turned it over. The name RAWLINGS was still legible, though faded. Slowly it came back to him, how that night with Eric the woman had been babbling something about circles. Only it wasn't "circles." It was the Circle. She'd been talking about The damn Circle.

Terry went to the store for me and the circles got him, she'd said. *You be careful of those circles, too.* She'd warned him, but who'd listen to something like that? And poor Terry? It was pretty obvious what happened to him, that he'd never be coming back.

"Ma'am, do you remember where you got this envelope?"

"Terry gave it to me to hold. It's important. Terry needs it."

Doug weighed the envelope in his hand. It was heavier than the ones he'd gotten before. "Is your last name Rawlings?"

"Rawlings, Terry Rawlings, my son. Born July 7, 1962, died October 22, 1999, thirty-seven years old."

She knew that Terry was dead, but still wanted him to have the envelope. What a sad, sad story. "What happened to Terry, ma'am?"

"Terry went to the store. The circles got him. He's coming back for me, Terry is. He loves me." The woman began rifling through her things.

Push her too hard and she'd crack. But he had to know.

"Ma'am, what do you mean, the circles got him? Was he kidnapped?"

"My Terry." She pulled out an old newspaper clipping. Doug read the headline. "Investment Banker Missing" it said. "My Terry."

Doug scanned the article. A few key words jumped out at him: "high-ranking partner," "body never found," "no evidence left behind." Doug didn't have to guess what happened to Terry. "Ma'am, you're talking about the Circle, aren't you?"

"Stay away from the circles," the woman said, rocking, "*Stay away from the circles.*"

"Yes, yes. But why are you so afraid?"

"Terry asked me what I needed at the store."

The whole box was rocking with her now. Time was running out.

"Milk, I told him. Just milk."

"But ma'am, why circles? *Why circles?*" And why hadn't the Watchers gotten to this woman, Terry's mother? Was she too little of a threat?

The woman backed away, all the way into her box. Her words were now only mumbles punctuated by sobs.

He looked into the blue envelope, at the *Welcome to The Circle* at the top.

"The circles took my boy," the woman sobbed one last time.

Doug stood up. He'd gotten everything he could possibly get from Terry's mother. Maybe she'd know enough to use the money he left her for some food, perhaps a room for a few nights. It was a dangerous city for people who lived in cardboard boxes.

Or for investment bankers who killed for sport.

Liz had given up hope that Doug would show. She'd never been stood up before and was at odds with the feelings of insecurity it brought on. The candles had burned down and the roast duck was nothing but a lump of charcoal. Her dress was a mass of wrinkles. She felt dejected and angry and more hurt than she'd ever felt in her life.

Doug looked at his watch. He was late for his dinner with Liz. Really late. Forgotten about Liz. How was that even possible? He took out his new smart phone. "Liz? Hi. No, no, I'm okay. ...I just...something came up. No, really, I mean it. It's my fault. Is it too late? Well, okay, yeah, yeah, I understand. Yeah, dried-out duck can't be too appealing.... But really, I really do want to see you. Yeah, okay, I guess I'll just go home tonight. But, please, let's make another date. Yeah, okay, I'll call you tomorrow....

Doug put away his phone. Matthews' idiotic voice rang in his head. *Dude, I coulda told you that. Do a good deed, lose your babe in the process.*

42

When it was built in 1870, the building that now housed one of New York's most prestigious restaurants housed several hundred Southdown sheep that grazed across the street in what was known as Sheep Meadow in Central Park. Over the years it had reincarnated several times, but never so successfully as in 1976 when a ten million-dollar renovation, complete with chandeliers, antiques, and original artwork, soon made what was now Tavern on the Green the shining palace it was today.

High vaulted ceilings accentuate the Tavern's beauty and splendor. This restaurant is the only one in the country with a full-time horticultural staff and greenhouse. Doug took it all in. The artwork alone must cost in the millions.

He looked at his watch again, possibly the twentieth time in half as many minutes, and cast nervous glances over his shoulder at the long red awning leading to the entrance. Outside, several horse-drawn carriages waited for new fares. The lawn sculptures of various animals, topiaries, if he wasn't mistaken, were impressive, but not to his taste. The big one to his right could have been a man or a gorilla; either way its close presence made him slightly ill at ease. Every so often he checked his inside jacket pocket.

Suddenly the lights went out and hands were cupped in front of his eyes. Not here—in public? Who would take that kind of chance? He made a fist.

"Guess who!"

Cripes! Liz. Not some crazed killer, but Liz, the woman of his dreams. *When did she get here?* "Liz, I was starting to worry about you." He got up and kissed her on the cheek. She was tantalizing in a dress he'd never seen before, backless, metallic silver and blue. It was hard not to stare. In fact, it was hard not to rip off her clothes right there in front of thirty-odd wait-staff and some of the most sophisticated clientele in the city.

He moved around the table and pulled out her chair. She sat, arranged herself, her purse, the size of a slim paperback, and smiled at him.

"You are so incredibly beautiful," he said.

"Thank you, sweetheart. I'm sorry to be late."

"I'm the one who should be sorry. I mean it, Liz. I bailed on you a few weeks ago and I feel terrible about it. I know how weird it is that I'd stop and try to help this homeless woman, but I really did feel I had to—"

"Doug, it's okay. I understand...sort of. But if that's what you felt you had to do, it's okay."

"To be honest, it was really all a ploy to make you jealous. Did it work?"

"Well, seeing as all of a sudden every homeless person I see on the street makes me think of you...yeah, I guess you could say it worked."

When they laughed together the ice was finally broken, but both of them still felt the other's persistent wariness. There was a lot at stake. "So, Ms. Too-Busy-All-The-Time, what have you been doing?"

"Work has been insane lately. I've been to six auctions this week alone, two yesterday," she said. *The truth? I researched the man who killed my father, then poisoned him, and watched him die.* Yeah, probably not.

"That sounds intense. Anything interesting?"

"Absolutely nothing, disappointing, really," she said. "Mostly contemporary art, and my client isn't interested in that stuff."

"I'm sorry to hear that."

"No, it's fine," Liz said.

Which it clearly wasn't.

The waiter, a trim gentleman with a sweeping white walrus mustache approached with a bottle of wine. "I understand it is the lady's birthday. Will this vintage do, sir?" He presented Doug with a bottle of Opus One, Mondavi Rothschild, 2003, Nappa Valley Meritage.

"Doug, you remembered my birthday! I'm flattered," Liz said.

Doug pointed to a wine on the list in the leathered portfolio. "The lady and I would prefer a bottle of Screaming Eagle Estate, 1996, Cabernet Sauvignon, please."

"Very good, sir," said the waiter.

Liz peered over at the price. "Doug, what are you doing?" she whispered. "That's over three thousand dollars!"

"Oh, and that's not all," Doug added, reaching into his pocket.

Liz flinched. Suddenly she was down below the table top.

Doug jumped to his feet. "Liz? Are you okay?"

"Oh, yeah, sorry. It's these darn heels. Shows you what lengths I'll go to, to entice you...." Did she really think Doug would be going for a gun? Him? Here? She sat back up at the table.

Doug, nonplussed, simply looked at her.

"But what's this?" she said brightly. She sighed with relief when Doug refocused his attention on the box in front of them.

It was from Tiffany's, she knew that right away. One of the best-known gift wraps in all New York—probably around the world. Inside were two Platinum swing drop earrings, each with three-and-a-quarter-karat round sapphires and full karat round brilliant diamonds, sitting on a soft, white, velvety bed. She breathed in.

"Do you like them?"

"I love them." She got up and went around the table to give Doug a hug and a kiss. She knew the Tiffany's catalog by heart. The earrings he had just given her were worth a fortune. "Doug, are you sure you can afford this?"

"Don't worry about it, Liz, I told you, I have it." And I want you, he thought. *You. For the rest of my life.*

The waiter returned at that moment to prepare the wine for Doug's approval. Doug recalled Mr. Chemist's story about poison and wine, but this wasn't the day to worry about it with forty-two days left on his furlough. The freedom was liberating, but lurking at its edges was the painful reminder that he'd never have such a prolonged freedom ever again. Not without killing someone first. The waiter poured them each a glass with the pomp and circumstance Doug had come to expect from the establishments he'd been frequenting since joining the Circle. The waiter placed the bottle in a bronze stand next to the table and left as unobtrusively as he'd arrived.

Doug reached for his glass and raised it in the air, hoping Liz wouldn't see his slight wince at the motion. His shoulder had healed well, but it still gave him a nudge every now and then to remind him of his meeting with the Fink. At some point he'd have to come up with an explanation for why he suddenly had a scar where the bullet had been removed. If tonight went as planned, it'd better be fast.

"To Elizabeth Hughes. I could never have imagined that someone like you would happen to a guy like me."

"You are the most wonderful man I've ever met, Douglas Goodwin," said Liz, meaning it with all her heart. In another time, another place....

She took a sip of wine but hardly tasted it. "Can you excuse me for one second, Doug? I just need to touch up my makeup."

"Of course. But you look perfect to me."

Liz managed a smile, took one more sip of wine, and walked quickly to the back of the restaurant.

It was the one thing all men allowed all women: the freedom to "touch up" in the ladies room. In the bathroom, as big as many peoples' homes and decorated like a mini Versailles, Liz approached the mirror, where the sight of her deceitful self undid her. The tears ran, hot and stinging. *Shit. Shit, shit, shit.* She couldn't do this. She couldn't go back there with red eyes and a drippy nose. She placed her hands on the edges of the sink and focused on the tiles on the wall. An old trick, but a good one. Counting tiles stopped the trembling and plugged the emotional hole. And it was better than looking at herself, at the person she'd become.

Sniffling, she used a tissue to mop up the residual flow. She needed to get back. She forced herself to look at her reflection, but avoided the woman. Saw only the eyes, the lips, the nose, separate parts that could be anyone's.

She cleaned herself up, fixed her eye make-up, dabbed powder on her pink nose, and took a deep breath. *Make it good, sister. Make it good.*

Their entrées were on the table. Doug had waited for Liz to return before starting in on their seared yellowfin tuna. "Everything okay?" he asked.

"Of course, fine, just a little choked up." Liz sat down and took a long drink to steady her nerves.

"Good. Because there's something else I want to tell you."

"Oh?" Liz took a bite of her salad, which tasted like cardboard.

"I love you."

Liz almost choked on her hearts of palm.

"I just had to say it. I love you. It makes sense to me—*you* make sense to me."

The tears Liz had successfully bottled up escaped and ran down her cheeks.

"I keep making you cry," said Doug, putting down his fork. "I'm sorry, I didn't mean to—"

"No...no, it's not you..." She couldn't do this. "Listen, I...I have to go."

"What? Go? Go where? What are you talking about?"

"Doug," she said. She opened her mouth to speak, but then closed it again. What was the use?

Doug grabbed her arm. "Just because I love you doesn't mean you have to love me yet. I understand. I can wait."

"You don't want to love me, Doug. Believe me, I'm nothing but trouble. You need to get away from me while you still can."

"What the hell are you talking about, Liz?"

People were beginning to look up.

"You won't understand," Liz insisted, trying to keep her voice low. "You can't understand."

"You're right, I won't understand if you don't tell me."

"I *do* love you, Doug. More than I ever thought I could love anyone. I want you to know that."

"Then what won't I understand? Listen, whatever the trouble you're talking about is, we'll face it together." His face fell suddenly. "Oh, shit. Don't tell me," he said. "You're married."

"No!" Liz almost laughed—almost. "No, I'm not married."

"Then what?"

Liz tried to come up with something—anything—but had nothing.

"Look," said Doug, saving her. "What do you say we go back to my place, just the two of us, no—" he gestured to the room "—public. This wasn't the place for this. I should have—"

"No, it's not your fault," said Liz finally. "You're right. Let's go." She shouldn't go with him. But she couldn't stay away.

"Good. I'll go pay the bill."

"I'll get my wrap."

Liz took a last long gulp of the second most expensive wine she'd ever had for courage, then got her silk stole and stepped outside to wait. After a minute she stepped back inside the vestibule. She wished now she'd brought a bigger purse. The fashion statement she was carrying didn't hold but the bare essentials—and none of them were what she needed right now.

Doug and Liz were sitting on the couch watching *Casablanca* on the classic movie channel. Doug was trying not to think about how he wanted to rip the metallic dress from Liz's body, how her scent was driving him wild, how being this close to her was wreaking havoc on the area below his belt. He'd removed his jacket and tie and shoes, rolled up his sleeves. Liz had changed into his old U Colorado T-shirt, the one she borrowed the night they'd first met and had never relinquished. Even in an old T-shirt and sweatpants, the woman was so gorgeous and so sexy, Doug felt like a teenager about to have his first sexual experience.

"Um, ah—" he started.

"What do you—" she said.

Him. "You first."

Her. "No, you first."

They laughed weakly.

"Okay," he said. "I'll go. You know, we don't have to watch this. If you're tired, we can shut it off. Um, you could sleep here…I mean, if you wanted to…I can sleep on the couch…."

"I *am* tired and my stomach's a little upset…but it's nothing, really," Liz said, seeing Doug's face fall. "Probably just nerves. In fact, I'm feeling better by the minute." She came out from under Doug's arm and maneuvered onto his lap.

Doug literally swooned with anticipation.

She took off her T-shirt. Her nipples were already hard and willing.

Doug ran his hands across her back, shoulders, and breasts. He was breathing hard. He wanted her, so much it hurt.

Doug's shirt came off and she was kissing his chest then his face again. She wrapped her arms around his neck. "I love you, too," she whispered.

His words come out a croak. "You do?"

"I do. You make me feel like I'm the only woman in the world."

"You *are* the only woman in the world—for *me*. I love you, Liz. And I'm the luckiest man in the world. To hold you, to sleep with you, to make love with you. It's all that matters."

Liz reached down and unbuckled Doug's belt. Her legs wrapped tighter and tighter around him. If he didn't move, he'd die from the wanting. He slipped his fingers down into her panties and she groaned.

"Bedroom," he managed.

"Yes."

He carried her in his arms, her legs still wrapped around his waist, to the bedroom. They barely made it to the bed.

Two hours later, sated and exhausted, Doug rolled over to nestle at Liz's back. "I love you," he said again.

"Love you, too," she said. Within a minute her breathing was deep and steady, catching every minute or so with a thought or a snatch of dream.

Doug was content to stay awake and watch her sleep, but finally he couldn't keep his eyes open any longer. His last thought before dropping off was that the woman lying naked next to him was everything he's ever wanted.

Doug woke up with a start. The bathroom called, but Liz was peacefully sleeping like a baby. He slid out of bed as carefully as he could, slowly covering her body with the sheet.

His foot caught on the blanket. "Shoot." Down he went, hitting the floor with a loud thump, making enough noise to waken the dead. When Liz didn't budge he ran to the bathroom, urinated a long stream, then flushed.

He climbed back in bed. Just lying there watching her sleep makes him want her as if he hadn't had her at all the night before.

"Liz," he whispered. "Come here, baby...." He put his hand on her shoulder. "Liz?"

Why was she so cold? "Liz. Wake up. Are you okay?"

There was something wrong. Gently Doug turned her over. He kissed her face, her forehead. What? "Liz?" She was cool to the touch. She wasn't breathing.

"Liz!" he moaned. "Wake up!" Panicking, Doug administered CPR. He pounded on her chest, breathed into her cold mouth. Nothing. He kept going. Over and over until he was so tired he couldn't continue. He let out long wails of frustration and horror.

He reached for his phone and dialed 9-1-1.

"911. State your emergency,"

"My girlfriend isn't breathing. I tried CPR, but...."

"Address?"

"2110 West 62nd Street. Apartment 4B."

"A unit is nearby. Should be there any minute. Stay on the line, please."

What just happened? How could Liz be dead? It was impossible. She was young, healthy. She was there, in his arms, all night. He loved her. She loved him.

No, Liz wasn't dead. He wouldn't accept it. In another minute she'd be up and about, teasing him, holding him.

He rocked her in his arms back and forth, back and forth. If he stopped, it would be over. If he stopped, she'd be dead.

Doug held Liz in his arms until the doorbell rang less than two minutes later. They must have been around the corner.

Doug opened the door to three paramedics in surgical masks and pointed to the bedroom. Doug had covered her nudity with the sheet. They moved quickly into the room and began doing whatever it was they usually did, but this time they were doing it to Liz's lifeless body. He sank down to the floor in the hallway. He couldn't watch. The tears flowed noiselessly.

There was a part of him that saw and listened, but it was a part that couldn't feel, couldn't think. If he did he'd never make it.

They were done in a few short minutes. They shook their heads: *She's gone.* He looked at the clock. 5:48 AM. How long had she lay dead next to him? Maybe that was what she was trying to tell him—that she was sick...dying. But why now? And what would he do without her?

The EMTs loaded his beautiful Liz onto a stretcher. Doug opened the door for them, but didn't want them to leave. If they left, it would be real. He got up to follow.

"Mr. Archer, you should stay here," said one of the technicians.

Doug's came out of his fog. "What? What did you say?"

"Mr. Archer, please step back. Let us do our jobs."

"What the hell did you just call me?"

No. Not Liz. NOT LIZ!

A seething rage began to boil. "What are you talking about?" He grabbed the man closest to him by the jacket. "What—the hell—are you talking about?!"

"Sir, calm down." The man went to remove Doug's hold. Doug didn't give way, but his hold on the stretcher was weakening.

"I said, tell—me—what's—going—on."

The men looked at Doug's face and then each other.

"The body must be disposed of, sir," the first man said. "I believe you know the rules by now."

Doug looked at the EMT's jacket. "Johnson" was embroidered on the pocket.

Oh, my God. No!

He'd bet everything he had that the other two were Smith and Williams.

Doug let go of the man's jacket. Weak, he dropped to his knees. Liz. But how...why? It didn't make any sense.

Last night. The waiter. There was something about him. But, no, he was on leave. He'd only had eyes for Liz. Her eyes, her mouth, her legs.

The red wine, it had to be. Oh, my God, it was in the wine. Liz had drunk more than he had. He'd been preoccupied with her, caught up in the story he'd made up where they could be together forever.

Mr. Chemist. The bastard must have been after him, poisoned the wine. The small amount he'd drunk must not have been enough to affect him the way it did Liz. Enough to kill him, at least. But he was still on furlough. Did Mr. Chemist ignore the rules to go after him?

"You can't have her," he said.

"Mr. Archer, please," said Johnson.

"You can't have her, I said."

"Mr. Archer, don't make this any harder than it is already," Johnson repeated.

Doug caved, slumping down against the wall. Johnson was right. There was nothing he could do.

His life was over. Everything he had left to live for was gone.

43

"We had an arrangement!" Doug screamed, heading straight for the shadowed corner.

"Yes, we did," Mr. Black nodded.

"You gave me a furlough—ninety days!"

"Indeed I did."

"Then why the attempt? That's against the rules. Why was I being hunted?"

"There were no such attempts," Mr. Black stated calmly.

"Bullshit!" Mr. Black's calm demeanor wasn't helping.

"What makes you think there was such an attempt made?"

"My girlfriend is dead, that's how. He missed me and got her." Doug's voice was rough with anger and pain.

"Who missed you…exactly?"

Doug took in the room with a sweep of his head. Mr. Chemist was looking at him with—what was the look on his face—pity… distain?

He's got a lot of nerve showing up here after what he did. What is he, waiting for me? Putting off his own furlough to look at me like that?

A low growl started in Doug's throat, percolating until it left his mouth in a hideous howl. "You!" he screamed. He charged Mr. Chemist, grabbed him by the neck, forced him against the wall and proceeded to punch him in the face—his jaw, his nose, his eyes. "Why?! Why? Why?" The single word punctuated each strike again, and again. "Why her, why Liz!?"

Mr. Dart and Mr. Lion pulled Doug off Mr. Chemist, now bleeding from the nose and mouth, but Doug managed to free himself and charge once more. A man possessed, it took another two members to pin him down before he could do permanent damage. Doug didn't recognize them. Probably new recruits. He continued to struggle to free himself, but they were strong and had pinned his arms to his sides. He was slobbering like a baby.

Mr. Chemist spoke through bloody lips, already swelling. "Liz? I'm afraid I don't know anyone by that name," he said.

"Don't bullshit me, you asshole. You missed me. You went after me and you missed and you killed her. Do you understand now? She wasn't involved in this sick little life we have here. She was a civilian, an outsider, and you killed her. You killed her, trying to get to me."

Mr. Chemist took out a handkerchief to wipe his face. "You're on a furlough, Mr. Archer. Going after you would be against the rules."

"You killed an innocent woman."

"Mr. Archer, that's enough," Mr. Black ordered from the back corner.

"Screw you!" he shouted back.

Mr. Black snapped his fingers in the direction of the back of the room. Immediately EMT-worker Johnson appeared through the door holding some kind of object. It looked familiar.

The fight drained from Doug's body all at once. What the hell was going on? Why did he have Liz's purse?

"Recognize this, Mr. Archer?" Mr. Black tossed it to Doug. Mr. Lion, Mr. Dart, and company let him go and he caught it mid-air.

"Open it," said Mr. Black.

Doug did as he was told. His hands were shaking. A blue envelope, folded over twice, was inside. Doug unfolded it. "DE LA FLEUR" was written on the outside in thick block letters. Inside the folder was a picture of him.

Him, Douglas Goodwin. The stupidest man in the world.

He didn't need to see the rest to know what it was.

"This is bullshit, you planted this," he said, feeling faint.

"Did I?" Mr. Chemist asked. "You say I killed an innocent woman? Everyone in the Circle is as guilty as the next. Once you're in, you forfeit any innocence you may have had. You know what that picture is telling you."

"No," Doug croaked. "I don't believe it."

"She sought *us* out," said Mr. Black.

"No!"

"She would've killed you at the end of your furlough." Mr. Chemist suggested this quietly.

Doug threw the purse against the adjacent wall; the papers and picture skimmed across the floor. "No! You don't know what we had! We loved each other!"

"Indeed you did. There was never any question of that," Mr. Black said. "In fact, she wasn't at all pleased when she received her assignment, when she found out who you were. She intentionally stayed away from Tasker's to avoid seeing you here. She stayed away from *you*, in fact, as long as she could, I imagine. She put herself in grave danger."

All those "disappointing auctions," the time she stayed away. He'd assumed she was avoiding him because she didn't want to be with him.

"She certainly loved you, Mr. Archer. But you need to understand one thing. Your precious Ms. Hughes was no more than Madame de la Fleur to us, a mark, a target, from the moment she killed Mr. Cufflinks."

Doug couldn't speak.

Liz killed Cufflinks?

"Revenge, you see, Mr. Archer, is a dish best served cold. Madam de la Fleur's father was—"

"Don't call her that."

"Fine," said Mr. Black, shrugging. "Ms. Hughes' father, Orson Hughes himself, was a member of the Circle as well—that is, until Mr. Cufflinks hunted him down. Ms. Hughes begged to be let into the Circle. She went through the initiation just like the rest of us...and she knew the rules. She was going to complete her task—no matter the target, no matter how hard it would be."

There isn't a pain worse than the death of a loved one. Doug knows that. But those words, and the reality behind them...if only she had come to him. They could have fought their way out together. They could have brought the whole miserable Circle down. *Oh, Liz, why didn't you tell me? Why?*

"Scotch. Leave the bottle."

The bartender did as he was told.

"I didn't ask for it. I didn't want any of it. Where's the justice in it? It's nothing but a demented spiral into death and destruction."

"You say that now," the bartender said, "but something tells me you'll come to your senses eventually. Out there," he said, pointing to the door, "is death. In here is safety. Don't forget that. Besides, I hate seeing good people lose it 'cause of one bad day."

Doug looked at him, a stranger he'd known for months. One bad day? Was this asshole really saying what he thought he was saying?

At Doug's look, the bartender backed up a step or two. "Look, stay here. Keep the bottle. But maybe it's time to stop being a herbivore."

Doug didn't have the energy to kill the guy, much as he wanted to.

His head dropped to the bar. His hand reached over to the bottle and he poured himself a tall shot. And then another. *The best thing that could ever happen to a guy like me.* And now she was dead.

Mr. Chemist emerged from the parlor pinching a handkerchief over his bloody nose. There were plenty of stools to choose from, but he took the one next to Doug.

"Screw you," said Doug.

"You know, Mr. Archer," said Mr. Chemist, ignoring Doug's snarl. "I'm not completely without tact. A man knows when a colleague, or friend—" at Doug's glare he took it back "—a colleague, then, has fallen in love. You should know that I broke a rule for you. A personal rule."

"You..." said Doug, pausing to down another shot, "are not my friend. You are not my colleague. I don't want to hear your screwed up logic. Get away from me."

Mr. Chemist stayed. "When I got involved in the Circle, I told myself that I'd never sacrifice an opportunity. Never pass up a kill."

"You didn't, you prick!" Doug fired back. "Liz is dead!"

"But I did, Mr. Archer. Although I didn't sacrifice myself as much as I sacrificed you. I could have killed her at dinner. Right in front of you." Mr. Chemist let the image sink in. "Or I could even have let her kill you first."

Doug blanched. He's refused to think about that part of the equation.

"Instead, I gave you one last night with her. Are you hearing me, Mr. Archer? I gave you this night, so you'd have one last night together to remember. It took some doing, too, slow-acting poison, not altogether reliable, but this way you had a whole night before it was over. I did that for you, Mr. Archer," he said again, slowly, letting it penetrate.

"Thanks, pal," Doug said meanly. "I guess I owe you one."

"Mock me now, Mr. Archer, but contrary to what you may think, I wasn't nearly as elated as I usually am after tagging a mark."

"She has a name, you hear me? She has a name. Elizabeth Hughes."

"Ms. Hughes, then. I hear you, Mr. Archer. Be that as it may, my gift to you might very well have killed you—and possibly me—in the very near future. Madame de la Fleur was as ruthless as they come. The way she killed Mr. Cufflinks was extreme, direct, and yes, ruthless. He undoubtedly suffered a great deal, according to The Watchers that had to clear the scene. Someday, Mr. Archer, you'll thank me for the memories you created together."

Doug is suddenly very afraid that Mr. Chemist might be right.

44

Doug scanned his phone's GPS. Several blue dots were scattered on the screen. As he left the island via the Brooklyn Bridge, the search radius automatically expanded to accommodate his search field. He checked the alarm setting, still set to beep if there were an approach within 1,000 yards.

The F-150 was running smoothly, almost by itself. He plugged the phone into the charger and continued south down the highway. The green of the trees and the black smog emitted by the tractor trailers seemed only a slightly more colorful microcosm of his life. Only a few days left of his furlough, nearly a month since Liz's death. Since he'd found out Elizabeth Hughes was a member of the Circle, the member who'd had Doug as her target.

What were the chances that the woman of his dreams would not only have a father who was a member of the Circle, but would join up to seek revenge? And the chances that she'd fall in love with another man in the same sick organization? Astronomical at least.

Of the countless thoughts forever running through his mind, *Why didn't she tell me? Did she really love me?* and *Would she really have killed me?* were the ones that got the most play. He was headed for Virginia, toward the mountains, a final tribute to the woman he'd loved, hoping to recover enough to have his head on straight when his status as a target was reinstated.

After the seven-hour drive and a long hike into the dense growth, Doug sat on the edge of the cliff where he and Liz had picnicked and made love. Where she'd towed him out of the water after his reckless macho jump. In his left hand was his UC T-shirt, the one she'd appropriated the night they'd first been together, the one she'd kept ever since, the one she'd worn the last night of her life. In his right hand was a picture of the two of them. They'd mugged for the camera, he'd flexed his muscles, and she'd sprung into the frame at the last minute before the timer went off. The waterfall, the magic, the passion...a lifetime ago.

Her swimsuit, the heat, the long walk back up the mountain, barefoot. Making love under the stars. Never again. He was here to say goodbye to her, but also to Douglas Goodwin, Jr. a man with needs and desires, a man with a conscience, a man to whom truth once mattered.

Doug got up to pitch his tent. When he knocked the last peg into the ground, he looked over his shoulder at the waterfall, then turned in for the night.

In the morning the balm of nature that had always been part of his life reasserted itself. He smelled the smells, felt the breeze on his skin, drank the ice-cold water so clear he could see to the bottom of the stream by the tent. He felt himself let down in a way that had become foreign, lost. He fished for his meals and cooked over the small campfire surrounded by a circle of rocks. Maybe he'd stay there forever.

It was after midnight on his third day in the mountains of Virginia. Doug was fast asleep in his sleeping bag when his phone alarm, still plugged into his car charger and a distance from his campsite, beeped.

Electronic gadgets don't belong in the wilderness. They can't quench your thirst, they don't keep you warm, and they can't curb your appetite. Besides, the slightest sound can frighten away a prize buck. Old habits die hard, too, and electronics always stay behind in the vehicle.

Doug came awake instantly. That wasn't his phone he was hearing. There was the sound of rustling leaves and a branch snapping. The hairs on his neck were standing on end. An animal in his food supply, hanging from a high branch? He peered out into the night. No, his knapsack was still hanging there, secure.

It was pitch black, the only light from the moon. He had his flashlight. He could head back to the truck. Dangerous, but it could still be the smart thing to do. He bent down to retrieve his hiking boots and laced them up in the dark. He picked up his flashlight and his hunting knife to stick in his belt.

There was a sound of tearing nylon. Inches from his head, a long blade slashed through the thin tent material, just missing him. The hunting blade was in Doug's hand and locked before he'd rolled away from the side of the tent. He made a cut in the back as he heard a second swipe ripping apart the fabric a few feet away.

Doug didn't make it out of the tent before his attacker had a hold of his leg and was pulling him down. The man was over him now, his knife reflecting in the moonlight. Doug feigned movement to the left and then rocked back on his tailbone to kick out with his legs. The attacker's knife slid out of reach. He lunged at Doug with his body, tackling him to the ground.

The tent threatened to collapse around them. Doug dropped his knife as he took a blow to the jaw. His face was forced into the hard ground as the attacker pressed all his weight onto Doug's back. The pressure of the assailant's arms made his neck feel as if it would snap at any second. Doug was losing the battle. In a minute he'd lose the war.

Clenching his jaw and grinding his teeth, he used every last ounce of strength to push up with his arms. Doug let the hunter think he was weakening for a second, then pushed back with all the momentum he could muster. With a grunt, the killer landed on his back. He'd lost his grip on Doug, but was back on his feet in an instant and looking for his fallen knife. He made his move when he located it by the Coleman lantern. He picked it up and lunged for Doug again.

Doug felt the elbow at his throat and was suddenly flat on his back. The guy was coming for him again...relentless. Doug waited. When his assailant put all his weight behind his attempt Doug slid the knife from his side.

He waited for another agonizing slow-motion second to pass. Then, as the masked man attacked, Doug turned the blade upward.

The sound of the blade entering flesh was the only sound. Doug felt hot breath on his neck. He was alive, but suffocating. He threw off the body and held his blade to the hunter's jugular. Not that it was necessary; he was nearly gone.

It was as he'd suspected. The upper body strength, the dexterity, the silent command of his surroundings. "Tell me. How did you find me?"

Mr. Lion coughed blood and attempted the ghost of a smile. "You're slipping, young Goodwin, your furlough ended yesterday."

Doug felt as if there were a hole in his chest. "But—here—"

"It's like I always told you, kid. Be a Boy Scout...prepared for anything."

Doug knew this man had just tried to kill him. He knew he would have gotten no mercy. But his eyes filled anyway with the sure loss of another...colleague? Mentor?

"Wait," said Doug.

"Don't look so shocked, kid. We know there are no friends outside those walls."

Was Doug imagining the sadness in his voice?

Mr. Lion's breathing was labored. His hourglass was running out.

"...So, was I right? Does it get easier?"

"No," Doug whispered. "It doesn't."

"It will kid," Mr. Lion said, "it will.... Now, finish the job, Doug Goodwin."

"Doug Goodwin doesn't exist anymore," said Doug, and knew in the moment he said it that it was true. Mr. Lion, and the Circle, had been successful.

"Well, then, Mr. Archer, finish off Mr. Quinn Phillips. ...Mr. Lion...hasn't been a man...for a long time...only a killer... I don't want my grandson to remember me that way."

Taking Doug's two hands in his own around the knife, Mr. Lion forced the knife down into his chest and blew out his last breath.

Doug wakened to a crisp morning, dew drops glistening on the leaves and overgrown brush below. He packed up everything he'd brought on the trip and stood at the edge of the falls looking down, holding the CU T-shirt to his face, smelling in the last scent of his beloved Liz. Finally, resigned, he extended his arm, let go of the scrap of fabric, and watched as it floated down and swirled in the foamy water, finally disappearing as abruptly as her life had been taken from him.

Doug knelt before the now cold body of Mr. Lion, made the sign of the cross, and kissed the golden cross around his neck. His father's cross. Mr. Lion had been like a father figure in a bizarre sort of way, so it seemed fitting. Doug took out his knife and carved "Quinn Phillips, 58, RIP" into the tree against which Mr. Lion now rested. As Doug began the hike back to his F-150, a team of three forest rangers approached his campsite. "Williams, Johnson, and Smith, I presume," he said, "what took you so long?" There was no answer. There rarely was.

"Up that hill there, next to the falls. Leave the inscription, if you don't mind."

Williams nodded. Doug didn't look back.

"What's going on?"

"What do you mean?"

Doug and Mr. Necktie were sitting at the card table, playing a game of Kozel. Mr. Chemist, Mr. Combustion, and the new recruit, Mr. Thunder, were playing a restrained but heated game of pool. Doug's mind wasn't on his game, but on the recent days' events and on how many people died everyday as a result of the Circle's far-reaching tentacles.

"You've been quiet all afternoon, Mr. Archer. And you haven't complained once. Something must be wrong."

"There really is no loyalty in the Circle, is there?"

Mr. Necktie looked disappointed. "Depends on what kind of loyalty you're looking for. Mr. Dart saved your life—in here. Out there you wouldn't have gotten a second's reprieve. Out there, loyalty can only mean one thing—that you can trust in the allegiance of the kill. I wish I could tell you otherwise."

"I still don't know how I can...."

"You'll figure it out," said Mr. Necktie, echoing many others. "Or you'll die trying."

45

The woman in the leopard-skin top and shiny black skirt wrapped her legs around the man in the four thousand-dollar Bottega Veneta suit. Not that she knows its exact price, only that the man wears it well and smells expensive, like he's been dipped in eau de Ritz or something. It's a perk of her plummy job that the men are in shape and clean and treat her with respect— usually—at least to the degree she has any right to expect. She gets her monthly check-ups, too, medical care if she needs it, and as long as she doesn't ask questions she can shop 'til she drops. She does wonder from time to time where they go...the men, that is. Sometimes they're there for days, sometimes for months. Most of the time they're not around any longer than that. But she does what she's told and doesn't ask. No point in stirring the pot, not when she's got it so good. She even gets to make her own rules. Her own personal favorite is the no-kissing thing. Not all the girls feel that way, but she does. Kissing is way too intimate for her liking. On the other hand, she's willing to do a lot of things that the other girls wouldn't touch with a ten-foot pole.

Take this client here, for example. He was cold and clinical, and got into some of the kinky stuff, so she's the one he asks for to fill his requirements. Today he'd suggested a rendezvous in an unusual place, under the highway. Heightened his excitement or something. Whatever. She didn't get it, but doesn't mind, either. Like her long-dead mother always said, variety was the spice of life.

She leaned into him as he leaned up against the black Cadillac Seville. It was time to take it up a notch. He'd paid for her for the day, but the position was giving her a cramp. She maneuvered her knee up into his crotch and listened to him moan. When his hands went to her breasts she undid a couple of buttons so he could feast his eyes on her ample bosom in the new Wonderbra she'd purchased at Nieman Marcus. Next trip she was going for the matching thong and garter belt. She doesn't know who pays the bills, but she's never had it so good in her life...clothes, shoes, rent, all paid by the man upstairs, whoever he is. Checks come from the bank and, as long as they don't bounce, who cares?

As he buried his face in her cleavage the woman in the leopard-skin top manifested a mewing sound or two to indicate her excitement. He deserved the best, the kind of money he was spending. Which reminds her, she has a manicure scheduled later. The polish has chipped off a couple of nails on the right and she has her image to think about. Hmmm, that new Vampire Red would be nice this time. Oh, and a pedicure, too, to match.

Mr. Dart was breathing heavily. Even through the binoculars Doug could see that. Should he wait? Give the guy the pleasure of release? A meager approximation of what Mr. Chemist gave him that night with Liz....

The woman in stiletto heels and a short skirt was rubbing herself against Mr. Dart, encouraging his excitement, whispering words in his ear. Doug had a clear shot across the highway and under the overpass. He's known for a long time how Mr. Dart likes his sex—raw and often in public places, where it either increased his risk of danger from his hunters or maybe just increased his sexual thrill. He'd gotten comfortable with Doug's apparent ongoing choice to abstain from the hunt. None of that mattered to Doug. Either way, it now gave him the edge.

His finger was steady on the trigger of his crossbow. He had plenty of patience. Years of lying in the snow or heat for the perfect shot at a buck had trained him well. He wasn't in any hurry anyway, and really would like to allow his colleague, Mr. Dart, the few final moments of his last happy ending.

The woman felt her client's hands go around her neck. With anyone else she might be afraid, but this client was a gentleman. He liked to play around, but never hurt her much. She took it as a signal to cup her palms around his genitals. He responded... right on cue.

Mr. Dart's hands went around the woman's neck. Anyone else might be concerned that he was about to strangle the woman, but Doug knew the signs. The woman was a professional, and she'd had Mr. Dart several times before, four by Doug's recent count. He watched her shift to accommodate Dart's needs. Doug shifted to accommodate his own.

Mr. Dart enjoyed this particular woman more than any other in their stall of thoroughbreds. She read him like a book, but still managed to surprise him with her creativity and willingness to explore the unconventional. Today, for example, under this overpass by the highway...it was so real, so coarse, so completely raw for the intimate act of sex.

He breathed in her scent—like an animal's, really, but an expensively coiffed and draped animal. He felt her heat, her rump, her breasts. Just the way he liked it.

He went for her neck. His arousal was a throbbing pulse ready for release. Her neck was white and smooth and soft. Power drove his need and he pummeled his erection in between her thighs.

The woman felt his explosion of liberated desire. As least that's what he'd call it. The way his hands lessened their hold on her neck, the way he collapsed into her. She swore she heard him catch his breath, the way it might catch if he were trying not to cry. But this client wasn't a crier. Not like some of the others.

Doug saw the act of letting go and knows it for what it is: completion. He fired. Mr. Dart's head exploded, the shaft of the arrow almost making it completely through his skull, but not quite, when the fletching caught on its path.

Mr. Dart jerked back suddenly. The woman was surprised. Normally he was not quite so quick to separate, not that he was the warm-and-fuzzy type either. She was about to ask if everything was okay...and saw pretty quickly that it would never be okay again.

She screamed, pushed him away, and vomited.

Doug felt for her; it was too bad she had to be there for the messy part.

She screamed and screamed and screamed, as if by screaming she could bring Mr. Dart back to life.

No one could hear. Doug's distance from their location rendered him and the general public essentially deaf. The traffic above continued its relentless pursuit, unaware that a mere fifty feet below a human life had been snuffed out like a bug under a tire.

Doug reached under his shirt and kissed the golden cross around his neck. He took his time packing up his gear. There was never any hurry with the Watchers so close by.

Goodbye, Mr. Dart. Goodbye, Douglas Goodwin, Jr. With one shot, Mr. Archer has killed you both.

The Circle has finally won.

The Circle always wins.

EPILOGUE

The two men entered Tasker's and looked around. They're young and cocky, there for some action.

The bartender knows them for what they are. "What'll it be boys?"

"Two of whatever you have on draught," said the one with the cowlick and the face of a baby.

"Two beers it is," the bartender said, dispensing the drinks with swift efficiency.

Baby Face pulled out his wallet.

"Put your money away," the bartender said. "First drinks at Tasker's are always on the house."

"Cool," said Baby Face. The wallet disappeared.

"Yeah, thanks," said the friend, "appreciate it." He took a big swig and licked his lips.

"Who's that?" Baby Face pointed to the picture of the bartender's father.

"My father, rest his soul," said the bartender, making the sign of the cross. "This bar's been in my family for five generations. Before him, there was a picture of his father. When I die, they'll take that one down and put up one of me. But enough about me. Let me welcome you to Tasker's, boys. You got names?"

"Sure," said Baby Face, sitting down on a stool. "I'm Greg, this is my friend Ryan."

His friend stayed standing, shifting from foot to foot gulping his beer.

The bartender nodded. The boys' attention was already elsewhere searching out the female element in the room.

"Hey, where's the bathroom in this place?" asked Ryan. "Back in a minute, dude."

Greg nodded distractedly. "Nice place," he said, watching a well-dressed man with a silver walking cane stroll through the bar with a young woman on his arm. "Wow, lucky old fuck."

The bartender smiled.

The man approached the wall and suddenly a panel slid open to allow him and his companion pass through to another room. "Hey, what's back there?" said Baby Face, his eyes big.

The bartender left the door open just long enough to make sure the young man saw what he was intended to see.

"Oh," he said, "you know, a lounge for our more...*distinguished* guests."

"How does one get to be 'distinguished' then?" asked Greg, envy seeping out of every pore.

The bartender glanced down. The photo underneath the bar was a perfect match. It was Baby Face all right, from the blue eyes to the cowlick to the smug attitude.

The bartender let the door close and watched the disappointment register on the new recruit's face. "I could let you find out for yourself."

"What, are you kidding? Sure."

The bartender nodded. "You seem like a good kid. Tell you what, I'll vouch for you."

Baby Face picked up his beer, ready to go. "I guess I should wait for Ryan, though. I don't know what's taking him so long."

"Oh, no worries. I'll send him back when he gets out."

The door swooshed open; the sound of luxury and promise.

"Go ahead," the bartender urged.

Baby Face mumbled a thanks and was off and running faster than you could say *the Circle owns you from this day forward.*

Greg took a long look around the VIP lounge. He was too busy checking out the tail to notice the many pairs of eyes taking in his height, his weight, his physique, his age.

The expensively tooled leather chairs, the billiards table, the smell of cigars and perfume...it's like an opiate.

"Care to join us?" One of the dart players was waving him over.

"Sure," said Greg, taking the proffered cigar, "thanks."

The man nodded. "First time?"

"Yeah, the bartender said—"

"Sure," said the man. "We're playing Cricket. This is Mr. Stealth—your partner—and I'm Mr. Archer."

Stealth? Archer? Were these guys fucking with him?

"Greg," he said awkwardly.

"This is Mr. Spata," said the man, gesturing to another associate. "He's visiting for a few months from Italy."

"Ciao," said Mr. Spata putting out his hand.

"Greg, Greg Connors," the young man said again. These guys were weird. He didn't like weird stuff. And where the fuck was Ryan?

"Yes, but your other name?" asked Mr. Spada.

Was the old guy hard of hearing? Greg repeated his name yet again, not as patiently as before.

"Ah, excuse me, Mr. Spada," said Mr. Archer, "but I believe young Greg here is a new recruit." He turned to Greg, a kid with the face of a baby. "You don't know why you're here, do you?"

Confused, Greg looked at him. Wasn't he here to play cards and get laid?

The guys words began to sink in. "New recruit for what?" Greg asked, suspicious. He didn't like the vibe here. And there was no way he's gonna be corralled into joining anything—even a men's club, or whatever this was. The dues alone'd probably put him on the streets.

"Please, Mr. Connors. Come with us. You should meet Mr. Black." Mr. Archer put an arm around Greg's shoulders.

Greg recoiled. "Get your fuckin' hands off me. Where are you taking me?"

"Why, to Mr. Black," Mr. Archer said, taken aback.

"Yeah...no. I don't think so," said Greg. This was getting creepier by the minute. "I'm just going to get going. I have a friend waiting for me."

"You see, I'm afraid that's not possible, Mr. Connors. You're not going anywhere."

"Wadaya mean, I'm not going anywhere? Who do you think you are?"

Mr. Archer smiled. "Today, Mr. Connors, I am your dearest friend. Tomorrow? I could be your biggest adversary. Let's start at the beginning, shall we?"

"The beginning?"

Mr. Archer nodded. "As with all circles, this one has no beginning and no end."

Greg's baby face fell, taking on the distinct pallor of a man in front of a firing squad.

"Trust me, it will all make sense in time," Mr. Archer said. "Welcome to the Circle."

ACKNOWLEDGMENTS

This book has been in the making for almost two decades. It would not have been possible without some truly amazing people. To my mother, Bernadette, and my grandfather John: You never got to see this published, but you never doubted that one day it would be. This is for you! To my father Stan: for your endless support and encouragement. Thank you for always believing in me. To Maria: for putting up with me during this whole crazy process; for always finding the time to read my next chapter; for your love and support. Thank you from the bottom of my heart! To my three amazing daughters: for slowing me down; for the joy you bring me every day. Thank you for being you. Never stop dreaming! Always remember these two things: you can do anything, and your daddy will always love you! To Greg: for refusing to read *The Circle* until it was published. Thanks for the extra motivation! To Danielle: for your constant reads and re-reads. Thank you for your honesty after each one. To my whole family, especially my two wonderful nieces, thank you for your love and optimism. To my editor, Heidi Connolly: for your patience with a novice, wannabe author. You helped me take my crazy story and make a book out of it. Thank you for making this dream come true!

To my students, past, present and future: Anything is possible. And, finally, to every person who reads this book: Thank you for taking a chance on me.

ABOUT THE AUTHOR

The Circle is Stephen J. Galgon's first novel. He began his writing journey at Fairleigh Dickinson University where he received his bachelors and masters degrees, and completed *The Circle* while working as a middle and high school teacher. When he's not writing or teaching, he works as a volunteer for the National Brain Tumor Society. Steve and his family live in New Jersey where he is currently at work on *The Circle's* exciting sequel.